KILL

Strega was
into his sta

They were face to face, Maria and Strega, inches apart, Strega staring at her with a wild mix of admiration and terror. Maria brushed her lips across his. She smelled his sweat now, and she tasted his fear. Her own breath was hot, her tongue silky.

"Accidents happen," she whispered. "What would happen if my revolver accidentally discharged right now, into you? Accidents happen. They do happen." She bit his lip gently. "I could have done it, Jonnie. I could have killed you today. . . ."

BLUE JUSTICE

KILLER WITH A BADGE

...was suddenly next to her, sucking air
into his starved lungs.

BLUE JUSTICE

BLUE JUSTICE

Jeannine Kadow

A SIGNET BOOK

SIGNET
Published by the Penguin Group
Penguin Putnam Inc., 375 Hudson Street,
New York, New York 10014, U.S.A.
Penguin Books Ltd, 27 Wrights Lane,
London W8 5TZ, England
Penguin Books Australia Ltd, Ringwood,
Victoria, Australia
Penguin Books Canada Ltd, 10 Alcorn Avenue,
Toronto, Ontario, Canada M4V 3B2
Penguin Books (N.Z.) Ltd, 182–190 Wairau Road,
Auckland 10, New Zealand

Penguin Books Ltd, Registered Offices:
Harmondsworth, Middlesex, England

Published by Signet, an imprint of Dutton NAL,
a member of Penguin Putnam Inc.

First Printing, July, 1998
10 9 8 7 6 5 4 3 2 1

PUBLISHER'S NOTE
This is a work of fiction. Names, characters, places, and incidents either
are the product of the author's imagination or are used fictitiously,
and any resemblance to actual persons, living or dead, events, or locales
is entirely coincidental.

For Alice Weiss and Marcy Posner

One

Maria Alvarez kicked a stone on the edge of the East River. It skipped down the sloping embankment and scuttled into the fast-moving water. Maria leaned over to watch it sink and wondered what it would feel like to lose herself in the same water. Rocking back on her heels, she sat down on the hard-packed earth and lit a cigarette. It was nearly midnight. The lights of Manhattan were a thousand stars trapped on the river's surface.

A siren wailed far away. Police, she thought. She knew the sound. Maria Alvarez was the law, and the midnight blue NYPD uniform she wore proved it. She reached up and caressed her shield, then unpinned it and held it up to catch the spill of city light behind her. Embossed across the top were the words CITY OF NEW YORK POLICE and across the bottom, the number 2153. There was another Alvarez out there with an NYPD shield, but that Alvarez was a higher-ranking, more important officer. Maria loved him and hated him at the same time.

"Alvarez." She spoke her name, *his* name, out loud, and although she spoke softly, it sounded like a curse: "Alvarez."

She turned the shield over and over in her small hand. Maria Alvarez was the law, but she was a victim too and that irony was not lost on her—not with her silver handcuffs hanging empty at her side when they should have been slapped around someone's wrists and cranked down tight—when she should have been able to use the law to arrest that someone and lock him away for a long, long time.

Weren't criminals—*perpetrators of crimes*—sent to

prison? Wasn't that the law? Wasn't that justice? How
was it that the perpetrator of a lifetime of crimes walked
free? Some people were above the law? Well, now she
was too. *And justice for all.* Maria Alvarez had re-
invented the concept. Most of the time she felt good
about her brand of justice. Occasionally she did not. This
night was one such occasion. Tears burned in her eyes.
"Alvarez, you're really fucked up," she whispered, not
knowing which Alvarez she meant.

Maria gripped the little shield tightly, driving the
sharp metal points into her flesh. She bit the inside of
her cheek to keep from crying out, then squeezed hard
until she felt the warm wet of her own blood seep
through her fingers. She dropped the shield. Bloody-
handed, Maria fumbled with the buttons of her uniform
shirt and slipped it off. Gun belt, pants, and heavy regulation shoes followed. She wore no undergarments. Her
generous skin was damp and flushed, as hot as the August night around her.

Maria Alvarez stood up and picked her way over the
rock shards and tin cans littering the riverbank. At the
embankment edge a long metal pipe jutted out a hundred feet across the water and cleared the river surface
by a neat twelve inches. She grabbed hold of it and
swung her body down into the water. The pipe was slick
with algae. Her hands slipped for an instant. She tightened her grip, then shimmied out to the end of the pipe,
where the water was deep and the current strong.

The sludge-scarred river whirled around her. This was
no cleansing bath. The cold water was fetid and foul, as
dirty as she was. It slapped up against her chin, filled
her nostrils with a rank perfume, lifted her long Spanish
hair and fanned it out in a wide circle. The river raced
around her thighs and rushed between her legs where
countless hands and faces—and countless other things—
had been. She spread her legs slightly, reached down,
and opened herself roughly. The river water filled her
up. It was an urban douche. A fitting baptism for God's
wayward subject.

A hard object bumped against her shoulder blades,

then drifted off. Another object lodged in the crook of her neck just under her ear. She shrugged it free and watched the bloated, hideous mass of a drowned rat sail off, its sharp face locked in a Halloween death grin. Maria Alvarez laughed. If she let go, she would end up like the rat. She couldn't swim.

The tidal flow pulled and tugged at her hanging body, urging her down, hungry to sweep her away. She had simply to release her hands, give herself up to the current, let it wrap her in its rolling watery embrace, and lull her into a long, liquid slumber. How would it feel to breathe and inhale water instead of air? How would it feel to tumble and spin, to have wide-open eyes yet see nothing, to drop and fall until drowning obliterated consciousness?

Exhilarated, she eased her arms out from the pipe into a full stretch. Her head sank below the oily surface. One hand slipped free. She touched her breasts. Her nipples were hard buttons in the icy water. It would be so easy. All she had to do was let go. Five fingers held her between life and death, five slim fingers.

It would be so easy to let go and be free!

Her feet kicked awkwardly in celebration, a useless giddy flailing.

Her lungs began to ache.

Let go, her brain screamed. *Drop the second hand, do it!*

Her black hair billowed around in the force of the current, covering her face. She clawed it away.

Let go now!

Her pulse thundered, the aching inside turned to fire, her chest threatened to explode. Maria opened her mouth. Water rushed in. Panic wiped away exhilaration. The primal survival instinct kicked in. Her free hand surged up on its own accord, five digits spread wide reaching for life, five crimson fingernails raking the air, grappling for the pipe, and finding it. She gripped hard and pulled. Her head broke the surface. She choked and coughed, then sucked summer air into her starved lungs.

Blood from her cut palm dripped down to the water,

where it spread, a fast red stain, liquid on liquid. The
pain told her she was still alive. Maria Alvarez screamed
with anger. Her screams turned to profane words hurled
at a deaf night sky. She kicked and shouted, "Fuck, fuck,
fuck," all the while holding two-fisted and tightly to the
algae-slicked pipe. "Fuck, fuck, fuck," she yelled, "fuck
you, Alvarez," again not knowing which Alvarez she
meant.

Finally, when she was tired and her voice hoarse,
when her shoulders ached from the effort of hanging
above the cold water's surface and when her fingers
turned numb, she worked her way, hand over hand,
along the length of the pipe back to the river's edge,
where she stumbled out onto land.

Maria clambered on her knees in the dark, her bare
buttocks two white orbs gleaming in the black summer
night. She scooped up her gun belt, uniform, and shoes,
groped like a blind man for her shield, then stood and
staggered a few feet before falling down. She rolled over
onto her back. She gulped air, but the death need rose
high in her chest and she cried: "When?"

When would she finally be able to drop the hand?
Fire the shot? Drag the steel blade over her china blue
vein? Vault wingless from a rooftop?

She lifted her gun, fired once into the air, then pressed
the burning barrel to her right temple. The hot metal
seared her skin. She tossed the gun aside and put her
fingertips up to feel the wound, a round welt rising.

She had seen what a gun did when it was pressed to
the temple and fired. The gunshot explosion sends flames
and gases out with the bullet—gases that invariably become trapped between the skin and bone and, having
nowhere to go, burst the skin open in a ragged star
shape. Maria had seen the telltale star on human flesh.
She had seen the star and she had touched it too, and
she knew now that it wouldn't be the drowning or the
steel blade or the wingless flight, but a perfect constellation of one that would set her free.

She would shoot the star. It would be the final fuck-
you. Maria's final justice.

*   *   *

At midnight on the same Thursday night in August, Officer Ed Gavin walked up to the entrance of the city morgue at the corner of First Avenue and Thirtieth Street in Manhattan. The first floor of the six-story structure was ablaze with lights. Night was the busy time here, when the wagons came and went, making their sad deliveries of the dead.

Gavin entered and went directly to the reception room where he waited for the chief medical examiner to come fetch him. The place still spooked him after all these years. There was something unnatural about having so much death collected in one space. Gavin had an irrational fear that death would find him there, that somehow someone would run in off the street, shoot him point-blank in the heart, and leave him to die, literally, on death's doorstep.

He looked back at his new partner, hovering in the reception room doorway, and felt reassured. Jon Strega's powerful six feet four inches in uniform made him an effective and convenient guard dog. As far as Gavin was concerned, that was all the kid was good for. Looking at Strega, he started to get mad all over again. Almost three decades in the NYPD, and here he was playing nursemaid to a prim twenty-four-year-old rookie. *Rookie.* A four-letter word that happened to be spelled with six, and this one was ass-deep in *proper police procedure.*

Strega had the patrol manual memorized from cover to cover, and he quoted from it liberally. He probably slept with the fucking thing under his pillow. He was a jabbering fountain of youth spouting the kind of rookie enthusiasm that would disappear forever once he got his first look at a disarticulated female corpse stuffed in a trash bag. Until then Strega was green enough to run around with his hand on his holster John Wayne style, believing the NYPD was the last word in justice. Believing there *was* such a thing as justice.

Worse still, the kid was a goddamn living Ken doll. He had the same chiseled face, the same perfectly bal-

anced broad shoulders tapering into a tight torso, and
the same bright smile as Barbie's boyfriend. Jon Strega,
however, was Italian. He was aftershave-ad handsome
and young enough to be Gavin's son—not that anyone
would ever make the mistake of thinking they were
related.

Gavin was a big man, five eleven, with a barrel chest
and broad shoulders. He had a solid build from a lifetime of boxing for sport, but he'd let up over the years
and now his muscle was soft and his body slack. Gavin
couldn't remember the last time he'd worked the heavy
practice bag hanging in his basement. He wondered if it
was even still there.

Despite the boxer's body, his features were finely
drawn, delicate almost, and his eyes were a surprising
shade of bright blue which deepened in color when he
was angry or sad. Gavin had two deep folds to either
side of his mouth and a shock of steely white hair. It
seemed his hair had turned the day Alex disappeared,
and the furrows on his face appeared the day he found
Danny dead. Gavin liked to think his hair would turn
blond again one day when Alex found her way home.
The facial furrows, he knew, were there to stay. Danny
was never coming home.

The reception room was hot. Gavin fanned himself
with his hat and tugged at his collar. Forty-two days
of record-breaking heat and no end in sight. He hated
Manhattan in August. Two days out with the wet-nosed
kid behind him, and Gavin knew he hated his new partner too.

The rookie had a degree from one of those uppity
East Coast universities where the ivy was thick enough
to choke you if the bullshit academics didn't first.
Princeton this and Princeton that, Strega yakked up a
nonstop Ivy League storm. What did Strega think he
was going to do with his ivy green education in the red-
neck New York Police Department, recite Shakespeare
instead of Miranda *if* and *when* he ever arrested some-
body? Sure, Gavin thought, in the NYPD a diploma

could be useful—if you were partial to parchment toilet paper.

The fact was, Gavin missed Donovan. *Daniel Donovan.* Lifelong friend, partner for twenty-nine years, then poof—just like that—he was out of this world and into the next. God's idea of a joke, Gavin thought, the second part of a double whammy—his partner dead and his daughter Alex gone missing for five long years now—in exchange for which he got pretty boy Strega hanging on his heels, looking to learn. Well, Gavin wasn't in a teaching mood. All he wanted to do was have a fistfight with God—if he could find him.

The chief medical examiner poked his head out the door. "Come on back."

His name was Lang, and he was a kindly middle-aged man who looked positively ancient. His hair was gone and his face was wizened. Gavin supposed it was from a lifetime of looking at violent deaths—the fine work of knives, guns, drunk drivers, rapists, and all the innumerable forms of torture a twisted human mind could think up. Lang was obese. He waddled when he walked, with a cigarette perpetually hanging from his lips. Gavin guessed Lang didn't much fear dying of lung cancer, given what he saw day in and day out.

Lang led him downstairs into the basement, then down a long, cold hall which was the mortuary. Fluorescent lights flickered above. Lang moved slowly along the wall of steel refrigerators—Gavin had once counted a hundred and twenty-six of them—then stopped and tugged one open. He pulled a metal sliding table out. Like hundreds of times before, despite the chill of the room, Gavin began to sweat. His heart hammered in his chest and his stomach felt weak. Lang threw the white sheet back and watched Gavin's face.

Gavin stared. She had been pretty. Shoulder-length red-gold hair. Slim-hipped like a boy, but full-breasted. Her face was oval and her skin unblemished. Her mouth was wide and her lips full. She was the right age and she was very pretty, but she wasn't Alex.

Gavin shook his head. Lang pulled the sheet up and

pushed Jane Doe back into the refrigerator. Gavin
looked up at the digital thermometer blinking over the
door. Thirty-five degrees. It was always winter inside
those steel bins. Spring never came.

"Sorry," Lang said, "the picture you gave me is old
now. Hard to know how she might have changed. This
one's been here a long time now, nearly two weeks unclaimed. No ID. She goes out for city burial tomorrow.
It was a long shot, but I thought you'd want to look."

"Thanks. You were right to call."

Lang sighed. "I'm doing two bodies back to back tonight. Just finished the first. The second's waiting."

ME's rarely did autopsies at night. "Must be important for you to work this late."

"Diplomats. Suspicious deaths. The chief of detectives
is pushing me for an answer."

"I can find my way out."

Lang touched his sleeve lightly, then waddled down
the hall to the examining room.

Gavin stood alone watching the banks of steel refrigerators. What was he waiting for? One of the doors to
swing open, Alex to pop out? How many Jane Does had
he looked at in the five years since Alex had disappeared? Two hundred? Five hundred? More? They
haunted him, those young dead girls who looked as if
they were sleeping peacefully. They crowded his dreams,
parading along with their white, waxen faces and empty
eyes, all different heights and weights and arrangement
of parts, all those lovely young girls with the one shared
name—Jane Doe. For every one of them there was a set
of parents somewhere, most likely frantic with worry and
grieving as he was. He wished he could send this girl
back to her rightful home and bring her parents peace
of mind—a peace he knew he might never have.

Gavin walked slowly back up to reception. Strega was
waiting with a puzzled expression on his eager young
face, wondering what they were doing spending their
meal break at the morgue. Gavin let him wonder. He
marched straight past the rookie and out into the night.

"There's a great twenty-four-hour diner not far from here," Strega said when they were back in the car.

"Fine with me," Gavin replied, "so long as it takes plastic."

"It doesn't. You want to stop at an ATM?"

"I don't have an ATM card."

"I do. Couldn't live without it. All my accounts are linked up so I can transfer and withdraw money, even pay bills."

"Well, tech head, Shelly and I don't have everything linked up. In fact, I've got our savings at a different bank from the checking, and our credit cards from a third bank altogether, not to mention some hard cold cash buried in a cement block in the backyard."

"Money can't grow inside a cement block. You should buy stocks instead."

"Stocks?" Another four-letter word spelled with six.

Strega nodded. "West Entertainment's a hot pick right now. Small company, cash-rich, debt-free, and ripe for a takeover. It's a sure bet."

"I'm not a betting man."

"Then dig your cash out of the cement. Put it in the bank where it can earn interest."

Gavin had heard enough. "Ever hear of something called the Great Depression? The banks could all go bust again, and when they do, you'll wish you had a little something stashed in your mattress."

"Contemporary economic theory holds that a repeat of the crash is impossible," Strega stated as he checked out a leggy hooker striding by. She blew him a kiss. He frowned. "I'm glad I landed in the Nineteenth Precinct."

"Now, why would that be?"

Strega missed the sarcasm. "The Nineteenth's not like downtown here. It's got class."

Gavin snorted. "Where I come from class is another word for expensive."

Gavin and Strega were assigned to the Nineteenth Precinct on Manhattan's ritzy upper East Side, and the Nineteenth was nothing if not expensive—the million-dollar apartments, twelve-dollar cheeseburgers, twenty-dollar-an-hour parking lots—hell, Gavin thought, in the Nineteenth the hookers were so expensive they weren't called hookers at all. They were *call girls* and they had class, all right. No mini-skirts, no vinyl. *Call girls* dressed in Armani. No street walking either. *Call girls* traveled in limos. Five-dollar blow jobs? Forget it. Five-hundred-dollar minimums and on the upper East Side hooking wasn't even a cash business. Most *call girls* took plastic—Visa, MasterCard, some even accepted American Express—which reminded him.

"Let's go," Gavin ordered.

"Where to?" Strega asked, yanking the patrol car into gear.

"Any place that takes Visa."

"Ten-four. The River Diner on First." Strega turned on the siren.

"Strega, what's the deal with the siren?"

"I'm hungry. That qualifies as an emergency to me."

"Fuckin' rookies," Gavin mumbled. "Everything's a toy. The car, the siren, the radio, the women." He glared out the window at the late-night riffraff humming along the sidewalk. The riffraff glared back, insolent and unafraid.

They pulled up in front of the diner, and suddenly Gavin forgot about Strega and the riffraff and even the young Jane Doe in her icy steel bin. The early edition of the *Daily News* had hit the stands, and the headline chilled him to the bone: *NYPD Suicide Binge Claims Number 16.* Another cop blown away by his own hand. Sixteen since the first of the year and this was only August.

"Damn shame," Strega said, eyeing the same headline.

Damn shame? All that Princeton education and that's the best he could come up with?

"Suicide's the ultimate act of despair," Strega went on. "He must have been one unhappy guy."

Unhappy? What could an over-educated rookie possibly know about the kind of despair that was driving seasoned cops to eat their guns like M&M's?

"I heard that's how your partner died," Strega said.

"Did he ever give you any indication he was that depressed?"

"Fuck you, Strega," Gavin said, clumsily wiping the tears running down the furrows on his old face.

Maria skimmed across town in her old Toyota Celica, cutting from the East Side to the West Side. She turned south on Ninth Avenue, out of the midtown business district. The neighborhood began to grind down fast. Corridors of big glassy skyscrapers gave way to the strip bars, low-ticket retailers, and grimy residential buildings of Hell's Kitchen. It was an apt name for a rough pocket of Manhattan. A creeping urban decay chewed the glass out of windows and littered the sidewalks with broken whiskey bottles and used needles. Summer smells were strong. Urine. Garbage rotting in the August heat. Simmering asphalt. Mixed in was the sweet, acrid smell of reefer smoke rising from Maria's ashtray.

Maria could have lived in a good neighborhood—she had the money—but she preferred Hell's Kitchen. There were no doormen or suit-and-tie neighbors here to witness her comings and goings, to see things she didn't want seen. The Kitchen was full of misfits. Broken people. Like herself. Even though she was a cop, she felt at home here. The Celica hit a pothole. Her teeth cracked together. She took the last five blocks slow, easing around the potholes where she saw them, bumping gently through them when she didn't.

At Forty-fifth Street, she turned right and pulled into a no-parking zone two blocks shy of her apartment building. Maria tossed her NYPD ID plate on the dash, got out, and locked the door. She started down the deserted sidewalk. Spray-paint scrawls covered the building walls around her. Some of the graffiti was good, like the twenty-foot-high mural of a black woman holding the world on her bare, straining shoulders. Most of it was nothing more than illegible urban screams in chaotic confetti colors.

Two angry screamers materialized out of the shadows, shaking cans of spray paint. One was short and pit-bull squat, the other was Doberman lean. Stiff braids spiked out from their heads. Oversized hip-hop jeans rode low on their hips. Identical sleeveless grunge gray sweatshirts showed off their bulging, vein-corded arms.

The lean one began to work his fist. Open, shut, open, shut. Maria looked from fist to face. A bright pink scar raced in a half moon across the cheek, cutting down into his upper lip. Fist flexor pulled his mouth back in a grin, and the flayed skin puckered, the half moon collapsing into itself. His partner wore a matching scar, fresher and angry red. Scar or gang mark? Maria's pulse began to race. Rings of sweat pooled under her arms. She had been waiting a lifetime for this.

The half-moon brothers came close. They fingered her NYPD uniform and snickered. The lean one spoke in falsetto. "Who-wee. Ain't she pretty, all dressed up in a nice suit."

"She's one stacked mother," the squat one sang out.

The pair circled her, whistling. The lean one clucked. The squat one making wet sucking noises. Circling, circling, forcing Maria to turn in a circle to track them. A knife flashed, then another. "Hey, pretty cop," one of them whispered, "you want me to make your pretty face ugly or your big tits tiny?"

Carved muscle, dead eyes, and stilettos herded her into an alley. "Nice purse, copper girl," the squat one whispered.

Maria had fifty bucks in her leather shoulder bag, and fifty bucks was worth a life.

Hard cement dug into Maria's shoulders, trapping her. A building in back of her and two human sawhorses in front, just like the night she had watched her mother die, cut to pieces on a Spanish Harlem sidewalk. The memory stirred around in her stomach, and for an instant she was a terrified five-year-old again. Then eagerness swept away her fear.

This time she would get them.

One of the knives dove through the air and rested against Maria's throat. It was a tickle at first, the lightest brushing of metal against flesh. She silently cursed her-

self. At the river she had dropped her service revolver
in her purse instead of putting it back in her gun belt
where it belonged. It was ironic and stupid. Stupid
enough to laugh. The teasing tickle at her throat
changed to a flat pressure, and the threat was suddenly
metal chill and not funny at all.

Her head exploded with the memory of a different
knife, one that had sliced her mother's throat in an easy
arc, carving a jack-o-lantern grin in her perfect Spanish
flesh. The old images unreeled. Maria remembered her
mother's mouth open and screaming, her slender fingers
holding onto a red patent purse in which she carried
twenty dollars in small bills. A pair of smirking black
faces, the killers' greedy hands yanking the purse away,
her mother's beautiful face crumpling in death.

That time in Spanish Harlem, Maria had cowered on
the pavement, waving her scrawny arms and crying useless tears. The attackers had laughed at her fear, at her
helplessness. *She wasn't helpless now. She wasn't going
to let them cheat her out of her final act.* Maria opened
her bag, hoping to slip her hand inside and find the gun.
Her wrist snapped back in pain. Fist flexor had her in
his iron grip. He twisted. The pain was white-hot.

"What you got in there, copper?" he whispered, his
breath damp and sour in her face. "You got a gun, cop
lady?" He studied Maria, looking for a telltale flicker
of fear.

If they see your fear, you die.

Maria sneered at him. Defiant. Unafraid. "Fuck you."

He dropped her wrist and lay his knife blade flush to
her cheek. He kneaded her chest with his free hand.
"Drop your purse, copper girl."

She let it fall to the ground and smiled in anticipation,
eyeing the knife. She didn't need the gun, not when she
could kill him with his own weapon. Maria had learned
to use a knife after her mother's murder. Her father had
taught her, first with a rubber toy. When she had the
moves right, he rewarded her with a real blade, Spanish
steel, shiny and sharp. She remembered the look of in-
tense concentration on his handsome face, his big hand

closing around hers, adjusting her grip, turning the weapon in her small palm until she had it right.

Get the knife.

Fist flexor kicked her handbag aside. "She's packing," he barked back at the squat one.

Suddenly, Maria snapped her knee up high and hard into his groin. He spun off her and doubled over clutching his crotch, screaming. The knife clattered to the ground. Maria snatched it up as the squat one came at her, shouting, "Hey! Hey! What the fuck did you do?" She swooped down on the helpless lean one, locked her arm around his neck in a powerful chokehold, and pressed the knife to his cheek. "Back off," she spat at the squat one as she increased the pressure against her prisoner's windpipe.

He edged forward anyway, eyeing the steel against his brother's face, weighing the intent of Maria's threat.

"Toss the blade!" Maria ordered.

"You're dead meat, copper lady," the squat one whispered, coming now straight on and fast, blade whirling through the air, ready to take her.

She jerked the lean one's face back and swiped the knife across his scarred cheek.

The lean one screamed. His voice was shrill. "Do what she says! I'm cut, man! I'm fucking bleeding!"

The squat one tossed his knife. It skidded over to Maria. She kicked it away. Her bag lay between them. The squat one eyed it, hungry for the gun he knew was inside. He dove for the bag. Maria ripped her blade across fist flexor's neck, across the carotid arteries, then shoved his slack weight aside and threw herself at the squat one, plunging the bloodied knife in high on the sternum. He cried out once, then fell to the pavement, silent and still, as silent and still as Maria's own mother had been.

When they come at you, Maria, you look here, at the chest, not at the waving hands or the flying feet, not at any one of the hundred things your opponent will do to distract you. Focus on the chest. When the time is right—you'll know that like you know how to breathe—you

thrust out and up. Always up. You must be confident.
You must move to kill, not to nick or scar or tear, but
to kill."

"Killing's wrong, Daddy. It's a sin."

"It's self-defense. Do you understand that?"

Maria looked at the two prone bodies. It was self-
defense, open and shut. Self-defense, not her own brand
of justice. Not this time. Maria glanced at the phone
booth on the corner, knowing she should call the local
precinct house. She hesitated. Calling in would mean
hours of questioning, statements, and a possible Internal
Affairs investigation.

It was two o'clock in the morning. Maria was tired.
She felt brittle and shaky. The reefer had worn off. So
had the blow that made her feel a hundred feet tall and
invincible, like the Statue of Liberty walking free. Maria
was back to feeling human. Her body shook. Her head
pounded. She wiped the knife handle carefully, wrapped
the hand of the squat one around it, then grabbed her
bag and hurried out of the alley and down the deserted street.

She crossed Eleventh Avenue and saw a group of people hanging out in front of her building. It was Angel
crowding the stoop with a half dozen neighborhood boys
collected around a boom box playing rap. Angel was
tiny, five-two in stocking feet, and she was young. Eighteen years old. *Maybe.* She looked like she was fifteen,
a baby-doll fifteen, sugar sweet and pretty, with the kind
of long, luxurious wavy hair that made a man want to
bury his face in it. A lot of men did. It was a privilege
they paid for.

"Hey, Maria," Angel sang out, hiking her Day-Glo
mini-skirt up. "Looking sharp tonight. Sure I can't interest you in some no-charge fun?"

Maria knew she was showing off. She didn't mind.
Angel was her best friend, her only friend, really. Angel
was a friend and sister and daughter all rolled into one.

"So what do you say, girl?" Angel teased. "You coming with me tonight?"

"No, thanks," Maria laughed. "You're not my type."

Clucks of disappointment ruffled the air. Angel's rag-tag bunch of friends wore low-slung, frayed denim shorts and open shirts that put a half mile of teenage male midriff on display. Six backs arched, feet tapped, and six pairs of eyes turned on Maria. They gave her long appraising looks. Eyebrows lifted in approval.

Maria swung up the stairs and inside. The dim lobby was small. One stride put her across it and in front of the old caged elevator that was crammed between a stingy staircase and cracked wall. She pulled the iron gate aside. It screeched open, a banshee shriek that echoed up the long, narrow column of surrounding stairwell.

Maria looked down at the elevator floor before stepping in. A dozen flaccid, wet condoms stuck like dead balloons to the floor. Milky fluids oozed out and mixed with spilled cheap champagne. House drink, Hell's Kitchen special, no graceful glasses or umbrellas to dress it up.

Some hooker was using the elevator to turn her tricks. Sure wasn't Angel, Maria thought. If there was such a thing as a class hooking act, it was Angel. Scrubbed fresh to gleaming, baby powder sweet smelling, she handled business discreetly in the privacy of her own place on the fourth floor. Maria threw the elevator grate shut and trudged up the stairs to her apartment on eight.

She unlocked the door and stepped inside.

He was waiting for her. There, in the yellow canvas butterfly chair. His cigarette tip glowed orange in the dark. The tip flared, and Maria knew he was inhaling. She closed the door softly. He ground the cigarette out, then was up and across the room, wrapping her roughly in his arms. His stubble scraped her cheek.

Maria wanted to tell him to get out. To leave her alone. To go to fucking hell. She squeezed her eyes shut instead. It was all mixed up, the loyalty and the hate and the love. And the fear. *The fear, the fear, the terrible fear.* She was scared of him. She was scared of all the things he had done to her and all the things he hadn't but might.

Maria used her imagination to block the fear. She

imagined she was standing at the top of a snow-covered mountain where the world was chill and clean, where she felt free. She imagined an eagle swooping by close enough to hear the feathery beat of its flapping wings—*shhwoo, shhwoo,* the sound of freedom.

But Maria wasn't free. She was imprisoned in this man's embrace, and the only sound she heard was the noise of his heavy panting breath. *The eagle,* Maria thought. *The eagle.* With her eyes still closed tight, Maria concentrated on the eagle, on those wide, beating wings, willing the great bird to dip down, pick her up, and fly her away.

Yes! She was airborne now, flying higher and higher until the ragged human panting faded and then even the rush of the great beating wings stopped. Maria was with the eagle, gliding on a thermal, soaring effortless and free in a splendid silence, carried on the wind, rising high, past the burning globe of a white-hot sun, into the hush.

The hush.

The magnificent hush of freedom.

The hush of feeling fearless.

"Fuck me now," he whispered in her ear.

The eagle tumbled through the sky, away from the sun, falling fast out of the hush, out of the quiet, away from the white light, dropping her back into the dark, to *him,* back to where his hot breath was loud in her ear, where his stubble scratched the skin on her breast, and where his thigh was jammed up high between her legs.

Where the fear was so strong, Maria wanted to die.

Gavin didn't bother to change out of his uniform at the end of the tour. He said a curt good-night to Strega in front of the precinct house and ducked into his old Ford Tempo. A fist rapped on the window. Annoyed, he looked up, thinking it was the rookie. He was wrong. It was Detective Lieutenant James Quinton Ballantine, commander of the Nineteenth Precinct detective squad. He was a huge man as round as he was tall, bald, thick-lipped, pale and ponderous. Officers called him Q-Ball when he wasn't within earshot. Now Q-Ball was peering in, looking grave. Little rivers of sweat ran down the channels in his face. Gavin opened the window.

"Glad I caught you," Ballantine said. "Got a minute?"

Gavin shrugged. "Guess so."

"Let's talk inside."

Gavin followed him back into the station house and up the stairs to the squad room, where one tired detective punched two-fingered on an old Smith-Corona. A light burned in Q-Ball's glassed-in corner office. Q-Ball, tight-lipped with intent, wound through a clutter of metal desks to reach it. He unlocked the door. The locked door struck Gavin as odd, but before he could think it through, Q-Ball was ushering him in, closing the door, dropping the bolt back in place, and snapping the Levelors closed. The air was hot and stuffy in the small space. Q-Ball's chin glistened in the dim glow of a desk light.

"Sit down," he said unceremoniously.

Gavin lowered himself into a low vinyl bucket chair facing Q-Ball's desk, and watched the big man switch on a little blue desk fan. The blades whirred softly, spinning up to high speed, and though it barely tickled the air, the frail breeze was relief enough to make Ballantine close his eyes in appreciation.

The regulation metal desk was swamped with meticulously organized stacks of files. A large empty bulletin board leaned on the credenza behind the desk. Gavin was puzzled. On the few occasions he had visited this office, the desk had always been empty and the bulletin board full.

"So, Ballantine, you ask me up here for a Thursday night poker game?" The feeble attempt at humor fell flat, and Gavin was sorry he'd tried. Didn't have to be a detective to read the expression on Q-Ball's face.

Q-Ball sank into his swivel chair and laid his big palms against his pale cheeks. Gavin crazily thought Q-Ball was going to cry; then the hands dropped down on a stack of manila, his face closed up, and the moment was gone. Ballantine spoke in a flat, colorless voice. A recitation of facts.

"The P.C. made a public statement this evening which all the news broadcasts carried. The standard stuff about his 'regret' over these 'unfortunate' instances of suicides. Then more standard stuff about the kind of pressure cops are under these days, what with drugs and gang wars and all the rest. Compassion for the families, and so on and so forth. It was all very proper, subdued, and quick. No questions from the press, nothing. Case closed. The buzz inside One Police Plaza? Damage control. Now that the proper public acknowledgment has been made, the P.C. wants the story buried fast. Close the case files, cross your fingers, and hope it doesn't happen again."

"He's right. It's an ugly subject."

"That it is. But the P.C.'s motivations are purely personal. A bunch of cops committing suicide makes a new police commissioner look bad. Especially one who made department morale his number one priority when he took office."

"He had to. Morale is in the gutter."

"Which is exactly why he wants to sweep this thing under the rug."

"What's wrong with that?"

"Nothing—if what we're looking at are sixteen legitimate suicides." Ballantine leaned in close to the bright desk lamp. His pupils shrank to pinpoints. He lit a cigarette. The match striking filled the silence. The sulfur tip sparked a split second before Gavin began to understand. Ballantine flipped the spent match into his wastebasket and waited while comprehension worked its way across Gavin's face. Then he sat back away from the light and pulled on his cigarette. "I've been a detective for eighteen years. That much time out there looking at what human beings do to each other gives you a feel for things."

Gavin gripped the vinyl seat of the bucket chair and asked in a low, tight voice: "What are you telling me, Ballantine?"

"I'm telling you I got a feeling about these so-called suicides. My gut tells me there's more here than a freak blip in statistical averages."

Gavin felt his throat constrict. Enough sly implication. He had to nail it down. He forced himself to speak, and when he did the one word sounded like a croak: "Homicide?"

Ballantine nodded. "Dressed up like suicide."

Gavin was stunned. The possibility ricocheted around in his head, scaring him and relieving him at the same time. *What if Donovan hadn't killed himself?*

Ballantine continued: "When I tried to share my gut feeling with the chief of detectives, I was politely told all the cases are considered closed. When I insisted they be reopened and the evidence reevaluated, he turned cranky and impolite, shouting all sorts of threats. It was a very loud verbal rap across the knuckles. Ouch. The chief thinks my suspicions are too far-fetched to risk the media feeding frenzy a homicide investigation would invite." Ballantine sat back. "An investigation would keep the suicide story on page one of the tabloids for a long, long time. The P.C. would just like to close his eyes and have the whole thing go away."

"However."

"However, I'm not in the mood to stick my head in the sand like the pussies at One Police Plaza. I've been doing some off-hours investigating of my own, which incidentally is in flagrant disregard to orders. Keep our conversation here private, Ed. I got my ass hanging out in the wind, hoping it doesn't end up full of buckshot. If word of my private investigation gets back to the P.C. or the chief of detectives, my pension turns into pigeon food."

"Why are you talking to me?"

"You and Donovan were tight. Twenty-nine years kind of tight."

Gavin merely shook his head. He didn't trust himself to speak.

"I figure maybe you've got a personal interest in finding out if I'm right. I want you to help me." He reached over and turned the bulletin board around. It was covered with a large map of the five New York City boroughs. Brightly colored push pins punctured the map in various places. Ballantine gestured to them. "Sixteen pins. Each one marks the location of a suicide."

He swiveled back to the desk, picked up a sheaf of white paper, and shook it at Gavin. "Computer printout of all the vital statistics of each victim. Age, birth date, rank, marital status." He dropped the sheaf, then passed a hand over the files covering his desk. "Crime-scene files on each victim, which I'm not supposed to have. But I've got chips out, fifteen years worth of favors done scattered throughout the Department. I finally called them in and got these copies of all the suicide case files." He picked up one of the twelve-by-fourteen envelopes off the top of a stack and dropped it across the desk in front of Gavin.

Gavin read the name neatly typed on the label in Courier 12 Bold: DONOVAN, DANIEL D. He felt that cannonball feeling in his chest again.

Did someone kill you, Danny boy?

The envelope sat unclaimed.

Ballantine ground his cigarette out. "Danny's file. Complete autopsy report, police reports, all the paperwork. The CSU photos are in there too. Look through them. See if they jar your memory."

"I spent the last two months trying to forget what I saw."

"Which is why I want you to study these. Maybe there's something there we didn't catch, something only you might understand."

"What am I looking for?"

Ballantine shrugged. "I'm not sure. A puzzle piece that doesn't fit, something out of whack. I didn't know Danny well enough to read his living room. Read it and tell me your old friend left a message that says this is something more than a suicide."

Gavin shook his head sadly. "Lang read the gunshot wound, and it said suicide. I think Danny just plain killed himself. Nothing in those pictures will make me think otherwise." Gavin shoved the folder back across the desk. He remembered Strega's words and repeated them to Q-Ball. "Suicide's a desperate act, an act of grief."

Ballantine pressed. "So what could've made Danny that sad?"

"He went home early one day and found his wife screwing the teenage boy who lived next door. She filed for divorce, took everything Danny had, then tried to get custody of his little girl. In my book, that's cause enough for genuine grief."

Ballantine picked the folder up and held it out. "And maybe someone pulled the trigger for him. All I'm asking is for you to keep an open mind."

Gavin looked from the file to the map covered with bright push pins. Color codes for men who just couldn't take what life was offering them anymore. His gaze dropped to Ballantine's weary face. What if Q-Ball was right? What if life had served up a little unexpected side dish? Didn't he owe Danny the benefit of doubt no matter how infinitesimal that doubt might be? Death was cold and it was for a long time. Life was here and he had a chance to bring a little dignity back Danny's way. He reached out and took the file.

"Take your time," Ballantine said. "A few days, a week if you need it."

"I'm not much of a detective," Gavin said, standing up. "You know that. I couldn't even find my own daughter."

Ballantine's face softened visibly. "But you tried, Ed. God knows you tried."

Gavin nodded curtly. He slammed the door on his way out.

Gavin dropped the CSU file in the trunk of the old Tempo. *Take your time,* Q-Ball had said. Gavin would look through the file, but not yet. Not tonight, and maybe not tomorrow. Maybe not even over the weekend. He wasn't ready to relive the horror.

Not just yet.

TWO

The Nineteenth Precinct station house is located on East Sixty-seventh Street, smack in the middle of the upper East Side. It is a tony neighborhood defined by designer boutiques, doorman buildings, and three of the richest avenues in the world: Fifth Avenue, Madison Avenue, and Park Avenue. Bounded by Fifty-ninth Street on the bottom and Ninety-sixth Street at the top, the Nineteenth Precinct runs west to the border of Central Park and east to the East River.

Jackie-O lived in the Nineteenth. Mariah Carey, Woody Allen, Paul Newman, Itzhak Perlman, and Madonna still do. The mayor of New York City lives in the Nineteenth, and the police commissioner lives there too. Every major foreign embassy is located in the Nineteenth, and so is the reigning embassy of beauty, the Ford Modeling Agency. The Nineteenth houses more priceless art per square foot than any other place in the world, in museums like the Guggenheim, the Whitney, the Metropolitan, the Frick, and Cooper-Hewitt. A stone's throw away from the precinct house, art fortunes are routinely auctioned off in the venerable establishments of Sotheby's and Christie's.

In cop talk, the Nineteenth is referred to as the One-Nine. Cops outside the One-Nine call the precinct "Club Med" because the murder rate is almost nonexistent. Most of the serious crime committed in the One-Nine is white-collar. The rest is confined to robberies, burglaries, and car thefts. No wonder. There are more Mercedes, Porsches, Jaguars, and limos per square foot there than anywhere else in the country. Violent crime is an oddity, something seen on television or reported in the *Times,* something that happens *somewhere else.* The Nineteenth is a cocoon for the insulated, rich, pampered people who live there.

Inside the NYPD, any cop that requests assignment to the One-Nine is considered to be a cop without ambition, a wheezer who wants to coast along until pension time, not a real cop at all. Patrolmen with ambition transfer out of Club Med whenever possible. They request rugged details like the buy-and-bust tactical narcotics team down in the bowels of lower Manhattan. Or they request assignment to the Twenty-fifth Precinct in Spanish Harlem, where a patrolman stands a good chance of taking a bullet and along with it, a meritorious commendation. Such commendations get ambitious officers noticed. These are the politics of promotion, none of which usually apply in the One-Nine, not unless you are the captain of the precinct house. Then you are looking at an instant promotion to the rank of deputy inspector upon assignment to the One-Nine. The citizens living in the precinct are too rich and powerful themselves to deal with a simple captain. They insist on rank, and the New York Police Department brass is happy to oblige.

Even the precinct house itself is different. It sits on a gracious block of refined historic brownstones. The front of the four-story structure is solid red brick, except for the window frames, which are painted bright blue, the same cheerful Mediterranean blue as the patrol cars. A gracious arch sweeps across the facade, and a charming "welcoming arms" staircase leads up to the main entrance door. In the early nineties the hundred-year-old station house was totally renovated to include central A.C., a spacious, fully equipped gymnasium, and the biggest, slickest locker room in the Department.

The only amenity the architects did not add was a real parking garage. The deputy inspector and a few high-ranking lieutenants have parking privileges inside an adjoining courtyard. Everybody else competes for the limited spaces on the street.

On Friday morning, Gavin turned his beige Ford

Tempo down Sixty-seventh Street and lucked out. The one remaining parking space was in the shade. He pulled in, tossed his NYPD ID plate on the dash, and got out. It was six forty-five in the morning, but the merciless heat made it feel like noon. He trudged into the station house and wondered why it was so hot *inside*.

The desk sergeant on duty was a big black officer named Bell. He sat high up at the elevated desk that kept him out of reach of belligerent taxpayers and hostile prisoners, looked down at Gavin, and raised a hand in greeting. "Morning."

"Hey, Bell," Gavin said. "It's like the Bahamas in here."

"A.C.'s on the fritz."

"It's brand-new."

"So what? It's on the fritz. Guy's looking at it, says the contractor didn't hook up the ducts right, or some goddamned thing like that."

"They going to fix it?"

"Might take some time. Might have to rip out part of the ceiling to get to the problem. Who knows? Could be out for two days or two weeks. Fucking contractors."

"They'll milk the job for all they can get."

"They always do," Bell agreed. "You pulling the eight-to-four tour?"

"Just when I was getting used to steady nights."

The phone rang. Bell answered it and waved Gavin off.

Gavin went down the hall toward the locker room. He paused by the stairs leading to the gym. Guilt gnawed at him. He used to get in three decent workouts a week, pumping iron and hitting the boxing bag. There was time now for a few good sets of bicep curls, maybe some leg work. No reason not to. Not a reason in the world. Except for the fact that he wasn't in the mood and hadn't been for some time. Like so many things, it just wasn't the same without Donovan. Gavin walked away.

He was early for the tour change. The locker room was empty. Water dripped in the shower stalls. The sound of his footsteps echoed around him. Gavin opened his locker and undressed methodically. Jeans folded once over a hanger, then placed on the left. T-shirt placed carefully on the locker shelf. Sneakers on the locker floor, socks spread out on top.

Gavin took the regulation Kevlar bulletproof vest from its hanger and slipped it on. Next, he pulled out a fresh shortsleeve uniform shirt and counted the five gold military-style stripes on the left sleeve. One stripe for each five years served, and Gavin was going for six—six stripes, after which he would take a long walk into the sunset of his life. Gavin had loved being a cop—until Donovan died. Now finishing out thirty years was just an ego thing. He and Donovan had made a crazy pact when they were rookies together, swearing to serve three decades and earn six stripes. Five stripes weren't six. Twenty-nine years and seven months wasn't three decades. It had to be thirty years.

Gavin shrugged the shirt on. The ritual of dressing for the tour still pleased him. The uniform was symbolic of strength and bravery, of law and order, of America itself, and of course, of his commitment to the NYPD. That commitment was like a marriage, he thought, for better or worse, and he had seen both sides in his twenty-nine years. He pulled his dark pants on and zipped up. As much as he thought he wanted out, the prospect of quitting scared him. He picked his gun belt out of the locker and slung it around his waist, liking the bulk of it. It was heavy, omnipresent, a constant reminder to him of the weight of his responsibility. What was it going to feel like to not be a cop?

A small color snapshot of his daughter was pasted to the inside of the locker door. He ran his fingers over her smiling face. It was another part of the daily ritual, touching the picture of Alex for luck even though it seemed like his own luck had run out the day she disappeared.

Gavin closed his locker and drifted down the row to number 46, Donovan's old locker. He said the name and it came out a whisper. "Daniel Donovan." The urge to spin the combination lock was irresistible: 36-24-36.

Donovan's big laugh came back to him: "*Easy enough numbers to remember. I'd like to meet her, whoever she is.*" Gavin yanked down on the lock. It didn't open. It wouldn't ever open to that set of numbers again. Regulations called for a lock change upon reassignment of the locker.

Gavin had been the last one to use Donovan's combination when he collected Danny's personal effects. A freshly pressed uniform with five stripes on the left sleeve of the uniform shirt. Two sets of carefully folded clean Fruit of the Loom underwear. A shave kit. Jumble of old sneakers in various states of disrepair. NYPD gym shorts and a T-shirt that said *Look Better Naked.* Couple of fishing magazines saved for a never-to-happen retirement in the country. Spit-polished dress shoes. Old *New York Times* sports pages. Metal basket full of worn bars of soap that had one more shower left in them. Beach towel with a life-size hula girl stamped across it. Frayed jeans. Keys, chewing gum, the Holy Bible.

And, the snapshots taped on the inside of the door. There must have been fifty of them, all together documenting the growth of Donovan's first three kids from diapers to sullen Generation X quasi-adults. The fourth was still a child. She was five years old, a late-life surprise who had adored her daddy and won his heart. Katy Donovan. Danny's pride and joy.

Gavin hadn't offered Danny's personal effects to the widow. She didn't deserve them. Neither did the older kids, a ratty threesome who called cops "pigs." Imagine that. Katy was too young to understand, so Gavin placed the items lovingly into a box which he carted home and shoved back into the far reaches of his closet. One day he would be able to take it down and look through the odds and ends of Donovan's life without feeling a kick in his kidneys. One day, but that day would be a long time in coming. Gavin pressed his forehead against the cool steel.

Mike Kelly drifted down the row. He was a tall, well-built man with jet black hair and bright blue eyes. Kelly was an imposing man in uniform, and his uniform, like

Gavin's, had five stripes on the sleeve. He put a hand on Gavin's shoulder. "We all miss him, Ed. He had a heart bigger than this whole goddamned squad put together. He gave to everyone who needed the love."

"And didn't have enough left over for himself." Gavin punched the locker.

"Maybe. But he was a great cop and an even better man. Keep that in mind." Kelly moved down the row to his own locker.

Gavin went for one more spin, counting the numbers out loud. "Thirty-six, twenty-four, thirty-six."

"You need something out of my locker, Ed?" Strega asked.

Gavin hadn't seen him come in. He pulled away from the locker. "Roll call's in five minutes. Don't be late." He turned to leave.

Strega grabbed him by the elbow. "Listen. I'm sorry about Donovan. I know having a new partner must be hard for you."

"You don't know shit." Gavin shook his elbow free and stalked out.

Strega looked at Kelly. "No matter what I say, it's the wrong thing."

"Cut Ed some slack," Kelly said. "He and Danny were like family. He's still grieving."

Forty-three officers with foot-post, patrol-car, and station-house duties split between them attended the Friday morning roll call. The crowded room hummed with cop talk, hand radios buzzed, and from time to time someone laughed. Maria Alvarez took a seat in the front row. She removed her hat and held it in her lap. A skinny young cop dropped down in the chair next to her. He had a chipped front tooth and little close-set eyes. Acne scars pocked his face like craters. Cops around the One-Nine called him Moon.

"Looking good, babe," he whispered, smiling at her boldly.

Maria felt a mixture of pity and disgust for Moon with his big, horsy laugh, his clumsy ways, for the earnest, eager expression on his dog-ugly face and the fact he wanted to be a cop at all. Mostly she felt disgust for the way he looked at her with such evident naked desire. Maria preferred shy cops.

The kind who were afraid to fuck her because she was the P.C.'s daughter.

Her eyes scanned the room. Kelly. Mike Kelly was one of the shy ones. Kelly was afraid of her, and looked at her secretly, hiding his interest. Then there was the new cop Strega, who didn't look at her at all. He wasn't interested or afraid—yet. Maria turned back to Moon and winked at him, then brushed her teasing hand across his thigh. His eyes widened, his jaw dropped. The craters flushed red. *Men are so easy,* Maria thought, directing her attention to Ballantine, who was milling through the room, passing out Xerox copies of a composite sketch.

Q-Ball handed her one. Maria studied it. Unlike Moon, the suspect had no identifying facial scars or marks. His eyes were neither too close together or too wide apart, and his teeth were even. He was not ugly, but not handsome either. It was, she thought, an unremarkable face.

"Most criminals, most killers even, are average looking," her father had taught her when she was older and he was preparing her to be a cop. *"A good detective is not fooled by appearance. He knows what an average face can hide."*

Maria knew Ballantine was a good detective. Some, like her father, even considered him great. She wondered what Ballantine saw when he looked at her face.

"Our suspects are male," Ballantine rumbled. "So far we've got a rough composite on one of them. Caucasian. Late thirties. Approximately six feet tall, sandy blond hair, clean-shaven. His buddy has dark hair, but our witnesses can't agree on his height, weight, or what his face looks like. They do agree that both suspects were well dressed."

"What do you consider well dressed?" Moon asked.

"They sure as hell aren't wearing worn-out sneakers

and Levi's like some slobs I've seen around here," Ballantine snapped.

The craters flushed red again. Moon chewed on a fingernail.

"Well dressed means well dressed," Ballantine boomed, shaking the composite sketch in the air. "Business attire! Coat and tie! White shirt! Shoes with those little tassels on the front, just like a thousand men who work in office buildings in this area. And therein lies the problem. *These perps don't stand out.* They're wearing those little tasseled shoes while they're working Madison Avenue, looking for the lunching ladies who think a carrot is something you wear, not eat.

"It goes like this: The blonde works the neighborhood. When he finds a woman wearing impressive jewelry, he discreetly follows her until she's vulnerable. Then he sticks a gun in her ribs and steers her right into the front seat of a waiting vehicle. He does not get in. The car takes off with the woman inside, alone with the driver. The car doors are locked, windows are sealed shut. The driver is armed. He informs the victim that she will not be hurt—if she cooperates. He then drives her to an out-of-way place, confiscates her jewelry, lets her out, and disappears.

"So far this team has nailed six women, in six separate incidents, all on Madison Avenue in broad daylight. The bitch of it is, each time a different vehicle is used. Stretch limo, Mercedes sedan, Jaguar, Porsche. You name it. They are all most likely stolen. The composite you have is of the perp who canvasses the neighborhood. He moves fast and smooth, makes it look natural as can be. Risky? You bet. What if one of these ladies screamed? Put up a fight? He's counting on fear to keep them quiet. So far he's counted right. Each of the victims cooperated. Each was released uninjured.

"I've received numerous calls from the mayor. He lives here in the One-Nine. His wife's afraid to go out to lunch. She's upset. The mayor's upset. Hell, even the P.C.'s upset. He lives in our precinct too. He wants the perps behind bars, and I plan on giving the P.C. what he wants."

Ballantine stared at Maria—*the P.C.'s daughter*—driving his point home, but for an instant she was afraid Q-Ball had another reason for staring at her. Did he know? Could he look right through her and see how her skin was bare under her uniform? Could he see the small packet of white Colombian snow shoved deep in her pocket? Did he know about her alley fight, how when cornered alone she had gone after her attackers like a warrior, drawing her blade across one man's throat, then driving it deep into the second man's heart? Did he know about her midnight trips to the river? And if he did, could he possibly know about her other secrets? *Be careful with Ballantine,* she thought as he finally turned away from her.

The squad room door opened, and Deputy Inspector Wilson blew in. He was a magnificent-looking man, tall and fit, with a full head of thick silver hair. This morning Wilson was immaculately dressed in a trim dark blue suit, crisp white shirt, and a sleek yellow silk tie. His back was ramrod straight, and his lean, handsome face was set hard with anger.

Ballantine eased aside. "Good morning, Inspector."

"It's not," Wilson said, snapping open the *Daily News* and holding it high, pointing at the banner headline: NYPD SUICIDE BINGE CLAIMS NUMBER 16. "Steve Prince from the One-Seven. Eighteen years on the street and he decides he's had enough. Every year the average number of Department suicides sticks to around eight or nine. One freak year we had fourteen. Obviously, we would like to see that number be zero, but the number's going up instead of down. Sixteen suicides this year and it's only August." Wilson's voice cracked. He paused to regain his composure, then went on.

"The Department understands the special psychological pressures that come with policing New York City, and the Department stands behind you all the way. That's why Psychological Services was created. It's there so officers under stress have a place to go. The professional counsel Psych Services offers is free of charge and available to any officer of any rank who wants it. The problem is, no one's using it. If you have something on your mind and you don't want to go to Psych Services, come to me. Please. I can guarantee you confidentiality." Wilson slapped the newspaper down on a desk and marched out.

Maria watched Ballantine and Gavin exchange a long look. She wondered what it meant.

The tour sergeant tossed out the tour assignments, putting Maria on foot post. She was a floater who teamed up with various partners on a rotating basis, filling in for cops who were on vacation or out sick. When she wasn't buddied up, she worked alone on foot, which was fine with her this morning. She had too much on her mind to spend eight hours in a patrol car making small talk. Maria also felt tired, and she knew she needed regular hits of blow to stay alert. It was easier to do alone. Safer too. Her drug habit was a secret.

One day when Wilson read her name instead of Steve Prince's, and when the cops here talked among themselves about the *Alvarez incident,* she wanted them to remember her as a model cop. They would remember how she always arrived promptly for roll call and how she sat straight up, attentive and alert. They would remember the sharply pressed pants and starched shirt of her immaculate uniform and how she wore it with pride. They would think back too on how she sat with grace, her small, lovely hands resting lightly on the hat in her lap with no sign at all that she wanted out of this life.

The tour sergeant dismissed. The room emptied, but Maria hung back, watching her fellow cops file out. Moon loitered, eyeing her up and down, his big Adam's apple pumping hard. "Listen," he finally said with a lustful grin, "you want to grab a beer with me tonight?"

"No," Maria said coldly. Moon scratched his head and wandered off. He looked back at her once or twice, wondering, she guessed, if he had imagined her bright smile and her promising hand heavy on his thigh.

When she was finally alone, she picked up Wilson's

abandoned newspaper and studied the picture of Steve
Prince. It was a good shot. Prince looked proud and sure
of himself. The cause of death was described simply as
a single gunshot to the right temple. Maria touched the
fresh welt on her own temple. Although the squad room
was hot, she shivered.

She put her hat on, tucked the composite sketch in
her uniform pocket, and tossed the newspaper in the
trash on her way out.

Gavin posted his copy of the composite sketch up
front in the patrol car, where it would serve as visual
references throughout the tour. He sat back in the passenger seat and waited for Strega.

Mike Kelly stopped by and stuck his head in the window. "Number sixteen. What the hell's going on?"

"I have no idea." And he didn't. Danny's CSU file
was still sitting unopened in Gavin's trunk.

"Here comes your new partner," Kelly said. "Try to
have a good day." He slapped the roof of the car and
walked off.

Gavin watched him go, reluctantly. He and Kelly were
the old dogs in the precinct, the only two cops with five
stripes. They should have been teamed up after Donovan's death, but Gavin was told he was more valuable
partnered with a wet-nosed rookie he could *teach the
trade to.* An old dog teaching a new one the game, and
in Gavin's opinion that included all the special goodies
the academy never covered—the off-the-book tricks, like
how to put the Yellow Pages on a perp's head and
whack it with the nightstick so there was plenty of pain
but no incriminating marks or bruises.

The problem was, Strega was such a by-the-book kid,
he wasn't going to be much interested in the kind of
tricks Gavin had to teach. Strega had announced he
wanted to do everything right—whatever *right* was. He
wanted to climb the NYPD ladder straight up to Detective Heaven. In his own intent words, Strega had said
he wanted to be the best cop on the job and a hero too.
A goddamn hero.

Well, Strega didn't look much like a hero walking across the street to the car. He looked unsure, nervous as hell, and a little scared. He even hesitated before getting in the car. Strega dangled the car keys in front of Gavin and asked primly: "Would you like to drive today?"

"Do I look like I would like to drive today?" Gavin mocked. "You drive today and every day. That's your job. I ride shotgun, handle the siren, the loudspeaker, the paperwork."

"Procedure calls for four hours driving and four off. Officers are required to alternate. We never switched yesterday. I did all the driving."

"You got a problem driving eight hours?"

"Not really, But procedure—"

"Fuck procedure. Just drive. I never drive."

They spent the top part of the tour cruising the sector. Strega was still learning the neighborhood, and it was Gavin's job to make sure he knew it. They inched up Madison Avenue, hugging the left curb.

"A lot of people call this the Silk Stocking District," Gavin explained. "The ladies are rich, the stores are expensive." He pointed at a small, elegant shop on the opposite side of the street. "See that place there?"

Strega nodded.

"Stockings cost more than a hundred bucks a pair." Gavin shook his head and pointed at a different shop. "See that?"

Strega looked and nodded.

"Six hundred bucks for a pair of prescription eyeglasses. See that wine shop? You could spend five hundred bucks on a bottle of wine, or you could spend the same five hundred on a pair of shoes in the store next door." Gavin chuckled. "You show up on Madison Avenue with ten grand in hundred-dollar bills, it'll last you approximately one block depending on where you stop in. Ten grand used to get you a down payment on a house. Here, if you're lucky, it buys you a party dress."

They rolled along in silence. Then Gavin started pointing and talking again. "This block here starts the heavy fashion stuff. Bunch of Italians, no offense intended."

"None taken," Strega replied.

"Versace. Armani. Valentino. Ungaro. Gianfranco something. And here you got the French guys, one guy's a Saint, the other's an Oscar. I can't pronounce their last names. Hell, the only French word I can say is croissant. Over there you got Ralph Lauren. American first name, Frenchy kind of last name, if you ask me. Guess that's why he's on the French block."

They turned left at Eighty-seventh Street, then left again on Fifth Avenue. Gavin pointed out the Metropolitan Museum, sitting low and graceful on the edge of Central Park. "Technically, the museum's in the Central Park Precinct, but we help keep an eye on it."

They cruised slowly, hugging the curb. Gavin pointed at an imposing pre-war structure opposite the park. "See that swank apartment building?" A smart green awning fanned out over the sidewalk. A liveried doorman stood at attention. Two limos waited out front.

"Nice place," Strega observed.

"Tell that to the taxpayers. The P.C. lives there."

"So?"

"So, it's out of line. The P.C.'s been on the job six months, and he's taken to the good life like he was born to it, which he wasn't. Expensive restaurants, big society events, Armani suits. Last week he had dinner with Robert De Niro. The *Times* ran a picture of the two of them on the front page. The P.C. thinks he's a fucking star."

"He is. He's a politician."

"He's a cop. Cops shouldn't be stars."

Strega stopped for a light.

A sidewalk newspaper vendor flashed a copy of the *New York Post.* Gavin locked in on the headline: 16TH COP SUICIDE: GOOD NIGHT SWEET PRINCE.

Strega saw it too. He shook his head and started in. "Put a man in uniform, throw him out into a hostile urban environment where little kids are dealing drugs, turning tricks, and getting murdered, and tell him to deal with it. Some cops can adjust. Others can't. They feel threatened, useless, and finally, hopeless."

"What makes you an expert?" Gavin sniped.

"I took a lot of psych courses at Princeton."

Sigmund Freud. Alive and well and in uniform.

Gavin's eyes narrowed to slits. He aimed them out of the window at the sea of cars idling in the hot sun. "Fifth's a fucking parking lot," he muttered. "Turn back over to Madison when you can."

Strega complied.

"Slow down," Gavin ordered on the approach to Seventy-seventh Street and Madison Avenue. "It's our job to check in with all officers assigned to foot posts in our sector. We got one on foot post here. Officer Alvarez. Maria Alvarez. That's Alvarez as in Ramon Alvarez, the show-biz P.C. She's his daughter. You can practice your Princeton pop psychology on her."

Strega eased the car to a stop alongside the curb.

A young Spanish woman strolled across the sidewalk. She was not tall, but she had generous hips and a lush chest. In between bust and hips, her tiny waist was cinched tight with the regulation gun belt. A pair of aviator style Ray-Ban sunglasses hid her eyes. She took her hat off and leaned down next to Gavin's window. Her dark hair was pulled back slick against her head, showing off her striking face. She was beautiful but hard-edged. Her heavy lips were painted circus red. She wore the same bright red on her long nails. Her perfume was strong. Something musky cinnamon. It mixed with the sharp scent of female sweat and another richer smell that Gavin couldn't identify but didn't find at all unpleasant.

"Quiet day here?" Gavin asked.

"Quiet and hot," she answered. "Too hot." Her face was moist with perspiration.

"On your next day off, go to Jones Beach," Gavin quipped. "Take a swim."

"What if I don't know how to swim?"

"Then put your bikini on, stay home, and turn the a.c. on," Gavin replied. He noticed a dark mark on the side of her head. "What happened?" he asked, pointing.

She quickly put her hat back on, covering the mark. "Ran into my locker door. The heat makes me clumsy."

Gavin thought the injury looked more like a burn than a bruise, but he kept his observation to himself.

Maria took her Ray-Bans off and studied Strega. Her face lit up. "Who's your driver?"

"Officer Jon Strega. He's new in the One-Nine. New in the Department."

"Nice to meet you, Jonnie Strega." Her dark eyes flashed. She reached across Gavin and held a slim hand out to Strega.

Strega took it briefly. "Nice to meet you, Alvarez."

Gavin studied the arm stretched across him. Her shortsleeve uniform shirt exposed the bare skin of her arm. It was covered with a fine down of dark hairs.

Alvarez withdrew her hand, fooled with her gun belt. "What do you think of the One-Nine so far?"

"Seems like a good precinct," Strega answered coolly.

"In my opinion, it just got a whole lot better." She arched a dark eyebrow and looked down at Strega's lap. A raw, predatory expression flickered across her face; then she blinked and it was gone. "The One-Nine's as good as it gets. You don't have to worry about getting beat up here, and the shopping's good, if you can afford it. If you can't, don't let it get you down. Some of the best things in life are free." She tapped a red fingernail on the door. The air was charged.

Gavin couldn't help looking at the red fingernail. He wondered what it would feel like crawling down his spine.

"So, you live in the city?" she asked Strega.

"West Side," he acknowledged.

"Very upwardly mobile," she teased. "Are you a yuppie, Jonnie?"

"Nope, I'm a cop just like you."

"Oh, I doubt that you're at all like me." A low laugh rolled around in the back of Alvarez's throat. She put the mirrored Ray-Bans back on.

Gavin looked into them and tried to read her expression. All he could see was his own mouth moving as he spoke. "Time to go," he was saying. "We'll stop by later." He pushed a button. The window slid up. Alvarez pulled away.

Gavin watched her small, dark figure edge back into a patch of shade under a store overhang. "Alvarez likes you, Strega."

"Is that good or bad?"

"Do you like her?"

"Not my type."

"Then you're in trouble. Alvarez doesn't like the word no."

"You have personal experience?"

"Unfortunately, Alvarez never liked *me* the way she likes *you.*"

"Lucky you."

"From the talk I hear, you might consider buying a cod piece."

Strega glanced back at the sidewalk. She was leaning against the building, hands on her hips, grinning at him.

"Let's go," Gavin ordered. "Take a run down to the bottom of the precinct."

Strega moved back into the traffic flow.

Gavin thought about Maria Alvarez. A few months earlier, out of the blue, she had set her sights on Donovan. It was just after Donovan's wife dumped out of the marriage, and he was vulnerable. Maybe Maria thought he was an easy target, a quick toss, good for a laugh and a couple of free meals. Or maybe she just felt sorry for him. Who knows. The whole thing was puzzling. Donovan wasn't a great catch, so what sexy little Maria saw in him was anybody's guess. From the talk Gavin heard, she had a voracious appetite for young, good-looking cops like Strega. A shy, middle-aged guy like Danny? Well, it just didn't fit. Nonetheless, according to Donovan, she had thrown herself at him.

At first Donovan laughed it off, though Gavin secretly believed his partner was flattered by the attention. Then, all of a sudden just before he died, Donovan clammed up. He got grouchy and snappy whenever Gavin introduced the subject of Maria Alvarez. As far as Gavin knew, they'd never had so much as a beer together, let alone a date. Two weeks later, Daniel Donovan was dead. Gavin had forgotten the whole Alvarez thing—until he saw her eyeing Strega. He wondered now if there had been something between Danny and Alvarez that he had missed.

"What else is there to know about Maria Alvarez?" Strega asked.

"She's the P.C.'s daughter," Gavin replied. "A golden child, hatched from big-time NYPD stock. Ramon Alvarez started as a beat cop here in Manhattan, and he was a star from day one. Some say he's heading straight for Washington. Hell, Ramon has all the right stuff. He's a self-made minority kid from the slums, a widower who raised his daughter alone, and a good-looking son of a bitch to boot."

"What happened to his wife?"

"She was murdered up in Spanish Harlem when Ramon was a rookie. Maria was five years old."

"Jesus."

"It gets better. Maria was with her mother when she was killed. Saw the whole goddamn thing. Ramon turned his personal tragedy into a one-man anti-crime crusade. He never misses an opportunity to talk about it. He loves the limelight, the public loves him, and the mayor loves him because the *public* loves him. He's the most charismatic P.C. this city's ever had. Not only that, Ramon Alvarez is fearless, and he's got more decorations than you can hang on a Christmas tree to prove it. His one disappointment in life? No sons. Just Maria, but it worked out okay. She's got *cojones* as big as his."

"How's that?"

"Maria graduated top of her class at the academy. Beat the pants off every other candidate in target practice. She set a record: highest target scores in the history of the academy. She's fearless too, like her father."

"Define fearless."

"She was standing on a subway platform late one night, off duty, when some punk pulled a knife and made a move to steal an old lady's gold necklace. Maria beat the shit out of him, bare-handed."

Strega whistled.

"She's got guts and she's ambitious. Maria Alvarez isn't afraid of anything or anybody. Last I heard, she was gunning for the buy-and-bust team. The minute she lands a high-profile assignment like buy-and-bust, she'll sail up through the ranks. Maria didn't go to college like you, but she's smart. Maybe not book smart, but she's smart. And she likes you, Strega."

"What makes you think that?"

"She made it very clear to you back there. She was ready, able, and willing. Maria Alvarez all but hauled you out of the car and jumped you on the sidewalk."

Strega shook his head. "No, thanks. Like I said, she's not my type."

Hell, Gavin thought, if he were in Strega's place, he'd take what was offered. Why not? Life was short and Maria was a walking firecracker. She could probably make a dark night feel like the Fourth of July. Lately, Gavin was more interested in Maria than a married man ought to be. He had fantasies, lots of them. They were ribald, raucous things that popped into his mind at all hours of the day and night, distracting and arousing him, charging him up. He was charged up now, plenty, thinking about little Maria Alvarez, about what she could do to him with her generous red mouth.

The hand radio sat on the seat next to Gavin. It crackled from time to time with the sound of Central tossing out jobs to other precincts. The One-Nine shared a frequency with the Two-Oh and the Two-Four on the upper West Side, as well as the Central Park precinct. The three sister precincts were active. The One-Nine, however, was quiet. Something started to beep. It sounded like a small alarm clock. Strega pulled a black square box out of his pocket and flipped it open.

"What's that thing?" Gavin asked.

"Stock Genie," Strega said. "The world's smallest money maker."

"Money maker?"

"The Genie acts as an extension of my mainframe computer at home, which I've got linked to the stock tickers. I program the Genie to beep me if any of my stocks hit a certain number, high or low. When it beeps, I look at the little screen here, see what the stock's doing, and decide whether to buy, sell, or hang on. If I want to place an order, I call my broker. Since I ride around in a car all day, my broker can't reach me. The Genie's the only way I can stay on top of my portfolio. Great, isn't it?"

"Peachy," Gavin said, yawning. He was bored silly by anything financial. He let Shelly handle all the money stuff. It was a good division of labor. He made the money, she managed it. Big purchases, like new carpet or the custom tile job in the bathroom, he had to approve. Once a year he asked how much they had socked away for retirement, At the last annual review in January, things were humming along on schedule, heading for the magic number that, coupled with the handsome pension six stripes worth of duty paid out, would let him live out his retirement in Florida in relative comfort.

The Genie beeped again. Gavin looked back at Strega. "What's it telling you now?"

"West Entertainment's ticking up. But I'm not going to sell yet."

"Why not?"

"Entertainment companies create programming for the multi-channel media universe. As that universe expands, so does demand for product to fill it. West Entertainment's prime for a studio takeover. If the company goes into play, the stock will really fly."

Gavin scowled. Strega had no commitments. His paycheck was one hundred percent his. If Strega wanted to play stocks like a roulette wheel in Vegas, what the hell. As far as Gavin was concerned, he'd rather go to Vegas. Same odds, but in Vegas at least he could ogle the dancers.

"So how long have you been in the One-Nine?" Strega asked.

The worst thing about having a new partner was the life-story bit. "Two years and change."

"And before this?"

"Prior to assignment in the One-Nine, Officer Edward S. Gavin spent twenty-seven years pulling alternate day and night tours in the notorious Three-Four up in Washington Heights. Now, there's a precinct with ambiance. Crack heads, psycho-whores, domestic violence, armed robbery, murders, beatings, gangs burning rival gang members alive, child abuse, drug rings, the occasional family dog dipped in scalding water. You ever get bored, try spending a summer afternoon in the Three-Four and see if it doesn't make you lose respect for the so-called human race."

"Is that why you transferred out?"

"No," Gavin said.

"Does all the misery you've seen depress you?"

"Oh, no, no way are you going to start psychoanalyzing me. I'm not interested in your Princeton pop psychobabble."

"What've you got against Princeton?" Strega asked lightly, stopping for a red light.

"You just don't fucking get it, do you?" Gavin slouched in his seat and studied the people moving down the sidewalk.

Suddenly, he sat straight up, bird dog sharp, focused on a flash of long red-gold hair in the crowd. He tracked it, hoping to see the face that went with it. The girl tossed her hair and turned slightly. Gavin glimpsed her profile. It wasn't Alex. This "girl" was thirty-five, not eighteen, older by far than Alex would be now. *Idiot,* he thought, watching her walk away, *thinking you'll find Alex on the street, thinking you'll ever see her again.*

Thirty blocks down Fifth Avenue, the Empire State Building sparkled in the sun. Gavin looked up at the building's sharp point sticking high in the sky and thought, *Is Alex up there with you, Danny boy? Can you both reach down and touch the spire?*

Three

Gavin didn't say much to the rookie for the rest of the day, which isn't to say the rookie didn't have much to say to Gavin. He did. Only Gavin never really became a part of the conversation. It was a speech, a monologue, a one-man ramble. Strega started with his bright academic success, and when he exhausted that subject, he rattled happily along, challenging conventional investment theory, reviewing books and cinema offerings (it was always *the cinema* or *a film,* never the movies or a flick). Gavin grunted now and then, and barked out orders from time to time—*Turn left. Turn right. Stop*—while Strega went on. And on. And on.

By the end of the tour, Strega was deep into a verbal political dissertation in which he concluded—quote—*full employment is the panacea to urban chaos*—end quote.

"What do you think?" Strega asked earnestly.

Gavin grunted and fiddled with the a.c., which was already turned up to high. "It's almost four," he muttered. "Let's call it a day."

"Sure thing." Strega turned up Third Avenue.

"Fuck," Gavin said, staring out into the sea of metal bumpers choking the street. The five-minute trip back to the station house would take thirty.

"Nineteen Ida," Central's rapid-fire female voice called out over the radio.

Gavin glared at the radio. He didn't want to take any calls this close to quitting time.

"Nineteen Ida, do you read me?" Central's tone was sharp and urgent.

Gavin reluctantly picked the radio up off the seat. "Nine Ida John."

"Ten-thirty in progress," Central reported. "Two men armed and dangerous, shots fired. Proceed with caution. Melissa Stewart Bridal Shop, 982 Madison Avenue, Seventy-seven at the cross. All other units in the vicinity, please assist."

"Nine Ida John," Gavin confirmed. "Ten-four." He punched up the control panel as he talked, sending out the thousand electrical impulses that set the roof lights to spinning and revved the siren up to a full undulating wail. Adrenaline flushed out his late-afternoon apathy. A ten-thirty was an armed robbery in progress, and it was a rare event in the One-Nine. Old reflexes from his hell-chasing days in the Three-Four kicked in. "Get us out of this parking lot, Strega," he snapped, looking at the hopelessly clogged street. "Show me you can do something besides talk. Show me you can drive."

Suddenly, the car shot forward. Gavin threw a sideways glance at Strega. He was impressed by his young partner's utter concentration, the perfect calm and determination with which he made the speedometer soar and lift, past thirty, past forty, to a shaky point between forty-five and fifty. Strega pulled the steering wheel, left, then right, then left again in a steady samba in and out of the cars, finding holes to slip through where Gavin saw no opportunity at all. Not bad, Gavin thought, not bad at all for a rookie driver on a jammed main street at rush hour on a summer afternoon.

Strega raced up Third, not easing up, not slowing a bit, even when they were right on top of west-bound Seventy-seventh Street. Strega pulled hard on the steering wheel, slowed for the eye blink it took to drag the car around into a left turn; then his foot was back on the accelerator, pressing down, hungry to get to the scene.

Or so Gavin thought.

He looked again at the young determined face next to him and realized he had mistaken fear for anticipation. The fear was there and it was strong. It was in the set of Strega's eyes, the line of his mouth, the busy jaw muscle, and the white of his knuckles.

Strega made a hard right on Madison. The force of gravity threw Gavin against the passenger door. The radio clattered to the floor. In the time it took Gavin to sweep down and pick it up, Strega had sailed down the last two blocks and was braking hard in front of the bridal shop.

An EMS unit was already parked out front, emergency lights turning and rear doors spread wide. One blue-and-white unit was jackknifed up on the sidewalk, two doors flung open like wings and the roof lights still spinning, slowly and in counterpoint to the EMS lights. The empty vehicles indicated to Gavin that the ambulance attendants and officers were inside, and that the perps had fled the scene. Gavin knew the Department brass would show up soon, outraged and incensed that anyone at all had been shot there on the most prestigious avenue in the city.

A handful of spectators buzzed across the street. For the moment they were hanging cautiously back, but Gavin knew in a half hour's time, they would be fighting to get as close as possible. Dead bodies did that to people. Murder was a circus. Everybody wanted a ringside seat.

Gavin got out and sprinted up the sidewalk. Strega followed. Gavin identified the first patrol car as they went by. "Kelly's here," he said to no one in particular.

Two teenagers, feeling brave or reckless or both, edged in and pressed their faces up to the big plate-glass shop window, hoping to get a glimpse of real-life murder—like it wasn't good enough to see it a thousand times a week on TV.

The sister cry of another EMS unit filled the air.

While Gavin shooed the teens away and Strega cleared a wide passage on the sidewalk for the second set of paramedics, a third radio unit blew in and parked broadside across Madison, closing the street off to traffic. Two officers got out, neither of whom had five stripes or more on his sleeve. Gavin pulled rank and shouted orders over the piercing sound of sirens that seemed to be coming now from all points in the city.

"Secure the area," Gavin ordered. "Get the tape up and keep the crowd behind it. Strega, you guard the door."

It was a heavy, ornate door with a gilded handle, and it was slightly ajar. The handle would have to be bagged on the wild chance that the perps had left prints going in or out. Gavin hoped the cops inside had been smart enough to avoid touching it. Sometimes in the panic of a possible crime in progress, officers forgot. Gavin leaned against the door and pushed with his shoulder. It opened. He took a step forward, then stopped. The carnage stunned him.

Twenty-nine years of walking in on every kind of human horror, unimaginable and imaginable, ought to season a man, give him an iron stomach and balls of steel.

Ought to.

Gavin's head reeled with twin desires. He wanted to cry. He wanted to buckle down to the ground and throw up. Instead, he walked inside, beating back the pressure against his eyeballs and the jack rabbit in his stomach.

What had been a bridal shop was now a grotesque modern art exhibit. Performance art. Mixed media. Human blood and silk taffeta. Expressionism, and the expressionism wasn't abstract. It was quite definite. Cold-blooded murder always was. Blood splattered the ivory walls, stained a pair of gold satin divans, and pooled cherry red in the vanilla cream deep-pile carpet. Music filled the shop: Sinatra crooning "Love and Marriage."

In the back of the shop, a row of eight mannequins dressed in white bridal gowns had been transformed into a gruesome chorus line of defiled virgins. One of the smiling brides was one-armed. Another had her plastic chest blown open. Blood soaked the fronts of their frothy gowns, and little bits of bone and flesh hung tenuously in the mess. It was human blood and the brides weren't human, so where did it come from?

Gavin cranked his reluctant head slowly to the right and looked down at two bodies splayed out on the floor. He called on twenty-nine years of regimentation to keep him steady. His brain clicked into automatic. Procedure kept him sane. He began to process and codify the information in front of him.

One man, one woman. Both Caucasian, middle-aged, well dressed. Gavin guessed an assault rifle had done the damage. Where the woman's face used to be, there was nothing but shards of bone and ragged flaps of flesh. An assault rifle, he reasoned, would create the kind of explosive wound that would account for the substantial human organic matter splashed around the store. The woman's arms lay out wide at her sides, the way they must have been when they lifted and spread at the moment she took the impact of the gunshots and fell back. Her right hand still clutched a white pearl-encrusted wedding veil.

The EMS teams worked on the father. His head was intact. From what Gavin could see as he was loaded onto the gurney, his midsection wasn't.

"Is he alive?" Gavin asked one of the paramedics.

"Technically speaking, yes," the young paramedic said, shuttling the gurney out.

Gavin looked back down at the mother's body. It would remain on the floor until the crime-scene unit and the medical examiner arrived. It seemed callous to just leave her there in plain view, but she was no longer a mother, she was evidence. Evidence could not be moved until the crime-scene unit said so.

Gavin turned away and scanned the shop. Bullet holes riddled the walls. Those too were evidence for CSU. The bullets would tell them what kind of weapon had been used, but they couldn't give names or identify faces. They were silent witnesses.

A live witness, a young woman dressed in a pink Chanel suit, was balled up on the floor in one corner of the store, sobbing. Mike Kelly knelt next to her, patting her shoulder and murmuring words of comfort. The woman refused to look at him. "Go away," she pleaded. "Just go away."

Another young woman sat on a gold satin chair talking to Maria Alvarez. Gavin guessed from the expensive Chanel suit that the hysterical woman with Kelly was the bride-to-be and the simply dressed woman with Alvarez was the store clerk. Sinatra crooned on. "The Shadow of Your Smile." The clerk was visibly shaken but composed. Gavin went to her. "Where's the music system?"

She pointed at the stock room.

"Go turn it off." He watched her leave, then said to Maria: "What the hell happened here besides the obvious?"

"Two gunshot victims," Maria stated, flipping through a fat sheaf of notes. "Mr. and Mrs. Ben Evans. Residents of New York City. I was the first officer on the scene."

Gavin was impressed with her neat, tight handwriting and, judging from the volume of notes, the thorough manner with which she had gathered information.

"The woman with Mike Kelly is Cynthia Evans, the daughter," Maria explained. "The woman talking to me was Karen Smith, the shop manager. Sometimes Melissa Stewart, the designer, comes in and sometimes she doesn't. Today she didn't. Karen worked alone. The Evans family entered the shop at approximately three-thirty this afternoon. The daughter is getting married in December. They were here to pick out the wedding dress. Ben Evans told Karen they wanted the best. Money was no object. Karen told me she could have guessed that herself."

"Why?" Gavin asked.

"Mrs. Evans was wearing important jewelry. A five-carat diamond ring on the right ring finger, a thick platinum diamond-encrusted wedding band on the left ring finger, a three-carat solitaire set in white platinum above the wedding band, a matching white platinum choker-style necklace set with three square-cut diamonds, a matching wrist cuff also in white platinum, also set with three five-carat square-cut diamonds.

"The family split up. Mrs. Evans looked at veils while Karen showed the daughter dresses. Ben Evans sat on the gold divan reading the paper. The entrance to the shop was secure. The door operates on a buzzer system. That's standard procedure here. At approximately three fifty-five, two men rang the buzzer. Karen saw they were conservative-looking individuals wearing expensive suits and carrying a couple of big Armani shopping bags, so she buzzed them in. One man was blond, his partner had dark hair. Karen said he looked Spanish or Italian. Something Latin. They entered the shop and pulled automatic weapons out of their shopping bags. Karen is not well versed in arms identification. She thinks the weapons were machine guns. I couldn't get a more specific description out of her.

"The Latin perp covered Karen and the daughter. The blonde approached Mrs. Evans and jammed his weapon in her neck. He ordered her to remove her jewelry. She refused. Ben Evans stepped in and attempted to block her body with his own. It was a bad move. The blonde lost his temper.

"First, he opened fire on the store, spraying the walls, the ceiling, and the mannequins, after which he shot Ben Evans. When Ben Evans hit the floor, the blonde opened fire on the mother, aiming for her face. When he finished, he leaned down and calmly helped himself to her jewelry. He even took her earrings off. They were pierced earrings with special security screw backs. It took some work to get them off. He put the jewels in his pocket, then signaled his partner. They backed out of the store. The daughter's uninjured. Karen's uninjured. The mother's obviously DOA. I don't know what condition the father is in."

"Looks pretty bad," Gavin said.

Maria glanced at the grieving daughter and frowned. "This should have been one of the happiest days of her life."

"What kind of security does the shop have?"

"Just the buzzer system. Karen said they never needed a guard or a camera here. Sales transactions are done by check or credit card. There's no cash on the premises. The only items of any value are these dresses. Who's going to try and steal a wedding dress? They're too big to stuff in a handbag."

"What about prints?" Gavin asked.

"Negative. Karen says the perps didn't touch *anything,* not even the door handle. When she buzzed, one of the individuals pushed it open with his shoulder. On top of that, they were wearing gloves. She remembers thinking how weird it was that they were wearing leather gloves in the summer."

"No prints, no video. What about a getaway car?"

"Negative. Karen didn't see anything."

"You talk to the daughter? Maybe she saw something different."

"The daughter?" Maria looked over again at the hysterical girl and shook her head. "It'll be days before she talks."

"You were on foot post across the street. Did you see anything?"

Maria hesitated before answering. "No."

"You did a good job in here," Gavin said, meaning it. Her work was cohesive and organized, and she was remarkably unfazed by the destruction around her. "Be sure to give Ballantine your notes."

Maria nodded and stepped away.

The small shop was filling up fast. It was built for a bride and her family of two, not for the NYPD family with its dozens of department specialists. The door was propped open. Someone had thought to properly bag the handle, not that it mattered now. Four homicide detectives in slick suits breezed in. Gavin knew them from the One-Nine.

A fifth homicide detective arrived alone. Gavin lifted a hand in greeting. It was Cybil Hansen. According to the gossip, she was Ballantine's rising star. She played the game smartly, dressing down the truth of her gender and working twice as hard as the men.

A half dozen more patrol cops spilled in behind her and milled around, gawking at the rare sight of a cold-blooded murder in the One-Nine. Inspector Wilson marched in and ordered the gawkers out. He was followed by the crime-scene-unit specialists, more brass, and finally, an imposing, immaculately dressed, handsome Spanish man. It was Ramon Alvarez, and he was taller and better-looking in person than his pictures suggested.

The CSU techs swarmed through the store with their gear. They began digging bullets out of the walls and scraping the carpet, picking over the mother's body with tweezers, searching for fibers or any other small puzzle piece that might help them put names and faces to the men who had turned a woman cold with death on a hot summer day.

Gavin watched the CSU photographer walk the boundaries of the murder scene and circle the corpse. First the photographer was dipping forward, then he was standing back, flat-footed then tippy-toed, working every perspective, shooting all the angles, sending out shocks of white strobe light and capturing for future reference—capturing forever—the exact position and horror of those dreadful human remains.

Should a suspect ever be arrested and charged with the murder, Gavin thought, the photos would be blown up poster big and put on a display in front of a jury of the suspect's peers. Twelve ordinary people would sit and calmly look at them. They would listen to the defense spin a hundred excuses explaining away the fact that the man in front of them had shot a woman point-blank in the face with an assault weapon built for war.

Gavin spotted Q-Ball's shiny head bobbing along the perimeter of the room. Q-Ball cornered Maria. He asked her a question. Gavin was too far away to hear. He watched Maria answer. Q-Ball asked another question. Maria shook her head no, then said something and shook her sheaf of notes at the detective. From what Gavin could see, Q-Ball was making her angry. He must have pushed a hot button, Gavin thought, for Alvarez to lose her cool that fast. Then Q-Ball leaned in close to her, grasped her shoulder, whispered something. He looked at her hard. Maria flinched, then answered. Ballantine patted her shoulder and pulled away. Maria hurried out of the shop. Q-Ball looked around, spotted Gavin, and bobbed his way.

"Gavin," Ballantine bellowed, "I'm dividing the neighborhood up. You and your partner take Seventy-two, three, and four, Madison to the river, and turn it upside down. If they ditched the weapons, chances are they did it around here. I got a foot-post officer who witnessed them traveling east, so don't bother looking west of Madison."

"Alvarez *saw* them?" Gavin exclaimed.

"She sure as hell did," Ballantine replied. He was about to say something else when he saw Kelly and the hysterical woman. "That the daughter with Kelly?"

Gavin nodded.

Ballantine waved Kelly away, then crouched low next to the sobbing figure and geared his raspy voice down to something soft and new. He spoke quietly in the young girl's ear and gently wound his arm around her. While Ballantine was stroking the auburn hair—stroking and murmuring—the girl's hysteria ebbed, and Ballantine won himself a sad, beautiful face looking up from the floor for the first time. Ballantine blocked her line of sight with his massive body, shielding her from her mother's remains. She started to speak. Ballantine's head moved up and down in sympathetic encouragement. He had a talking witness, and he would slowly, gently pry all the information out of her. It was more than Q-Ball's job. It was his talent. He had a special way, something magic, that made people talk.

Gavin left the store.

The crowd outside had quadrupled in size. Reporters pressed in against the police line, frantic for information. Spectators lined the sidewalks, standing shoulder to shoulder, ten deep. Blue-and-white patrol cars, ambulances, and detectives' cars filled the street for a full city block in either direction. Gavin wiped his forehead. The sun blazed down, the asphalt felt soft. It gave way under his feet. A waft of heavy cinnamon perfume tickled his

nose. He knew without looking that it belonged to
Maria Alvarez.

"Why'd you lie to me?" he asked.

Alvarez stood close to him. Her red lips were bunched
up in a pout. She picked a piece of lint off his uniform.
Her fingers rested on his arm long after the lint was
gone. He didn't mind the weight of her touch.

"They went right by me." Her voice was flat and
colorless.

"Why'd you lie to me?" he asked again. He looked
at her and saw his troubled face reflected in her mirrored
Ray-Bans.

"Because I felt stupid," she said. "I didn't want anyone to know how I fucked up. Correction. I didn't want
my *father* to know."

"What happened?"

"It's a bitch out here in this kind of heat," she said,
sighing. "There's no shade on this corner, so I stepped
away from my foot post around to the side street there.
See that little tree? Well, that's where I was. Cool and
comfortable. When they came around the corner, they
weren't even walking fast. They just strolled by like they
didn't have a care in the world. Even smiled at me and
said: *Hello, hot one, isn't it?* Can you believe that?"

She looked up at the sky. "*Hot one, isn't it.* And stupid
me, I answered, *Yes, it is. Have a nice day, gentlemen.* I
watched them walk away and thought about how sexy
the blond one was. I even wondered what he'd be like
in bed. By the time the call came over the radio, they
were long gone."

"Can you describe them?"

She shrugged. "The blonde didn't look anything like
the composite, but I didn't get a long enough look to
work up a new sketch. They were both wearing sunglasses and suits. I've already told the Q-Ball everything
I know. Shit. I really screwed up."

"It happens, Alvarez. Don't bust your own chops. Wilson and your father will do it for you."

She flashed him a bitter smile. "Thanks a lot."

"I've got to go pick up my rookie partner. Q-Ball put us on alley detail."

"Me too," Maria said. She looked at Strega across the street, working the police line. Her expression changed. "You ever get tired of Strega, I'll partner with him anytime, Ed. Anytime." Alvarez walked away, tapping her baton against her full hip.

Gavin felt a pang of disappointment watching her go. He wanted to see her ample lips go soft, her eyes go bright with interest looking at *him,* the way they did when she looked at Strega. Well, it wasn't going to happen, not in this life. He forgot about Maria and focused on the job at hand.

Gavin wound his way through the snarl of emergency vehicles and tapped Strega on the arm. "Come on. Alvarez saw them go east."

"She *saw* them?"

"Even told them to have a nice day. Thought about asking the blonde for a quickie. They're long gone by now. Q-Ball wants us to work over all the alleys in a four-block radius from Madison to the East River. We look under every car, in every bush, and toss every garbage can."

"What are we looking for?"

Gavin thought of the shards of bone sticking out of the dead mother's face. The jackrabbit jerked in his stomach again, and his palms turned clammy. "Weapons," he croaked.

Maria worked her assigned search sector alone. She was meticulous in how she dug through the trash. She peered in cereal boxes, opened every plastic garbage bag, picked through newspapers, patting them down, feeling for metal, wishing, hoping she would find the weapons so she could offer them to her father. *There,* she would say. *I did it.* It would redeem her, for Ramon Alvarez had certainly heard by now how his cop daughter had let the killers walk right by.

Maria folded down cross-legged on the cement. She took her mirrored Ray-Bans off and looked at her own eyes. The pupils were full black moons wrapped in a skinny band of brown iris. It was the blow, she thought, making her unsteady. Volatile. Paranoid. Standing there cornered in the bridal shop, with Q-Ball's bright blue eyes boring into hers, she had lost it. She had thought, for a moment, he was God.

She slipped her Ray-Bans back on, not that she needed sunglasses. The alley was dim in the late afternoon. It reminded her of how in a dead-end gooseneck alley like this, in the dingy light of winter, he taught her—back when he was rookie young, before the decorations, the stripes, the rapid promotions, before the drivers, the political notoriety, and his picture on the nightly news. Maria remembered how bare-armed in the December chill, fingers numb but gripping the knife handle tight, Ramon Alvarez taught her to kill.

Gavin rummaged through an old dumpster off the East River Drive, the last in their designated search area. It was seven o'clock in the evening. "No way the shooters dumped their weapons," he announced. "Not around here, not anywhere."

"You think they'll be back?" Strega asked.

"My fiver says they're planning another hit again, and chances are it'll be on Madison Avenue."

Strega looked up from a small trash can. "I hope you lose the five."

"So do I." Gavin peered back into the dumpster. "Nothing in there but last night's dinner," he said, kicking it with his big black shoe. He heard a tiny cry. Something feline and high-pitched. Gavin turned away and started for the squad car.

Strega held him back. "Wait. Did you hear that?"

"No," Gavin lied.

Strega kicked the dumpster and listened to the distinct, pitiful cry.

"Come on, Strega," Gavin complained. "We're NYPD, not ASPCA."

Strega dug through the garbage and pulled out a wrinkled paper bag. The bag was stapled shut. It was moving.

Strega ripped the bag open. A tiny orange kitten looked up at them. One ear was folded back. Its eyes were two pools of terrified blue gazing out of a little triangular orange fur face. It mewed again. The skinny little body was shaking.

"Hey, buddy," Strega said. He gently popped the folded ear back in place and cradled the kitten next to his chest.

"You a Save the Whales type?" Gavin sniped. "You got a bleeding liberal heart under your capitalist skin? Or did you read somewhere that *virile but gentle* is in?"

"It's a kitten, Ed. We can't just leave it here."

"What are you going to do with it?"

Strega held it in the air and flipped the tail up. "It's a he, see? I'm keeping him." He carried the kitten to the car.

Gavin followed, cranky and impatient. "How are you going to drive with a goddamn cat in the car?"

Strega turned his hat upside down in his lap and settled the kitten inside. "He's a good boy. He'll stay right here for the ride in."

"What are you going to call it?"

"Sigmund. As in Freud."

"Figures," Gavin muttered.

The kitten crawled out of the hat and settled into Strega's lap. Gavin listened to the little feline motor going happy and strong. Strega was just that kind of guy, Gavin thought on the ride back. Kittens and women went soft and gooey around him. Correction. Kittens went soft and gooey. Women went savage. Gavin remembered Maria Alvarez's feral expression when she had looked at Strega. Some guys, he thought miserably, had all the luck.

At the precinct house they ran into Maria Alvarez sitting on the front staircase, smoking a cigarette. She was still in uniform. "Hey, Ed. Hi, Jonnie." She looked at the kitten traveling in Strega's arms. "Cute cat. You an animal lover, Jonnie?"

"As a matter of fact I am."

"What do you know? So am I." Alvarez blew a smoke ring up at Strega. "You free for a drink tonight, Jonnie?"

"No."

"Too bad. I thought we could celebrate." She blew smoke through both her nostrils.

"Celebrate what?" Strega said. "The big fuck-up? I heard they went right by you."

Her red lips tightened in anger. She stood.

Desk Sergeant Bell poked his big head out the door. "Maria. Your dad's looking for you. He's up in Wilson's office."

Alvarez dropped her cigarette, ground it out with the heel of her shoe, and stalked inside.

"Why'd you pull her chain like that?" Gavin asked.

"Manipulative psychology. I'd rather have her mad at me than in love with me. Hey, do you like Chinese food?"

"If you're buying, then I like Chinese food."

"Why am I buying?"

"You're a big-time stock trader. Can't you afford to throw a couple of egg rolls an old man's way?"

"The Empire Palace on First," Strega said, grinning. "Best Chinese on the East Side, and it's close enough to walk."

Wilson's office was spacious and immaculate. The inspector wasn't there, but Ramon Alvarez was. He had made himself at home in the big leather swivel chair. He was clean-shaven, polished, perfectly tailored, and mad.

Maria stood in front of the desk, waiting for him to speak. She shifted uneasily, keeping her eyes focused on the black and gold cuff links flashing against the starched white of his French shirt sleeve.

He cupped a cigarette to his lips and lit it. "How could you do it, Maria?" His voice was dangerously low. "How the fuck could you let them walk right by?"

"I'm sorry."

Ramon slapped a hand down on the desk. "Sorry isn't

good enough. You're an Alvarez. You don't fuck up. Am I clear?"

"Yes," she managed.

"You have my reputation to live up to. You fuck up, it's a reflection on me, you understand that?"

"I understand," she whispered, curling her sharp fingernails into the soft cushion of her palms, biting down hard on the inside of her cheek, blinking back tears.

"Oh, shit," he said, rising. "Don't cry, Maria."

"I'm not crying."

"Yes, you are. You look like your mother when you cry." He ground out his fresh cigarette. "I just want you to be the best, baby, that's all."

Ramon came around the desk and folded his arms around her. She stiffened. He pulled her tight. The starched cotton of his shirt scratched her cheek; the black and gold cuff links pressed into the side of her head. He was rocking her now, like she was a baby again, rocking and shushing, stroking her hair, telling her not to cry. She couldn't help it. He scared her.

He turned her head so it fit in the crook of his neck, and she smelled the heavy musk of his aftershave, the mint on his breath. His cheek scraped hers. Her eyes were wide open, and she was looking at his hair, at the way it feathered back close to his head, black and glossy as a crow's wing.

He pulled back slightly, tipped her chin up, and looked into her eyes. She willed them to be opaque. Flat, still, brackish pools. He tapped her on the nose. "Don't fuck up again," he whispered. He brushed her forehead with his lips. Then he was out the door.

Maria's nerves were on fire. Her knees felt weak. She leaned against Wilson's desk. A stack of files slid to the floor. She scooped them up. Jon Strega's personnel file was on top. She sat down and opened it. The first document was a big black-and-white head shot of Jon Strega. She put it aside and flipped through the rest of the file, reading about him.

When she finished, she picked up the photo.

Strega smiled out at her, young and confident, world-by-the-tail smug. He looked like he was laughing at her. She could *hear* him laughing at her. *Stupid Maria. Dumb Maria. Daddy's little fuck-up.* Her hands shook.

Strega's hair feathered back from his face, black and glossy as a crow's wing.

She wondered if he wore musk. If his breath smelled of mint. If his cheeks would scratch the skin on her breasts. She wondered what he tasted like. Felt like. Looked like sleeping.

She wondered if he kept his eyes closed when he came.

Four

Gavin started in on the special. *General Tso's chicken.* General Tso would have been happy: The chicken was tasty and there was enough of it to feed Tso's entire army. The Empire Palace was a cut above the standard Manhattan Chinese. Classy ceiling halogens shot down pinpricks of light onto crisp white tablecloths. A giant green ceramic dragon curled around the dining room walls, his mouth wide open and breathing fire. Except for the dragon and one table of four, the dining room was empty.

A young Chinese waitress materialized next to Gavin. She moved silently on black ballerina slippers. Although she wore a very proper high-necked pajama suit of turquoise silk—gold filigree embroidery running through the raw silk and a row of thirty-five tiny mother-of-pearl buttons climbing from the tunic hem line to collar rim—her lips curled up in a little smile that promised all sorts of improper acts *if* you could get beyond the thirty-five buttons. Who had the patience? Maybe, Gavin thought, that was part of the game. The slow, tantalizing revelation of porcelain skin, the maddening precision and concentration needed to open *thirty-five* miniature mother-of-pearl buttons.

Strega introduced the girl: Ming, like the vase. As far as Gavin could see, she was just as delicate. Ming leaned over and picked up his empty beer bottle. Her long black hair fell over her shoulders and brushed the table. She moved back on quiet ballerina feet. The mother of pearl winked at Gavin, thirty-five shell eyes in a turquoise sea. Strega was watching her too. His expression was something between admiration and lust, caveman subtle and about as refined.

Gavin pointed his fork at Strega. "You obviously come here for more than the food."

"She *is* beautiful," Strega admitted, slipping the kitten a piece of chicken.

"You telling me a guy like you doesn't have a girlfriend?"

"Past tense. Had. I *had* a girlfriend. A Sicilian bombshell."

"What happened?"

Strega smiled ruefully. "She learned the remote-access code to my answering machine, tapped it in one day, and didn't like what she heard."

"What'd she hear?"

"A female voice that wasn't hers." Strega shook his head. "Sicilians are jealous and hotheaded. She hasn't talked to me since. Thing is, I can't stop thinking about her. You know what I mean?"

Gavin frowned. He knew. He thought about Maria Alvarez all the time lately. He remembered how standing right up next to her, he swore he could feel the heat coming off her body. He thought about the way her dark, glossy hair was slicked back tight to her head, and how when she turned slightly, biting the tip of her pen, he could look right into her ear, at the fine, small-boned structure of it, at the way it whorled in like a seashell. He remembered the pulse point on her neck, thumping steadily, and how she had the kind of teeth you see in milk ads.

"Hey," Strega said, "are you okay, buddy?"

For some reason Strega's concerned expression made Gavin mad. "You're not my buddy," he snapped. "I had one for twenty-nine years. A good man. Decent. I spent more hours of my life with him than anyone else, including my wife. As far as I'm concerned, he's the only buddy I'll ever have. All the rest of you are just drivers. Got it?"

"I got it, all right." Strega pulled out his Genie and began to fiddle with it.

Gavin pushed the chicken around on his dish, wondering why he had such a short fuse lately. The Maria fantasies, he thought. It had to be the goddamn fantasies putting him on edge, making him feel wound up like a top, making his teeth ache and his toes curl. He felt guilty for blowing up. He decided to make an effort to be more civil, more congenial. "You really make any money with all that hocus-pocus?" Gavin asked.

"Enough to rent a good apartment instead of the usual substandard housing rookies have to live in. Enough to furnish my place in style, buy a Jeep, pay parking and insurance in the city, and have some left over to play with."

"No kidding." Despite himself, Gavin was impressed.

"You should get a computer and a Genie. Start trading."

"I can't even set the clock on my VCR. I'm too old to learn computers."

"No such thing as too old. You're what, fifty?"

"Fifty-one." Exactly thirty-three years older than eighteen, the age Alex would be now.

"Fifty-one's young," Strega said.

Sure, Gavin thought. *It's young,* says he who doesn't lie awake at night wondering if his prostate's enlarging or his veins are shrinking, if his heart is slowing or his blood pressure's rising. *It's young,* says he who still has his full complement of hormones, a head of hair to go with them, and who is not yet a full decade away from his teenage years.

"How old were you when you got married?" Strega asked.

"Twenty-one. Shelly was nineteen." One year older than Alex would be now.

"Do you have kids?"

"No," Gavin lied.

"What was she like when you met her?"

"Shell?" Gavin stared into his beer, remembering her. "Funny, beautiful, tall, hair down to her waist. She filled out a mohair sweater like Jane Russell. Still does. We had chemistry. It was strong enough to drag us straight to the altar. Nothing mattered. We just wanted to be together. We had this dumb blind faith in the future and in each other."

"Looks like you were right." Strega did some mental arithmetic. "Thirty years?"

"This last June." The month Donovan died. Happy anniversary. Gavin's laugh was hoarse with emotion. "We were a couple of starry-eyed kids who just couldn't wait. Nothing was more important than getting married. I don't know now what we were in such a goddamn rush for. Living on a rookie cop's salary wasn't easy, but we did it."

And did it and did it and did it, Gavin reminded himself. There were no rules, nothing was off limits. There was no time, place, or way that was wrong. Everything was right. *They* were right. He used to turn around in the shower and find her standing there, naked and proud, proud to be Mrs. Gavin, proud to be his wife and the mother of their child. All that changed when Alex disappeared, and Gavin supposed that was why he had fantasies—to make up for what he was missing. Gavin kept these thoughts to himself, but the memories of Shelly softened him, and his surliness slipped away. "You know," he mumbled, "Shelly's the only girl I've ever had."

"In the biblical sense?" Strega asked, amazed.

Gavin nodded shyly.

"One woman in your entire life?" Strega was open-mouthed like the dragon on the wall.

Gavin nodded again. He felt an odd pride. Fidelity was an odd accomplishment.

Strega's forehead knotted in concentration. "Some psychologists say man isn't monogamous by nature and that when forced to live monogamously, he creates a subliminal world in which fantasy satiates his need to roam."

Bull's-eye. Score one for the Princeton psych department. Gavin felt the familiar surliness creeping back up on him. "A walking, talking Ivy League textbook."

"Are they right?" Strega pressed. "Have you ever thought about another woman?"

Gavin wanted to scream the truth. *Yes! I'm thinking*

about her right now! How could he admit that his nightly dreams were rabid things filled with two or three Marias at a time, all shrouded faces, gleaming hair, bodies arching and preening in the suppleness of youth? How could he explain that his lechery frightened him? He was a one-woman man and that woman was Shelly, but they were so far away from each other and had been for so long, Gavin's libido was running wild. The chill in his marriage made him feel old. The Maria fantasies made him feel young.

Gavin's fantasies embarrassed him. One of Strega's Princeton shrinks would have a field day with them. *Strega* would have a field day. Well, Gavin thought, he wouldn't give Jon Strega the pleasure.

"Don't you wonder what another woman would be like?" Strega asked. "Aren't you curious?"

"Hell, no," Gavin snapped.

Strega nodded, but Gavin saw those intelligent eyes looking hard at him, and he knew the agile brain was working, reeling around, processing the information.

A moment later, Strega delivered the punch line: "Do you think Shelly ever wanted to sleep with another man?"

Gavin's breath caught in his throat. "Shelly with another man?" he sputtered. He had never considered it. "Jesus Christ." The possibility rattled him. "Guess she must have. I'm no prize these days. Maybe she fantasizes about Mel Gibson, someone like that."

Ming set down another plate of steaming food. She wore a little gold I Love New York pin. Gavin pointed at the pin and smiled up at her with what he hoped was an avuncular glow. "Wish more people in this city felt the way you do." Her ruby lips smiled back at him. Gavin felt the glow sour into something lecherous. "Why'd you come to New York, Ming?" His question came out like an order.

Ming's smile disappeared. "My father says a person can do anything in Manhattan."

"Are you happy?" Gavin asked gently. He was rewarded with a shy smile and a flash of intelligent brown eyes.

"Yes. Business is good. Next year I start college. One day I'll go to law school." Her smile widened into something priceless, then she left.

Gavin turned to Strega. "Why aren't *you* in law school, Strega? Why aren't you a hot-shot lawyer or an investment banker or a psychiatrist with your big Princeton degree? What the hell made you want to be a cop? You watch too much *NYPD Blue?*"

Strega didn't answer.

"Tough question?" The surliness was cranked up to full. Gavin felt good turning the tables, practicing a little amateur pop psychology of his own.

"No," Strega said quietly. "I decided to be a cop the day my father was shot. He was a detective with the Philadelphia Police Department. Killed in the line of duty."

The surliness fizzled. Gavin felt like an idiot. "How old were you?"

"Six."

"What happened?"

"My father was late coming home one night. My mother had the table set for dinner. She wore a flowered house dress that tied at the waist. After three kids she didn't have much of a waist left, but her face was the face of a Madonna—young and clear and beautiful. At seven o'clock the doorbell rang. She opened the door.

"Dave Riley was standing there. He was my father's best friend and partner. My mother knew right away it was bad news. She tried to close the door on him. Riley pushed it open and walked in. He took her by the shoulders and whispered something. She clapped both hands over her ears and dropped to the floor, screaming. Riley wrapped his arms around her. It seemed funny to me seeing another man hug my mother.

"I asked Riley where my father was. He said my father was shot in the line of duty when he jumped into the line of fire to push an innocent woman out of the way. He took a bullet in the chest. The killer got away, but the woman lived. My father died a hero.

"My mother opened her eyes and looked up at me, then over at my sister and the new baby girl. *Jonnie, your daddy's gone to Heaven,* she said. *He won't be coming home. He's gone to be with Jesus. You're the man of the house now.* I asked why my father wanted to be with Jesus instead of with us. She didn't answer. She just made me swear I would be a policeman when I grew up. In honor of my father. She said I owed it to him."

Strega tapped his chopsticks on the table. "My mother didn't want to live with bad memories, so we moved to New York the day after the funeral, but she never let me forget that promise. I graduated top of my class at Princeton, then went on to get an MBA and graduated with honors again. I wanted to be a lawyer, an investment banker, or even a psychiatrist. I never wanted to be a cop, but I'm not free to do what I want. I made a promise, so here I am in New York City, scared to death I'm going to get shot but wanting to be the best anyway. My father was. Like father, like son." He folded his paper menu into an airplane and sailed it across the table.

Gavin picked the airplane up and held it awkwardly in his hand while he considered what he had just heard. A cop had gone down in the line of duty, and this was his son. No matter that the tragedy had occurred nearly two decades earlier. No matter that it had occurred in a different city, in a different state. Strega was that cop's son, and the bond, the brotherhood of the police, stretched across city and state lines. It spanned across the generations. The bond was powerful and sacrosanct, stronger than place or time.

All the animosity and contempt Gavin felt toward his young partner simply faded away. Gavin sailed the airplane back across the table. A peace offering. He struggled to find the right response. Gavin was not by nature a verbal man. Although his thoughts were expressive, spoken words usually failed him. When he needed the adjectives, the nouns, and the verbs all perfectly placed, stacked one on top of the other in a perfect linguistic pyramid, when he needed words most, they failed him, and they failed him now. So he simply said, "I'm sorry, buddy."

"I thought you didn't have a buddy," Strega replied dryly.

Strega was smiling, so Gavin knew they had struck a truce. They finished their beers in silence. Gavin pushed the empty bottle across the table. He owed Strega a little soul baring of his own. He wasn't ready to talk about Alex, but he could talk about Danny.

"Donovan," he said. He spoke the word with a mixture of love, admiration, anger, and disappointment.

Strega held a hand up. "It's not quid pro quo."

"Donovan," Gavin repeated, "was one of the great ones. He wanted to make a difference, even in a hopeless place like the Three-Four. He cared about the people there and tried to bond with them. He used to get out of the car, go up to folks, and talk. Hell, patrolmen don't get out of the car unless they're going to lunch, and in the Three-Four you never even roll the window down.

"But Donovan was different. He used to say that to understand the problems of the precinct, you had to understand the good things too. He believed a cop had to know the decent people and understand what their lives were like. Every day Donovan got out of the patrol car, went up to the women sitting on the stoops, and said hello.

"At first the women ran away. Little by little they started to stay put, but even then they mostly just stared at Donovan. One day the women started to talk. It was like a dam breaking loose. Old and young, they giggled and gossiped with Donovan like he was one of their own. It was the craziest sight, a big white uniformed Irishman hanging on the stoop like one of the locals." Gavin laughed. "You know what, Strega?"

"What?"

"Donovan was right. He became part of their world. They trusted him. Told him things that helped put away a lot of hard criminals. They even started calling him Danny. The kids called him Big Three-D, short for Daniel David Donovan. *Here comes Three-D!* they'd yell. Those rat packs of kids loved him. He gave the little ones rides around on his shoulders and let them wear

his hat. He used to tell them to study hard, go to college.
Danny was one big father figure to a whole generation
of fatherless kids.

"Most of the older kids were too far gone for anything
or anyone to make a difference. Danny was tough on
the punks and the gangs. But the little ones? He loved
the little ones. Danny used to say, *If my friendship can
keep just one kid from going bad, why then, my whole
damn career in the NYPD's worth something.*

"Big guy like that, you don't ever think to ask how
he's feeling underneath all that Irish brouhaha. I guess
he wasn't feeling so good. It started two years ago, in a
botched raid when he took a hit in the chest from a
fifteen-year-old with an Uzi. It was a rough couple of
days. Danny made it, but came back scared. You can't
be scared and be a cop, Strega. Fear unbalances you.
First, you start making little mistakes, like going for your
gun a second too fast. Danny did. He got spooked late
at night in a dark alley when a black kid reached in his
pocket. Danny drew his gun and fired. The kid died.
Turned out he was just going for a cigarette. The kid
was unarmed.

"The next time Danny got gunshy. He hesitated reaching for his piece, and as a result one of the cops he was
backing up took a bullet in the leg. Oh, the guy lived,
but Danny felt responsible. *It could've been his head
instead of his leg,* Danny said. That's when he told me
he didn't have enough fight left in him to spend the last
year of duty in the Three-Four. It was too violent and
too brutal for a cop who was unsure of himself. Danny
requested a transfer to the One-Nine. I came with him.

"One day he went home early and found his wife,
Jillian, in bed with the neighbor's eighteen-year-old son.
She told Danny that it was his own damn fault. Said
Danny was a lousy lover. Jillian filed for divorce and
threw him out of the house. She threatened to keep the
baby, Katy, away from him if he didn't give her what
she wanted. Danny adored Katy, so he agreed to everything, with one exception. Jillian wanted custody of
Katy. Donovan refused. He didn't want his little girl

growing up in a house where his wife was screwing teenagers.

"They were locked in an ugly court battle. Jillian began to fire her lawyers every couple of weeks, then hire new ones. She was dragging Danny on a long expensive ride through hell. But Donovan told me he felt sure he'd win. Jillian was an unfit mother. Danny had character witnesses lined up, ready to tell the judge about Jillian's drinking problems and about her sleeping around. Danny was going to retire at the end of the year, like me. He would've been there for Katy, all day, every day. When Jillian threw him out, he rented a little shithole apartment to live in. Said it cost next to nothing. He was saving all his money to fight for Katy. With what was left, he was going to take little Katy away and raise her in the country, some place clean and pretty.

"I've thought a lot about it. I guess he ended up feeling like he failed in the Department and in his marriage. You heard Wilson this morning. Every year an average of nine NYPD cops commit suicide. Sometimes it's eleven, sometimes twelve, but usually it's eight or nine. The record was fourteen in a freak year. By May of this year there were fourteen suicides.

"Then in June, Daniel David Donovan had to go break the fucking record. He put his service revolver up to the side of his head and pulled the trigger. He became number fifteen. Goddamn Donovan always had to break some kind of record. Number of beers consumed in five minutes. Number of parking tickets written on a Friday. There was always some record to break. I guess number sixteen gets that honor now."

Strega waited for him to go on.

Gavin pulled the label off his beer bottle. "I found Danny. We were scheduled for the eight-to-four tour. He didn't show. I called him off and on until noon. Finally, I drove over to that little shithole apartment. He was on the couch wearing his uniform shirt and not much else. There was no note, nothing. Guess he had nothing left to say." Gavin finished his beer in one long swallow and signaled Ming for another.

"Why didn't Donovan go to Psych Services for help?" Strega asked.

"What the fuck did the academy tell you about Psych Services?"

"The facts. That more officers die by their own hand than in the line of duty. That the number one stress for a cop is in not being able to open up. He walks around full of repressed anger and guilt. He's busy defending a public that hates him. Most cops feel compelled to live up to their classic iron-man image. They internalize all the stress. Psych Services gives them a place to go, a place to open up before they break up."

"That's what they told you rookies?"

"They say something wrong?"

"They left out a few juicy details."

"Like what?"

"Like the fact that when you walk in the door of Psych Services, they'll strip you of your gun and take you off the streets. They'll stick you behind a desk, pushing paper. It's called the rubber-gun patrol. Within twenty-four hours every cop in the city will know you've been over to see Psych Services. From that point on, you'll be ostracized and ridiculed. You'll go back to the putty-colored Psych Services building in Queens once every six months for a *session*. You won't get any counseling between *sessions*. The chances of you ever going back on active duty are about zero. Go to Psych Services? Might as well cut your balls off. That's why Donovan didn't go."

Strega whistled. "I guess that answers that."

"You bet your ass it does." Gavin calmed down and said more quietly: "Now, why he didn't come and talk to me, I'll never know. All I could think after he died was, Danny, why didn't you talk to me? Just talk to me? We could've figured it out together, like partners, like friends." Gavin rubbed his eyes. The long line of muscle from his neck to his jaw flexed, his jaw screwed down tight, and he whispered: "Why didn't he just talk to me?"

Strega stroked the sleeping kitten and waited for Gavin to go on.

"At first I used to sit outside every night on my porch, thinking about Danny. I loved him like a brother, but I failed him somehow. Each night I took out my piece and held it like I was looking at it for the first time. It felt so heavy. I put the barrel up to my head and tried to understand Donovan. How bad does it have to be? I'd wonder. Losing him left the inside of me empty, like a cannonball had shot right through. One night I thought I was hurting enough to want out too. So I tried. I swear to God I closed my eyes and tried. I put the gun in my mouth, but I just sat there crying like a baby. I couldn't pull the trigger. That night on the porch I put my piece down, lit a cigarette, and cursed. For Donovan, for myself. For the whole damn bunch of us cops."

Gavin took a deep drink of his beer. "Anyway, Danny's dead. I'm alive and on autopilot, skating out the last of my thirty years. The three decades is mostly a pride thing, a stupid pact Danny and I made when we were rookies. Six stripes. Doesn't seem right, both of us falling short. So here I am, counting the days left, and pouring my heart out to an Italian kid half my age." Gavin laughed hoarsely. "You know why?"

"Why?"

"Because you've got principles. You're a man of your word. It takes guts to live up to your word. I admire that. So I want you to understand me. You may not necessarily like me, but at least you'll understand me."

"Gavin, you're a pain in the ass, a griper, a dictator, and one hell of a stubborn guy. I don't understand you, but I respect you. More puzzling still, I honest to God like you."

They walked back to the precinct house, the rhythm of their slow footfalls filling a comfortable silence. Strega put the kitten in his pocket for safekeeping. When they reached the Ford Tempo, Gavin offered his partner a lift to the West Side.

"No, thanks," Strega said. "I'll walk. I need the exercise."

Gavin glared skinny-eyed with envy at the lean, fit body in front of him that didn't seem to need any exercise at all. "Suit yourself," he said, amicably sour.

"See you Monday," Strega said, walking away, his hand still shoved in his pocket holding onto the kitten.

"Yeah, we've got the weekend off," Gavin shouted after him, "just like a couple of regular working Joes."

He leaned against the car and watched Strega until he was out of sight. Talking about Danny reminded him. He opened the trunk and took the CSU file out. It was heavy in his hands. He dropped it on the passenger seat, ducked into the Tempo, and headed home.

Gavin pulled into his driveway at midnight. The solar-powered clock on the dash blinked at him. He felt a wiggle of guilty relief knowing Shelly would be asleep. The feeling wasn't new. He had been avoiding Shell for a long time now.

It wasn't really Shell he was avoiding, it was the accusation in her eyes. She had never said the words, but she blamed him for not finding Alex. He saw it every time she looked at him. *You're a cop,* her green eyes accused. *Why can't you find our daughter?* They had a common wound, but he couldn't share his pain. It wasn't his way.

Now they lived side my side with the awkwardness of strangers and an invisible wall between them. It was as though when their child vanished, part of Shell vanished too and their marriage disappeared altogether. He knew how to organize a search, how to mobilize the FBI and the NYPD missing-persons unit. He knew how to look for Alex, but he didn't have a clue how to bring Shelly back to him again.

Gavin lit a cigarette. He cracked the window. Dank summer air drifted in. Gavin pulled on his cigarette and looked at his home. He lived in Ozone Park. Grim name, decent neighborhood, a civilized commute into

Manhattan, and a straight shot down Woodhaven Boulevard to the beach.

The house was a two-story "contemporary." Builder's lingo for cheap construction and second-rate materials. It sat mid-block, surrounded on all sides by identical contemporary clones. His house had central a.c., a woodburning fireplace, a nice deck in the backyard, and an attached garage. It even had a lawn. *Right.* A two-by-three-feet rectangle of dirt that wasn't big enough to mow. Not that there was any grass left to mow. The heat had burned it all away, leaving ugly little mounds of brittle scrub the color and texture of straw.

Nonetheless, Gavin liked his home. It was part of a tidy, well-kept neighborhood, one he felt comfortable in because it was full of men like himself. O'Malley across the street was a cop; Rigoni next door was an ex-cop. Paccione a few doors down was a cop. So was Paccione's brother, who lived across the street.

If you chalked up Alex's disappearance to a freak occurrence, well, then it was basically a crime-free neighborhood. The only other crime he'd ever heard of was domestic, specifically a little adultery over at the Barrone residence. The grapevine buzzed of daily UPS deliveries. The truck stayed parked outside the Barrone house for two hours at a time, three days a week.

If Phil Barrone had been a cop, the brotherhood would have stepped in and told him. But Barrone was a traveling salesman. Out Monday mornings, back Friday nights. The other men on the block sort of figured he had it coming to him, leaving Ellie alone like that. Sure as hell *he* fooled around on the road. Why shouldn't his pretty, lonely wife have a good time too?

The subject of sex nudged Gavin's thoughts over to Maria Alvarez. He closed his eyes and concentrated on the image of her, on the way her full breasts strained against her uniform top, on the way her baton tapped against her full hip when she walked. He pictured her wide white smile, her damp, flushed skin, and how her eyes had sparkled with interest when she looked at Strega.

Gavin revised the events. He imagined he was alone in the patrol car, stopping to check up on Maria. He imagined her wordlessly opening his door and sliding in, onto his lap, just so, and slipping her hand into his uniform pants. He imagined her hair loose, falling over her eyes as she leaned over to kiss the top of his head, then the back of his neck, and maybe his lips too. She would tug her uniform pants down, giving him the opportunity to be inside her. She would inhale sharply, surprised by the power of his hardness. Gavin would hold her tightly and look at her lovely face while he loved her. Devoured her.

Gavin opened his eyes. There was no pretty Maria smiling down at him, just the fat file sitting next to him, the photographs nearly burning through manila with their meticulous, raw documentation of Donovan's ugly death. Gavin flicked his cigarette out the window and got out. The cigarette glowed orange on the pavement. He kicked it into the street, then looked back at Donovan's file. He picked it up and went inside.

Upstairs in the bedroom, Shelly slept curled up in a ball like a child. Her bangs spilled down over her eyes. She used to have long red-gold hair, but when Alex disappeared, she cut it off—symbolically, he thought—and rolled it every night in tiny yellow Velcro curlers. When she got tired of rolling it, she got a perm that turned her hair into little corkscrews wound up tight to her head. Gavin thought it made her look ten years older, but he wisely kept his opinion to himself.

In the dim night shadows, despite the matron's mop, Shelly appeared fresh and new again. He studied her face and found a memory of the young sweetness he had fallen in love with in the curve of her cheek, the shape of her lips, the brush of her long lashes.

He sighed, then quietly opened the bottom drawer of his bureau. It was full of winter sweaters. Shelly wouldn't be rummaging around in it, not in the summertime. He shoved the CSU file back in under a pile of wool blends, closed the drawer, and undressed. From time to time Shelly made little sounds in her sleep. Gavin wondered what she was dreaming about. It seemed that most of the time he didn't even know what she was thinking about. He washed up in the bathroom, threw his clothes in the hamper, and padded back into the bedroom. He shivered. One thing about suburbia. The air conditioning was great.

Shelly's bare foot stuck out of the covers. Her foot was pale and small, and the nails were painted a delicate sea-coral color. When had she started painting them? A day ago? A year ago? He didn't know. A pang of guilt sliced through him for fantasizing about Maria. It had nothing to do with love. He loved Shell, but grief had killed desire and neither of them had tried to rekindle the flame. Tomorrow, he lied to himself, he would slip Shelly's robe off, and he would roll her roundly and well.

Maria's face popped back into his mind. A feeling of helplessness ran through him. He looked back at Shelly and knew it didn't matter much how guilty or shameful he felt or how hard he tried. He knew that all through the weekend ahead he would be thinking about Maria Alvarez.

He rolled over and fell asleep, dreaming of the lush-hipped Maria sitting in his lap, singing Spanish lullabies softly in his ear. Sometime later his dream changed, as it always did, to a nightmare of slim, dead girls, their white, waxen faces staring blankly up at him, their colorless lips moving in silent messages. He leaned close to those lips but heard only a wordless whisper. It was the sound of wind rushing through trees, gentle as a sigh, and the icy breath of death blowing cold against his cheek.

Strega dropped the kitten off at his apartment. He set it up with a makeshift litter box and a bowl of milk, then changed into a pair of shorts, slipped into a pair of Nikes, and went back out for a long run. He liked to run. More specifically, he needed to run. It wasn't for his body. Running was for his mind, to wipe it clear with the white-hot pain of punishing physical effort.

He ran straight into Central Park, where no sane man

would run alone late at night. Strega's need was stronger than his sanity. The talk with Gavin had brought back all the old sorrow, all the disturbing memories of loss, so he ran flat-out, as fast as he could, legs thrusting out in long, reaching strides, moving swiftly forward toward no visible goal. The destination was interior, a place where the edge to whatever emotional hurt he was hurting softened, where memory and reality blurred. Running secretly lifted him to a level where he had no past and no furture, and he was there now.

He could no longer feel his feet hitting the asphalt or see detail in the cityscape rushing by. He followed the pavement up to the runners track circling the big reservoir. The track surface was packed earth instead of asphalt. He completed one full circle around the reservoir, then left the track and sprinted across the slope of a wide, grassy field, springing over rocks, leaping over scrubby bushes. He veered off into densely wooded park land. Trees loomed out in front of him. He zigzagged through them. Suddenly he was out in the open again, and the sky above was a starless blanket of velvet black.

He ran faster. His lungs expanded and contracted. His pulse raced, his heart hammered, and the two thundering together were a pair of hummingbird's wings drumming frenetically, deafening him to thought, numbing him to all feeling, including sorrow. No longer was he the obedient son living to give meaning to his father's death. When Strega heard the hummingbird's wings he was free, unhitched from the earth, a feather lifting on a breeze, soaring and weightless.

Sorrowless.

He moved tirelessly forward, legs pumping in long, graceful strides, arms flapping loosely by his sides, chin tipped up to the sky. Jon Strega raced until he outran the spindly legged black-haired boy who while scratching a bony kneecap with a stubby fingernail asked the empty air around him, *"Where did you go, Vincent Strega? Why did you leave me?"*

Strega rounded the corner of West Seventy-sixth Street and slowed. He trotted the last block, feeling his pulse drop back into the limits of something human. His lungs relaxed, his legs throbbed, his head buzzed with the feeling of freedom, but then the questions seeped slowly back.

What would my life have been like if you hadn't died, Vincent Strega?

He loped up the walkway of the three-level brownstone where he rented the top floor and unlocked the main door. It opened into an entrance hallway and stairwell. To the right was the door to his elderly landlady's living quarters. She occupied the first two levels. He climbed the stairs to the third floor, unlocked his door, and stepped inside just as his phone started to ring. He picked it up. "Hello?"

"Number sixteen," a female voice rumbled. "Do you ever wonder what makes a man want to kill himself?"

"Who is this?" As if he didn't know.

"Life is full of mysteries."

"Alvarez."

"You'd make a good detective, Jonnie. I'm going to be a detective one day. I have a real talent for finding things out about people, things no one else knows, secrets. If you kill yourself, it means you have secrets."

"What do you want?"

"Did you know that in March of 1977 a Philadelphia detective put his service revolver up to his temple and blew his head off? His name was Vincent Strega. Why did he do that?" The line went dead.

Strega put the phone down. He walked across his living room and looked out the big picture windows. Over at the corner of Amsterdam and Seventy-sixth Street, in the bright lights that lit up the West Side all night long, he could have sworn he saw a small figure walk away from a phone booth and disappear from sight.

Generous hips.

Black hair slicked back tight against a small head.

A dark NYPD uniform worn snug against the full, round curves of a female body.

Five

Jon Strega tossed and turned Saturday night until his nightmares finally scared him awake. Sunlight streamed in his bedroom windows. The orange kitten slept peacefully at his feet. Strega's head throbbed. His heart raced. He zeroed in on a half-empty vodka bottle sitting bedside. Headache accounted for. A framed photo of Vincent Strega lay on the floor. They went hand in hand, the picture and the vodka. Looking at the picture, Strega felt like someone had kicked him.

Which she had, hadn't she?

The raspy words came back to him. *In March of 1977 a Philadelphia detective put his service revolver to his temple and blew his head off. His name was Vincent Strega. Why did he do that, Jonnie? Why?*

Alvarez was lying, flat-out. It was nothing more than a sick game of telephone harassment which, by the way, she had won. Strega had wasted Saturday night drowning his hurt and doubt in vodka. It was an adolescent reaction to an adolescent prank.

In the bright morning light, Strega tried to think it through rationally. His NYPD personnel file was full of information. Anyone who looked would find out his father had been a cop named Vincent Strega and that he had died in the line of duty. Strega's file would certainly be accessible to the P.C.'s daughter. One phone call and she would have a copy of the whole damn thing. She would know everything about him, right down to his academy target-practice scores and his cholesterol level. Gavin's admonition came back to him: *Why'd you go yank her chain like that?* And his answer: *I'd rather have her mad at me than in love with me.*

So, Strega reasoned, his little quip Friday night at the station house made her mad enough to go digging, and she inadvertently dug up an opportunity to rattle his cage. Well, she had rattled him well. To the victor go the spoils. Maria Alvarez was a worthy competitor. She had found the one place where Strega was unprotected, where the raw, unresolved grief from the loss of his father kept him stripped down bare, and she had gone right for it—a Spanish rapier swiped right across Achilles' heel.

Strega picked up the picture. He wished he could remember his father's face without the help of a photo, but his memory was muzzy, blurred by the passing of time. He had only the tentative imagery formed in his six-year-old mind to carry him through a lifetime. It wasn't enough. The wash of time left him now with nothing more than the occasional echo of Vincent's voice and a flash of his face. Strega stared up at the ceiling, and reached back into his memory, needing to remember his father. Snatches of old conversations drifted by: *"Jonnie—important to know who you are—I love you, Jonnie."*

He could hear the voice, but he couldn't see the face. He squeezed his eyes shut and tried harder. His father's features slipped by too fast to track, melted away before he could see the sum of the parts. Strega opened his eyes and studied the snapshot. A tall man, dark and strong, who looked much like Jon did now, was tossing a small boy into the air and laughing. The little boy was grinning, his hands were thrown up high in joy, and the man's arms were open wide, ready to catch the boy on his way down.

Their names were scrawled on top of the top of the photo: *Jonnie and Vincent—June 17, 1977.* It was the last time Vincent Strega would ever toss his young son up to the sky. On June 18 Vincent Strega was dead, and he had died a hero. He had not killed himself; he had not willfully abandoned his *son*. Jon Strega's father had

loved him. Proof was right there in the expression on
Vincent's face. It was the face of a hero, dammit. A
hero.

Go to hell, Alvarez.

Strega swung out of bed and walked down the hall.
His apartment was big by New York standards and reflected Strega's appreciation for quality. Quality cost
money, more than a rookie cop earned in a year.
Strega's knack for playing the stock market earned him
enough extra income to indulge his expensive tastes.

The living room was a bright, airy room with high
ceilings. An enormous picture window looked out over
West Eighty-seventh Street. Strega had bleached the
natural-wood floors, then squared out the living space
with a big antique carpet, an oversized fern green custom sofa, a big matching armchair, and an iron-based
glass coffee table made by a well-known metal sculptor.
The back wall was built out with floor-to-ceiling bookshelves crammed full of books from his Princeton days.

A solid antique farm table defined the dining area.
Strega used one wall to display his small, eclectic art
collection—a few top-quality black-and-white photos
mixed in with three small oil pieces from the 1800s and
two larger canvases by contemporary American painters.
After a particularly smart stock trade Strega had treated
himself to a pricy piece of modern sculpture. She was
white Italian alabaster, two feet high, all fluid lines and
melodic angles. He kept her displayed on a broad slate
pedestal that turned to allow for full rotation of her
body.

Strega was a capitalist, but he had the heart and soul
of a sculptor. With the help of a gifted instructor at
Princeton, Strega had nurtured his raw talent into something accomplished. Now he had a working pedestal set
up next to the north-facing picture window, and he spe-
cialized in sculpting faces. A massive gray clay head
filled the pedestal. It was covered with a Hefty garbage
bag to keep the clay moist. Strega turned the revolving
work platform around, removed the plastic, and studied
the clay face.

He had started to do a self-portrait, but along the way the face had turned into his father's. Strega ran his hand over the cool, damp earth, feeling the sharp plane of the cheek. He touched the lips. They were curved up in a smile. He had captured Vincent well—the deep laugh lines around the mouth, the pull of the cheek muscles, and merry crinkles feathering out around the eyes—but the eyes themselves failed him. They stared out blank, utterly void of human emotion. Strega had reworked them a dozen times, but each time they gazed back with the same empty expression. If the eyes were the windows to the soul, there was no soul in this piece, and without soul it was just a lump of wet earth. Strega turned the pedestal around so the sightless, hollow orbs faced the window. He dropped the Hefty bag over the head and went into the kitchen to make coffee.

The kitchen had the same natural-wood floors as the living space. It was fitted with a semi-professional six-burner stove and enough copper cookware to equip a restaurant. He scrambled eggs for the kitten, brewed coffee for himself, and went back down the hall to the bedroom. He put the plate on the floor. Scrawny Sigmund devoured the eggs.

Strega studied the photo of his father. Would the sun ever be so bright as it was in the picture? He tried to remember that day and the exhilaration *he must have been feeling* there in the father-son game. Something stirred, a different memory entirely. It was of his father, but there was no sun, no laughter, and no wide-open sky. He had had this feeling before. It would disappear for months at a time; then suddenly the feeling would be back fluttering around in the back of his mind, evoked by something in the way the light fell or triggered by a certain tone of voice. When it came over him, it was as though a cloud was passing over the sun.

Strega closed his eyes and tried to track the sensory trail. *Color.* Blue carpet in the afternoon sunlight. *Music.* Old jazz, scratchy and low. Then a long corridor stretching in front of him, and voices coming from a room at the end where a door was ajar. Voices, and something else. Before Strega could pin it down, the phone rang, chasing the fragile memory fragment away. He let the machine take the call. When he heard the caller's voice, he was glad he had.

"Hi, Jonnie? Cindy. In case you lost my number, it's 678-9879."

Sure, he had lost her number. Permanently. He had met her in a bookstore earlier in the year, a week before he laid eyes on the five-foot nine-inch Sicilian. At first Strega thought Cindy might be good company. She was pretty and the fact that she was in a bookstore indicated that she might have an interest in literature.

One dinner out and Strega discovered Cindy's idea of literature was *Cosmopolitan* magazine. She giggled too much and drank her wine too fast. Strega hated nothing more than dumb women who thought they could get by on a smile and a thirty-six-inch chest. Not to say he didn't like a great smile and a thirty-six-inch chest, he just wanted a high-caliber brain to finish out the package. It was an impossible combination to find. He was doomed to live with an alabaster lady for whom he could invent a package of attributes.

Strega corrected himself. Such a woman did exist, and she was not alabaster. She was a hot-blooded, hot-headed, brilliant, beautiful Sicilian named Rosemary De Cesare, a Merrill Lynch executive down on Wall Street. When Strega had opened a trading account with the firm, Rosemary was introduced as his broker. The connection was powerful and instant. When Strega asked her if she was free for dinner to discuss his investment needs, she said yes. Her expression assured him she was interested in much more than his investment needs.

He took her to a cozy Italian place where the tables were small. Rosemary was a fusion of round shapes, one rolling into the next. Her body was expressive and unfashionably full. Her left ear was pierced twice with two half-carat diamond studs. Her hair was blazing copper in color, and she had lots of it tumbling around her shoulders in wild curls. Her eyebrows, the same copper color as her hair, swept up and out over startling blue

eyes. When he asked why she didn't have Sicilian brown
eyes, she murmured something about a Viking ship gone
astray on the shores of Sicily many eons ago. More mur-
murs about ransacking and pillaging. Strega looked into
the Viking blue and saw they were in the pillaging mood.
He asked for the check.

They returned to his brownstone, fell straight into bed,
and stayed there for two full days. Her mind was as fit
and rich as her body. In between their lovemaking she
discussed theater, politics, investment theory, global eco-
nomics, literature, and classical music, Then, in a limber
display of her intellect, she recited a lesser-known work
by Baudelaire, in flawless French. For the first time in
his life Strega was completely in love.

Over the month that followed, they spent most nights
together. Strega wanted to marry her but wouldn't. As
far as he could see, marriage to a cop inevitably ended
in one of two ways: divorce or death. Since Rosemary
couldn't have marriage, she insisted on monogamy.
Enter little Cindy. Despite Strega's rejection, she called
from time to time and left long, chatty messages. Rosemary inadvertently heard one of Cindy's bubbly messages, and Mt. Vesuvius blew. That had been two weeks
ago. She hadn't spoken to Strega since.

The funny part was that Rosemary was jealous but
shrewd, as greedy in the office as she was in bed. She
didn't want to lose Strega's trading business, so she used
her assistant as a go-between and continued to place all
of Strega's trades. He tried everything to win her back.
Roses to her office, roses to her home, chocolates, expensive wine, and just for good measure, a magnificent
bra and panty set from the most illustrious Italian lin-
gerie maker in the world. She hadn't sent the gifts back.
That was a good sign. Her assistant told Strega she still
had pictures of him up in her office. That was a very
good sign.

Strega sat down at his desk. It was a big oak piece
that he kept pushed up next to a pair of windows over-
looking a small garden in the back of the building. A
hundred-year-old vine, thick as a tree trunk, climbed the

exterior wall between them. The windows themselves were old-fashioned with simple wing locks on the frames. An IBM computer sat on the desk. His big iron bed faced the windows. On the long wall to the right of the bed were two doors. The first opened into a big walk-in closet. The second opened into a large, sunny bathroom.

This bedroom was different from the austere bedroom of his youth. The Strega household changed when Vincent died. The furniture was quickly packed up, and the family moved two hours down the train tracks to New York, as though a change of place would erase the tragedy. Their new house was tiny and had none of the feeling of *home*. Three dinky bedrooms and hardwood floors throughout.

His room had been sparsely furnished with a stark, dark dresser, a single bed, and a wood crucifix. His mother's bedroom had been cheerless too, with the same dark furniture and the same obligatory crucifix hanging over her half-empty matrimonial bed.

Strega's mother spent her days in prayer. Strega turned to his grandmother for comfort. He lay against her big, pillowy bosom and asked the unanswerable questions: *If Heaven is there, why can't I see it? If my father is in Heaven, why can't I reach up and touch him?* She would tell him there were no answers for the big questions in life. Then she would hold him tight and cry with him.

One day she clapped Strega on the ears and said the time had come to live again. She filled the solemn house with big Italian arias, and she began to cook. The old woman chopped, diced, stewed, steamed, simmered, peeled, minced, baked, roasted, whipped, churned, blended, fried, and grilled her grief away. "*Ragazzo*," she bellowed, "a man *must* know how to cook. He *must* know how to feed himself. Your father, God rest his soul, knew how to cook. And so will you." She pulled him into the kitchen, threw him a tomato, and taught him to chop.

When she wasn't ordering him around in the kitchen, she was pulling him up onto her lap, running her hands

over his face, and telling him stories of Italy, the homeland. Her breath was peppery, and her rough hands
made a scraping sound when they touched his face.
Those days, she said of her youth, were the Old Days
when she worked the land with her own hands. It was
the time before America, before the Atlantic crossing,
before she could speak English. "America!" she whispered into his ear. "You can be anything here. Dream.
Jonnie, dream! Make your life count! Make your dreams
come true!"

And Jonnie had dreams, dreams that grew as he did,
dreams that filled his head and heart. *Smart as a whip,*
his teachers said. *He'll make a fine doctor or lawyer one
day.* But his mother used to sit by his bed each night
and tell him to forget those dreams. With tears running
down her face and the rosary running through her fingers like water, she used to say, "You must honor your
father and fill his shoes. You must make him proud,
Jonnie. Oh, Jonnie, my son, my beautiful son, do you
know you look just like him?"

Every night those same words, and the sound of the
rosary falling through her fingers like rain.

The telephone rang again. He picked up on the
third ring.

"Jonnie. You feel like having dinner with me tonight?"

"No, I don't, Alvarez. Not tonight, not ever."

"You'll change your mind. I'm getting ready for when
you do. I'm learning about you. I'm going to be an expert on the subject of Jon Strega. I'm off to a good start
by finding my way through the lies to the truth. Truth
is important, isn't it? You think any more about what I
told you?"

"Nice piece of fiction. You scored. We're even now."

"But, Jonnie, this isn't about getting even." She hung
up softly.

The memory of her voice scratched him like sandpaper.

Six

"Sleep well, Jonnie?"

Her breath was hot in his ear. Her hand slipped over his, and red fingernails dug into his skin. She was sitting in back of him, in the squad room, waiting for roll call to begin.

Strega twisted around. Maria Alvarez leaned forward, close against his chair, close enough for Strega to see the little clumps of mascara bunched up on her eyelashes. Her lips were thickly and perfectly glossed. They were curved up in a smile.

"You have good hair," she whispered, releasing his wrist and stroking the side of his head. "It's nice and thick."

Strega removed her hand. "Don't ever take the liberty of touching me again."

Her eyes lit up, her smile widened. She cocked her head to one side. "Are you frigid?"

"Get out of my life, Alvarez."

"Oh, I'm not in it, Jonnie. Not yet, anyway." A big black eyebrow arched. She ran her tongue over her red lips, then slouched back.

Gavin dropped into the seat next to her. "Hey, Maria, you see who's on the cover of *New York* magazine?" He held it up and read the headline. "RAMON ALVAREZ—THE POWER P.C. He must be happy."

"Sure, he's happy," Maria said, shrugging. "Who wouldn't be?"

"Your picture's inside with him. Nice shot."

"Thanks. I'm photogenic." She winked at Strega.

Strega turned away.

Inspector Wilson whipped in, immaculate in suit and tie as anyone that high up and with political ambition always was. He was followed by a sweaty and rumpled Ballantine. A female detective hurried after them. Strega had seen her around. Cybil Hansen. She looked like a college girl, but she blew away every other detective in the One-Nine when it came to brains. Hansen was Ballantine's rising star. He doted on her, and that was clear in the expression on Q-Ball's face when he handed her a stack of papers to pass out. All the scowling and glooming and dooming blurred, then shifted together into a whole new look. Pride, Strega guessed. And affection. Nothing out of order, just good old-fashioned avuncular affection. The master to the protégé.

Wilson spoke. "In light of the increasing number of suicides, the P.C. has ordered an overhaul of Psych Services. His intent is to make the service more accessible and more user-friendly. Starting today, each precinct house will have a Psych Services counselor on the premises. Our counselor is Dr. Fields."

A slight middle-aged man stood up. His voice was thin. "My goal is to understand the day-to-day pressure uniformed cops are under. I will start by talking to each one of you, confidentially, of course. I hope you will consider me a friend." He looked out at the silent, closed faces, then glanced at Wilson, looking for help.

Wilson stepped forward. "Like I said, Dr. Fields is now a member of this precinct house. You will cooperate and extend every courtesy to him." Wilson escorted him out.

Q-Ball paced up front, scratching his head, rubbing his eyes, and looking like if he had slept at all, it had been in his clothes. He picked up the *Daily News*. "Fucking tabloids. PIRATES OF MADISON AVENUE STRIKE AGAIN. Sounds like some kind of Kevin Costner flick."

Ballantine slapped the paper down. "The father died this morning. That makes this a double homicide. I don't need a shrink to tell me that you patrolmen feel the case belongs to my homicide squad. Detectives' problem, right? After all, you've got your own work to do, right?

Wrong." He stuck a finger out. "You signed up to protect and to serve, and today that means finding these scabs before they do a repeat performance."

He shoved his hand in his pocket. "We spent the weekend crawling around on the floor of the bridal shop with the best techs CSU has to offer, and we've got shit to show for it. Aside from a fist full of bullets, we don't have one fucking lead. No prints, no video, no fibers, no blood. Zip. Zero.

"Oh, pardon me. We do have a lead. I forgot to tell you that they hit again, Sunday morning, right under our noses. The blonde hustled a lady into a black Mercedes sedan on Madison and Eighty-ninth Street. His buddy took her for a drive to the Bronx, confiscated her jewelry, then let her out and took off. The victim says the blonde didn't look like the composite sketch. Says she was so scared, she can't remember what the driver looked like, only that he was wearing Ralph Lauren cologne. Same kind her husband wears. Now, aside from that *helpful* hint, we've got zip. Zero.

"Keep an eye on rich ladies getting into fancy cars. If a man's with her, check him out, make damn sure he isn't one of our suspects. We're going to nail these scabs, and when we do, I'll personally pay for the party here. Anything you want. Champagne? You got it. Girls popping out of cakes? You got it. Pardon me. I forgot we have female officers in the house. I'll get some guys to pop out of cakes too. Detective Hansen is passing out revised composites, for what they're worth. Foot posts, I want you to canvas every store in your district and hand these sketches out. Show them to every doorman and every cashier. Find him. Find his buddy. That's all." Ballantine left the room.

The tour sergeant stepped up. "Davis is on vacation. Alvarez partners with Kelly. Dismissed."

Strega filed out with the rest of the officers.

Maria was there, up ahead in the hallway, sashaying slowly along. She pretended to drop her pen and leaned over to pick it up, timing it so she was eye level with Strega's crotch when he walked by. Then she straightened and fell into step beside him. "Your daddy must've been a handsome man," she said softly.

Strega ignored her.

"You ever think about what happens when a bullet goes through the side of the human skull?" she whispered. "Did they teach you about that at Princeton? A contact shot to the temple *always* leaves a perfect star-shaped entrance wound. Vincent had one, Jonnie. Did you know that?"

Her hand brushed across his lips, then she disappeared into the ladies' room. He caught a glimpse of her expression. It wasn't hate, it wasn't lust, it wasn't any emotion he could identify, but what was stamped on her features was raw and real, and it scared him more than any one of her tasteless phone calls had.

Strega hurried out to the patrol car. Gavin was ready to go. Strega slid in. Maria crossed the street in front of them. She was with Kelly, laughing at something he said.

"Lucky Kelly," Gavin grumbled, watching her. "You ever go on vacation, I hope I land Maria for a tour."

"She's harassing me."

Gavin began to giggle. "Harassing you? You read those signals wrong. Maria's hot for you. She wants to rush you off to bed. You should feel flattered."

"I don't." He started the car. "I feel harassed."

"What is she, five-three, five-four? You telling me you can't handle her?"

"It's not that kind of harassment. She's mad at me."

Gavin yawned. "You asked for trouble when you yanked her chain. Take her out. Buy her a beer and apologize. Better yet, *I'll* take her out and buy her a beer."

"You do that," Strega said dryly, pulling away from the station house.

An hour into the tour, Maria felt shaky inside. She wanted to stay straight today, but she wanted the feeling, the great bright feeling, more. She rested her forehead against the cool glass of the passenger window. The city washed by, out of focus and fluid.

"You okay?" Kelly asked, stopping the car.

"Headache, that's all."

"There's a pharmacy. Can I get you some aspirin?"

"Thanks, Mike. That's nice of you to offer." She watched him lope across the street. When he was out of sight, she pulled the small foil packet out of her pocket. She leaned down, out of view, and took a hit, then wet her finger and dipped it in the powder and ran it over her gums. Her mouth tingled. The world steadied and brightened. Her head cleared. Her nerves came alive. She tucked the foil back in her pocket and sat up.

Maria looked out the window. The sidewalks were full of businessmen hurrying to work—hundreds of men in suits, a disproportionate number of whom were blond or dark-haired and who looked like the composites. The shooters were soldiers, Maria thought. Suits were their camouflage. *Self-defense is a kind of war,* her father had once said. *All the rules of war apply.* Maria wondered what the shooters thought they were defending and what their cause was. Maria had a cause, and her uniform was her camouflage.

"Here," Kelly said, swinging back in, handing her a bottle of aspirin. "Maria, should I take you back in? You want to take a sick day?"

She noted the thumping of his thumb against the steering wheel, and knew he was nervous with her. She studied the clean, clipped nails, the long fingers, and the soft, hairless skin on the backs of his hands, and imagined he was a courteous lover—attentive but restrained, lights out, afraid of his own needs.

"Maria?" he said again. "You want me to take you back?"

"No, thanks." She reached over and covered his broad hand with hers. "We don't want to miss our chance to work together, do we?"

She watched his pulse tick in his forehead and his face flush red. He was speechless long enough for Maria to figure it out on her own. She saw the hunger in his eyes and the hope too. She saw how he was shy and a little afraid, and her own heart quickened. She liked them this way. The game was more fun with men like Kelly.

Kelly's voice was soft. "I'm married, Maria. I moved out, but technically I'm still married. Just thought you should know."

"I don't have a problem with that, Mike. Do you?"

Kelly touched her hair and smiled shyly.

Strega was uncharacteristically testy all day. He was irritable, jumpy, and talked in nothing but monosyllables. All that expensive Princeton vocabulary was reduced to three primitive words: *Yes, no,* and *maybe.* Something was bugging Strega. It struck Gavin that maybe he shouldn't have brushed the Alvarez thing off so lightly. Maybe sexual harassment *was* unpleasant. Gavin didn't know. He'd never been harassed.

Unfortunately.

They rolled back to the precinct house at four. The hot locker room did nothing to improve Strega's humor. When Gavin offered to buy him dinner, the kid snapped no so fast it sounded like a gunshot. Then Strega muttered something *having to get his exercise,* going running or some damn fool thing in the heat. Gavin got the message. He shut up and stayed that way through the rest of showering and changing, saying nothing, but taking sneaky little sideways glances at Strega's iron body. The goddamned washboard belly, those long, graceful thighs. Then when Strega casually dropped the towel from his waist, Gavin's curiosity was stronger than his manners. He stole a peek and wished he hadn't. *Holy Moses.* The kid was prodigiously endowed.

Gavin sat glumly on the bench. No wonder, he thought, no wonder at all that Maria felt like harassing the kid. What a package. If a body like Strega's was the guaranteed reward, Gavin thought he just might take up running too. Even when he had been boxing regularly, he'd never had a body like Jon Strega's, and he certainly didn't now. Damn shame. Would've been nice to know for *just one second* what it was like to have Maria Alvarez in heat sniffing along after him. Oh, yes, would've been nice indeed.

"Later," Strega mumbled.

The rookie was out the door before Gavin could think of something useful to say. He leaned down to put his sneakers on.

"Gavin," a familiar voice called out.

He looked up. Mike Kelly was smiling down at him.

"Scale of one to ten," Gavin said, "how much would it bug you if some girl tried to sexually harass you?"

Kelly frowned. "Sounds like a question Psych Services would dream up."

"Have you seen the little weasel yet?"

"Fields? That's why I'm here late."

"What's he like?"

"Nervous son of a bitch. Bites his nails. His hands shake."

"What'd you talk about?"

"He asked me if I had any weird fantasies. Vegetables turning into guns, knives flying off the dinner table and killing the wife, that kind of thing. Christ. I told him any man going through a divorce has fantasies about killing his soon-to-be ex-wife. Other than those, I told him the only fantasies I have are the flesh-and-blood kind." Kelly sat down. Despite his light talk he looked low.

"How's it going, Mike, really? The divorce thing."

"Shitty," Kelly admitted. "You know, I still don't know why she wants out. She *says* she wants a normal life. Any idea what the hell normal is?"

Sure, Gavin thought. *A husband with a Monday-to-Friday, nine-to-five job. Business suit and an attaché case full of papers. Your wife doesn't want to be married to a cop.*

Gavin couldn't tell Kelly that. His job was to comfort, not to pour salt in the wound. The truth was, cops were a breed unto themselves. They spoke a different language, and the bond between them was stronger than the bond with their wives or children. Men like Kelly and Gavin were cops first, husbands and fathers second. Women sensed this. Some women hung on for the ride.

Others, like Kelly's wife, tried to hang on, but cracked along the way. Some, like Donovan's wife, Jillian, never cared in the first place.

Kelly was looking at him, waiting for an answer. He put a hand on Kelly's angular shoulder. "It's just one more thing to get through, Mike. Take it in stride."

"Yeah, well, the worst part is I got to start dating again."

"Fear of rejection?"

"You're starting to sound like the Psycho shrink. He's got Moon in there now."

"No, he doesn't," Moon said, breezing in. "I told him you have to be crazy to be a cop in the first place. He couldn't think of a dang thing to say back to me, so I left." He laughed his horsy laugh and sat down next to Gavin. "Good day, Ed?"

"No murders, no floaters. Guess that's as good as it gets around here." Gavin turned back to Kelly. "You rode around with Maria. She say anything to you about Strega?"

"No. Why?"

"I think she's got a thing for him."

Kelly shrugged and looked away. "She's entitled. She's a healthy young woman."

Moon hooted. "I hear she's especially healthy between the legs. Pink and juicy. The fifth major food group."

Kelly flushed. "Shut the fuck up, Moon."

"Hey, Kelly, I was just having some fun," Moon defended.

"Have it at someone else's expense," Kelly ordered. "Maria wakes up every day of her life knowing she's being judged as *Ramon Alvarez's* daughter. Try putting yourself under that kind of microscope and see how long you hold out before you do some crazy things." He punched his locker and walked out.

Moon smiled sheepishly at Gavin and skulked away.

Gavin was ready to go too, but he stalled. Hung back. Rearranged his locker. Fussed with his stack of folded socks. Closed the locker. Mopped up puddles of water. Picked up old newspapers off the floor like a janitor.

Puttered around. Finally, he stopped and looked at himself in the mirror. "Go home, old man. You can't avoid it. Go home."

Maria lay on her back, nude, spread-eagled across her double bed. She was too hot to curl her body up, so her arms and legs poked out over the edges and dangled in thin air. She was on fire. The blow always made her feel that way. It was early Monday evening. The digital alarm clock flapped along, tracking the minutes, and the air seemed liquid—the breathing nearly drowned her. Her only window was closed and sealed against the stench of rotting garbage in the alley below.

The building across the alley was almost close enough to touch. In the window facing hers, a bright blue tubular neon sign blinked BAIL BONDS—24 HOURS. It flashed all day and all night. She knew the rhythm and pace. Sixty flashes a minute. Three thousand six hundred flashes an hour. She had been watching it for exactly one hour.

She stared up at the ceiling. Some previous tenant had painted the bedroom ceiling black and filled the fake cosmos with a galaxy of painted silver stars—a hundred and five of them. They glowed in the dark. The black-painted universe had a crack in it, a jagged line of white plaster which had started small. Now it had grown and went from one side to the other. Maria wondered if the crack might eventually work its way down the wall and across the floor. She imagined that if it did, the room might break into two halves around her and swallow her alive.

She rolled over and snapped the TV on with the remote. Her father's face filled the screen. She punched the mute button. Ramon gestured a lot with his hands. Even though Maria couldn't hear the words, she could hear his voice. It was in her head. The resonance of it. The thunder of it. Now that thunder was directed at reporters and at a sea of unseen taxpayers watching the news. The thundering was about the Madison Avenue shooters. Crime made Ramon Alvarez mad.

The camera went in for a tight shot. Ramon's face

filled the screen. He was perspiring. He pounded his fist on the podium. His white teeth flashed. The black and gold cuff links glinted in the hot television lights. He was looking hard into the camera, as though he were looking right through the lens into Maria's room. Into her eyes.

Maria rolled over onto her back. The crack in the ceiling was bigger, but maybe it was the blow kicking in, making it seem that way. The blow exaggerated everything, even her father's face. Maria felt trapped. Trapped between the cracking universe and Ramon and the flapping numbers of the digital clock. She had to get out before the ceiling split wide open and swallowed her— before Ramon crawled through the TV set and caught her.

Maria dressed quickly, pulling her uniform on although she was off duty. It made her feel official. Safe. The gun belt was heavy against her hip. She hurried out of her building, trotted down the stairs and into the early evening. The blow made her feel strong. She walked fast, seven blocks, all the way over to Grand Central Station.

The city pulsed all around her. It was the end of a working day. She took it all in. Street vendors hawking cold sodas at inflation prices. Earnest executives hailing cabs, bicycle messengers whizzing by, powered by tree-trunk legs, pumping tirelessly, racing to an important destination, a deadline address, ferrying urgent documents and *get this there before six o'clock* packages. Everyone had a destination. So did Maria.

She entered Grand Central Station and hurried down to one of the crowded platforms. She picked him out instantly. Late thirties, expensive clothes—a well-cut Italian summer gabardine suit, a silk tie, and a gold Cartier watch Maria knew was real. He carried a burnished leather briefcase, a copy of the *Wall Street Journal,* and he wore a shiny wedding band on his left hand. Maria guessed the man was still in love and eager to get home.

A train rocketed out of the dark and screeched to a stop. The doors slid open, the travelers piled in. Maria stayed close behind him, close enough to touch his sleeve. He smelled good. He took a seat. The doors closed. The train shot forward.

Maria sat down behind him. An hour later, at an affluent suburban stop, he stood up and got off the train. Maria followed him out to the parking lot. A blue Volvo wagon pulled around. The driver was a beautiful woman, with a rope of pearls and her hair in a shiny chignon. Two small children frolicked in the backseat. The man got in and kissed his wife tenderly. The Volvo pulled away.

Maria sat down on a bench and watched the car until it was out of sight. She wanted to be that woman, that wife, that mother. Maria knew she never would be. She was broken. Busted. Hollow inside. Dirty inside and out.

Summer dusk drifted lazily down. Day slid into night.

A bicycle bell zing-zinged. The little bell was silvery and light. The summer song of carefree kids carried on a breeze. *All the outs in free-free-free.* The squeak of bicycle tires, the rattle of shiny bicycle fenders, the clank of a chain gear shifting down. A splash in a far-off swimming pool. The slap of a girl's jump rope beating the pavement. A swing set creaking, the occupant pumping hard to reach the sky. A rain bird rat-a-tat-tatting over a carefully tended lawn. A wood-paneled station wagon packed with little girls in camp clothes passed. A shiny Mercedes sedan slipped by.

Night closed in around Maria. She stood up, moved down the platform, and rode an empty train back into the city.

It was midnight. Grand Central Station was empty. She walked slowly. The energy from the blow had worn off long ago. From somewhere behind one of the many pillars, a man's voice rose in song. It was a rich, plaintive aria. Maria stood still to listen. The voice touched a high note; then the note changed to a cry, the cry cascaded down, and all the soaring beauty of the aria was lost in a low, throaty cry—a funeral dirge.

Maria followed the sound. She found a man. He was kneeling, his back curled in a perfect arc, his face buried in his old, shaking hands. Next to him was a metal grocery cart piled high with junk—pots and pans, old radios, blankets, pillows, and a woman's heavy winter coat in a bright shade of fuchsia.

The man laced his fingers and peered through them at Maria in her uniform. "You've come to throw me out," he barked.

"I heard you singing," Maria replied. "It was beautiful."

"Ha." The old man rocked up on his heels, the arc unfolded. He stood six-four in his flat, dirty, bare feet. He wore a striped button-down shirt, frayed at the cuffs and collar, and an old, stained red tie. His gabardine slacks were grimy and shapeless. Long strings of matted gray hair lay damp and flat to his skull. Even so, his eyes were kind, and leftover intelligence sparkled in them. "You're here to throw me out. All you coppers want to do is give homeless people hell. Ha. Well, go ahead. Throw me out."

Half mad, Maria thought, from a lifetime of disappointments or a week's worth of hunger. Maria pulled a five-dollar bill out of her pocket. She held it out to the man. "Here. Get yourself something to eat."

A spotted, bony hand plucked the bill from Maria's fingertips. The old man held it up to the light. "A five. It may last me five days if I'm careful and spend only a dollar a day. Thank you, dearie," he whispered, stuffing the bill in his pocket. He gripped the metal shopping cart handle and slowly pushed it across the deserted station.

Maria watched the old man shamble away. He stopped once, turned around, and raised his hands in a gesture of helplessness. "God's forgotten me," he cried.

"Me too," she whispered, fingering the service revolver in her gun belt. "Me too."

Maria thought about dropping in on Mike Kelly, but she went home instead. She had a present to deliver to Jon Strega.

Seven

Gavin pulled into his driveway at seven-thirty. In the neighboring yard an old metal rain bird gyrated slowly, sending out a worthless spit of water—worthless because the patch of lawn there, like his, had burned dry weeks before. He got out of the car and stood over his own square of dismal, dry-cracked earth. It depressed him. Was it too much to ask? That a hardworking man should have some little token piece of nature in his concrete world? He kicked the dirt patch and went inside.

The house was cool and quiet, and the drapes were drawn against the harsh late-day sun. "Shell?" he called out. No one answered. He wandered into the kitchen. A note was stuck to the refrigerator door: *E: Went to the movies. Leftover chicken in fridge. S*

Attached to the note was a set of complex instructions on how to microwave the leftover bird, and what to do to make a box of frozen potatoes edible. Gavin decided to mix up a scotch and soda instead. He roamed through the house with the cold tumbler in his hand, and when the tumbler was empty, he mixed up another. More scotch than soda this time. Pale gold poured over little chunks of crushed ice. A token splash of bubbly. He gave it a quick stir with his finger. Cheers. The nectar of the gods. High-carbohydrate dinner. Courage for the cowardly lion.

He carried the drink upstairs to his bedroom and set it on the dresser. He leaned down and opened the sweater drawer. It was stuffed to the brim with snowflake and reindeer motifs, cheerful winter garb in festive colors for a man who wondered if he would ever feel festive again.

He dug underneath the pile of wool. His fingers touched manila. He needed two hands to pull the folder out, it was that full and thick with information he didn't particularly want to look at.

Gavin sat cross-legged on the floor with the folder in his lap. He felt secretive, and the feeling was familiar. He struggled a moment, then realized why.

When he was a teenager, he used to hide girlie magazines in the bottom of his drawers. He used to lock himself in his room and page through them with a flashlight, the sweet fear of getting caught curling up in his throat. Oh, yes, he felt that same fear now. Fear because he'd been sneaking along, hiding all the evidence of Donovan's fate in the bottom drawer like he had something forbidden, something dirty.

Which it was, wasn't it?

Wasn't suicide dirty?

Profane?

Unforgivable for all eternity?

Donovan and Gavin were Catholic. Well, their version, anyway. They were obedient when it came to baptisms, weddings, and funerals. Disobedient when it came to confession, divorce, and birth control. They were *progressive* Catholics. Their indoctrination, however, had been Old World and thorough. All the lessons had been learned, all the rules and regulations for achieving eternal happiness drummed in. The Ten Commandments? Indisputable. Christ as the savior? Indisputable. Suicide as eternal damnation? Indisputable—with certain progressive modifications.

Forty years earlier, a man dead by his own hand would have been denied the honor of a consecrated burial. But the Church had *progressed* over the years in an attempt to keep pace with the evolution of man and his society, and Donovan had been granted a proper burial in the family plot. In cases like Danny's, the Church allowed for the possibility that mental illness played a role in the decision to commit suicide. In the Church's *progressive view,* mental illness liberated the poor soul from eternal damnation. If the *progressive*

Church was that forgiving, why couldn't Gavin feel the same way?

Was he mad at Donovan? Was that it?

Gavin reached for his drink. His hands shook. He sucked on a scotch-coated ice cube. Yes. The truth was, he was furious at Donovan. The earthbound life was hard enough. Why screw yourself for eternity by committing suicide? What if the *progressive* Church was wrong? After all, the Church was an institution run by mere mortals, and those mortals were betting that the act of suicide would be forgiven.

What if it's not, Danny? What if you're damned for all time? What good will it do you then, this magnanimous allowance to let you do your rotting in the family plot?

Gavin pushed himself up to a standing position. Holding the file tight to his body with one hand and carrying his drink with the other, he went downstairs to the dining room. Four recessed lights threw a soft, even light across the rectangular dining table. Gavin put the file down. Judging from the bulk of it, he figured he would need a lot of space to spread the photos out and study them properly. Ballantine had thoughtfully tucked a powerful magnifying glass inside. Gavin took it out and used it to look at his own palm. His life line appeared enormous—a deep, cavernous, prophetic crease in his flesh.

He squeezed his hand shut. He procrastinated. Freshened his scotch. Waited until the clock struck nine. For no reason. It just seemed he should know the exact hour that he witnessed Danny's death for a second time. When the clock chimes faded out, he opened the folder.

The first sheaf of papers contained the police reports, a copy of the death certificate, legal identification records, fingerprint cards, and the autopsy report. Gavin lifted the papers and put them to one side. The stack of CSU photos was underneath. It was three inches thick and bound with a fat rubber band. He peeled the rubber band off and pushed the rest of the file away. One by one he lay the twenty-nine photos, solitaire style, across the table, creating an arbitrary order to them. Wide shots first, followed by medium shots, and then the close-ups. When he finished shuffling the pictures around, his hands were shaking and his breath was shallow from the effort of trying to maintain a nice analytical perspective while viewing Donovan's self-destruction.

The color quality of the photos was good. It captured the exact shade of the gold shag carpet, the horrible aqua blue vinyl sofa bed, and the black of the fat, bloated flies crawling in and out of his friend's ear.

Gavin choked. He bit his lip and shut his eyes against the visual assault. It was too late. The mental playback button had already been pushed.

He remembered nothing of the frantic drive that June day, from Manhattan to Long Island, to the crummy neighborhood where Danny lived, only that he was somehow there, rapping on Donovan's door, calling out. "Danny? You okay?" Then, in the silence that followed, he jiggled the doorknob and found it unlocked. Gavin remembered stepping in to the tight, angular foyer and feeling puzzled at first by the high humming sound coming from somewhere inside.

"Danny?" he called out, with less authority than before.

He listened and heard nothing but the horrible high humming sound. Had Donovan left the TV on? Was the phone off the hook? Gavin turned the corner and stepped into the one-room living space. He saw the open window first, the turquoise drapes billowing out in a light breeze. Then the back of the ugly couch facing him. A thousand flies swarmed across the top rim and over the high winged armrests. A larger cloud of flies pulsed over the couch seat. The stench knocked Gavin back. It was the smell of a toilet overflowed, of sweet fruit gone bad in the heat, and of something else. Something his cop brain told him was blood. He pulled his T-shirt up to cover his face.

He peered over the high couch back and saw Danny toppled over sideways, wearing his uniform shirt and nothing else. He was barefoot. Hungry flies crawled up his pale, hairy legs. Gavin's mind lurched around, refusing to process the information in front of him. He thought Danny was asleep. His mind refused to register the gun that lay on the floor, next to Danny's ankles. He would remember that later. Gavin forced himself to look up from Danny's feet to where his head should have been.

The flies were feasting. On Danny's gray matter. Marching hungrily along and they had been marching for some twenty-four hours. The scientific facts were there. The eggs had been laid and the babies had been born—white, twisting things, curling their way along Danny's neck. Maggots. Laid and hatched in the single revolution of the Earth in which Donovan lay dead.

Gavin's eyes slammed shut. He wheeled around and blindly felt for the foyer wall, then for the door. He stumbled down the stairs, taking them like the sightless man he was. His eyes stayed sealed until he was out the lobby door and standing in the gentle summer afternoon sun. He threw up on the sidewalk. He threw up again crossing the street to the pay phone. His stomach continued to constrict violently while he dialed 911, but there was nothing left inside. The heaves were dry. Had he thrown up his heart as well? He must have—his chest hurt so much, a bright, burning feeling behind the sternum that was turning into an icy, iron grip.

He fumbled the numbers and dialed 199. He tried again, punching the silver number pad with a drunkard's exaggerated precision: 9-1-1.

The operator answered. A concerned female voice.

Gavin tried to talk, but his speech came out idiot thick, garbled, and unintelligible. *Murder* was the only word he could say whole.

The operator reassured him and told him to calm down. She asked him to give her the information and promised that she would send someone right away.

Right away, Gavin had repeated, is too late. *Danny's dead. Someone murdered him.*

How did Danny die? the operator had asked like she was talking to a child. *Where is Danny now?*

Good question, Gavin thought. Heaven or Hell or

stuck someplace in between. He managed to articulate
the address, and then the shock gripped him and he was
mute again. The receiver fell from his hand, hit the side
of the phone booth, and dangled at the end of its silver
coil. Gavin's body hit the side of the phone booth too,
flesh and bones potato-sack heavy, inert, and his eyes
sealed shut again as he slipped to the ground.

Gavin heard a noise and opened his eyes. He was at
home in his dining room, holding one of the CSU photos
in his right hand and the tumbler of scotch in his left.
The noise was the front door opening, then closing. He
identified Shelly's footsteps.

"Ed?" she called out. "You in there?"

He looked at the explicit pictures spread out on the
dining room table. "Don't come in," he ordered. He
didn't want to share Danny's death, didn't want to hear
the bromides, the clucking, the *Ed, he's dead, you've got
to let him go,* the *Ed, he killed himself and that's a fact
you have to accept,* and the horror on her face if she
saw the photos, then the *Ed, you shouldn't be looking
at these* as she scooped them out and took them away.

"You hear me?" Gavin shouted. "Don't come in.
Leave me alone."

He heard her sharp intake of breath, then her hurried
footsteps and the creak of the stairs as she climbed them.
A door slammed upstairs. Gavin went back to the mental replay of that day in June.

The EMS unit had arrived. The attendants had raced
over to Gavin and helped him up off the ground. Gavin
protested and screamed that he wasn't the one in trouble. "Danny." He pointed a finger at the apartment
house. "Two-C," he cried. "He's in Two-C."

The paramedics raced into the apartment building.
Gavin sat outside on the curb while the patrol cars flew
in, one after another, a flock of six blue-and-white birds
circling around one of their own. The M.E.'s van was
next, as welcome as the grim reaper. CSU arrived and
disappeared inside, and Gavin sat waiting two full hours
before anyone thought to come out and tell him Danny
hadn't been murdered.

"But he's dead," Gavin dumbly replied. "I saw him myself. I saw the flies." The godawful flies.

"He's dead, Ed. But he wasn't murdered. Danny killed himself," a cop told him.

Gavin couldn't remember now who.

The cop walked away. A gurney was wheeled out of the building, heavy with the full black rubber body bag. The gurney was loaded into the ambulance, the doors slammed, and the ambulance rolled silently forward, roof lights still. There was a branch of the county morgue close by, but all the important deaths went to Lang in Manhattan. An NYPD cop was considered important. Danny was going to Lang.

One by one the patrol cars pulled away. Later, the detectives and the CSU team reappeared. There was a momentary flurry of door slamming, engines firing, and then the homicide squad cars drifted away. Gavin looked around. It was sunset and there was only one car left. It took him a moment to realize it was his. He crossed the street, climbed the stairs of the apartment building, and stood outside Danny's door. It was closed but not locked. He learned later that no one could find the key. Someone had stuck a length of yellow crime-scene tape to the door in a token effort to keep the casual burglar out—not that there was anything worth stealing in the fleabag place, or anyone alive to steal it from. Gavin turned around and walked out. He threw up one more time alongside the Tempo, then drove home and went to bed for three full days.

Gavin was forced back into the living world because he was the only appropriate one to wrap up the hundred loose ends left by Danny's death. Donovan's will named Gavin as the sole executor. Gavin filed the obituary, made the funeral arrangements, and conferred with the priest in the delicate matter of choosing a sermon. He chose the grave marker and the simple words that would be engraved on it.

He made all the phone calls to the far-flung Donovan clan, and drove alone up to the streets of the Three-Four where folks still loved Donovan and cried to hear he was dead. He had Danny's phone turned off, the mail stopped, and he paid the final bills. To Donovan's ex-wife, Jillian, Gavin made one curt phone call in which he told her that she was not welcome in any part of Danny's death—not the funeral, and certainly not at the final closing of his apartment. If he could, Gavin said, he would charge her with murder; what she put Danny through was obviously what had killed him.

He filed the appropriate Social Security and IRS papers on Katy's behalf, and fought an unsuccessful battle with Donovan's life insurance company. The company sent an oily-looking agent—a Sherman Crane—over to meet with Gavin in the precinct house to discuss the claim. Gavin wanted the meeting to take place in his law and order environment. He counted on a certain subliminal intimidation factor—service revolver prominently displayed, handcuffs jangling, hand radio buzzing—to cow the company into sending Katy a check.

The pebbly-eyed claims adjuster heard Gavin out, then ceremoniously laid his ratty vinyl attaché case on the desk. He opened it, took out a white document, and displayed it so that Gavin could read it. It was a copy of Donovan's death certificate.

"Get to the point," Gavin ordered.

Crane simply smiled thinly and pointed to the death certificate, where the manner of Danny's death was legally recorded as suicide. "Under the terms of the late Mr. Donovan's policy," he recited, "Harvest Mutual has no obligation to pay out when the cause of death is suicide." He snatched the paper back, shaking his head vigorously from side to side. He pursed his cracked lips and made a clicking noise with his tongue. *Click, click, click.*

Gavin tried another tack. "The bullet was from his service revolver. It was an accident. He was cleaning his gun."

"Then why was the barrel pressed directly to his head? It was a *contact* wound. Says so right here in the autopsy report." He held the white report up again. A

surrender flag. "Suicide. That's a fact, Mr. Gavin. I only
deal in facts."

"He left a small, defenseless child behind. That's a
fact you should deal with."

"Nope, sorry, Mr. Gavin. As I said, in cases of suicide
we have no obligation to pay. None. Not a one." *Click,
click, click.*

"What about a moral obligation?" Gavin brought his
fist down on the table. "Katy Donovan is five years old.
She's fatherless. How's she going to go to college?"

"Life is not always fair, Mr. Gavin. It is not Harvest
Mutual's responsibility to cure all the injustices of the
world. We are a *business.* Mr. Donovan knew the terms
of the policy when he signed it. If he was as worried as
you are about young Katy's forthcoming education, why
did he go and kill himself?"

"This meeting's over," Gavin said. "Now. Get out."

Crane shrugged. The white death certificate disappeared into the attaché case. Crane stood and straightened his horrible orange tie. "Good day, Mr. Gavin."

Gavin watched him go, then slumped in his chair.
Damn it, Danny, he thought. Crane had a point. *Indisputable suicide.* Damn selfish way to finish yourself off.
Why didn't you drive your car into the East River? Walk
in front of an oncoming bus? Of all the hundreds of
ways to die, why couldn't you do something that looked
accidental? Then Katy would have gotten her check, a
nice tidy sum to help her get the right start in life.

As it was, by the time the funeral was paid for and
the leftover legal bills settled, there wasn't much left.
Gavin stuck the meager sum in a long-term Treasury bill
in Katy's name. It was a poor one, Katy's legacy. A
crazy woman for a mother, a father dead by his own
hand, and a miserable lump of spare change that would
hardly buy her college books when the time came. Somehow it didn't seem fair, and the injustice gave Gavin the
energy to get mad at Donovan all over again.

The anger gave him the courage to clear out Donovan's apartment.

He went back alone, carrying two boxes of Hefty garbage bags and a half dozen cardboard boxes. The door was still unlocked. Gavin pushed it open, took a step inside, and sniffed the air. It was stale and still, but thankfully full of medicinal disinfectant odors and industrial cleaners. He left the door open anyway and walked in.

The landlord had removed the aqua couch and the coffee table. The shag carpet had yet to be replaced. Several large rusty spots stained it. Gavin walked around them to the shelving unit. There wasn't much to go through. The furniture and appliances all belonged to the landlord, as did the dishes, television set, and drapes. He cleared the shelving unit in five minutes flat, tossing out Donovan's collection of paperback books, the stack of fishing magazines, and old *TV Guides*.

He put the framed photos of Katy in a small carton, then tossed in four crude crayon drawings that were hanging in the kitchen, thinking Katy might want them one day. She might, he thought, get a laugh at eighteen, looking back at her childhood art. There was one skimpy closet stuffed with clothes. Gavin filled up three Hefty bags for the Salvation Army and kept for himself the big straw sombrero Donovan used to wear on their summer beach walks. On the plastic hook on the back of the bathroom door, Gavin found one of Donovan's uniform shirts. He tossed it in the box with Katy's pictures.

The bathroom itself was full of the minutia of Donovan's day-to-day life. Shampoo, deodorant, toothpaste, mouthwash. Gavin threw it all out. He emptied the medicine chest of aspirin bottles, over-the-counter sleeping aids, Band-Aids, and tossed it all in the Hefty bag. Donovan's electric razor sat on the counter. Gavin reached for it, then pulled back. Somehow, the razor got to him. It was still plugged in and charging, a tiny token of the irrepressible human optimism that believes there will always be one more morning in which to shave. The things we take for granted, he thought. He yanked the plug out, dumped the razor in a trash bag, tied the bag, and hauled it out.

Gavin opened his eyes.

Ballantine wanted him to do more than remember. He studied the photo in his hand. It was a wide-angle shot of the living room, and there wasn't much to study. A TV set sat on the floor, the VCR next to it. There was a plastic shelving unit filled with paperback books. Gavin picked up the powerful magnifying glass. McBain, Daley, McDonald, all the big names in police and detective fiction. No surprises there. His eyes moved to the VCR machine. The little light was on. Danny must have been watching a film.

He put the photo down and picked up a series of bathroom shots. The magnifying glass worked well. He could see how the cap to the toothpaste tube was screwed on tight. He could even see the goddamn electric razor plugged in and charging.

The next series of shots documented the kitchen. It was a cupboard of a room, crammed with a short refrigerator, a two-burner stove, and a dinky sink. A jumble of dishes filled the sink. A pink plastic garbage can overflowed with empty soda cans and TV dinner boxes. The CSU photographer had opened the cupboards and documented the contents: a box of corn flakes, instant coffee, bag of sugar, bag of Oreo cookies, two bags of pretzels. Bachelor stuff. The inside of the refrigerator was a wasteland. One can of Budweiser beer, a quart of milk.

The photos went on to show every angle of the kitchen. The cabinets and refrigerator were closed. Four bright primary-colored crayon drawings were stuck to the wall. They were all variations on the same theme peopled by a cast of three: a stick-figure lady with yellow hair and a purple dress, a stick-figure man wearing a dark blue uniform and a yellow star-shaped badge, and a stick-figure little girl wearing blue pants. In the first drawing the three figures were standing together on a green lawn in front of a pink house. Smoke curled up from a crooked chimney. The stick faces all had wide red mouths that curved up in exaggerated smiles. Their stick arms were stuck out at their sides, holding hands with each other.

In the second drawing the yellow-haired lady stick had

her back turned to the man stick. The lady had no clothes on. The man wore the same yellow badge, but this time his hands were up in the air and tears were flying horizontally out of his eyes. The little girl stick was sprawled on the ground, facedown. Tears shot out of her hidden eyes, horizontally, off the page. There was no smoke coming out the chimney. The green grass had turned brown. The pink house was marbled with black.

In the third drawing the pink house was shrunken in size. It floated in the top corner of the page. The yellow-haired lady wore a black dress. She had big black-rimmed eyes and a giant red frown. She was staring out the window. A large room took up most of the rest of the page. In it a blue couch faced an open window. Turquoise drapes billowed out in a cartoon breeze. Outside the window, a big orange sun smiled in. The stick man with his yellow badge stood at the open door, waving his stick hand. The little stick girl stood outside, midway between the shrunken pink house and the wide-open door. Two heads grew out of her stick neck. One was frowning and was turned back in the direction of the shrunken house. The second was smiling and turned toward the big man with the gold star. She carried a suitcase that was half again as big as she was.

The last picture. One big room filled the paper. An aqua couch. A TV set with a cartoon rabbit on the screen. Big orange sun smiling in. Flowers raining down from the ceiling. Stick figures of the man and the little girl, holding hands, smiling, and tears in the shape of hearts flying from the eyes, upward, defying gravity. On this last drawing the crayon artist had thoughtfully given names to the two figures. Daddy. Katy.

As if that wasn't absolutely clear from the start.

Poor Katy. Poor lost Katy stuck now in the shrunken house with the black-eyed, yellow-haired monster. Donovan could have used the pictures alone in the custody trial and won. He hadn't needed a couple of high-priced lawyers at all. There would have been no more compelling argument, no more compelling closing statement, than Katy's crayon drawings.

Gavin put the photos of the kitchen down and looked through the living room shots again. There was Danny, alone, slumped on the couch, facing the TV. The entrance wound was on the right temple. There was a series of close-up shots showing the texture and markings around the entrance wound. It was a star-burst shape, irrefutable proof that the gun barrel had been pressed to the skin. When a contact shot is fired, the explosion gases shoot in and become trapped between bone and skin. The gases burst the skin open in a star shape.

Star light, star bright—the last star you saw that night.

The next close-up showed Donovan's right hand and the damning powder stains on it. Irrefutable proof. His hand had held the gun when the shot was fired. Gavin slapped the photo down and riffled through the papers, looking for the autopsy report. It had its own file, complete with its own set of photographs.

Gavin waited to open the file. He reminded himself that he had been present at an autopsy once. Then the corpse had been a guy in his sixties who had the misfortune of being an *innocent bystander* in the Three-Four one afternoon when all hell broke loose between the NYPD and a drug lord. No one knew whose bullets had killed the John Doe—NYPD's or the drug lord's or both. Gavin had been the lucky one, sent to the autopsy to ferry the bullets that were being dug out of the victim over to the crime lab.

Like anyone else, he was curious about what went on in an autopsy. He elected to wait inside the room and observe the procedure. The M.E. intoned all his observations into a microphone which recorded his words on audiotape. Of all the cutting and sawing and splaying, Gavin remembered most vividly how the M.E. had examined the heart. "Muscle of a twenty-year-old," the M.E. stated for the record. He then held the heart up, and a camera flashed, recording the visual evidence for posterity. "Could've gone on pumping for another forty years," the M.E. added.

Could've, should've, would've.

"No signs of arterial blockage," the M.E. continued.

"Lucky son of a bitch. Paid a lot of attention to his diet. So what, huh? The moral of this heart? Go eat a steak and a nice baked potato with heaps of butter and sour cream because *you never know* when your number's up."

Gallows humor. Gavin guessed a guy who spent his days digging around in the cavities of cadavers had the right. All the men in Gavin's family had died in their sixties of so-called natural causes. The English diet had done all the Gavin males in. Stews and puddings, suet and nice crispy, fat-cooked golden on the rim of a lamb chop, bacon and pancakes and eggs and butter stacking up on the arterial walls until there was no room left for the blood to squeeze through.

The M.E. continued cutting and sawing and lifting and weighing. After the first gruesome fascination wore off, the autopsy grew tedious. The thousand little details needed to document a man's death.

Gavin shifted his thoughts back to the present and opened the file. The photos stunned him. This wasn't some John Doe stretched out on the table. The prone white body was Donovan, photographed first in the NYPD uniform shirt he had been found in, then naked, and finally, horribly, splayed open by a big Y incision which put the entire inside of him on view. The chest organs were lifted out, examined, weighed, and then sliced open and examined again. Donovan's heart, right there, in a glossy photo, weighed and observed and sliced. How can you weigh a man's heart? Gavin wondered. As though the mass of the organ was relative to a man's capacity to love.

Gavin flipped through the rest of the shots. Stomach, kidney, liver, spleen, adrenal, pancreas—the hundred intimate facts detailing the man who had been his friend. Gavin sagged against the dining table and put his head in his hands. It was too much. As if death wasn't a horrible enough thing, as if the powerful gunshot Donovan had inflicted on his own head wasn't degrading enough. To have all his parts pulled out, weighed, sliced up, and eventually stuffed back in again sausage-style.

Suddenly, Gavin was mad. Furious. He hurled the

tumbler of scotch against the wall. How dare Ballantine ask him to do this? How dare he force Gavin to witness this final degradation? The powder burns were there on Donovan's hands. The indelible star was there on his temple. Herman Lang was the chief medical examiner. He had taken Danny apart, morsel by morsel, and decided without a shadow of a doubt, that Danny had been the one to shoot the gun.

How dare Ballantine subject Gavin to this?

He scooped up the reports and photos and shoved them into the folder. He marched out to his car and dumped the folder into the passenger seat. The anger was suddenly gone. Gavin felt tired and drunk. He walked slowly back in to the house, stopping on his way, to kick the dirt patch.

The bedroom was empty. A light spilled out from under the door of Alex's room. Shelly was on strike. He supposed he deserved it. No, that was Ballantine's fault too. The headache, the inevitable hangover, the grim parade of pictures and, to top it off, a fight with his wife.

Thanks a lot, Q-Ball.

Gavin toppled down on the bed, fully clothed, and shut his eyes. He fell into a troubled sleep. Around four-thirty in the morning, he woke up. His tongue was a thick wedge of sandpaper inside a parched, stale mouth. The scotch pounded behind his eyeballs. His head buzzed. He had been dreaming, as usual, about the parade of dead girls with their white faces. Then the nightmare had faded, and he had dreamed about Donovan.

In his dream they were sitting together on the aqua vinyl sofa, legs crossed Buddha-style, watching a video. The video played back the bumbled bust where Donovan took a bullet in the chest. The scene played in slow motion over and over and over again. Donovan clutched the shield on his chest and fell a hundred times.

Gavin stared at his bedroom ceiling. After looking at the photos of Donovan's death, he was not surprised he had dreamed vividly about his old friend. That and the fact that in the photo the VCR had been on.

The ceiling overhead seemed to spin. The VCR had been on, but Donovan had told him just the week before how it was out of order. It played pictures, but the sound came out Martian-style, warbled and incomprehensible. Problem with the heads, Donovan had explained. He said he had to wait to replace it. All his extra money was going to feed the lawyers, to pay for the custody battle of Katy Donovan.

"Nothing," Donovan said, "is more important to me than Katy. I don't care if I have to live the rest of my life delivering egg sandwiches to the lawyers. I want to win. I won't give up. So no VCR." Then the chuckle. "Maybe Santa will bring me one."

Why, then, was the VCR on?

Gavin rolled out of bed and fumbled for his sneakers. He tied them loosely and stumbled downstairs to the Tempo. The folder was on the front seat where he had dumped it. He turned the overhead light on and shuffled through the pictures. When he found the shot of the living room, the close-up of the TV unit, he held it up to the light. The VCR was clearly on. And, just as clearly, there was no tape in it. He could tell that by the LED read-out next to the VCR clock. The machine was empty.

He rifled through the other photos, searching for a cassette box. There were no videos at all in the apartment, which was not a surprise, since Danny didn't own any. The TV set was on too, a screen full of gray snow. It was programmed to display whatever was in the VCR, and since nothing was in the VCR, it displayed snow.

Something else bothered Gavin about the dream, the part where Danny had clutched his shield. Gavin had never found Danny's shield, not in the locker and not in the apartment. The shield was missing.

Ballantine. Gavin had to get to Ballantine. He looked at the dashboard clock. It winked at him: 4:45 A.M. He could be in the city by five-thirty. He knew Ballantine would be there.

*   *   *

Gavin pulled up in front of the Nineteenth Precinct house at 5:35. He had his choice of parking spots and took the one closest to the welcoming-arms staircase.

Inside, the desk sergeant on duty was an old cop named Kravits. He looked up, sleepy and surprised. "What brings you in this early, Ed?"

"Couldn't sleep. Must be the heat."

"Third time I've heard that tonight."

"Who else?"

"The P.C.'s daughter came in around two. She left pretty quick. Then Ballantine rolled in around five. And just a few minutes ago that creepy shrink showed up. Said he wanted to get an early start."

"He interview you?"

"Hell, no. He tried. But I put him in his place." Kravitz grinned, then stifled a yawn and went back to reading the early edition of the *News*.

Gavin sprinted up the stairs. He felt energized with a sense of purpose and walked briskly through the empty squad room to the glassed-in corner office. It was lit up. The blinds were open. Q-Ball was bent over his desk, scribbling on a legal pad. Gavin rapped on the glass. Ballantine looked up. His face was covered with a night's worth of shaving stubble; his tie was loosened and askew. Gavin had the feeling Kravtiz was mistaken. He knew Q-Ball hadn't been home at all. He'd been there through the night, thinking and scribbling, trying to fit the puzzle pieces together.

Ballantine waved him in.

Gavin locked the door behind him. He dropped the folder on Ballantine's desk and reached over to snap the blinds shut.

Ballantine leaned back in his chair and stretched. "You didn't happen to bring coffee and doughnuts with you, Ed?"

"Don't have much of an appetite."

"Why's that?"

"I've been through your file. Couple of things jump out at me. First, the VCR is on." He slapped the photo down in front of Ballantine.

Q-Ball perched a pair of reading glasses on his nose and studied the picture. "TV's on too, but all you see is snow."

"Exactly. You see snow because it was programmed to air a video. Thing is, nothing's in the VCR." Gavin pointed at the LED readout. "When a tape goes in this type of machine, this little light goes on. It's off. Nothing's in there."

"I'm not sure I get where you're going with this."

"The week before he died, Danny told me his VCR was out of order. It played pictures but no sound. He said he couldn't afford to get it fixed until the custody battle was over. Getting custody of Katy was the only thing that mattered to him. At the time he joked about being a prisoner of the fifty-five-channel cable network. 'Fifty-five channels,' he said, 'and there's still nothing I want to watch.' He used to like to rent old black-and-white cops and robbers films. He didn't own any. Always rented. So, why was the VCR on?"

Q-Ball chewed on his lower lip, and although the stubble still shadowed his face, there was nothing left of the exhaustion. He was awake and thinking. Alert. "You said several things hit you. What else?"

"Danny's shield. It wasn't in his apartment or in his locker. I know. I would have saved it for Katy."

"Anything else?"

"My gut feeling. Danny would have never checked out. Not while he was fighting to get Katy." Gavin felt a new excitement. "He wouldn't have killed himself and left her alone with Jillian. I don't know why I didn't understand that before!"

Ballantine yawned.

"What's wrong?" Gavin's gusto was blown flat by the bored look on Q-Ball's face.

"I just hoped for something more concrete, that's all," Ballantine said. "VCR. Missing shield. Gut feeling." He shrugged. "Not much to start a manhunt with."

Gavin exploded out of his chair. "What the hell did you expect me to find, the killer's driver's license lying on the carpet? His name written on the bathroom mirror? Christ. You ask me to read these shots and I read them. I'm telling you Danny didn't kill himself."

"Calm down." Q-Ball wasn't yawning now.

"I won't calm down. Not until you tell me you're going to bust your ass tracking down my so-called flimsy leads."

"Okay. Sit down."

Gavin sat down.

Ballantine stood. "First thing I'll do when I have time is check out the video-rental stores in Donovan's neighborhood. Could be an oversight. He could have rented some wildlife film that didn't require sound and taken it back before he shot himself. Anything else strike you as strange? Anything at all?"

"No."

Ballantine leaned across the desk. "You read the M.E.'s report? The autopsy report? The conclusions?"

Gavin looked sheepish. "No. I didn't make it past the photos."

Ballantine sank back in his chair. He watched Gavin's expression. "There were signs of sexual activity. Specifically, dried semen on Donovan's legs."

Gavin stared back at him dumbly.

Ballantine went on. "And he had enough cocaine in him to kill a horse."

Gavin shot up out of the chair. "Bullshit. Bull-fucking-shit. Danny never touched a drug in his life. I knew him like I know myself."

"You obviously don't know yourself very well," Ballantine snapped.

Gavin sucked air through his clenched teeth. "Goddamn you."

Q-Ball's two big palms went up in the air. "Simply stating the facts. I'm not implying that he was a big-time junkie, just saying he might have been a recreational user. Maybe he discovered the cocaine high made him brave, brave enough to face his misery and eat his gun. Wouldn't be the first time it's happened. Won't be the last."

Gavin shook his head. "Never. Not in a hundred years would Donovan cram that stuff up his nose."

"He didn't. He *mainlined* it, Ed. Right into the vein. A nonstop ride to Heaven, only this time he took it all the way. And let's not forget the sex. Could've played out like this: Donovan hires a pretty young hooker to take him on one last mystery dance. When they finish, he lets her out, then shoots up—once in his arm and once in his head."

Tears sprang up in Gavin's eyes. He wiped at them, clumsily, grabbed a fistful of photos, and shook them at Ballantine. "If you're so fucking sure of yourself, why'd you put me through this? Why?"

"I'm not finished."

Something in Ballantine's tone, the sharp look in his bright eyes, made Gavin sit back down and listen.

Ballantine continued. "Nine out of the sixteen suicides had mainlined cocaine. That's more than fifty percent and another reason I think the P.C. wants this thing squelched. All he needs is for the press to get a hold of the fact that his men in uniform are drug addicts. The tabloids would have a field day. It would be a p.r. disaster."

"What else?"

"I think there's some other explanation for how the cocaine got into those nine dead cops. And I think it's significant that those nine cops did not leave suicide notes. The other seven cops did. I don't think those nine men killed themselves. Something went down. The question is what." Ballantine closed his eyes, rubbed his temples.

Gavin stared at the map, at all the red push pins, markers for all the men who, like Danny, might have been murdered.

Ballantine spoke. "You on the eight-to-four today?"

"Four-to-midnight. Just when I was getting used to steady days."

"Get out of here. Go home. Take a shower. Grab a few hours' sleep. You look like hell. If you think of anything else, call me."

Gavin moved to the door. Suddenly the idea of
tracking down Danny's killer felt a lot like finding
Alex—impossible. He took a deep breath.

"You feel okay?" Q-Ball asked.

"Like a million bucks, Ballantine. A million fucking
bucks." Gavin yanked the door open and left.

Eight

"What did you do when they attacked your mother?"

"I hid my eyes."

"That's all?"

"And I cried. I was afraid."

"You must never be a hostage to fear. You must protect yourself and those you love." He put the rubber knife in her hand and wrapped her fingers around the base. "There's a distinct difference between stabbing your opponent and slashing him. Slashing is a way to issue a warning, if you have the luxury to do so. Slashing will create only a surface injury. It will not disable your adversary. Stabbing, however, will induce instant shock and weakness, followed by loss of consciousness and, possibly, death. Stabbing is the way to eliminate your enemy. With the knife, you are armed to kill." He took the rubber knife out of her hands. "And now?" he asked.

"You have the knife, Daddy. I am unarmed."

"If you think you are unarmed, you will die."

"But I am unarmed! You have the knife!"

"And you have your ingenuity. Learn to use it."

"How?"

"There are weapons all around you! Throw hot coffee or a rock or a trash can at your attacker, to shock him, to delay him, to distract him—to buy yourself time. You must use any man-made or natural weapon available to you, including your body."

"My body?"

"Yes. Your body is a weapon too. Kick him in the groin with your knee. Gouge his eyes with your fingernails. Kick him in the knees to break his balance."

"And then?"

"Make your move while he is immobilized in pain. Take his weapon." He put the rubber knife back in her hands. *"Justice never takes a life without cause, Maria."*

"I'm afraid."

"You must never show fear. If your opponent sees your fear, you die. Do you understand, Maria?"

"Yes, Daddy."

"Yes, what?"

"I understand."

Maria rolled over onto her back and stared at the stars on her ceiling. The lessons had been a long time ago, when she was small, but they had stayed with her.

Suddenly she remembered. Today was Tuesday. She wondered if Jon Strega would like his present.

The air was thick and the sky gray when Strega jogged over to the station house Tuesday afternoon for the four-to-midnight tour. He liked the late tour because it gave him the day free to concentrate on the stock market, and on this day there had been plenty to concentrate on. Rumors were flying on Wall Street. West Entertainment was in play. *Which just might drive the stock price way up.* Strega had acquired more West stock, but now, halfway through the park, he wished he had been even more aggressive. He stopped at a pay phone outside the station house and dialed Rosemary's office.

"Ms. De Cesare's office," a lisping male voice said.

"David."

"Hi, Jonnie," David said in a bored voice.

"I want to buy another two thousand shares of West Entertainment."

"Will do."

"Is Rosemary in?"

"She's still not talking to you." Singsong chiding. The schoolteacher to the child.

"Does she still have pictures of me in her office?"

"All over the place."

"Good. Tell her I called."

"Will do. Cheer-i-o."

Strega hung up and went inside.

"Strega," Bell shouted down from the duty desk. He took in Strega's soaked body. "You go for a swim in the lake?"

"Nope, I ran to work. Two six-minute miles. Decent pace in weather like this."

Bell shook his head. "I hope that witch doctor Fields is going to talk to you next, because you need some talking to. You're nuts. Running in a hundred and five–degree heat. Christ, you *got* to be mad."

Strega grinned up at him. "Use it or lose it."

Bell looked down at his own wide girth. "No way I can lose this. My wife says I got *love* handles, and she thinks they're sexy as hell." Bell waved him off.

The locker room appeared empty. Then Strega turned down his locker row. It was packed with a crowd of officers in various states of undress, staring at something. Strega zeroed in on Gavin's frozen face. "Ed, what's going on?"

"Strega, what the hell . . ."

The crowd parted. They were looking at his locker. It was closed and locked, but blood was oozing out of the bottom and dripping out to the ground into a matching puddle. Strega dialed his combination and opened the locker door. The crowd behind him erupted.

A large orange cat.

Hanging by a rope.

Orange body stiff with rigor mortis.

Pink tongue sticking out of an open mouth.

Single gunshot wound to the left side of the head.

Strega staggered to a trash can. Waves of nausea rolled through him, squeezing his insides out, leaving him weak and sweaty and scared out of his mind. Someone was clasping his shoulder, trying to talk to him, but all Strega heard was the echo of that one rumbling female voice saying, "His name was Vincent Strega."

"I am shocked," Wilson roared, "that a member of the Nineteenth Precinct would pull such a repulsive practical joke." He paced up and down in the squad room, outraged. Everything about him—his straight back, tightly clipped hair, buffed skin, square jaw— seemed enhanced in the heat of his anger. "What breach in security allowed someone to obtain the locker combination? And who was that someone? You can bet your asses I'm going to find out." He smacked the desk with his fist.

"Daniel Donovan's death is no joking matter," Wilson continued. "He was a respected, decorated officer of the NYPD. Much loved, much admired. His death was a tragedy. He should be alive and with us today, as should the other fifteen officers we lost this year to suicide. If any one of you knows something about this disgusting prank, this smear against Daniel Donovan, you let me the fuck know A.S.A.P." Wilson stared hard-eyed at the crowd of officers in front of him.

Strega knew something about the prank. He knew that it had nothing to do with Donovan. It had everything to do with a Philadelphia detective twenty years dead. Wilson was right about one thing. The person responsible was a uniformed member of the Nineteenth Precinct. Strega looked around. She wasn't there. Strega wondered what he should do. Find her? Confront her? Go straight to Wilson with the whole crazy story? Accuse the P.C.'s daughter? Wilson was an ambitious cop. He liked the game and he played it well. Wilson would not put his career on the line by alienating Ramon Alvarez.

Strega blinked. Wilson was talking directly to him. "Strega, get a uniform from loan-out for today's tour. I'll see to it your permanent uniforms are replaced and paid for by the Department. Tell my secretary what was in your locker. She'll have the new items for you tomorrow. You'll also be issued a new lock. The four-to-midnight tour stays put for roll call. The rest of you get out of here. Go back to work." Wilson marched out.

The room cleared. The tour sergeant ran through assignments.

"Alvarez is out sick today," the sergeant said. "Kelly partners with Moon. Dismissed."

Strega stopped to change into a loan-out uniform. His

locker was closed up with crime-scene tape which would stay put until CSU had a chance to dust for prints. Alvarez was too smart to leave prints. He folded his street clothes in a neat stack and carried them out to the car. Gavin waited in the passenger seat, pale and disturbed.

"Loan-out pants are too short," Strega said, sliding in. "I look like a geek."

Gavin just grunted.

Strega wanted to tell Gavin the prank hadn't been aimed at Donovan. "Ed, listen."

"Shut up."

"How do you know what I'm going to say?"

"I don't want to hear a word about the friggin' cat or Danny either. Not a word. No theories, no fancy Princeton psychological profiles of the perp, no ideas on who might've done it—nothing. So if you've got something to say and it isn't about Danny or the goddamn cat, go ahead and talk. Otherwise, save it. Can you do that for me? Can you just keep your mouth shut about the whole thing for the next couple of hours?"

Tears were spilling out of Gavin's eyes and snaking down his flushed cheeks. Strega knew this was not the time to talk. As Kelly said, the man was still grieving, and the cat, so graphically murdered, had stirred up the grief and made it fresh again.

The silence lasted for hours, through the setting of the sun and the dark falling over Manhattan. Every so often Strega took another look at his partner. The old cop was sitting stone still, sightlessly watching the city whip by. He was turned inward, Strega guessed, looking at some place and time in the past when his friend and partner was alive and well, and grief was still a stranger.

After the knife, he taught her to use a gun. He started with a water pistol, then a toy cap gun, then an empty service revolver. The service revolver was big and too heavy for her child's hands. She had to use a two-fisted grip.

"A wide stance will give you balance," he instructed. "You must aim to kill. A single shot to the heart or the

*head. The target rarely survives. Do not aim to injure.
Injured but alive, your opponent will be enraged and still
capable of disarming you. You must always aim to kill.
Do you understand, Maria?"*

"Justice never takes life without a cause," she answered.

"Correct. Self-defense is just cause. Never be a hostage
to fear."

Maria looked out the window. It was dark out. She
dressed quickly and left her apartment thinking about
Strega, only about Strega. He was working the four-to-
midnight tour. Maria wanted to be waiting for him when
it was over.

Nine

Ramon Alvarez straightened his Hermes tie and swung easily up the steps to Emilio's, the most expensive Italian restaurant in the city. A film producer was waiting for him inside. The producer was interested in the P.C.'s life story. He said it would make a *hell of a movie*. There was even talk of getting Scorsese to direct.

Emilio greeted him. "Commissioner Alvarez. I read the piece in *New York* magazine about you. Very impressive. Come. Mr. West is waiting."

Emilio led him through the dining room. It was an intimate space with dark wood walls, thick cream carpet, and only fifteen tables, all round, generously sized, and set with crisp white linen and heavy silver. A brilliant glass chandelier hung down from the ceiling. Three of the four walls were fitted with floor-to-ceiling mirrors, creating the illusion that the sparkling chandelier and elegant diners went on and on, into infinity.

William West sat at a big table in the back corner of the room. West needed a big table. He was a huge man. He wore tiny round tortoiseshell glasses and a tiny gray goatee, both of which were ridiculously out of proportion to his enormous face. The heavy prescription lenses made his eyes appear unnaturally large, almost owlish. His eyebrows were great, busy salt-and-pepper things, the same color as his bristly hair. His hands were tiny and plump. He gripped a fat cigar in one and a tumbler of vodka in the other.

"William, you're looking prosperous as always," Alvarez said, grinning.

West waved the cigar, not bothering to stand. "Commissioner Alvarez! Have a seat."

Alvarez unbuttoned his suit jacket and took a seat against the rear mirrored wall where he had a good view of the room. The P.C. liked to be visible. He knew half the people there personally. The other half knew him. Two men walked into the restaurant. Alvarez didn't recognize them. One was blond. The other was dark—Italian, maybe Greek. Not Spanish, Alvarez thought. Both men carried large Armani shopping bags and were well dressed in dark suits identical to the sophisticated lightweight Armani suit William West was wearing. Lawyers, Alvarez guessed, or possibly investment bankers.

Emilio extended a hand to greet them. The dark one seized the old man's elbow and spun him around, locking him in a choke hold. The blonde whipped two Uzis out of the shopping bag and tossed one to his partner.

Stifled screams rippled through the dining room.

"You folks stay quiet," the blonde said, "and the old man lives to see his hundredth birthday."

William West dropped his cigar.

Alvarez slipped his hand under the table, reaching for the cellular phone in his pocket.

The blonde pulled two masks out of his shopping bag. The first was a black-and-white photo of Giorgio Armani. It had been fashioned into a clever mask with the eyes and mouth cut out. The blonde tossed it to his partner, then slipped a Calvin Klein mask over his own face. It had the same eerie cutouts. Alvarez could see the wet of the gunmen's eyes and the pink of their lips.

Klein tucked the Uzi high up under his arm and quickly crossed the dining room, disappearing into the kitchen. Armani guarded the front door.

The P.C. inched his cellular phone out of his pocket and flipped it open under the table.

Klein herded ten kitchen workers into the dining room and ordered them to drop to the floor. Then he bent his knees slightly, as if for balance, tipped the nose of the Uzi up and opened fire. Klein's whole body worked with the weapon, bending backward and forward, then side

to side as he sprayed the room with bullets. At first the
sound was a soft spitting noise, then it was piercing, bullets zinging into glass and finally, glass exploding.

Alvarez punched numbers on his phone by feel. He
fumbled and tried again.

The rear wall of mirror behind the P.C. cracked, gunshot loud, and exploded out. Glass rained down like
hard confetti. Klein swung his body in a broad arc. The
second and third walls of mirror exploded. The chandelier was next, vibrating with every hit. It swung crazily,
then dropped to the ground and shattered, adding to the
glass storm. Diners covered their eyes and heads, men
and women screamed. The air was heavy with the smell
of gunfire, and without the gentle light of the chandelier,
the room was dim, lit only by the soft glow of candles
on every table.

Klein stopped shooting.

Muffled weeping and the crunch-crunching of the
killer walking over glass were the only sounds in the
room.

Klein held his Uzi up over his head. "This is not a
toy. It works."

Armani spoke. "My associate has a bad temper. I ad-
vise you to cooperate when he asks for your watches,
jewelry, and wallets."

A mobile phone rang.

"No one's home," Klein quipped.

The phone continued to ring.

"Who has the phone?" Klein yelled.

A woman held her portable up in the air.

"Like I said, no one's home." Klein aimed and
squeezed off one shot. The phone exploded out of the
woman's hand. The killer's head moved slightly, and the
cutout eyes focused on the woman.

"No," she whispered.

"You should've gone out for Chinese tonight."

His first shot hit her in the throat.

His next ten hit her in the chest. She jerked like a rag
doll. The last burst of gunfire spun her around and threw
her face first into the floor.

The P.C.'s ears ached from the blast. He snapped his own phone shut.

The dead woman's husband rose from the table, totally outraged. Klein pumped five shots into the man's chest. The look of outrage shifted to disbelief. The man tried to catch himself on the table edge, then fell over backward to the floor.

Someone whispered a prayer.

"Anyone else want to make a call?" Klein sang out.

Alvarez slipped the phone back into his pocket.

"Good," Klein laughed. "Now it's trick-or-treat time."

The killer held the shopping bag open with his left hand and hugged the weapon tight against his body with his right hand. He kept his elbows tucked neatly into his side, his rigid body ready.

One by one the well-dressed women and men went eye to eye with the Uzi and handed over the great timepiece names of the world—Rolex, Piaget, Cartier, Omega, Breitling. Cash rolls followed, then diamond earrings and rings, jeweled necklaces, sparkling bracelets. Klein worked his way back to the big corner table and shoved the Uzi in the P.C.'s face. Alvarez peeled off his gold Rolex.

"Cash," Klein whispered. "Don't forget your cash."

Alvarez dropped his money roll into the bag and looked up at the mask. Behind the cutouts he could see the pupils of the shooter's pale blue eyes. They were saucers, unnaturally large and drug-fever bright. Alvarez started to shake. He hated himself for feeling afraid. *If they see your fear, you die.*

Klein jammed the nose of the Uzi into the P.C.'s jawbone. The pressure increased, driving his head up, forcing him to look again into the handsome cardboard face of Calvin Klein. The eyes behind the mask changed. Recognition flickered.

"Look what we got here," Klein whistled. "The fucking police commissioner in person. I don't fucking believe it. Why don't you stand up and arrest me?"

The pressure under Alavrez's chin was agony.

"But, hey," Klein gloated, "you're just a suit. You're

not a real cop. If you were a real cop, you'd have a gun on you. You'd shoot me and be a fucking hero. If I kill you, you can't be a hero, can you? Ballbuster Alvarez. I heard all about you. I'm going to do you a favor. I'm not going to shoot you today. Catch me if you can, *Commissioner*." He pulled away and moved on to William West. "Your turn, big boy."

West complied. Diamond Rolex, cash roll, wallet, gold signature ring, Cartier pen.

A high-pitched alarm went off, shrill as a woman's scream.

The killer tensed and waved his weapon in a nervous arc. "What's that?"

No one answered.

He aimed the Uzi at the glassware on the P.C.'s table. When he fired, his knees bent again slightly, as if for balance, and his torso rocked. The champagne glasses exploded. The Perrier bottle, the wine goblets, the cut-crystal tumblers full of ice water, the flower vases, all exploded in split-second intervals, sending glass shards out with the velocity of bullets. The P.C. instinctively threw his arms up to shield his face. He felt a hundred pieces of glass slice through his suit jacket.

The burst of gunfire lasted a few seconds, then it was over. Alvarez cautiously dropped his arms and looked over at William West. The big man's face was badly cut, a hundred nicks, all bubbling up red and wet. West's eyeglasses had been knocked off his face. He squinted and groped blindly at the table.

The P.C. grabbed his hands and whispered: "Don't. The table's full of broken glass."

"I can't see," West stated in a perfectly calm voice.

The P.C. found the glasses and set them on the bridge of West's nose.

The alarm shrieked again.

The killer roamed the room, blasting more glassware and shouting. "What the fuck is that?"

A man stood up slowly, "It's just my beeper. I'm a doctor."

"Good for you. Put your beeper on the table."

The doctor complied.

Klein aimed his gun.

Armani shouted: "What the fuck are you doing? We're finished. We're out of here."

Klein hesitated. He trained the gun on the doctor. "Bang, bang," he sang. "You're dead." The nose of the gun dipped off the mark. The killer turned away from his target and went to the door.

Armani pushed Emilio away. "Face down, old man." Emilio crumpled to the floor. Armani addressed the room. "Stay as you are for ten minutes. Anyone comes out the front door, there won't be much the good doctor here will be able to do for you."

They backed out into the night.

Someone in the dining room coughed. Women wept. Another cellular phone rang. Alvarez stood up. "Ladies and gentlemen, please stay in your seats. I am Ramon Alvarez, the police commissioner of New York City." He flipped open his portable phone and punched in 911.

Strega chewed on a handful of Cheerios while he steered the patrol car down the empty center lane of Fifth Avenue. "Want some?" he asked, shaking the box.

Gavin shook his head. "No, thanks. I'm a Captain Crunch man myself."

Strega turned off Fifth and cut over to Third Avenue. The neighborhood was full of bars and restaurants, and the sidewalks were active. Gavin studied the face of every pedestrian who walked by, trying to forget the shattered feline head in Danny's locker. His eyes roamed over the crowd and zeroed in on a face that could make a man forget his own name. It was Latin. High, smooth forehead, cheekbones like butterfly wings, proud nose, crimson lips pulled back in a smile.

Her hair piled high like a young flamenco dancer. Her companion, a yuppie-looking, starched-shirt kind of milk and toast guy, trailed along beside her. Everything about him screamed privilege—Connecticut roots old and deep and thick, anchored by the family fortune and all that went with it. Prep schools, military schools, the *right* university, all Daddy's contacts, a closet full of stiff new suits and silky ties to go with them, and here he finally was, Mr. John Doe Junior from Connecticut, starting out on the good road of success in the Big Apple only to have his head turned by a wrong-side-of the-tracks kind of girl. One with no higher education—unless you counted what she had learned about men in her short life. Not a business suit or a string of pearls to her name, and the kind of roots she had stretched all the way to a shanty town in Mexico or Puerto Rico. Untrained in the art of subtlety, she was all loud lipstick, four-inch white patent heels, and big glittery hoops of phony gold hanging from each juicy earlobe.

She wasn't the kind of girl Mummy or Daddy would ever approve of.

She was the kind of girl who made a man wish for the short days of winter, darkness falling at four o'clock. *Hurry up, sundown,* Gavin thought. *She's going to take you on a special trip tonight in the backseat of your old Ford.* Her companion sure as hell drove a BMW 325-I with all the goodies. Bucket seats. Programmable CD. Air conditioning. But the backseats in the I-class Beamer were too small for a proper tumble. No wonder he looked frustrated. Mr. Milk and Toast stared hungrily at the girl. At least, Gavin thought, prep school hadn't dulled the kid's instincts. He was making big gestures with his hands, talking up a storm, devouring her with his eyes.

There was plenty on display to devour. No button-down shirts and Bermuda shorts for this girl, no sir. She wore a midriff-baring band of white jersey across her chest and a ruffled short white skirt that left her lithe dancer's legs nude in the summer night. She floated along, keeping even with the patrol car. Her midriff mesmerized Gavin. It was swaying gently, keeping time to her own private Latin beat. Her prominent rib cage was a flesh-and-bone metronome, and Gavin's pulse drummed with a matching rhythm.

There was something primal about the girl that reminded him of Maria Alvarez. A raw sexuality, a devil-may-care kind of roll to her walk. An impress-me-if-you-can tilt to her magnificent head, and a I'm-more-woman-than-you-can-handle set to her high, brown breasts. She was the kind of female that could make a guy forget the flies, forget the nightmares, the gunshot to the left side of a cat's head, and the star-burst hole to the right side of a man's head.

At the next block she turned a corner with Mr. Milk Toast, and they disappeared from view. Gavin had stopped thinking about her the instant before she made the turn. His mind was stuck on a detail, a record needle skipping over vinyl. The cat had been shot on the left. Donovan's entrance wound was on the right. Left, right. Right, left. Donovan was right-handed. If the cat stood for Donovan, why was the cat shot on the left?

Gavin slumped back in the seat. Ballantine's made me paranoid, he thought. Looking for clues where there was nothing but five pounds of dead feline.

The radio crackled. "Nineteen Ida."

"Nine Ida John," Gavin said into the handset, grateful for the distraction.

"Report of a ten-thirty in progress, Seventy-fourth Street between Third and Lex. Emilio's restaurant. Shots fired. Two suspects, male Caucasians, armed and dangerous."

Strega tossed his cereal box into the backseat and pushed the accelerator to the floor. He jumped a yellow light and raced up Third Avenue. Gavin put the roof lights on, but left the siren off. He didn't want the perps to hear him coming. He fondled his gun. An old hunger he thought was long gone growled inside him. He wanted to sneak up quiet as a mouse, tippy-toe up to the restaurant, slip inside, and blow the murdering bastards to hell. His fingers tapped a Latin samba out on the hard leather of his holster. Strega's voice interrupted his reverie.

"You know Emilio's?"

"Most expensive restaurant in Manhattan," Gavin answered. "Cash only. And my cash says our bridal boys are there."

Strega turned hard at Seventy-fifth Street. The car fishtailed and skidded to a stop.

Gavin resented the noisy arrival. He hoped it hadn't alerted the perps. He unfolded out of the car and gripped his gun with both hands. Strega followed. At the top of a small staircase, the restaurant front door was flung wide open to the night. Gavin glanced back at Strega. He knew his partner was scared and might crack if things got rough. The warning signs were there in the pale pallor of his skin, the visible tremor of his hands, and the sweat rolling down the sides of his face. The fear was edging toward panic. For an instant Gavin felt sorry for him. Then his mind swung back to the problem at hand.

Two gunmen with terrorist war weapons and a taste for killing. Reason enough, Gavin thought, to hang back and wait for backup before going in. He chewed his lip. Gavin hated to lose the element of surprise. The alternative was for him to go in alone and try to take them out with two well-placed shots. His service 9mm wasn't much of a match for the artillery inside, but with any luck at all, he could pull it off.

His eagerness stunned him. He thought he'd dumped his need to play power cop a long time ago in the Three-Four, when being a cop was still something fun to him, something noble and exciting, something more than a deck of time-clock cards he could eventually trade in for six stripes and a shitty pension.

He edged up to the molding around the front door, keeping his body pressed flat to the redbrick building facade. The stones were still warm from the day's sun. The heat burned through his shirt, into his skin. It was fire, he thought, the old fire of ball-busting law enforcement, and he welcomed it. Blow the bad guys away. Aim for the chest, shoot to kill. Stop their murdering hearts from pumping. One each, right through the main valve. Watch them do a scarecrow jig, a cartoon shake, watch them fall dead to the floor. His toes tingled.

"I'm going in," he whispered softly to Strega. He threw the weight of his body around the white molding and in through the open door. His legs spread wide, giving him stability. His gun was shoved way out in front of his body. It was a third eye, scanning the room, searching for the mark. His finger tightened against the trigger, ready to squeeze.

"Freeze," he shouted.

But everyone was already frozen. And no one there had an assault weapon aimed at him.

"You're too late," someone said simply. "They left ten minutes ago."

Gavin kept his gun raised. A little voice inside his head warned him this could be a setup. His perps might be in the kitchen or under a table, waiting to ice a cop.

"Put your goddamn weapon down," the voice ordered. "I told you they're gone."

Gavin looked around the room. Ramon Alvarez was standing up, pointing at him. The P.C., Gavin thought dumbly, lowering his gun.

Gavin advanced slowly into the room, crunching across the broken glass. The destruction frightened him—the buckled mirrors, the hailstorm of glass, the skeleton of a shattered chandelier in the middle of the floor. He passed a table splattered with red and looked down. One man, one woman. The man was on his side, the woman on her back, her pretty peach cocktail dress shredded with bullet holes.

Gavin crouched down to feel the woman's pulse.

"Don't bother. I called the M.E.," the P.C. said, moving across the room to Gavin.

The sound of approaching sirens drifted in through the open door.

Two waiters moved quietly around the room, handing out free booze. An old man picked his way through the glass and approached Gavin and Alvarez.

"This is the owner," Alvarez said.

"What a tragedy here tonight!" Tears streamed down the old man's elegant face. He looked at Gavin and clutched his sleeve. "Two gunmen. One blonde, one dark. Night and Day. Remus and Romulus. I thought they were customers. So nice-looking. Good Italian suits.

Then they pulled machine guns out of a shopping bag and put masks on to hide their faces. They took money, watches, diamonds. Everyone cooperated and still they murdered." He raised his fists to heaven. "May they burn in hell."

The sirens were out front now, and the air was filled with the sound of doors slamming and heavy shoes hurrying across pavement. Strega ventured in. Four pairs of patrolmen surged in behind him. Ballantine walked in next. His face, Gavin thought, looked like it had aged ten years. The skin under his eyes appeared to have come unglued, and his mouth hung down in a miserable frown. Circles of sweat seeped out across his shirt, over his chest. He spotted the P.C. and crossed the room.

Q-Ball introduced himself. "Lieutenant Ballantine, sir. You were here when this happened?"

"Unfortunately," Alvarez answered. "Where the fuck's Wilson?"

"On his way, sir."

"Take a look around," Alvarez ordered in a low, tight voice. "These witnesses are too fucking important to be dragged down to the precinct house and put through the wringer. Take statements here and do it fast. Treat these people with respect. Then when they're out of here, I want you on your hands and knees with the CSU techs, ripping this room apart until you find something that leads to the shooters. This is your crime scene, Ballantine," the P.C. said, poking the big detective in the chest. "Don't fuck it up." He wheeled around, then moved through the room to comfort people as he went.

Gavin watched in admiration. The ballbuster was gone, replaced by an elegant, concerned leader. Alvarez shook hands, patted shoulders, and hugged ladies. The destruction notwithstanding, Alvarez looked like he was campaigning.

"You just wait," Ballantine whispered. "Alvarez is going to milk this into a major media event of the year. The P.C.—a *survivor* of the biggest hold-up in the city this year. If that isn't story enough to get him elected

one day, I don't know what is." Ballantine shook his
head. "You and Strega were the first officers here?"

"Yes."

"Run it down for me."

Gavin repeated what the old man had told him.

Ballantine took a long, slow look around the room.
"Alvarez wasn't kidding," he whispered. "It's a fucking
Who's-Who in here. The most important names in Man-
hattan, and guess what? Most of them *live* in the One-
Nine. It's going to be one long night."

He rapped on a table. "Ladies and gentlemen, I'm
Detective Lieutenant James Quinton Ballantine. I'm
asking you to give us your full cooperation. I know you
all want to get out of here and go home, but you are
witnesses. One of you might have inadvertently noticed
something that could lead us to the killers. Normal procedure requires me to take you over to the precinct
house, but you will all be more comfortable here. Try to
not discuss what you saw amongst yourselves. Memory is
a tricky thing. By exchanging stories you may cloud your
own memory. I appreciate your cooperation."

Ballantine turned to Gavin. "I've got only one detective tonight. I doubled up the day shift, thinking these
boys would hit again during the day. Got that wrong,
didn't I? I need you and Strega to help with the questioning. Customers first. Waiters and kitchen staff last.
I'm going to need a pair of cops out front guarding the
door. Another two units to close the street off to traffic.
And tell them to keep the news vans the fuck out of
here." He looked at the patrol officers milling around.
"What do they think this is, a crime scene or a baseball game?"

Cybil Hansen walked in the front door and hurried
over to Ballantine's side. "Wilson just pulled up."

"Fuck." Ballantine mopped his forehead and worked
his way to the door.

Gavin moved through the room giving orders. He
looked for a place to take statements. The tables were
full. The only places with privacy were the rest rooms
and the kitchen. He told Hansen to set up in the kitchen

and Strega to set up in the ladies' room. He would take the men's room.

Gavin walked by a table and pocketed a garlic roll, wishing he had a cold beer to go with it. Wishing he hadn't been ten minutes too late. Wishing he'd had those two shots, one each, right into the hearts of the men who left a lady in peach and her husband dead, side by side, on a carpet of broken glass.

Strega started to take the last statement at twelve-thirty. All the statements had been the same. He doubted this last witness would have anything new to add. He read questions from the standard form. "Your name?"

"William West."

Strega looked up. The man's face was covered with tiny Band-Aids. "The chairman of West Entertainment?"

"The one and only," he sighed. "Can we get on with this?"

"It's nice to meet you. Sorry it has to be under these circumstances. I admire what you've done for the company. I'm a stockholder."

West's demeanor changed. He smiled, then stuck a hand out and shook Strega's vigorously. "Always glad to say hello to my stockholders."

Strega ran him through the complaint form quickly. West's answers were standard, until Strega asked him to describe the assailants.

"They were wearing Armani suits," West stated.

"How can you be sure?"

"See this?" West tugged on his own jacket lapel. "They were both wearing the same one. Three grand, from this season's Armani summer collection. Only so many places in Manhattan sell Armani. If I were you, I'd start with the stores that do." He stood up. "May I go now? My driver gets overtime after midnight."

"I'll need you to drop your suit off at the precinct house tomorrow. Our detectives will want to see it. We'll get it back to you."

"You can have it right now. I'll never wear Armani again." West removed his jacket and tossed it to Strega. Then he unzipped his slacks, stepped out of them, and gave them to Strega too. West was stripped down to his dress shirt, boxer shorts, shoes, and socks.

"Mr. West, there are television cameras outside."

"I know. If I'm lucky, the *Times* will print a nice big shot of me on the front page. It would be great publicity. Let's go."

Strega followed him out.

Detectives and department brass packed the dining room. Ramon Alvarez had Inspector Wilson cornered. Strega had never seen the P.C. in person. He was surprised. Alvarez was powerfully built. His face was square-jawed and rugged. There was nothing of the pretty Don Juan in it at all. He wore his thick black hair combed away from his high forehead. His eyes were large and dark, and they were flashing in anger. Crime made Ramon Alvarez angry. The voters loved that about him. They loved seeing a city official as mad as they were about handguns, gangs, drug rings, and drive-by shootings. Ramon Alvarez inspired confidence. Looking at him, Strega suddenly understood why it was most people in the Department just *knew* this man was going to be big one day.

At the moment Wilson was the focus of Alvarez's self-righteous anger. "How could this happen here in the One-Nine right under your nose, Wilson?" Strega heard him say. "Five blocks from the fucking station house. How? Tell me that."

Strega steered West away from the P.C. All Wilson needed was for Ramon Alvarez to see his dinner companion, the chairman of West Entertainment, a visible and influential citizen, stripped of his suit, face nicked and torn, walking humbly through the dining room wreckage in his underwear.

Strega guided West out the front door. West straightened his tie and went off, tugging at his shirt tails, looking for the television cameras.

"Hey, Strega," a woman said. "What happened to his clothes?"

Strega looked down. Cybil Hansen was sitting on the stoop, sipping a Perrier.

He dropped down next to her and tossed her West's suit. "Evidence. According to him, this was the same suit the perps were wearing. Couldn't get out of it fast enough."

"Takes all kinds, doesn't it?" she laughed, looking the suit over. She tossed him a bottle of Perrier. "Here, have some bubble water. We can celebrate."

"What are we celebrating?" Strega opened the bottle.

"The addition of one more Ivy Leaguer to the NYPD. I heard you went to Princeton. I went to Yale. Run it down for me."

"Princeton undergrad. Business major, eclectic minor."

"Define eclectic."

"Heavy emphasis on psychology and art, sculpture in specific."

"Interesting."

"It was."

"Something tells me you were an academic star."

"Good detective instincts, Hansen. Graduated top of the class, gave the commencement speech. Went on to get an MBA. Graduated top of the class again. Had more corporate recruiters circling me than I could count."

"And you're not arrogant?"

"Just a nice guy, I hope."

"Was one of the recruiters from the NYPD promising you a lifetime of lousy pay and crummy hours?"

"Something like that." Then, after a beat: "My dad was a cop. Detective, actually. Philadelphia Police Department. Rumor has it he was a hero."

"I hear a lot of past tense attached to your dad."

"He died in the line of duty. I was six years old."

"Shit."

"That sums it up."

"Now you want to finish your father's work?"

"I don't *want* to. My mother brainwashed me into believing it's my destiny."

"Guilt is the great manipulator," Hansen said, "and mothers are the masters of guilt."

"It worked," he laughed, shaking his head. "You should've seen her face the day I graduated from the academy. She glowed like I was one of the Apostles come to life. Looking at her, I knew I had done the right thing. She lives in Queens. I drop by for dinner once a week. She insists I wear this uniform."

"You're a dutiful and obedient son," Hansen teased.

"And an overachiever. Now that I'm here, I'd like to be the best cop in the city. Hero complex. Probably tied to my early life loss. Problem is, I'm scared of guns."

"No other siblings around who could fill your father's shoes?"

"No sons. Two girls. My baby sister's spreading the word of God to impoverished farmers in Chile. And my older sister is a Jesus freak with a low tolerance for stress."

"You won by default."

"Looks that way."

"Do those sisters admire you as much as your mother does?"

"My baby sister loves me. My older sister hates me. I never figured out why."

"Standard sibling rivalry."

"Guess so."

"Well, don't stop there," Hansen prodded. "Where's the rest of it?" Her eyes sparkled.

"What else do you want to know?"

"Are you married?"

"Nope. And I never will be, not while I'm a cop anyway."

"Why?"

"Do you want the truth or the standard reply?"

"Both."

"Standard reply: I'm a ladies' man who loves the challenge of the chase and the thrill of the catch."

"Poetic with a hint of self-importance," Hansen stated. "The truth?"

"I don't want Gavin to have to stand on a doorstep one day and tell my wife and children I'm never coming home. I have a cat instead. Something happens to me, give him some scrambled eggs and a new home. He'll forget about me in a week."

"You're willing to miss out on all the joy a family brings because of a statistical chance you might be killed on the job?"

"The statistics are pretty high, at least in my family. The way I look at it, marriage to a cop ends in one of two ways. Divorce or death."

"Pretty grim assessment."

Strega looked up at the sky. Death was out there, he thought, lurking around. It had tipped his own mother's life upside down, his too. If his father had lived, Jon Strega would have been an investment banker or the president of a corporation, but death held the trump card and he was a cop instead—*a cop who was afraid he would go down in the line of duty leaving a grieving wife and family behind.* He might not be able to cheat death, Strega thought. But he could cheat death out of a macabre repeat.

Hansen put her hand on his arm, bringing him back to the present. "I'm sorry," she said. "I have no business judging you."

"No apology needed, Hansen. But it's your turn now."

"Yale. Class of '88. Bachelor's degree in political science with an emphasis on government, secondary interest in philosophy. Graduated with honors. Gave the graduation speech. President of the debate team, the philosophy club, and student council. Edited the op-ed page of the campus newspaper for two years. Academic life agreed with me, so I went on to graduate school and collected a master's in government. Same stunning academic performance as undergrad. Graduated with honors again."

"Two degrees from Yale," Strega observed. "That makes you knee-deep in Ivy."

"Yes, sir, just like you." She was smiling. "I was going to be an expensive consultant to the screwed-up city governments of America. A well-paid living Band-Aid for urban detritus. Falling into bed at night rolling in money, but with my capitalistic conscience eased by the fact I was helping the country."

"So what happened, Hansen?"

"Love. I married a brilliant man. Only problem was, he was younger than me. He had three years of Columbia Law in front of him and no way to pay for it."

"You didn't."

"I did," she admitted.

"What happened to women's lib?"

"Hey, good men are hard to find. Actually, it wasn't entirely his fault. I signed up with the NYPD as a short-term thing to bring in some cash for us to live on until I found my dream job. Short-term somehow turned long-term, the dream job never appeared, and much to my surprise, I discovered that I have a talent for police work. In fact, I'm downright *gifted* as a detective. So here I am."

"What happened to the husband?"

She smiled wryly. "He passed the bar on the third try and landed himself a job in a personal-injury law firm. It's pretty low on the food chain as far as lawyers go."

"Bottom feeders."

She nodded in goodhearted agreement. "Ambulance chaser is the preferred derisory term. Good thing I fell in love with him for his body and his sense of humor, not for his strong moral values. America's litigation happy, and my husband sees nothing wrong with getting his piece of the pie." She laughed. "Funny, isn't it? I was going to save the system, reform it, make it strong. All my husband wants to do is suck it dry. Sue cities for holes in the pavement in which people trip and break their ankles. That kind of thing." She sighed. "Anyway, he swears he's got a knack for finding the right kind of people with the right kind of messy injuries. One day he'll be the big breadwinner, and I can retire and read Agatha Christie novels. In the meantime, my social conscience feels good knowing I'm out here trying to catch the bad guys."

"You think you'll ever catch these guys?" Strega asked, pointing at Emilio's.

Cybil looked thoughtful. "They're smarter than the average bear. Greedier too. Big jump from a wedding dress shop to a restaurant with sixty-one diners. But in my book all criminals are dumb. Eventually, they make a stupid mistake and we nail them."

"What about whoever broke into my locker?"

"Same thing, I guess. Technically, it was a crime. That makes whoever did it a criminal. Eventually he'll make a stupid mistake and we'll nail him."

"Or her," Strega corrected.

Cybil gave him a sharp look, then nodded her head. "Or her."

"Murder isn't gender specific," Strega explained.

"Nope."

"Lizzie Borden. Case in point."

Hansen laughed.

Gavin walked out of the restaurant. "What's so funny?"

"The concept of Lizzie Borden with an Uzi," Hansen said.

"Cheerful thought, Hansen," Gavin said.

"Don't look at me," she said, smiling. "It was your partner who politely reminded me that all murderers are not men."

"He took a lot of history at that fancy college he went to." Gavin dropped down on the stoop. "Hell of a night. Bet you didn't expect to see real murder here in Club-Med, did you, Hansen?"

"Slow down, Gavin. I didn't *choose* the One-Nine. It chose me. Or, more specifically, Ballantine did. He's taken me under his wing and promised to teach me all his sneaky detective tricks. Here's a little amateur psychology for you, Strega: I'm the son he never had, the daughter he wishes he had. He's going to retire soon, and part of him can't bear to just walk away from the Department without leaving something of himself behind. So, I'm his protégé, and I'm honored. There's no better detective on the job than Ballantine."

"If he's so good, why is he coasting in the One-Nine?" Strega asked.

"Because he earned the right to coast a little his last few years, that's why," Hansen said sharply. She put a hand on Strega's arm and softened her tone. "He's got a drawer full of commendations, almost eighteen years of brutal crimes solved. You know what they say: If you're guilty and you're in the line of sight of the Q-Ball, he'll sink you—right in the corner pocket."

"I hope he can sink the motherfuckers who turned this place into a shooting gallery," Gavin said. "What if these two incidents were random hits? What if the shooters disappear now? He'll never catch them, will he?"

"I don't believe in random events," Hansen said.

"Big statement," Strega replied. "Philosophically, you could argue it either way."

"Maybe," Hansen conceded, "but these are not random hits. They've targeted this neighborhood. Ballantine's right. They'll be back."

Gavin rose. "Come on, Strega. We've still got a couple hours' work to do at the station house filing these statements. The way I see it, we'll finish in time to report in for the eight to four."

"Carpe diem, Strega," Cybil sang out as they left.

"Seize the day," Strega explained to Gavin. "Latin."

"I know, don't tell me," Gavin grumbled. "You studied it at Princeton."

Strega walked out of the precinct house at three o'clock in the morning. Sixty-seventh Street was deserted. Halfway down the block, he heard the tap-tap of ladies' shoes behind him. He looked over his shoulder. Maria Alvarez quickened her pace and fell into step with him. She was poured into a pair of white jeans and a white spandex T-shirt. The dark circles of her breasts showed through. She wore high white patent heels. Her hair was loose around her shoulders. It was much longer than Strega had imagined.

"What's the matter, Alvarez, couldn't sleep?" Strega said. He didn't stop walking.

"We're making progress, Jonnie. You're showing interest in my sleeping patterns. You should try sleeping with me. You might like it." She laid her hand casually on his ass.

"I don't fuck uneducated cheap women."

The hand dropped away.

"I thought you were out sick today," Strega said. "What'd you catch? Cat-scratch fever? Feline leukemia? Rabies?"

They stopped and faced each other in the half-light spill of a dim street lamp. Her face was flushed and damp. The tip of her tongue pressed against her red glossed lips. It reminded him of the pink cat's tongue sticking straight out of the slack cat jaw. "Where've you been, Maria? Did you take a little trip to the dry cleaner's to get the blood out of your uniform?"

She pulled one of her hands high to slap him. He grabbed her wrist and cranked down tight. "You keep harassing me," he said, "any more phone calls, any more dead animals, and I'm going straight to Internal Affairs and get you booted right out of the Department. What's your daddy going to think about that?"

To his surprise, she giggled. Her hand twisted around and gripped his own. She pulled her body in so close she had to tilt her small head up to meet his eyes. He felt the brush of her breasts against his shirt. A length of full, round thigh pressed against his. Her eyes were dreamy. "Think twice before you start making accusations, Jonnie. Think about this. You lied."

She rose up on her toes, pressed her cheek against his, and whispered into his ear. "You told the Department your father died in the line of duty. When the Department finds out you lied about that, why will they believe your accusations against me? When they find out your own father was a liar, a cheater, a *criminal,* Jonnie, why will they believe anything his lying son says?"

Her tongue darted out and explored his ear. It lapped him in lazy circles, then pushed deep inside, probing.

Shivers ran down Strega's back. His loins felt heavy. The tongue was moving now, in and out in a lazy, steady rhythm. Her hand dropped to the front of his trousers and squeezed him. Strega felt dizzy. Her perfume was heavy. Cinnamon and musk.

"You want me, Jonnie. You don't want to admit it yet, but you do want me. You'll start wondering what my body looks like. Then you'll start wondering what it feels like. You won't be able to not think about me, Jonnie. You'll come to me, begging for it. You'll see."

He raised his hands to force her off him, but she dropped back suddenly on her own accord.

Strega turned and hailed a cab. The door scraped the curb getting in. "Eighty-seventh and Columbus," he ordered, scraping the door shut. The cab accelerated away from Maria Alvarez. Two blocks flipped by. Strega looked back. A figure in white stood in the middle of the street. Hands on hips. Strega knew she was laughing.

Ten

Maria felt exuberant. It was more than the blow. It was the expression on Jon Strega's face, the way his voice sounded low and tight and scared—yes, scared—and the way his body tightened when she got right up next to it. He was so different from the others. So different from shy Mike Kelly. Strega didn't go for her. He didn't even know he wanted her. That was the best part. The fact that he *thought* he didn't want her when Maria knew deep down inside he did. Want her. His body wanted hers.

She swung up the stoop of her building and kicked a pile of beer cans out of the doorway. The game was different with Jon Strega. The difference electrified her. She climbed up the narrow stairwell, listening to the usual din coming from the surrounding apartments. Late-night television. Music. And on the fourth floor, something else. A girl. Screaming.

Angel. It was Angel. Maria reeled around the banister and raced down the hall to Angel's door. It was unlocked. Maria pushed it open. Rock music thundered in the dimly lit space.

Angel cowered, naked, in a corner on the far side of the room. A short, beefy white man towered over her. He was stripped down to a pair of yellowed, bagging underwear and cowboy boots with sharp pointed toes. His skin was sickly white. A heavy matting of black hair crawled over his shoulders and back. His legs were bulldog short but powerful, and he was using them to deliver precise, deadly kicks to Angel's small body.

Angel tried to ward off the blows, but her fear was a

red flag to the bull over her. The more she screamed, the harder he kicked. Maria could see by the intent curve of the hairy back that the bulldog was having fun. He grunted happily with every kick.

The music and Angel's shrieks drowned out the sound of Maria's heels tapping across the bare wood floor. Angel's eyes flickered up to hers. The bulldog turned to see what Angel was looking at. Maria picked up a brass candlestick and swung it hard at the fleshy face. She heard his skin split with the first blow. She swung again and heard his teeth break with the second blow, and his squat nose snap on impact with the third blow.

The stocky bulldog legs gave way. He toppled over face first. Maria rolled him over onto his back and kicked. "How does it feel?" she shouted. "Does it feel good to get kicked? Or is it more fun being the one who does the kicking?" Maria drove her sharp heels into his bulbous sides, his fleshy beer belly, and finally, powerfully, into his groin. The bulldog body lay inert.

Maria felt for a pulse. She was disappointed when she found one.

"You going to arrest him?" Angel croaked.

"If I do, you'll have to talk to a detective. Do you want to do that?"

"No. I ain't talking to no detectives." Matter-of-fact, the way Angel was about her position in life. "Just get him out of here."

"You have a gun?"

Angel nodded her head. "In the bedroom dresser drawer. I couldn't get to it."

"Is it registered?"

"Shit, no." Then, after a beat: "I got some handcuffs in there too if you want them."

Maria found the gun. It was a Saturday night special, fully loaded. She tucked it in her waistband, yanked a soiled sheet off the bed, and grabbed the handcuffs on the way out.

The fat man was coming to. He drew his knees up to his injured groin and sniffled. Maria cuffed his hands behind his back, tossed his balled-up clothes at him, then threw the sheet down and wrapped him in it, binding his arms and legs straitjacket tight.

"Crawl," she ordered.

"Can't," he blubbered.

"Then roll!" She kicked him. "Now! Go!"

He started rolling, across the floor. Maria steered him out the door, down the hall to the staircase. The fat man stopped short. His fish eyes widened in terror.

"Roll!" Maria ordered, prodding him with the gun. "Now! Go!"

He rolled over the edge. Maria watched him tumble down. At the bottom he lay still, but he was groaning. Maria knew he was conscious. She trotted down the stairs and kicked him sharply. "Go! Roll!" She shouted him into motion again, rolling him out the door, down the deserted sidewalk to her Celica. She popped the trunk and unwrapped him. He stood up uncertainly. "Get in," she ordered in a dead voice.

He eyed the gun in her waistband and whimpered.

"I said, get in!"

He crawled in. She slammed the trunk.

Maria threw his balled-up clothes into the backseat and drove swiftly across town, up the East River Drive to Harlem, where she left the highway. She bumped across the river bank to an isolated promontory. She grabbed the clothes, went around and opened the trunk. "Get out."

He lumbered out clumsily. She aimed the little Saturday night special at him. "Don't hurt me," he begged. "Don't shoot me."

She pistol-whipped his flaccid face and gripped his fleshy chin. The red lips bunched up into an O. "You get off on hurting women?"

"No!"

"Liar! Liar!" Maria sneered, squeezing his fat cheeks hard. She released him suddenly. "Walk."

He stared at her, dumbly.

"Walk!" Maria shouted again.

He shook his head no.

She fired at the ground near his feet. *"Walk!"*

He jumped and walked jerkily away. "Where we going?" he called out.

"Swimming," Maria said. She marched him down the embankment to the river edge.

The bulldog looked at the water, then back at Maria. "I can't swim," he whined.

"Neither can I," Maria said, firing a single shot into his heart.

He fell back into the river. Maria watched the fat-bellied corpse bob in the swells. The swells eased the corpse out into the tide, and the tide carried it swiftly away. From time to time, in the distance, the white belly crested on a swell. Maria watched the belly for a long time. She watched until it shrank to a tiny pinprick of white on the rushing black water. When the body disappeared from sight, when there wasn't even a speck of white visible on the rolling river, Maria tossed the gun and his clothes into the water and walked away.

Inside Angel's apartment, Maria shut off the stereo and flicked on the lights. Angel huddled in the corner. Maria wrapped her in a blanket and scooped her up. Angel's hair smelled like honey. She was feather light in Maria's arms.

Angel squirmed. "I can walk."

"This is a full-service rescue."

Angel stopped squirming. She tried to smile, but her smooth coffee skin was split and bleeding around her mouth. One eye was swollen shut. The other eye peered up into Maria's face. "You moonlighting as a female Clark Kent or something?"

Maria carried Angel upstairs to her own place, set her down on the bed. She grabbed two towels, soaked one in cold water and wet the second towel down with warm water. She knelt next to Angel and placed the cold compress over her injured eye. "Hold that there," she instructed.

She used the wet warm towel to gently wipe the blood off Angel's face and neck. She worked her way down past an ugly bite mark on Angel's left breast to the split

skin on her rib cage, then over the bleeding cuts on her
thighs and shins. From time to time Angel inhaled
sharply.

Angel looked so small. She was small, smaller than
Maria. Maybe five-two standing soldier straight. Her legs
seemed too fragile and thin to have survived such a beating without actually breaking. Her breasts were high and
round and surprisingly full on her scrawny girl's body.
Even so, Angel was just a girl, fifteen or sixteen, a runaway from the South, with no real family. She had been
in and out of a dozen foster homes, enough to know
bad as things were in the real world, they were better
than foster care. Now, here in the city, she sold drugs
and she sold her body, but Angel said somehow she
felt free.

Maria sat on the edge of the bed and lifted the compress. She wouldn't know until morning how serious the
eye injury was. She put the compress back in place, then
covered Angel with a pink rayon robe.

"What if he comes back?" Angel whispered.

"He's not coming back," Maria promised. "Who was
he?"

"He was sent," Angel managed through chattering
teeth.

"Who sent him?"

"Zeke."

"Who's Zeke?"

"Operator who wants me to stroll for him," Angel
spat. "Guys like Zeke want to own you. They try to
scare you into working for them. If you do, they own
you forever. They take most all of what you bring in,
then hand some back like you should be thankful. I'll
never work for Zeke. I'll never work for no one. But
I'm afraid now, Maria."

"Why didn't you tell me this before?"

"Thought he'd leave me be."

"Where can I find Zeke?"

Angel looked so hopeful. Then her one good eye
teared up and her head sagged. "Forget it. You'll never
find him. Zeke changes his first name and don't use a

last name. And I never seen his face. He sends messengers. That one tonight was a messenger. He'll send another to hurt me again."

"You won't do him any good beat up like this."

"No, but word gets around. He'll use me as a lesson, to set an example to other girls." Angel buried her face in her pillow and cried.

Maria took a hairbrush off the dresser. Slowly, as gently as she could, she brushed the knots out of Angel's long hair. The brushing calmed Angel. After a time her shoulders stopped shaking, but her eyes were still wide with fear. "I'm afraid," she whispered.

Maria lay down and wrapped her body around Angel's.

"I wonder what men are like outside of Hell's Kitchen," Angel mused.

"They're all the same, Angel." Maria thought of Jon Strega, of his cocksure smile and his sneering contempt for her. "They're all the same," she said again, tears running down her face. She was crying for herself. For Angel. For all the broken women out there.

They lay easily together in the dark for a time, like sisters, which they were in a way. Angel looked up to Maria. They took care of each other and were close, like family. It was an odd family, the hooker and cop, but Maria loved Angel just the same. And Maria didn't love anyone. Not even herself. Especially not herself. Angel's one good eye drifted closed. Maria stroked Angel's head and hummed an old church hymn, soft and low, and she was still humming it long after she heard the deep, steady breathing of Angel asleep.

Eleven

Maria Alvarez was present at the Wednesday afternoon roll call. Strega saw her arrive late. She slipped into a chair behind his, hat in hands, eyes turned demurely down.

Ballantine paced up front, swatting the *Times* against his thigh. Wilson stood off to one side, looking like he had slept like a baby. If composure was a politician's asset, Strega thought, then Ballantine was no politician—not with that grizzled face creased with fatigue and those eyes marbled red from sleepless nights. Strega knew how it went. The mayor hammered the P.C., the P.C. hammered Wilson, Wilson hammered Ballantine. Pass the buck, buck the responsibility, lay it on someone else's shoulders. Q-Ball was at the end of the line, and the burden he carried—the run of violence in the One-Nine—made his broad shoulders droop.

Ballantine started in. "For those of you who've had your heads in the sand, our perps hit again last night. Emilio's restaurant. The P.C. was there, for Christ's sake. This time the shooters hid their faces behind a couple of cheap masks. Same automatic weapons as in the bridal shop. The bullets match. Two DOA's, a man and woman, multiple hits to the chest. The M.E.'s still digging the bullets out.

"Neither the restaurant nor the bridal shop had security cameras or guards. By this afternoon I'll have a list of every high-ticket place of business in the precinct that doesn't have a security camera or guard on the premises. I'm going to plant plainclothes officers at as many of those addresses as I can. From the witness statements, we know the blonde is the trigger-happy one of the pair. We also know they are the same perps who are working the Madison car-and-driver scam. I guess the ladies who were taken for a ride are lucky Don Juan was driving and not his blond buddy."

Alvarez kicked Strega's chair. It was a light tap at first, barely noticeable. She kicked it again, harder, in a staccato rhythm. Morse code.

Kick-kick-kick. Kick-kick.

"Don't think for a minute they've given up their day job," Ballantine went on, "At noon today, another woman was forced into a luxury car in broad daylight on Madison. Same drill as all the prior incidents. They nailed another lady at two-thirty. They work smooth and fast. To anyone watching, it's just another lady getting into a car. The cars are always different, and now the blonde changes the way he looks. This morning he was wearing a mustache and beard. This afternoon he was a clean-shaven redhead."

Kick-kick-kick.

Q-Ball snapped the newspaper open and held it in the air. "They get a big kick out of coverage like this." He poked a finger at the headline: NO ONE IS SAFE. "The P.C.'s asking the press to drop the story for a few days. That's like asking a dog not to lift its leg on a hydrant. This is a hot story, it sells papers. If any of you are approached by a reporter, the magic words are *no comment.*"

Kick-kick-kick. Kick-kick.

Inspector Wilson stepped up. "Most of the stores and restaurants along Madison Avenue are members of MARRA—Madison Avenue's Retail and Restaurant Association. The association was one of the largest single contributors to the mayor's election campaign last year. I don't need to tell you what kind of pressure MARRA's putting on the mayor. Go out of your way to be visible in your sectors. Get out of the car. Talk to people. Make the citizens in the One-Nine feel your presence." Wilson checked his watch. "The mayor's waiting for me at Gracie Mansion." He strode out.

Ballantine followed.

Kick-kick-kick. Kick-kick.

Strega turned around. She was looking into a mirrored compact, lining her lips with total concentration. She went back and forth over her lower lip with the pencil, darkening and smudging. Then she rubbed her lips together and smiled into the mirror.

Strega turned back around.

Kick-kick-kick. Kick-kick.

The duty sergeant ran through the usual housekeeping and scheduling details, then dismissed. The room emptied. Strega hung back. Alvarez fussed with her hair, rummaged in her handbag. Strega steeled himself for a confrontation, but she ignored him and walked easily away, swinging up to Kelly's side and walking with him out the door.

The scent of cinnamon and musk lingered in the air, then that was gone too, and Strega wondered if he had dreamt the whole encounter the night before, and maybe the kicking too. He remembered how her breasts had looked, dark and full under the transparent white net shirt, and it suddenly occurred to him that she was probably just as naked under her uniform. Thinking about her body disturbed him.

Hansen approached with her arms folded across her chest. "Ballantine asked me to investigate your locker incident," she said flatly.

"So?" Strega asked.

"So, where were you at six o'clock Saturday night?"

"At home." Drinking fermented Russian potatoes.

"Anyone with you?"

"Nope." One cat, an alabaster lady, and a clay head.

"You go anywhere or see anyone around that time?"

"What's this all about?"

"Why is your name recorded on the ASPCA log dated Saturday?"

"You've lost me, Hansen."

"According to the ASPCA, you adopted one of their pets. A cat. An orange striped male cat named Frederick. Frederick was very much alive and in good health when you took him out of the shelter. He didn't have any holes in his head."

"You think *I* did it?" Strega said. *The savior of abandoned kittens?* "Are you out of your mind?"

"No—the question is, are you?"

Strega took her by the shoulders. "Do you honestly think I did it?"

Hansen hesitated. She tapped her foot. Looked him in the eye. Her arms unfolded and fell to her sides. All the anger went out of her. "No. You don't strike me as a schizoid kind of guy. But I'm not so sure my opinion's going to be good enough for Ballantine. And what the hell's your name doing listed at the ASPCA?"

"I don't know." Oh, yes, he knew.

She eyed him suspiciously. "Anyone out there have a reason for framing you?"

"Maybe."

"A name would be helpful."

What would Alvarez do if Hansen started stirring things up? Could she get Hansen kicked off the job?

"Strega, I'm waiting."

"I decided I don't want you involved."

"Dumbass decision. Is it because I'm a woman?"

"You know that's not true."

The sincerity in his voice soothed her. "Okay, tell me this. Do I tell Ballantine what I know, or do I let it slide and make this the one case out of a hundred I can't solve?"

"I can't tell you what to do."

"Come with me down to the ASPCA. Let's see if anyone there ID's you. If no one does, I drop it and Ballantine never hears another word. If someone does ID you? Well, then, to hell with my instincts. You can talk to the big man yourself." She wheeled around and left.

The sun was a fat white circle in the hazy summer sky. It reflected off the hood of the squad car and flashed into Gavin's face as he and Strega skimmed up Madison Avenue. Gavin wondered how many times a year he watched the same rows of shops flip by. Day after day, week after week, month after month, he gazed out the car window looking for something that didn't fit. Something out of order. Something wrong.

There was something wrong now. Barney's department store was closed, and it was a weekday. All of the elegant boutiques, restaurants, and art galleries were shuttered too. They had banded together and closed for the day in protest. The owners were marching at City Hall, demanding better police protection and more cops in the One-Nine.

As if that was the answer. As if solving crime was a question of manpower.

It was impossible to predict where or when the shooters might hit again. The One-Nine didn't need more cops. It needed a lucky break, Gavin thought, looking out at row after row of dark, empty designer boutiques and restaurants. At the top of Madison, a travel agency was lit up and open. A GO HAWAII promotion filled the giant display window. A life-sized motorized plastic hula girl was dancing a stiff version of the hula.

Strega turned off Madison Avenue and slipped down a dignified residential street. His Genie beeped. He took it out of his pocket, studied the screen, and smiled. "West Entertainment's on the move."

"You finally going to sell?" Gavin idly asked, watching gracious brownstones flip by.

"No. In fact, I bought some more of it yesterday."

"Do me a favor," Gavin said suddenly. "Take me past the travel agency again."

"You thinking of taking a trip?"

"Something like that."

Strega circled around to the travel agency.

Gavin got out and went up to the window. Inside, paper fish dangled from the ceiling. A plastic fake sun glowed. Giant cardboard seashells covered the floor, and cheerful signs promised once in a lifetime bargains: 5 NIGHTS, 2 ISLANDS—$899.00 W/AIRFARE. Gavin scanned it all, but his eyes locked in on the hula girl and her mechanized swaying hips. She fascinated him. Something wiggled around in the back of his mind. He couldn't pin it down. He gave up and ducked back into the patrol car.

"Let's go," he said.

It was noon. Strega said: "You in the mood for Chinese?"

"Sure," Gavin said, looking back at the dancing hula girl.

He tried to understand what he found so compelling about a plastic doll in a grass skirt. He thought about it all through lunch at the Empire Palace and was so preoccupied thinking about it, he barely noticed Strega picking up the check. Gavin was still brooding when Ming came back to the table, frowning, holding out Strega's gold VISA card.

"I'm sorry, Officer Strega, but your card's no good."

Strega checked the expiration date. "It's valid for another year."

"The machine rejected it. I called the authorization number. The lady told me your card was reported stolen. I said I know it's not stolen because you're sitting right here in the restaurant. She said, so what. It's reported stolen. She told me to keep the card, call the police. I told her I don't have to call the police. They're already here."

"Must be a computer error." Strega put cash on the table and stood up. "Ed ..."

Gavin waved the apology away. "Happens to everyone." He smiled at Ming as they left, but her red outfit only reminded him of the hula girl in the red flowered bikini top.

At the end of the tour, at five minutes to four, Gavin figured it out. They took one last spin up Madison. The hula girl was still dancing.

"Stop the car," Gavin ordered.

He walked up to the window. The hula girl's lush hips were moving in a circle. She smiled out at him. Her bikini top was a Hawaiian flower motif with red and white orchids sprawling all over her majestic plastic bosom. She was the quintessential hula girl.

And she looked just like the ones on Danny's beach towels.

Gavin put his hand on the window as if to touch her. "Thank you," he said. He jogged back to the car, knowing he had to get to Ballantine.

The blinds were open. The big detective was hunched over his desk, alone in his fish-tank office, scribbling on a pad of paper. Gavin rapped on the glass. Ballantine looked up, annoyed at the interruption, but he waved Gavin in and gestured for him to take a seat even though there was no place to sit. The vinyl bucket chairs were piled ten deep with file folders, and every available surface was obscured by a hurricane of paper.

"Throw those folders on the floor," Ballantine grumbled, waving at one of the chairs.

Gavin swept the folders off and sat down.

Ballantine stretched. "Looks like World War Five in here. Jesus, thanks to these shooters, I'm working twenty-three hours a day. I grab a one-hour cat nap here on the floor, then get up and start all over again."

He pinched the bridge of his nose. "I don't have enough men. The chief of detectives says the full resources of the Department are mine for the asking, so I ask. The shooters are terrorists, I say. Give me a hundred detectives, fifty for the day tour and fifty for the night tour. I want to cover this precinct in wall-to-wall detectives. I want one of my men standing next to whatever lady or in whatever room they decide to hit next.

"Christ, I want to be standing there myself the next time these sons of bitches pull their Uzis out, but what does the chief say to me? 'Sorry, Ballantine, these unfortunate attacks appear to be random incidents. The perps are probably long gone. We do have budget parameters. It's only August. There are going to be a lot more crimes to investigate before the year is out. We can't spend all the money at once, and we sure as hell can't spend it all in one precinct, even if it is where the mayor and the P.C. live. Best I can do is ten extra men. Five for each tour. All overtime must be approved in advance.'

"Then he has the balls to stand up and stick his hand out like I'm going to feel like shaking it, and he says, 'Ballantine, you're going to do a fine job anyway. You've got a nose like a hound dog when it comes to tracking killers down.'" Ballantine snorted. "Like flattery's going to make me want to catch these guys more. Fact is, he hates the mayor and he hates the P.C. He wants to see them fried in the press. Fuck politics."

"Sorry to interrupt." Gavin stood up to leave.

"Sit the fuck down."

Gavin sat.

"I was just blowing off steam. What do you have for me?"

"The hula girl towels."

"The *what*?"

"Danny owned three giant beach towels with hula girls on them. He said a guy his size couldn't use standard-size bath towels. Said it was like drying a wet elephant with a Kleenex. He had one hula towel here in his locker and two at home. The two at home weren't in the CSU photos."

Ballantine rummaged in the mountain of files for Donovan's file. He pulled out the bound stack of CSU photos, picked up a magnifying glass, and went over each shot.

"CSU was thorough," Gavin said, while Ballantine looked. "Every inch of the bathroom was documented, and nowhere, not in the open cupboard, not on the plastic hooks on the back of the door, or in the hamper was there a single hula girl towel, let alone two."

"Maybe Donovan dropped them off at the local laundromat."

Gavin shook his head. "Danny did his own wash at a do-it-yourself place down the street. Twenty-five cents a load. Said he saved money that way. Everything was about saving money to pay for the fight to get Katy away from Jillian."

"We should check the laundromats anyway." Ballantine tossed the photos aside.

"You won't find them."

"What makes you so sure?" Ballantine asked in a half-interested, distracted way.

"The killer took them when he left."

He had Ballantine's full attention now. "Slow down, Ed. Give it to me step by step."

"The towels are gone because the killer used them to clean himself up after the shooting."

Ballantine scowled. "There's no trail of blood leading from the living room to the bathroom."

"The killer could've worn a special outfit, say, a workman's uniform, for the shooting. Then he stepped out of it in the living room, balled it up, and walked naked into the bathroom to shower off the rest of the blood—the blood in his hair and on his hands. He wrapped the bloody uniform up with the soiled towels and carted the whole package away in a plastic trash bag."

"If he threw his uniform away, what was he wearing when he walked out the door?"

"He came with a change of clothes in a sack. A plastic sack, a gym bag, who knows?"

Ballantine let the hypothesis sink in. He mulled it over, then shook his head. "Ed, I got to tell you, it's a flimsy theory."

Inspector Wilson walked in and eyed Gavin. It was a *what the hell are you doing in here* kind of look. The schoolmaster to the student.

Ballantine answered Wilson before he could ask the question. "We were just discussing the incident with Donovan's old locker."

Wilson lost interest. "With all due respect, we've got more pressing issues to deal with. Ed, you understand."

"I do." Gavin moved to the door. "Good night."

No one heard him. The two men were already deep in conversation, Wilson the aggressor, pressing, demanding, stalking from one end of the office to the next, letting his mask of perfect control slip, showing his anger and frustration.

At least, Gavin thought, walking through the busy squad room, at least Wilson had witnesses to ID the shooters. He had descriptions, details, approximate heights and weights. He had an entire team of detectives and the whole patrol squad out on the streets looking.

Gavin and Ballantine, on the other hand, were flying blind into a place darker than night.

Twelve

"You've done well," he said one winter day. "Now that you understand the fight, you must understand death. You must not be afraid of death. If you are, you will make the wrong decisions when you fight. You must be fearless to fight well. And to be fearless you must confront death."

He took her to the city morgue one night after hours and left her alone in a big, chilled room, where the sickly sweet smell of disinfectant made her eyes water and her stomach churn. She went to the wall of metal, to an unmarked door, and opened a steel refrigerator. She rolled an empty long metal table out and climbed on, laying flat and stiff on her back. The steel was cold against her live skin and hard against her head. She held her breath and tried to be still, as still as the silent, lifeless bodies she knew were all around her in those other cold steel vaults.

Maria Alvarez lay on her back on the bed, as though it were that long metal table. She turned her head and looked at the picture of Jon Strega she had pinned to the wall. It was the picture she had stolen from his personnel file, the one in which he smiled out, young and confident, world-by-the-tail smug.

Jon Strega was waiting for her.

Maria left her apartment and walked up to Central Park. She admired the buildings stretching up all around the park, scraping the sky. She walked north, to the reservoir, where she knew Jon Strega liked to run. In the shrubbery lining the runners' track were plenty of places for a small woman to conceal herself. Maria chose a place where she knew the ground was soft. She sat down and waited.

At seven o'clock, she saw him. He loped along gracefully, like a gazelle, long-limbed, agile, and swift. He ran shirtless with his chin tipped up to the sky and his arms flapping loosely at his sides. He ran as though he were in a trance, his pace constant, footfall after measured footfall thumping down onto the hard-pressed earth.

One, two, three, four, five times around he went, his pace and intent expression never changing, the bright blue nylon running shorts snapping smartly against his thighs. His long, molded runner's legs were hard-carved and solid, as carved and solid as his belly.

At the end of the fifth circuit he veered off into the dense wooded park land, on a cross-country sprint Maria guessed would lead him home.

She stood up and took a walk around the track. The clouded sky muted the late daylight. The reservoir looked ethereal. The water shimmered gunmetal gray, wrapped by the seasonal scarf of park trees. Today the scarf was green, a thousand shades of green—gray green, lime green, silver green, forest green—and the tree branches were heavy with the weight of those green summer leaves. Come fall, the leaves would turn the colors of fire—red, orange, amber, riotous yellow—and a ring of fire would wrap the gunmetal water, a circle of flaming autumn splendor, a splendor Jon Strega would never see.

Come fall, he would be dead.

Gavin sat at the kitchen table, waiting for his dinner. He skimmed the newspaper headlines, read the weather forecast. A hurricane was blowing up the Eastern Seaboard, and it was heading straight for Manhattan. He tried to concentrate on the details, but he saw hula girl towels where he should have seen words. Gavin shoved the paper away.

Suddenly, he felt like an idiot. Chasing after ghosts, chasing after a murderer no one even knew existed, going whole hog with not one single solid piece of evidence. Feeling like an idiot made him feel powerless, like he was looking for Alex again. Feeling powerless

made him mad. He was mad at Ballantine, mad at
Danny, Wilson, Strega—he was mad at everyone, including his wife.

He looked over at Shelly. She was standing at the
stove, making a hell of a racket cooking Chinese style
in a big wok. She had a lot of makeup on. Shelly didn't
usually wear makeup unless they were going out. On top
of that, she was dressed in a sleeveless dress that went
up to mid-thigh. She wore high-heeled sandals that tied
around her ankles, Grecian style. The dress was black.
It begged the question: "Going to a funeral?"

Shelly threw her cooking utensils down. "Why do
you ask?"

"You're dressed in black."

"Someone doesn't have to die for a woman to wear
black." She turned around. Her hands dropped to her
hips. Combat stance. "You don't like it."

"You just look dressed up. Fancy. That's all." He
broke open a packet of chopsticks and rubbed them together. "Anyway, it's too short for a funeral."

She turned back to the stove, shoveled the food onto
a couple of plates. "Short is *in*."

The meal was Chinese, but he was in a kamikaze
mood. "For college girls maybe."

"I got the message." She slapped his plate down in
front of him.

Gavin looked at it. "I give up, Shell. What is it?"

"Vegetables."

"Why don't they look like vegetables?"

"I wokked them in low-sodium soy."

"Oh." He pushed them around with the chopsticks.
"Is there something after this?"

"Fruit."

"Fruit."

"Edward."

He knew he was in trouble. Whenever she was mad
at him, Shelly called him Edward—just like his mother
had. He was too old and too tired to be mothered.
"Well, vegetables don't do it, not for me. I'm going to
microwave a pizza."

Shelly pushed her plate away and left the table.

Kamikaze pilot hits target. Shit, he thought, listening to her take the stairs two at a time. A door slammed upstairs. He went over to the fridge and pulled out a beer. He drank the entire bottle in one long swallow. He took another bottle out and nursed it while he opened the frozen pizza box, slid the pie into the microwave, and zapped it. When the timer dinged, Gavin tilted the beer bottle high, finished the last swig, and reached in the fridge for a third.

He leaned against the counter and ate his pizza, looking out into his dining room. Big polished wood table, six chairs. Little lace doilies carefully placed under a fake silver candelabra. Six chairs and no one in them. He and Shell never ate in the dining room, not anymore. Gavin finished the pizza. He picked up his beer bottle and wandered around. What was the point having a house with a den, dining room, and living room when all they used was the kitchen and the bedroom?

The living room looked like some kind of altar to Alex, which it was in a way. The walls were crowded with framed pictures: first step, first bath, first Easter dress. He looked at Alex's winsome, smiling face. *Alexandra Gavin.* A perfect baby and a star student. Honor roll. Junior high counselors buzzing about her scholarship potential. Big-name schools bandied about—Yale, Harvard, even Princeton, for crying out loud.

The photo gallery stopped at age thirteen, the year she had disappeared. Gavin studied the last shot. There was nothing awkward or teenage gawky about Alex. She was so pretty, with long hair that hung down to her waist, the same color as Shelly's. Gavin wondered what she might look like now if she was miraculously alive.

Five years older. Would I even know her? Did she grow up tall? Is her hair long or short? Did it lose its red-gold color and turn the color of wheat, like mine used to be? Does she need braces at eighteen or is her smile perfect? Does she ever drive by the house in secret? When she passes a pay phone, does she ever think of calling,

*just to let us know she's okay? Or is that she can't? That
she is, after all these years, dead.*

He snapped the lights out, put his beer bottle in the
kitchen trash, and wandered upstairs to see what
peacemaking could be done. Shelly sat cross-legged on
their big bed, grazing through television channels with
the remote. She was wrapped in an old ratty bathrobe
and had her face scrubbed clean. The black dress was
crumpled on the floor.

He sat down next to her. He put his hand under her
chin and tilted her face up. Her eyes were full of accusation. "Shell," he said, "I didn't mean to criticize your
cooking."

She pushed his hand away and gave him the side of
her face to look at. "I'm just trying to help you lose
some weight, Ed. You know you need to. Why are you
so stubborn?"

"I like to eat. Makes me feel better."

"You've been doing nothing but eating since Danny
died. You going to just keep eating until you explode?"

"Maybe."

"What about how I feel?"

"It's my body."

"I happen to be married to that body."

He stood up. "I'm taking a shower."

"Good. Walk out. Don't talk about it. Don't talk
about what's really eating you alive."

"And what might that be?" he asked sarcastically,
moving to the bathroom door.

"The fact that Danny's dead and that he did it to
himself."

Her voice stopped him.

"He didn't even talk to you before he did it, did he?
And that hurts you more than Alex disappearing. Isn't
that what this is all about? Danny hurting you?"

He spun around to face her. She was getting off the
bed, shrugging out of the bathrobe, pulling her black
dress over her head and smoothing it down over her
hips.

"You probably wish I'd been the one to blow my head

off," she went on. "Then, at least, you'd still have Danny. You're stuck with me instead. Life's a bitch, isn't it? Or maybe it's just that I am." She grabbed her sandals and handbag and ran out the door.

"Shelly, wait." Gavin ran after her, down the hall, down the stairs, and out to the front porch. She was in her car, firing the ignition up. "Now who's running away?" he shouted. The big station wagon rolled backward out of the driveway, rocked to a stop, then lurched forward and roared off. Gavin watched the taillights disappear around the corner.

"Now who's running away?" he shouted again, foolishly, to the empty street.

Walls in a marriage went up one brick at a time. Gavin figured he and Shelly had only a handful of bricks left before the wall closed them off from each other for all time.

He went back inside, plopped down on the living room sofa, and waited to hear the sound of the old wagon rattling back up the driveway. An hour passed. He knew Shelly was out looking for Alex, driving the way he sometimes still did, around and around all night long, cruising the waterfront docks, the bus stations and nightclubs, rolling slowly, searching the faces of the swivel-hipped hookers working the bridges, and into the city, skimming up and down the avenues, alongside the West Side piers where the homeless wandered, looking, always looking for that one sweet face, so much like her own, with green eyes and a spill of red-gold hair.

Nothing that night pleased Strega. Not the spicy pasta he cooked or the rich red wine he drank with it. Not the art hanging on his walls, the kitten curling around his ankles, or any one of the many comforts in his home. Even his evening run had failed to cheer him. He sat on the couch in his running shorts and a Princeton T-shirt, nursing a vodka, feeling anxious and disturbed.

At the end of the day he had gone with Hansen to the ASPCA. A clerk there remembered the orange cat

and said a black kid, a messenger, had picked it up in
the name of Jon Strega.

Kick-kick-kick.

And earlier, at the Empire Palace when he was told
his credit card was canceled.

Kick-kick-kick.

What was the message? What was the point? Strega
felt lost. He knew enough to know human emotion was
unpredictable. Despite centuries of philosophical and
psychological investigation, emotion remained a wild
card. Love, hate, fear, guilt, joy, dread. When the emotion card popped up, life changed.

Strega himself was a living example. Guilt had driven
him into a job he didn't want. He had found love with
Rosemary and he had been happy. Without her, without
love, he was miserable. Now fear had shown up in the
shape of Maria Alvarez. She scared him. He had the
feeling she could do anything at any time. She was an
emotional terrorist, and she was using his father as the
weapon. Strega walked over to the clay head of Vincent
Strega. He looked at it from all angles, watching it, as
though it might suddenly speak.

The phone rang. He picked up.

"Jonnie. You look good in those running shorts. I
watched you running earlier. You're fast. Did you know
I was there? Watching? You went around the reservoir
five times. I counted. And now? Is the vodka relaxing
you? Is it helping you? Are you talking to Vincent, Jonnie? Or is Vincent talking to you?

"You know, you look just like him. Is Vincent telling
you his secrets? Is that why you're standing so still next
to him? Or are you just standing there trying to imagine
what he looked like when he died—what happened to
his handsome face when the bullet exploded into it.
How's it going to be, Jonnie? Is it going to be like father,
like son?" The phone went dead.

Strega whirled around and looked out the big picture
window. He knew she was out there. At the corner.
Across the street. Maybe standing in his own garden
talking from a cellular phone. She was out there, close,

close enough to see the clay head of Vincent Strega.
Close enough to see Jon Strega. She knew what he was
wearing, what he was drinking. *She knew what he was
thinking.* She was out there and she hated him.

Strega snapped the lights out. He stood in the dark.
The world was spinning out of control, tipping off its
axis. He felt he was going to slide into the random chaos
of Maria Alvarez's universe, where there was no gravity—where he would be unable to keep himself from
tumbling and hurtling into the great dark core of her
hate.

He was scared.

The kitten swiped his ankle. Strega scooped him up
and stroked him while he looked out into the night. He
shook himself out of his irrational thoughts. Gavin was
right. He had to walk up to her and apologize.

Tomorrow, he promised himself. *Tomorrow, I will
confront her and put an end to this.*

The phone started to ring again. He let it ring.

Tomorrow, he promised himself, *I will put an end to
this.*

Gavin woke up alone in his king-size bed. Bright sun
slanted in through the Levelors. He rolled over and
looked at the clock. It was eleven. The house was quiet.
He had waited up until he heard Shelly come back,
around dawn. She was sleeping in Alex's room. He
guessed she would sleep well into the afternoon.

Gavin was scheduled for the four-to-eight tour. He
planned on leaving the house at two o'clock. That left
three hours—three free, fun hours—to do whatever the
hell he wanted, just like a kid on summer vacation, only
it was too hot to play outside and there wasn't really
much he wanted to do inside.

In summers past he and Donovan used to spend free
mornings like this one at Atlantic Beach, ambling along,
admiring the girls, What a sight they must have been,
he thought now. Two old cops dressed in Hawaiian
shirts, kicking their bare feet in the shallow water like
kiddies. Donovan used to wear his crazy hat for those

walks. It was a straw sombrero, two feet in diameter, and it had a little red string that tied under Donovan's sizable chin. The first time Donovan put it on, Gavin fell down in the sand laughing.

"Go ahead," Donovan sputtered, "go ahead and laugh. This just happens to be functional." Donovan's pale Irish skin burned easily. Gavin's skin burned too, but he made do with a New York Giants baseball cap.

Donovan.

When you grow up with someone, Gavin thought, and stay close over all the years, the person becomes like an appendage, an arm or a leg, and losing it's just the same—sometimes you're sure the appendage is still there, you can even *feel* it there. It was that way with Danny.

Sometimes Gavin felt *sure* Danny was out there, in the next room or a phone call away. Walking through the station house, Gavin would suddenly expect to see Danny loping around the corner with his wide Irish grin. In the locker room from time to time Gavin could feel Danny's big hand cuffing him on the shoulder. When Gavin turned around, Danny was never there, but Gavin's shoulder tingled just the same. Sometimes, Gavin even heard Danny laughing, and that's when he missed his friend the most.

Gavin closed his eyes. Danny's face popped up, clear as day. Gavin smiled. It was the face of a St. Bernard, loyal and doleful, with big soulful eyes that grew sadder as time went on. The job got to Donovan more than the average cop. Unlike the average cop, Donovan never lost his ability to feel or his ability to hurt. He never lost his humanity.

Gavin opened his eyes and stared at the ceiling. His New York Giants cap sat on the dresser. Gavin didn't need it this summer. The only walking he planned on doing was to the refrigerator and back. He reached for the remote and flicked the television on.

A local weatherman was pointing at a map and talking about a hurricane named Emma that was blowing up from Florida with a hundred and fifty mile an hour winds. Gavin half hoped it would blow right through Ozone Park, pick him up like Dorothy, and blow him the hell away, to Oz maybe, where the wizard would throw back a curtain and show him Danny and Alex standing there, alive and well. Gavin pulled on an old robe and went downstairs. His stomach was growling. He didn't know whether to feed it breakfast or lunch, so he decided to have both.

He poured a bowl of Captain Crunch breakfast cereal and ate it while he waited for his coffee to heat. He made a chicken sandwich on sourdough to go with the coffee, then ate the sandwich standing up. Gavin left his dishes in the sink and wandered across the living room carpet. It was freshly vacuumed. His feet left big imprints. He looked out the front window. The morning newspaper lay on the pavement outside.

He opened the front door, squinted in the bright sunlight, and walked down the driveway. The cement burned his bare feet, and the sun burned his face. He got the mail out of the mailbox and flipped through it. Credit-card bills, checking statement, phone bill. Shelly dealt with the bills. He never even opened them. He leaned over to pick up the newspaper. His feet were sickly white. Blue veins, fat as worms, pushed out against his skin. He grabbed the paper and straightened.

A little kid pedaled one of those big three-wheeled plastic bikes down the sidewalk. The bike had long plastic streamers flying out of the handlebars, and they were hanging limp in the still summer air. The kid looked at Gavin, stuck his tongue out, and pedaled furiously away.

Gavin thrust his arm up and gave him the finger, but the little monster never looked back. When the kid and his bike were out of sight, Gavin dropped his hand back down to his side. The street was deserted again. A dog whined. A sprinkler gyrated on the scrubby lawn patch next door. Gavin ambled back into the house. As he was closing the front door, he spotted a big brown UPS truck lumbering down the street.

The truck stopped in front of Ellie Barrone's house. A man in a brown UPS uniform hopped out and loped up to her door, empty-handed. The front door opened. Ellie Barrone kept her body wedged behind the door, but Gavin could see she was wearing a nightie. She smiled at the driver and pulled him into the house. Her front door closed.

Gavin shut his own door and dropped the stack of bills on the kitchen counter for Shelly. He considered going to work for UPS when he retired. The fringe benefits looked pretty good. On the other hand, how did he expect to service dozens of hungry housewives when he couldn't even service his own?

He went upstairs, back to bed. He punched up the pillows and looked at the local news. The anchorman was frowning. A picture of Ramon Alvarez popped up over his shoulder.

"Alarmed by the record-breaking number of suicides among New York Police Department officers, Police Commissioner Alvarez set in motion a major overhaul of the Psychological Services branch of the Department. He made this statement this morning."

The camera cut to press-conference footage. Alvarez looked prosperous and sharp in a banker's blue suit, crisp white shirt, and red suspenders. "Sixteen suicides," he proclaimed, "is sixteen too many. Psychological Services is supposed to be the place officers can go for help. Obviously, we're not delivering the kind of support our officers need. I've ordered a complete reorganization of Psychological Services effective immediately. The changes will guarantee officers who need it get support."

Gavin snapped the television off. Alvarez was wrong. It was going to take a homicide investigation, not a Psych Services reorganization, to prevent more *suicides*. Unfortunately, there was no such investigation. There was no one on the case but Ballantine, and he was too busy with official homicide investigations to do much vigilante work. Ballantine didn't have the time.

But Gavin did have the time. Hell, he had nothing but time. Gavin shot up out of bed.

*   *   *

He went first to Danny's grave and talked, fool that he was, as if Danny could hear. Then he sat quietly for a while, feeling the sun on his face and some of his old rage against God for taking Danny away.

Next, he stopped by the school and pulled up next to the busy playground. He got out, stood by the fence, and picked her out of a crowd of kids. Whatever the game was, Katy was winning, and jumping up and down with glee. She was all Danny. It was in her big blue eyes and golden hair, but mostly it was in her laugh. Katy was laughing now. The sound came ringing out across the schoolyard, and for a second, Gavin thought, it was Donovan's laugh ringing out across the years, full of love and joy.

Katy threw the ball into play. A little boy lurched forward and kicked it hard. The ball shot high into the sky and sailed over the fence, landing at Gavin's feet. He picked it up as Katy was running on her skinny legs toward him, running and laughing, then colliding with the chain-link fence, shaking it hard and looking up at him with a mischievous smile.

"Hey, Gavin! Are you coming in to play?"

He shook his head slowly. "No, honey, not today." He tossed the ball in a high, easy arc over the fence. Katy caught it and ran away, giggling.

Who killed your father, Katy? Who?

Gavin whirled around and jogged back to the car. He had to get to Ballantine.

"I want to catch this guy more than I want to nail the masked shooters. You know why?" Ballantine asked.

"Because he's killing cops?" Gavin guessed.

Ballantine picked up a half-eaten ham sandwich. "That's a big part of it. But I got to be honest. It's more. The ultimate murder is the one that no one thinks is murder. This guy's going around icing cops, and no one knows it. The killer's watching the P.C. blame Psych Services. He's laughing at us!" Ballantine slapped the sandwich down.

"I'm going to nail him," Ballantine promised. "Don't

think for one minute that I've shuffled this thing to the bottom of the deck. I'm going to nail the fucker sooner or later. Simple as that. Unfortunately, it's going to have to be later." Ballantine gestured to the stacks of paper on his desk. "The shooters are taking all my time."

Ballantine's office was shrouded in the now familiar half-light. The blinds were snapped closed and the door was locked. Gavin heard the muffled noise of the busy squad room outside—phones ringing, detectives shouting, typewriters clacking.

"I have time," Gavin said quietly. "I can help. But all I've seen is Danny's file. You've studied them all. Tell me what you have so far."

Ballantine flipped the bulletin board over. "Take a look at the map." The map was punctured by push pins in two colors—blue and red. "Sixteen suicides in all. As I said, I think nine of them are homicides. Of those nine, four were right here in Manhattan. Uptown, downtown, West Side, East Side. There's no pattern. The other five are scattered across five different boroughs. They're all over the place. I think our killer has gone to great trouble to make sure there's no *geographical* similarity."

"Why?"

"Simple. By spreading them out, he's created a series of *random* suicides. *Unconnected, unrelated deaths.*"

"How do you tell the killer's work from legitimate suicides?"

"Look at my map. Blue pins are for the legit suicides. Red pins are for the homicides. Remember Sullivan in January? He stood on a sidewalk in Queens, surrounded by spectators and television cameras, put his gun in his mouth, and fired. We know that one's legit." Ballantine pulled a blue pin out of the bulletin board. "One cop on Staten Island locked himself in his garage and sucked carbon monoxide until he died. Legit." Ballantine pulled out another blue pin.

"One cop took a bottle of painkillers and jumped off the Triboro Bridge in front of ten witnesses." He pulled another blue pin out. "One cop in Queens hung himself in his basement. He left a note and a video recording of his suicide." The fourth blue pin came out. "In Queens, a cop went home and found a letter from his wife saying she had left him. He walked in the bathroom, filled the bathtub, got in with his clothes on, and slit his wrists. He left a note." Ballantine pulled the fifth blue pin out. "One Manhattan cop went to the top of the Empire State Building, put his gun in his mouth, and pulled the trigger—in front of twenty-five witnesses. Legit." He yanked the sixth blue pin out.

"A Brooklyn cop found out Internal Affairs was going to come down on him for skimming drugs off his busts. He stood on the front stoop of the precinct house and shot himself in the heart." He yanked the seventh blue pin out. "That's seven legitimate suicides, and nine I don't think are legit, including the last one, number sixteen."

Gavin looked at the pin map. The remaining nine pins were red, and they were scattered across several boroughs. "One of those is for Danny?"

"It is. So now you have to ask yourself, what did Danny have in common with the other eight men besides the fact he was a cop?"

"I'm listening."

"They were all in uniform at the time of death, and like Danny, I found out their shields are all unaccounted for. In each instance the fatal wound was a single gunshot to the side of the head, right or left, depending on the manual orientation of the cop. They all died at home. In each case home was a small, shitty apartment because these cops lived alone. None of them left notes. They were all divorced or in the process of getting divorced. And—this may be a long shot—they were all Catholic."

"What else."

"There's evidence of the drug thing in all nine officers. Like Donovan, there was a fresh needle mark on every arm and a whopping dose of cocaine in every body. All nine of these officers died wearing nothing but their uniform shirts. And all nine had their own semen on their bodies. That bugs me. Was the killer gay? Did he set these cops up with a woman? Did he set the cops up with an easy lay, watch the sex, then kill? Who's the whore he set them up with? Where is she? Did he kill her too?"

Ballantine paced around the small room. "Fact: A serial killer collects trophies. We can consider the missing shields 'trophies.' Fact: A serial killer never changes the way he kills. He is specific, right down to the rituals he practices after killing. Maybe he writes the victim's name in blood. Maybe he goes to church and confesses. Maybe he jerks off. What did this killer do? Why did he choose these nine cops?

"The nine pins are spread randomly over the city, but I don't believe they're random choices. Are they revenge killings? Did these nine cops arrest the same guy in different parts of the city at one time or another? I'm cross-checking the last five years' worth of arrest records for each of these nine officers, and I'm looking at every parking ticket or moving violation they issued. I'm poking around to see if there are nine Jane Does who showed up dead around the times of these nine killings. Like I said, maybe those Jane Does are hookers who were present when our killer blew our cops away."

"What about the drugs?"

Q-Ball inclined his head. "Is the killer someone who was busted for possession? Is the killer a drug dealer who's holding a grudge against the NYPD? I don't know." He picked up a stack of the suicide files. "The connections are here, somewhere in this mountain of paper, in these CSU photos. We're looking at the goddamn connections and we don't see them." He dropped the folders. "I keep running this thing through and coming up empty. Odd little pieces that don't fit, like why are all the victims Catholic? Is it a fluke? Or did the killer know they were all Catholic?"

"Whoever did it takes the time to shower and change his clothes."

"A regular Mr. Clean and one cold-blooded son of a bitch. If he took out a whore at the same time, we're looking at eighteen murders." Ballantine went back to the pin map and flipped the bulletin board back around to face the wall. "Look, Gavin. If you really want to help, you can play detective on your own free time. But remember one thing. This investigation is off the record. Don't tell your partner or any other cop about it. If word gets out, I'm the one who takes the fall. Not you."

"Tell me what to do."

"Start with Donovan's apartment building. Talk to the neighbors. Maybe someone saw something. Canvas the video stores, and the laundromats too on the off chance the hula girl towels are sitting unclaimed somewhere. Go around to all the local bars, restaurants, and mini-marts. Talk to anyone who might've seen Donovan on the day he was killed. Maybe he was with someone."

Gavin stood up and turned to leave.

"One more thing, Ed."

"What's that?"

"Talk to the local hookers. Maybe one of them's missing. Maybe Danny was set up."

Maria Alvarez was present at Thursday afternoon's roll call.

Strega saw her sitting in the back of the room by herself, snapping her chewing gum and flipping through the *New York* magazine with her father's picture on the cover. He sat down next to her, waiting for his chance to apologize. She ignored him.

The tour sergeant ran through roll call and assignments. "Alvarez partners with Kelly. Now, special business. There's a fund-raiser at the Met tonight. Make sure the limos don't jam up Fifth Avenue. Double parking's okay if there's a driver present. Triple parking gets a ticket. Ballantine, any special security precautions we should know about?"

"No," Ballantine said. "The museum isn't in keeping with our shooters' profile. The Met's got more security than most third world countries."

Roll call was dismissed. The room remained full, buzzing with a dozen different conversations. Gavin was up front chatting with Kelly. Hansen was talking to Ballantine.

"Maria," Strega started.

"Jonnie?" She began to twist one of her earrings. It was a small gold stud. She twisted it to the left, then to the right, then unscrewed the back and pulled the stud out.

"I'd like to start over with you," Strega offered. "I owe you an apology."

She studied his face looking for sincerity. "Aren't you the little gentleman." A laugh rumbled deep in her throat. "Your mama taught you nice manners."

Strega felt tremendous relief. It was working. He rushed on with an explanation. "I was having a bad day, and you were in the line of fire, so to speak."

"You insulted me on a couple of occasions. I guess you're used to being around more beautiful women than me. You know, Princeton types."

"You're wrong, Maria. You *are* a beautiful woman. My not wanting to go out with you has nothing to do with your looks."

"Just my brains, like you said." She laughed again, but a split second later the laugh was gone and her eyes had narrowed, and somehow her lips were next to Strega's ear and she was whispering: "But I'm smarter than you give me credit for." She held her right earlobe with her left hand and stretched it tight. Then she pressed the sharp stud into the virgin flesh high up on the lobe.

Strega winced. He waited for her to pull back, but she clenched her jaw and punched the stud all the way through. Pain washed over her face. Bright blood bubbled up around the gold. Maria calmly secured the stud with the earring back, and started to twist the stud around in its new, raw red hole.

Then, suddenly, she shot out of her chair and slapped Strega across the face.

"One more dirty comment," she shouted, "and I'm filing harassment charges. This is the last time I'm going to tell you, Strega. I'm *not* going out with you. I'm *not* going to bed with you."

A hush fell over the squad room. A couple of officers tittered. Kelly moved toward Maria protectively. Maria waved him away. Hansen looked at Strega and shook her head. *Not smart,* the head shake said. Ballantine scowled.

Gavin ambled over to Strega. "You've got two ladies pissed off at you now," Gavin whispered, "one Italian and one Spanish. You should stay away from Latin women."

Thirteen

The night air was heavy and smelled of rain. Black thunderheads rumbled as Ramon Alvarez hurried up the broad esplanade of the Metropolitan Museum. Limos jammed the street behind him, waiting three deep, engines idling, windows rolled up tight against the hot summer air. In front of him, the Metropolitan was ablaze with lights. The twin oval fountains were lit and flowing. A brilliant banner stamped with gold lettering unfurled from the roof: SEEING RED—FUNDING THE FIGHT AGAINST AIDS.

This was the most important fund-raiser of the year, with five hundred of the city's richest, most influential citizens attending. It was a place to woo politicians and the men who make them. Ramon Alvarez had plenty of wooing to do. He was planting the seeds for his own brilliant political future.

The P.C. wore a tuxedo, like all the men around him. But unlike them, Ramon Alvarez was alone. He had no wife, no girlfriend, no casual date. His public image was carefully cultivated. He was a grieving widower, even after all these years. The press and the public liked that.

He gave his invitation to one of the many door guards. The crowd swept him in through the Great Hall and into a splendid banquet room filled with fifty round tables set for parties of ten. Each table had a living centerpiece—a model wearing a red evening dress designed for the gala by the world's top fashion designers. The gowns were going to be auctioned off after dinner and the proceeds donated to AIDS research.

Ramon Alvarez worked his way through the room to

his front-row seat. He looked up at the centerpiece and
raised an eyebrow. The model sat on a red velvet stool
in the middle of the table. He recognized her. Chriska,
the eighteen-year-old girl who had zoomed to the top of
the modeling world. She wore a red Valentino back-
baring dress and strappy red evening shoes. Her rich
black hair was stacked high. One length of it tumbled
down her ivory back. The Cold War is over, Alvarez
thought. Russia won.

He sat down. The mayor sat to his left. A well-known
opera diva sat to his right. The governor faced him. The
P.C. chatted through dinner, talking local and national
politics, art and music, fashion and film, all with ease.
When the dessert plates were cleared, the lights dimmed
and a band began to play. One by one the fifty centerpiece models stood up.

Chriska rose. Her red dress floated lightly around her
body. She swayed to the music and blew kisses to the
men. The music pulsed. Then, underneath it, there was
another sound. An odd popping noise. Firecrackers, Alvarez thought, smiling up at Chriska, happy there were
firecrackers for her. Chriska smiled down at him. Suddenly, she stumbled. Alvarez gasped. The right side of
her face was gone. The firecrackers, he realized, were
really bursts of automatic weapons. He looked at the
room. The models were falling, one after another,
plucked off like ducks in a carnival shooting gallery.

Alvarez turned back to Chriska. Her magnificent Russian body swayed to the left, then fell hard, collapsing
into the astonished police commissioner's lap. The lights
went out.

The patrol car windshield wipers slapped back and
forth. The FM radio buzzed with updates on Emma's
progress. The heart of the hurricane was drifting off to
sea. Emma was going to slide right by Manhattan and
do nothing more than flick the city with her tail. Even
so, the tail was full of fury. It had all the feel of something tropical blown up from the Florida keys—a hot,
whipping wind and raindrops as big as golf balls. The

wipers slapped away at the golf balls, but they were coming down too hard and too fast. Strega was forced to pull over and wait it out.

The police radio buzzed softly with the sound of Central tossing out assignments to other precincts. Strega worked through a bag of chili tortilla chips. The jalapeño smell filled the car, but it was the steady crunch-crunch of Strega chewing that grated on Gavin's nerves. The noise reminded him too much of Donovan, of how they used to cruise the streets of the Three-Four passing a bag of corn chips between them, talking sports, Department politics, or sometimes not talking at all, just enjoying an easy silence between two old friends and letting the crunch-crunch of their shared corn chips say it all.

Hell, Donovan had invented an entire system for rating foods on the basis of the crunch. Over the years they had crunched their way through every major food group. The thousand little things that bonded two friends together, sealed the friendship, and stamped it with its own unique imprint. It was the little stuff Gavin missed most—like the corn chips.

Strega took another handful of chips and crunched. Some things were still sacred, Gavin thought. Shoot the messenger: "Can't you eat something that doesn't make so much noise?"

Strega looked thoughtful as he munched. "Ice cream's quiet. How about that?"

"As long as you don't get one of those waffle-cone things." Donovan had awarded the waffle cone a nine on his crunch meter.

Strega helped himself to more chips. Gavin rubbed a peephole in the fogged window glass and peered out into the dark. Shops were closed, shuttered, and locked for the night. The sidewalks were empty and the streets nearly so. Hurricane Emma had chased everyone inside. A taxi cab splashed by. A long, dark Mercedes limo sailed up the street.

Gavin stifled a yawn. Funny, he thought. Thursday nights in the Three-Four, a patrol cop was always ready for the worst. Thursday night was game night, when the streets doubled as an asphalt playing field where ugly urban gang sports were played. He remembered the burn of a thousand pairs of eyes turned on him, looking down from windows and out of cars, a thousand pairs of eyes, accusing and hateful, burning right through the dark night at two white cops cruising by.

Gavin was relieved when Danny wanted to be transferred out. Gavin was scared too. What chance did you have of staying alive in a neighborhood where life was worthless? Once the cops had been hated and feared there. Then they were just hated. Then they were hated and hunted. When Danny said "Let's bail," Gavin was happy to go.

Central's rapid fire voice filled the patrol car, snapping Gavin back to the present. "All units in the vicinity of the Metropolitan Museum, ten-thirty in progress. Shots fired. All units, respond forthwith."

Forthwith. *Get your ass over there as fast as possible.*

Strega accelerated out into the street.

Central spat out more information. "Undetermined number of suspects, armed and dangerous. Approximately five hundred civilians inside. Proceed with caution."

Strega rubbed the foggy windshield. "Our shooters?" he asked.

Gavin shook his head. "Could be a copy-cat crime. So far the bridal boys have been careful to hit places with no security. The Met's a fortress, which makes me wonder how the fuck anyone with a machine gun got past museum security in the first place."

Strega jumped a yellow light, then made a hard left flying west down Eighty-sixth Street. Gavin could swear the car was aqua-planing. No way the tires were touching pavement, not with the stomach-in-throat kind of feeling he had. Strega shot through a red light.

"Take it easy," Gavin complained, gripping the dash.

"Don't worry," Strega said, keeping his eyes on the rain-slicked street in front of him. "I'm good at this."

Eighty-sixth Street dead-ended into Fifth Avenue, and
Strega went into the left turn hard. The momentum
knocked Gavin into the side of his door. He heard the
sickening grate of metal against cement curb. A lamp
post loomed.

"Shit," Gavin swore, closing his eyes, anticipating the
impact. He felt Strega make a gutsy correction. The car
lurched and bumped and skidded; then it stopped. Gavin
opened his eyes. They had jumped the curb and were
sitting on the museum esplanade, a foot shy from a sparkling oval fountain.

"Told you I was good," Strega said. He put his hat
on and got out.

Gavin followed. The rain blew down sideways into his
face. He squinted. Fifth Avenue was a sea of red. There
were the red spinning lights of two dozen patrol cars
and ambulances, the red taillights of a hundred limos,
and the rain-slicked black asphalt reflecting it all.

Gavin turned his face into the wind and looked up at
the museum. A red banner unfurled from the roof and
billowed out like a spinnaker. Gavin turned and ran to
join Strega at the curb. Deputy Inspector Wilson's car
was jackknifed up on the sidewalk. He was standing on
the hood in a yellow rain slicker and shouting orders
through a bullhorn to the cops crowded around him.
Mike Kelly and Maria Alvarez were there.

"We going in?" Gavin asked Kelly.

"Negative," Kelly replied. "We don't know if the gunmen are still inside, and we don't know how many of
them there are. The mayor's in there. So is the governor
and the P.C. We may have a hostage situation. Wilson's
waiting for ESU."

ESU was New York's version of a SWAT team. Gavin
had worked with ESU on drug raids and knew the unit
would show up in heavy armored vans packed with assault weapons: Heckler & Koch MP5 9mm submachine
guns, Ruger Mini 14 carbines in two lengths, Remington
660 rifles with telescopic sights, not to mention a couple
of tear-gas guns and body-length bulletproof shields that
looked like turtle shells. ESU men were rigorously

trained in war tactics like bomb chemistry and hostage negotiation. There was no one more capable, Gavin thought, moving back through the crowd of cops, looking for Strega.

Maria watched Wilson. It was exhilarating, standing in the wind and the rain listening to the inspector's powerful voice organizing the scene.

Wilson singled out four officers from the Central Park precinct. "I want yellow tape up now. Run it all the way around the perimeter of the far sidewalk there. No civilians or newsmen inside the tape. I've got what looks like forty uniformed officers in front of me.

"The first ten of you I want working with the cops in the street. Get the limos out. We need space for emergency vehicles. The next ten, man the police line. You two mounted officers work the police line too. The rest of you sit tight. We got five hundred guests inside and who knows how many more service and museum personnel. When they start coming out, try like hell to contain and organize them."

Maria shivered with excitement. Ramon Alvarez was inside the museum. She hoped the shooters had shoved their Uzis into his chest and fired. She hoped the P.C. was dead.

"The injured get priority," Wilson went on. "Get them to the ambulances. Write down their names and addresses as well as which hospital they're being taken to. Uninjured witnesses go into those transport vans over there. The vans will shuttle witnesses to precinct houses. Five hundred people is too many for any one precinct. We're going to break it out to fifty per precinct spread across ten city precincts."

Maria reached for Kelly's hand in the dark and turned her face up to look at him. She knew right away that he mistook her anticipation for fear. He didn't know how much she welcomed the danger, how much she loved it.

A half dozen blue-and-white vans marked POLICE EMERGENCY SERVICE roared up over the curb side and across the museum esplanade. The doors opened. Men in helmets spilled out, dozens of them, slinging automatic weapons over their shoulders and holding man-sized shields in front of their bodies.

The unit commander approached Wilson. Wilson leaned down. They exchanged a few words, and then the commander and two truck loads of his men stormed up to the museum and disappeared inside. A dozen soldiers veered away into the park and a dozen remained, stationed at the foot of the stairs, weapons drawn, ready to act as a human net if any of the killers were foolish enough to try for a Fifth Avenue exit.

One soldier jumped up on the hood of the car and spoke rapidly to Wilson. The inspector nodded, then bellowed into his bullhorn. "Central Park is now closed. We've got units at every park entrance. Aviation's coming in too, the whole goddamn cavalry."

Maria heard the bass *thwump-thwump* of chopper blades. She looked up. Six choppers whacked their way across the turbulent sky, toward the museum, Emma's gale-force winds tossing them like paper cups. They swayed crazily in the air but moved stubbornly ahead, blasting the museum roof with premier-sized spotlights. A celebration, Maria thought, watching the lights swinging left to right. Ramon is dead. When there was no more roof to search, the white-bellied birds dipped away and crisscrossed the dark park land behind the museum.

Suddenly, the museum doors opened.

"Go!" Wilson shouted.

Maria dropped Kelly's hand and raced to the stairs.

Gavin stood frozen for an instant, watching the panic, the stampede of people coming out of the museum—men in tuxedos, women in ball gowns, waiters, waitresses, security guards—running for their lives, past the officers, and right through the yellow crime-scene tape. Gavin plunged into the crowd.

A tall silver-haired man slipped on the rain-slicked steps. Rampaging feet kicked him. Gavin struggled to help him up. He stumbled with the weight. Strega appeared. "I'll take him," he said, lifting the man easily.

Gavin saw red fanning out across the victim's white dress shirt.

The man gripped Strega's collar. "Are you my son?"

"No," Strega said gently, "I'm a police officer. I'm here to help you."

"You look just like him. I want to see my son." The man shuddered once. His head fell back. Strega stared down at the slack jaw and the eyes open to the rain, and his own face turned the color of stone.

Gavin wanted to say something comforting, something wise, but a new tide of victims swept them apart.

Maria worked through the night, in the driving rain, never tiring—showing proper respect to her superiors, to Wilson. She was solicitous of Kelly, her partner, her one link to herself tonight, to Maria the cop, the good cop, the hardworking cop, dedicated, focused, caring, intent.

She felt strong, good, the way she might feel all the time if she did not have the dark, the pitch, the hollow, the wide, frightful place inside her. But now she moved swiftly and surely through the crowd, proud and graceful, offering help, hurrying victims to the waiting ambulances, murmuring words of comfort, lifting the wounded with a strength that belied her small size. She carried the victims, one after another, gently handing them over to the waiting medics, who stretched their hurt bodies out on gurneys on stark white sheets. She watched and waited while the gurneys were loaded into ambulances and ferried away.

She was proud of herself for her work. She was a model officer, confident and able in her smart uniform, the uniform she wore with pride. Suddenly, she froze in mid-stride. She saw him. *He is alive,* she thought. He did not die inside the museum. The shooters did not shove their muzzles up to his warm flesh and fire. There he was, walking, tall and angry, with purpose, bloodstained but alive. He slowed once he saw her. His face changed as he looked at her. Although they were a good distance apart, Maria could see the glint of his wet white teeth.

Reality cracked. Split. Shifted. Hate, fear, and rage washed over her. She felt Janus-faced. Her vision blurred. Her arm hurt. Kelly was standing next to her, gripping her elbow.

"Maria," he shouted over the hard, hissing rain. "Are you okay?"

She tilted her head slowly to look at him, at Kelly, at his jet black hair and the water streaming down his face like sweat. He looks like *him* with all that false concern, the voice ripe with worry, when all he must have been thinking was when she might finally spread her legs wide, like the wings of a gull, full and white and wide for him. Only for him. Always for him. For him and his fine face, the sweat streaming down his cheeks like rain.

A young woman slipped on the staircase. Strega crouched down beside her. She wore a red silk gown with a matching stole around her shoulders. Her face was chiseled perfection. It moved his sculptor's heart. Her eyes were closed. Strega circled his arms around her protectively. "Are you hurt?" he asked.

Her eyes were large liquid pools of blue. "No," she said. "I felt something terrible, but it's gone." Her blue eyes went blank, and her long body slumped into his.

Strega pushed the stole aside. The silk dress was torn, revealing her rib cage, and her flesh there had been ripped away. He touched raw bone. Strega lifted her. She was taller than Rosemary, but lighter by twenty-five pounds and her perfume smelled of lilies. He shouldered his way through the mob. Breaking free, he ran with her in his arms, across the esplanade to a waiting ambulance. He laid her down on a gurney.

"She's bi-fib," a medic shouted, ripping her dress and going to work on her chest.

Strega couldn't help but look at her body. The lines were long and fluid. She had none of Rosemary's rich, voluptuous curves. She was fragile as a foal and her waist was tiny. Strega knew he could circle it with both hands. The rain bounced off her skin. She looked violated with her breasts bare, the shattered bone sticking out of her sternum and the big man pounding on her. The rain soaked her hair flat to her head, and her face had turned a sickly white. Her eyes were open wide to the sky.

A voice whispered in his ear. "Is that how you like them, Jonnie? Cold and dead? You can do whatever you want when they're dead."

He whipped around. Her pupils were giant. Her hand was on his waist, then it was on his chest, then it was on his lips, touching them, caressing them. Suddenly, Maria Alvarez dropped her hand and disappeared into the crowd.

Strega turned back to the girl. One of the attendants was passing his hand over her face, brushing off rainwater and closing her wide, staring sky blue eyes. Then the bright white sheet covered her, and the attendants lifted the gurney and carried it away. The red silk stole lay forgotten on the ground. Strega picked it up and smelled lilies. He folded his body down on the curb. His stomach tossed and turned. He hung his head and retched. A hand touched his shoulder. Hansen dropped next to him, held out a bottle of water.

"Drink," she said. "It will help."

Strega drank. Hansen was wrong. His stomach lurched again and the water came up.

Hansen sighed and patted his back. "I feel that way too, Strega."

A young woman grabbed Gavin's elbow. She wore a filmy red gown and red high heels. She towered over him. "My best friend's still inside. Help me find her."

Gavin had a hard time hearing. The choppers were back, circling the museum, blades straining in the heavy wind. Gavin saw Strega heaving in the gutter and started for him. Hansen waved him away.

Gavin turned around and tried to find the tall girl in red, but the esplanade was suddenly full of tall girls in red. Medics were pouring out of the museum with the dead and injured models. Gavin watched them stream by. A girl in red lurched down the stairs carrying another

girl in her arms. The rain beat down, pasting their gowns
to their bodies. The faces of some were white with fear;
the faces of others were white with death. They were
the girls of his nightmare come to life, parading past
him, and the nightmare was hideous.

A gurney rumbled by carrying one of his nightmare
girls. Blood oozed from a bullet hole in her chest. Then
a dozen more gurneys slid past, and Gavin stood frozen,
looking at all the young, slender beauties stretched out
on starched white hospital sheets—white sheets made
long enough to throw over their pale, waxen faces.

Strega stumbled out of the gutter, feeling ashamed. It
was the fear. He was *so afraid,* like he was walking
around in mine fields, waiting to step on one. Next time
or the time after, it would be him. The bullet would tear
through *his* sternum, shred *his* bone and heart, and leave
him to stare sightless at the deep black sky. *Just like his
father.* Yes, any day, he knew, he could go down just
like his father. A young girl with sky blue eyes was dead.
Next time it might be him.

He smelled perfume. No lilies now. Cinnamon and
musk. A pair of heavy regulation shoes appeared next
to him. He looked up. At Alvarez. At her wet black hair
whipping loosely in the wind and the water running
down her cheeks in rivers. Her uniform stuck to her
body like she was wearing nothing at all. He thought
she was crying. But Maria was smiling, so the water on
her face must have just been rain. An ambulance pulled
up next to her. The flashing emergency lights sliced
across her face, illuminating her smile.

She leaned in close, whispered in his ear. "It's a bad
trip, seeing all this death, Jonnie. Does it make you
afraid? Does it make you wonder how it was for Vincent
at the end?"

How did she know?

"Was it like this, full of cops and cars?" she whispered. "Was it raining that night too? Or was it still?
How did Vincent Strega die? Who was holding his hand
when he slipped from this world into the next? What

did his face look like? Did he live long enough after the shot to feel pain? Did he live long enough to feel regret? Or did he die instantly? The answers are all in Philadelphia, Jonnie. I'm surprised you haven't asked the questions before now. Maybe you just didn't love Vincent enough to care. Or maybe you loved him too much. Either way, you owe it to yourself to know how it was.''

She put her fingers on his lips and separated them. She slipped a finger into his mouth, running it over the hard enamel of his teeth, up over his gums. Then she slipped the finger out and put it in her own mouth. She sucked it slowly. She put her wet, sucked finger up to his temple. "The answers are in Philly. I promise you, Jonnie. It's not the way you thought." She dropped her hand and walked away from him, the gun belt heavy on her lush hips, the rain water running down her head, the wind whipping her hair.

Strega's gums tingled. He ran his tongue over the gums, and then his tongue tingled too.

Kelly passed Gavin and raised a tired hand in greeting.

A familiar *thwump-thwump* filled the air. Gavin looked up. Another chopper, this one with a big NEWS FIVE stenciled on its belly, hovered above, swaying in the wind, spinning its white searchlight over the esplanade. *Whores,* Gavin thought.

Sirens wailed, close in and far away.

The News Five chopper banked away from the museum and drifted off.

Gavin walked wearily across the pavement, following Kelly. Kelly stopped suddenly. Gavin stopped too. Wilson had Strega backed up to a wall. He was shouting and poking the rookie in the chest.

Maria Alvarez stood a few yards away, on the museum staircase with the P.C. Although Gavin couldn't hear the words, her agitated gestures were clear. She was upset. Maria was pointing at Strega and shouting hysterically. Ramon Alvarez looked over at Strega and frowned. He put an arm around Maria and pulled her close. He brushed a strand of hair out of her face.

It was a disturbing tableau, father and daughter standing in the pouring rain, staring at Strega, hatred stamped on both their proud faces. There was something else there too, but Gavin couldn't pin it down.

Then a new wave of victims spilled past him, sweeping him along, away from Kelly, Maria, and Ramon, and his troubled young partner.

Hours later, Gavin looked up at the sky. Emma had blown out. The rain had softened to a light drizzle. The wild winds had died down to a tree-tickling breeze, and the sky was empty, free of the swaying white-bellied birds. The last ambulance had pulled away. The ESU vans were gone. There were more cops inside the museum now than outside, and without the wave of victims spilling across the esplanade, an uncanny quiet descended over the crime scene.

One man sat alone on the bottom step of the big staircase. Gavin approached. It was Ballantine, head in hands, smoking a cigarette, looking beat. Gavin dropped down next to him.

"The senator was in there tonight," Ballantine said, wiping his forehead. "The mayor was in there. The fucking P.C. was in there tonight. Fuck."

"They get hurt?"

"Miraculously, no."

"The museum's got state-of-the-art security," Gavin mused. "Cameras, round-the-clock guards, motion detectors, the works. How did the shooters get in?"

"They put on a couple of tuxedos and walked in with everybody else."

"How did they get their weapons in?"

"Guitar cases." Q-Ball laughed roughly. "They said they were with the band. The scabs had the place cased. They knew exactly what room to go to, and they sure as fuck knew what to do once they got there. The room was fitted with surveillance cameras. Guards in a safe room were watching the whole dinner on the surveillance video monitors.

"The shooters waited until the lights dimmed and the band began to play. Then they opened fire and took the surveillance cameras out. With the monitors suddenly down, the safe-room guards didn't know if there were two gunmen inside or twenty, so they stayed put. The shooters planned it that way. They knew they had the twin advantage of surprise and uncertainty. They knew they would have museum security bamboozled."

"There were other guards inside the museum. Why didn't they nail the shooters when they made a run for it?"

"Like I said, the scabs were wearing tuxedos. When they finished looting, they blasted the dining room lights out. They must have put the money and jewelry in a couple of spare guitar cases. Then, when the crowd ran out the doors, the shooters ran with them, carrying their guitar cases. They looked like a pair of scared musicians. It was brilliant. Fucking brilliant. A Trojan fucking horse. In the panic they slipped out, right past us."

"Where do you think they are right now?" Gavin asked.

"Long gone. It's a big fucking city."

"What are the odds of catching them?"

"Thousand to one," Ballantine admitted. "A *million* to one, even if we put every goddamn genius detective in the Department on the case. It's going to be a solid brass investigation led by the chief of detectives himself. Wouldn't be surprised to see the FBI in on it too."

"What about the art?"

"Untouched. Stolen works from the Met would be too hot to try to fence." Ballantine shook his head. "Nope, the scabs went in after the rich folks' jewelry and watches. There were enough diamonds in there to live a hundred lifetimes on. This is how it goes now. Their weapons will be dumped in the East River before midnight. Then the shooters sneak out of town, quiet as mice, with all the goodies stuffed in a bag. The stolen cash is untraceable.

"The jewels will be fenced, little by little, over time, but not in New York. There are plenty of big cities a train ride away. Baltimore, Washington, Philly. Without the jewels, without the guns, without the perps themselves, we've got no case. Simple as that. We'll never fucking find them."

Ballantine flipped his cigarette into the darkness, stood, and lumbered back up the stairs into the museum.

At seven o'clock Friday morning, Strega sat bleary-eyed in the squad room, punching keys on a typewriter. His stomach felt raw from too much black coffee. He typed slowly, reluctant to make any mistakes that would cost him time correcting errors. Precinct houses were time warps, and despite the architectural renovation this station house was no exception. The squad room was littered with old manual typewriters.

Strega had one last statement to file. Dozens of Styrofoam cups, stale ashtrays. and half-eaten donuts littered the metal desks around him. It had been an ironic scene—the squad room cluttered with women in ball gowns, the men in their tuxedos, and the cops clacking away on this antequated equipment.

A few tired patrolmen sifted through, moving slowly, finishing their paperwork. Strega pushed his coffee cup away. The smell made his stomach rock. He tried to focus on the typewriter. The face of the dying man popped up. *I want to see my son.*

Strega thought of his own father. What happened when he went down? Was some rookie cop holding Vincent Strega while his life seeped out all over Philadelphia cement? Did Vincent ask for his son? What were his last words, and who did he speak them to? Alvarez was right, Strega suddenly thought. He knew nothing about the final minutes of his father's life. No one had ever told him. *He had never asked.*

Alvarez's voice ricocheted around in his head. *The answers are all in Philadelphia.*

*   *   *

"You know, Strega, it's ironic," Gavin said later when they were both slumped on the locker room bench.

"What's that?"

"I worked the Three-Four for more than two decades. When Donovan and I transferred to the One-Nine, I thought it was a free ride to retirement."

"Looks like you guessed wrong."

"In this last week I've seen blood, violence, and murder just like the old days, and I wonder. Maybe it's me, maybe it's following me. Maybe it will follow me the fuck into retirement. I can see it now. There we are, Shell and me, tottering around in Florida. I tee up at the tenth hole and get mugged by a kid with an Uzi. *Hand over your driver. And your teeth.* I can't fucking wait." He tied his shoelaces. "I'm going to go home and sleep. After that I'm going to go prowling around like Dick Tracy and try to put a few pieces of the puzzle in place."

"What puzzle is that?"

Gavin stopped short, realizing he had spoken his thoughts aloud. He looked Strega over. To hell with Ballantine's code of secrecy. "You want to come along? Wear your uniform. I could use the help. Come at seven and I'll throw in dinner. I'll do better than that. I'll grill up some of my world-famous chicken."

"I'm happy to help, but what am I helping you do?"

Gavin scribbled a map on a scrap of paper. He printed his telephone number, then handed the paper to Strega. "You're going to help me find out who killed Donovan."

Fourteen

He came for her at dawn. She knew he would. He took her hard and fast, then left without a word.

When it was over and he was gone, Maria cowered nude in the yellow canvas butterfly chair, turning her shield over and over in her small hand. The doorknob rattled. He's back, she thought, frantic but frozen. The door opened. It wasn't him. It was Angel who came creeping in, bolting the door safely behind her, kneeling by Maria's side. Angel didn't ask, and how she knew Maria couldn't guess. But Angel knew. Maria rested her cheek on her knees. Angel stroked her hair.

She and Angel were bound by hate—Angel hating every nameless man plunging into her, and Maria hating one man the most, the smiling man, the cajoling man, the man who whispered her name at the same time his wandering hands traveled her body, making it his own.

Angel never asked questions, never asked why Maria didn't just say no. *No* was a powerless word, a begging word—*No, No, No* cried in counterpoint to his own chant, *Maria, Maria, Maria*. The word no was nothing. Angel knew that. She had said no to one man, and that man had sent someone to beat her. Angel said no and look what happened to her. The only question Angel ever asked was the one she was asking now, leaning in, her battered lips close to Maria's, candy sweet on her breath.

"Why don't you just kill him?" Angel hissed.

Angel left the question out there, hanging, and Maria loved her more for not pressing—for not talking at all now. It was Angel's turn to heal. She held Maria and rocked her for a long while, then left as quietly as she had come.

Sometimes Angel's love was almost enough to make Maria forget her hate. Almost, but not quite. The hate brought on the need, and the need had risen now as it sometimes did when he finished with her. Maria put her shield in her mouth and bit. The sharp points drove into her tongue and cheek, but through the pain she still felt the need. She spat the shield out.

The need. The need. The terrible need.

Maria rose from the chair and walked swiftly down the hall, her thighs hurting from where he had been rough. She dressed quickly in a fresh uniform and left the apartment. It was seven o'clock on Friday morning. It was time. Her lover was waiting—her lover with his soft, shy hands. It was time to play the game.

Strega left his brownstone Friday evening. The night felt heavy around him as he walked the short block to his parking garage. José was the attendant on duty.

"Hey, Officer Strega, how you doing?" José jogged down the ramp and reappeared a few minutes later behind the wheel of Strega's new black Jeep. He hopped out and patted the hood. "She's a beauty!"

"Thanks," Strega said, getting in. He tooted the horn, rolled out of the driveway, and turned left.

A beat-up white Celica fell in behind the Jeep. Strega noticed the car because it was low-slung and had windows tinted so dark, it was impossible to see in. The Celica trailed him across town to the Midtown Tunnel. It vanished at the toll gates, but reappeared ten minutes later, right behind him on the expressway, riding up tight on the Jeep's tail. Strega tapped the brakes in a warning. The Celica pulled closer. Strega changed lanes. The Celica drifted over behind him. Strega slowed down, hoping it would pass. The Celica hung back. Strega accelerated. The Celica did too. Every time Strega glanced in the rearview mirror, the Celica was there, white and low, the front license tag missing.

The exit sign for Gavin's town loomed. Strega put his

signal on as if he were moving left, but he veered off to the right at the last second, shooting down the exit ramp. The Celica sailed on down the expressway. Strega relaxed. It had been nothing more than a simple game of cat and mouse. He'd let it unnerve him for no reason at all.

Gavin slept through the day Friday.

He woke in the early evening, dressed in faded NYPD gym shorts, old laceless sneakers, and a worn out T-shirt, then went down to the kitchen and piled a tray high with ingredients for his summer barbecue. He carried the tray out to his rear deck.

Gavin hummed while he prepared the pair of chickens for the round potbellied barbecue. Grilling was a summer ritual. He loved painting the sweet sauce on with a long brush, poking the coals with a long-handled fork, and pushing the splayed birds around on grill slats thick with years of barbecue goo. He grinned to himself. So what if it was a hundred and five degrees outside? It was summertime, and certain joys even the heat couldn't take away.

In years past Donovan used to sit there on the deck with Gavin, shouting out opinions on Gavin's grilling technique, taste-testing the barbecue sauce, and wrapping ears of sweet summer corn in foil to be grilled up in the bed of smoldering charcoal. Jillian, his wife, used to show up most Fridays with all her frenetic party-time energy, as put on and fake as her spidery eyelashes. She'd mix up a pitcher of gin and tonics, or margaritas or daiquiris—the drink changed each summer—and work away at it all by herself until the heavy glass pitcher was empty. In the early years the pitcher lasted through dinner. In recent years the pitcher was empty before the chickens ever made it off the grill.

Everyone saw the signs of trouble. Jillian drank recklessly, as though the acrid Jack Daniel's or gin fizzes could bring her something her gentle husband couldn't. Even Danny knew the summer she left him—his last summer alive—that her leaving was a blessing in disguise. *With the exception of Katy,* Gavin corrected him-self. That last summer Danny would sit there by the grill doing all the *me-grims* and the *glum-glums* before dinner to get it out of his system.

"As if the no-good, pot-head teenage boys Jillie sleeps with aren't enough," Donovan used to complain, "she's got to give Katy a parade of stepfathers named Jack Daniel's, Johnnie Walker, and Tom Collins." At this point Donovan would suck his cheeks in and chew on them while he watched the flames lick the chicken skin black.

Then he'd slap his big hand down on the wooden deck railing and say: "Well, hell. I'm going to win this one, Ed. I'm going to get Katy away from Jillian, and when I do, I'm going to devote the rest of my God-given days to raising her right, to giving her a good life. I may not be able to change the world, but I can make a difference with my own little girl. I can do that, can't I?" Gavin would nod quietly and flip the chickens. Donovan would point out how the birds needed another brush of sauce, and then, while Gavin was painting the goo on, Danny would cheer up. "My Katy's an angel, isn't she?"

"Through and through," he'd agree.

Donovan would nod then and boast some more. "Pretty and bright, a hell of an artist, and she's only five years old. Look what she drew for me yesterday." Danny would chuckle and unfold a child's crayon draw-ing out of his pocket. Sometimes it was a picture of bright-beaked birds, sometimes of multicolored tigers, but her favorite subject was by far and away her own huge daddy. Thinking about the crayon drawings re-minded Gavin of the collection of Katy's work he'd found hanging in Donovan's kitchen, of the powerful hope in the last drawing, the great big smiling sun and her giant daddy smiling next to it.

Gavin poked the chicken with his cooking fork and cursed the fact that his Sherlock Holmes act would be at the mercy of the tour schedule—one that had him down for a string of eight-to-four tours starting the next day, Saturday, and running straight through to the following Thursday.

Gavin wanted to call in sick for a week, and then spend that week doing nothing but trying to come up with the one piece of evidence that would lead him to Donovan's killer. Gavin wanted to find the killer and string him up by his toes, kill him slowly and painfully, then leave his murdering corpse swinging in the trees for the fat, hungry flies. Yes, that was it. Leave the motherfucker to decompose in a cloud of feasting flies.

Gavin's insides churned. The American justice system was too hit-or-miss to send Donovan's killer into it. Gavin wanted to invent a new kind of justice, and there was only one kind for the sick son of a bitch who had murdered Danny. Revenge was the word—an eye for an eye. Old-fashioned but satisfying.

Gavin's vengeful euphoria hollowed out. Fantasy was fantasy, but the fact was—as Ballantine had pointed out—Gavin had nothing to go on but his sneaky feelings of wrongdoing. No leads, no names or faces or smoking guns with which to identify the murderer. Gavin brooded, and forgot about the chicken.

The front door chimed. He leaned into the kitchen, where Shelly was finishing a plate full of steamed veggies. She hated grilled chicken. Something about the fat content. "Get that, will you?" he said. "It's Strega."

With Strega's help, Gavin hoped he might turn over enough rocks to see something scuttle out.

When Shelly Gavin opened the door, Strega had to hide his surprise. She was tall, slim, and very pretty as he expected, but her clothes were not. Rosemary liked fashion and made enough money to indulge herself, so Strega knew what expensive women's clothes looked like.

Shelly Gavin's were clearly top of the line. She wore a smartly cut raw silk tunic over matching pants and a silk scarf he could have sworn was a real Gucci. He looked at her feet. Shoes didn't lie. Hers were beautiful Gucci leather sandals. Four hundred dollars a pair.

Strega knew the price. Rosemary bought all her sandals
from Gucci. But Rosemary was a big-time stock trader,
not a cop's wife. Cops' wives didn't dress that way, not
where Strega was from anyway.

"Mrs. Gavin?" Strega asked.

"Shelly to you, if you're Ed's new partner," she replied, waving him in.

"What if I'm a salesman and not his new partner?"
Strega quipped.

"Then you call me Mrs. Gavin, and I'd be tremendously disappointed because Ed said his new partner
might drop by. I'm secretly dying to meet him. Ed said
he's quite a guy. Couple of Princeton degrees in his back
pocket, literate, amateur artist, hot-shot driver."

"That's a pretty accurate summation."

"But not complete. Ed forgot to mention that you're
a hunk." She smiled sweetly up at him. "Besides, if
you're a salesman, what are you doing wearing an
NYPD uniform?"

Strega laughed and held out a bottle of wine. "A small
offering from my homeland."

"Since when do they make chianti in Philadelphia?"
Shelly said, taking the bottle.

"Ed's giving all my secrets away. Women find me
more attractive if they think I'm fresh off the boat."

"Strega, something tells me it isn't your rugged roots
women find attractive." She closed the door. Shelly
steered him into the kitchen and pointed. "He's out
there grilling his world-famous chicken. I've been ad-
vised this is a working dinner. I'll leave you two alone."

Strega joined Gavin on the deck. "Didn't know you
liked to cook."

Strega was dressed in a freshly pressed uniform—
knife-creased pants, starched shirt, even his five o'clock
shadow looked sharp. Next to Strega, Gavin felt like a
slob. He ran a hand over his sweaty face and pointed
his cooking fork at Strega. "I don't cook. I barbecue.
There's a difference."

"How's that?"

"Cooking's a year-round homemaker-type thing.

Barbecuing goes back to man's primitive roots, when a man hunted down his food and grilled it over an open fire."

Strega pointed at the grill. "The clan will go hungry tonight if that's all you brought in from the hunt."

Gavin followed his look to the smoldering chickens. "Damn." He lunged for the birds with his fork.

"It's too late," Strega observed. "I can cook dinner. Do you have any Italian food in the house? Tomatoes, garlic, olive oil?"

"The only things remotely Italian in this house are a stack of frozen pizzas and, of course, you. We'll pick up some takeout and eat in the car." Gavin untied his apron.

"The mystery continues," Strega said, following Gavin inside.

"I'll be right down." Gavin disappeared upstairs.

Strega wandered into the living room. There was a gallery of photos on the wall. He studied them. Single subject. A girl. All the usual shots documenting her life. What surprised Strega was the big color shot of a trim and fit Gavin grinning like crazy, with his arm around the subject. The girl's face looked a lot like Shelly's.

Gavin reappeared dressed in his uniform. "Let's go," he said from the doorway.

"Who's this?" Strega asked, pointing at the picture.

"That's Alex." Gavin turned and walked out.

Twenty minutes later, they were sitting in the Tempo in a low-rent neighborhood eating Chinese. Gavin kept the engine running and the air conditioning pumping, and in between mouthfuls of spicy shrimp, he gave Strega the rundown on the streak of suicides in general and Ballantine's suspicions in specific. Then, over fortune cookies, he gave Strega his own take on Donovan's death.

"So what do you think?" Gavin asked when he finished laying it all out.

Strega looked out at the grim apartment building across the street. Ten stories of prefab concrete squares.

Donovan's building. Q-Ball's renowned detective's instincts aside, Gavin's theory sounded like a long shot, a
wild-card hope born of frustration and anger. It smacked
of wishful thinking, Strega thought. If Gavin could prove
Donovan hadn't killed himself, Gavin would free himself
from a lifetime of guilt—a lifetime of regret—from feeling like he had failed his friend.

"What does Shelly think?" Strega asked, hoping to
deflect the original question.

"She doesn't know about this investigation," Gavin
said flatly.

"Why's that?"

"She'd give me a hard time, tell me Danny's dead and
buried and isn't coming back. Hell, she'd accuse me of
wishful thinking or some damn thing like that." Gavin
shook his head and tapped his chopsticks on the steering
wheel. "That's Danny's old building across the street."

"So you said. What are we doing here?" Strega asked.

"We're going to go door to door and talk to everyone
who lives there. Someone must've seen or heard something that night. When we finish here, we'll hit the video
stores. So, what do you think?" Gavin repeated.

"If Hansen's right, every criminal eventually makes
one dumb mistake." Assuming there was a crime committed in the first place, which Strega still doubted.

Gavin nodded his head enthusiastically. "That's all we
need. One dumb mistake. One solid piece of evidence I
can take to Ballantine." He tossed the shrimp boxes into
the takeout bag and threw the bag in the backseat.

"The building's got no security buzzer," Gavin stated.
"Open access to the lobby and the elevator. Open access
to the stairwells. According to the M.E.'s best guess,
Danny died in the afternoon of June twelfth. That was
a Monday. I found him Tuesday the thirteenth."

Gavin handed Strega a clipboard and a stack of notes.
"Keep track of every apartment number and whether or
not someone answers. Slip these notes with my name
and phone number under the doors of the empty apartments. We'll take alternate floors. You start with one.

I'll take two, which was Danny's floor. You take three, I'll take four, and so on. Let's go."

Gavin left Strega on the ground floor. He took the stairs up to the second floor and started at the end of the hall, working both sides in a methodical manner. There were ten apartments on the floor, and Danny's was in the middle. Gavin found people at home in the first five apartments, but those tenants all had day jobs and each of them had been working the Monday afternoon in question. Gavin hoped to find a housewife, a senior citizen, or a night-shift worker.

He went to one of the apartments next door to Danny's and rapped loudly. There was no answer. He rapped again and put his ear to the door. There was no television on inside, no barking dog, no music. This tenant, he thought, was one of the most important possible witnesses. Gavin scribbled a note with his name, home phone number, and the words *urgent police business.* He slipped the note under the door and moved to the apartment on the other side of Donovan's.

A television blared inside. He rapped loudly.

"Who is it?" a female voice called out over the racket.

"Police."

He heard the peephole scrape open. A moment later, the chain rattled and the door opened. A tall young woman in shorts and a Ferrari T-shirt looked out at Gavin. "Something wrong?" Her face was scrubbed clean, and her carrot red hair hung down to her waist.

"We're investigating the death of officer Daniel Donovan. He lived next door to you."

"Yeah," she said, twirling a length of hair around her finger. "I knew him. He was Irish, like me."

"Were you home on the afternoon of June twelfth?"

"No, I'm a teacher. I work weekdays, so I wouldn't have been here. It was a shock to me. He was a quiet neighbor. Nice man too. Always telling me to get a better lock on my door."

"Did you see him with anyone unusual before his death?"

"I never saw him with anyone other than his little

girl, Katy." She smiled. "She's one cute kid. You know little Katy?"

"Yeah."

"I felt real bad when I heard about Danny. He loved his little girl so much, you could see it. Doesn't seem fair her having to grow up without him."

"No, it doesn't. Did Danny ever give you any laundry to do?"

Her face clouded. "Weird question. I'm a teacher, not a maid."

"Sorry." Gavin wrote out his name and number. "In case you think of anything, give me a call."

She reached for the paper. "Sure. Hey, why is there an investigation? I mean, Danny killed himself."

"You saw him with Katy. Was that a man who'd desert his daughter?" He watched her face absorb the innuendo. "Like I said, you think of anything, anything at all, give me a call."

"I will."

Her door closed. Gavin turned to Danny's door. He touched the number 2C, then made his way down the hall back to the stairwell and up to the fourth floor, where he started rapping on doors again. The young teacher's words stayed with him: "He loved his little girl so much."

Danny did, Gavin thought. He sure did. He would have never left Katy. Never.

Two hours later, he and Strega stood under a street lamp, flipping through their notes.

"Ten apartments were empty," Strega said. "Here's the list if you want to check back with those tenants. Danny died in the afternoon. Almost every tenant I spoke to works day jobs. The five who don't are retired and hard of hearing. They don't go out much, and when they're in, their TV's are turned up so loud they wouldn't hear a gunshot if it went off right next to them."

"I came up with the same thing," Gavin sighed.

"However, one of the empty apartments was 1A."

"So?"

"So 1A is across from the exterior stairwell. The living room window faces the stairs. The tenant could have seen Danny come in with someone. I put a note under the door."

"Okay. Let's hit the video stores."

Gavin pulled out a map and pointed to a circle in red ink. "This marks a five-mile radius around Donovan's apartment building. According to the yellow pages, there are seven video stores within this circle. The closest is Blockbuster over at the mini-mall. That's about three minutes away. Knowing Danny, my bet is that it was the only place he ever went for tapes."

The manager of the Blockbuster shop was a young, clean-shaven man in his twenties. A name tag on his white oxford shirt identified him as Fred. "We've got one Donovan," Fred confirmed, peering at the computer screen. "A Daniel, D. 145 East Garden Street, 2C."

"What can you tell us about his video-rental activity?" Gavin asked.

Fred tapped on the keyboard and studied the screen again. "I've got a record going back to January of this year. Lots of kid-vid. Preschool stuff. In the three months between January and March, he went through our entire oldies collection of black-and-white detective movies. In March and April it looks like he had a thing for Bogart. Rented *Casablanca* twice. More kid-vid. Muppets, Sesame Street, Barney, that kind of thing. Then in the middle of May, all the rental activity stopped. Surprising. According to this, he used to rent four or five videos a week, sometimes more. The last rental was May 16. A Tuesday. He rented one film. Disney's *Lion King*. He returned the film the next day, May 17. That's it. Nothing since then. Strange isn't it?"

"Not really," Gavin said.

"Why's that?" Fred asked.

"His video player broke down."

"Did he get it fixed?"

"Didn't have a chance. He died three weeks later."

"Jesus," Fred said. "How?"

"That's what we're trying to find out," Gavin said.

"I guess I should put Mr. Donovan in the inactive file."

Gavin blinked back the tears. It happened from time to time. Out of nowhere. That cannonball feeling, like the fact that Danny was dead hadn't really sunk in. He focused on the video playback monitor in a corner of the store. King Kong squeezing Fay Wray in one fat, hairy fist. She kicking and flailing, staring horrified at the big ape mouth that wanted to swallow her into eternal darkness.

Danny, what was the last thing you saw before your life was snuffed out? Was it a face, Danny? Was it?

Then Strega was tapping him on the arm. "Come on, Ed. There's nothing more to learn tonight."

They drove in silence back to Ozone Park. When they passed the junior high school, Gavin slowed and checked the sidewalks as he always did, automatically looking for Alex.

He remembered the hours of that first night when she hadn't come home, how he and Shelly had waited, thinking she was out somewhere late, having fun, forgetting to call. He remembered watching the sun rise and seeing Shelly sitting scared in Alex's room. Then the stream of cops clomping through the house. Ballantine setting up at the school, interrogating Alex's friends and getting nowhere, learning nothing they didn't already know: Alex loved her family, her friends, her school. She wouldn't have run away.

He remembered the long, frightening hours of the next night, the frantic circling of the schoolyard, roaming the neighborhood side streets, calling and looking, beating on every door in a five-mile radius, and after that, the second night and then the third long night which became the tenth long night, then the twentieth, then the fortieth night, after which he stopped counting but never stopped looking.

There were nights even now when Gavin saw Shelly standing by the front window, standing and staring, and he knew she was still waiting. Waiting, waiting, waiting. After all these years she was waiting for Alex to come home. She was like him, he thought. She just couldn't give up.

"My daughter's name is Alexandra," he said suddenly when they pulled into the driveway. "Alex, for short."

"I didn't mean to pry," Strega said.

Gavin ignored him. "Five years ago, she went to school one day and never came home. She didn't turn up dead or alive, she never turned up at all. She just *vanished*. She was thirteen years old."

Strega nodded and let Gavin go on.

"The city eats them, Strega. Young girls. One way or another, it devours them. Danny helped me. Ballantine was in the One-Four then, but he helped me too. We organized search parties and mobilized the missing-persons unit. Q-Ball even got the FBI involved. We circulated pictures to every hospital and medical examiner's office in the country. We posted them in bus stations, airports, train stations, and on the nightly news in a hundred and fifty cities. We got Alex's picture printed on milk cartons all around the country.

"She was a milk carton kid. Thirteen years old, smiling out at hundreds of thousands of people as they poured milk on their breakfast cereal. All those people, and no one called with one goddamn lead. Not one phone call, not even a crank one. She just disappeared, like we had dreamed her, like she was never here at all."

Gavin took a deep breath, then went on. "Shelly got it in her head once that Alex had gone off to join a cult. When the Branch Davidian compound burned, she stayed glued to the TV, half crazy, thinking Alex was in there burning alive. The FBI gave us a full accounting of every member in the compound and pictures of most. I even spoke to a survivor on the phone. Alex had never been there.

"Every year more than a hundred thousand kids are snatched up by strangers. Hundreds of those kids usually turn up dead. Most, like Alex, never turn up. Someone must have snatched her off the street, on her way home.

Who was it, Strega? Who grabbed her? A man? A woman? A pair? What did they look like? What did they do to her? Did they stuff her in a box and bury her alive? Did they lock her in a basement? Is she still there, pounding on the walls, five years of her life gone, spent in the dark? Or did some man grab her? Toss her in his trunk and drive her out to the Long Island potato fields and rough her up just for fun. Is she buried out there with the potatoes?

"No, it's easier thinking she just up and left. Ran away, eloped, married, changed her name. I'd rather think she left on her own accord, even though I know she didn't. It's just too damn hard thinking it through any other way. Shelly cleans Alex's room and changes the bed sheets once a week, all for the day Alex comes home."

Strega knew enough not to offer false reassurance.

"She's never coming home, Strega. And the worst part's not knowing for sure what happened. That's the worst part—not ever being able to bury her, to say good-bye, to let go. To just goddamn let go. Danny? At least I know where he is. He's accounted for. Alex isn't. There's no finish, no resolution, no end. Just a lifetime of uncertainty and quiet.

"And, Christ, is it quiet. Alex was always tromping through the house, making a racket, fooling around with my boxing bag, playing music, running hair dryers, talking, shouting, jumping around, laughing. Now it's just so quiet, Strega. So goddamn quiet."

Gavin punched the dashboard and stared out at his house.

Shelly came down the drive and leaned in the open car window. "Phone call for you, Jon."

Strega looked at her in surprise. "No one knows I'm here."

She smiled. "Your lady friend's pretty anxious to talk to you. She called three times while you were out. The phone's in the kitchen."

Strega followed her inside. He picked up the phone. "Hello?"

"Hi, Jonnie."

Alvarez. His breath caught in his throat. Forget how she knows I'm here, he thought. Just clear the slate. "Maria." He tried to sound light and joking. "You'll make a hell of a detective one day."

"I know I will. You're my first case. Look how I knew just where to find you tonight. And I'm continually learning new things about you, Jonnie." She paused. He heard the scratch of the match, the flare-up of flame. He swore he could hear her breathing a cigarette to life.

She exhaled softly, then went on. "For example. Your girlfriend's tall, like you, and she's dark, like me, but bigger. Not fat, just stacked in all the right places. Big job at Merrill Lynch. Rosemary De Cesare. Hot-shot stock trader. She must be smart too, unlike me. Remember?" She took another drag on her cigarette. "Remember how you called me dumb?"

"Leave Rosemary alone," Strega said evenly. "This isn't about her."

"You're right, it isn't. It's about you and me. We have a lot in common, like having heroes for fathers." She laughed softly. "It's not easy, is it? Always trying to live up to their big reputations, always trying to be as good as they are." She was rambling now and sounded like she was high. "You don't have that kind of pressure anymore because you know the truth about Vincent. He wasn't a hero at all. What kind of hero goes and kills himself? Do you feel free now, Jonnie, or do you feel damned?"

She was so quiet for a moment, Jon thought she had hung up. Then her rich voice was back on the line again, deep and dreamy. "Did Rosemary pick out the Ralph Lauren sheets or did you? A matching set of expensive blue checks. Designer sheets, fancy music. You both must think you're a whole lot better than the rest of us."

He heard her put the phone down on something hard, like a counter. "Alvarez?" Music drifted down the line. Pavarotti singing an aria from *Madame Butterfly*. It was the first disc loaded in his programmable player. "Alvarez?" he shouted into the phone.

The line went dead.

Strega slammed the receiver down. He ran his hands over his face. They came away wet.

Gavin walked in. "What's wrong? Why are you screaming Alvarez's name?"

Strega ran his hands over his face again. "She's in my apartment, Ed. She's *in*."

Strega put his key in the door and slipped the bolt back. Gavin had offered to come, but Strega said no, knowing Maria would be long gone. Strega's heart raced anyway. He opened his front door and stepped in.

The stereo was still on, glowing in the dark, filling the room with Pavarotti. Strega flicked the light switch. The living room was neat and orderly, exactly as he had left it. His art collection was in place. The alabaster sculpture was untouched. He searched the kitchen, then the bedroom. He threw open the closet. His clothes hung neatly in front of him. In the bathroom he threw the shower curtain back. The tub was empty.

There was no Maria and, he suddenly realized, no kitten. Sigmund was gone. He went back to the bedroom and looked under the bed. Like a kid's nightmare, he thought, standing up. No monsters under the bed. Right. What was she then, the invisible man? How had she gotten in? Or out, for that matter? The bed pillows were out of place. He picked one up. It smelled of cinnamon and musk. He stripped the blue-checkered pillowcase off, then on impulse, stripped the bed too.

He looked at his desk. The picture of Rosemary was gone. His computer was on. Block letters glowed on the screen: *Vincent has a message for you.*

In the living room, the pedestal was as he had left it, covered and in front of the big windows. He pulled the plastic bag off. Vincent's clay head had been turned to face him. A wet red liquid streamed down the side of the face. She had dug a ragged hole into the left side of the head, gouged the mouth into a gaping silent scream, forced the chin up, stretching the clay throat into an arch of agony. The skull structure had been pummeled flat as though an angry child had struck it repeatedly with an open palm. The eyes were no longer expressionless. She had plunged a marble into each socket. The eyes stared up now, red balled with terror.

And, on one clay cheek, she had crudely scratched the words: *Jonnie Strega.*

Gavin went down to the big boxing bag hanging in his basement.

Danny had liked the bag. He used to fly around it, surprisingly fast, big fists hammering out, punching like pistons, working up a sweat while Gavin coached from the side. Alex liked it too. When she was little, he taught her some of the footwork and a few elementary jabs. She used to dance around the bag, squealing with delight, throwing punches like a pro.

Gavin danced around it now, warming up, light on his feet despite the extra weight. He curled his bare fists and focused on the bag. He took a shot with his right fist, then his left. He worked them, right-left, right-left, throwing his body weight into each punch. His arms felt good. Loose. Warm. Strong. The rhythm came naturally and built fast.

His arms became jackhammers. Alternating jabs, uppercut to the chin, straight jab to the face, right cross, left cross, a jab in the eye, then one to the Adam's apple, followed by body blows, left-right, left-right. The cadence of his rhythm buzzed in his head.

Come on, God, come on!

He hit the bag, danced the dance, working his pulse up until it thundered in his ears and he was wheezing, his lungs working hard for air and hurting. Then he moved faster still, punching harder, willing his stubborn cop heart to blow up.

Come on, God, take me. Come on!

Waiting for the lightning flash down the left arm, inviting it, expecting to feel the cold foot of God grinding down hard against his chest, pushing, pushing, an icy pressure, squeezing the life out of him. It never came.

God wasn't playing, not on this night anyway. Gavin

gave up. He slumped down, hands on his knees, dripping sweat and tears on the hard slab floor.

Maria Alvarez sat down on her bedroom floor in front of a full-length wall mirror. It was five o'clock in the morning, and she was still in uniform. She touched her reflected face, the eyes, chin, and throat, and pressed her cheek against the cool mirror. She pulled her service revolver out of her gun belt. It was heavy in her hands.

She stood slowly up, unbuttoned the uniform shirt, and pressed the full flesh of her belly and breasts to the mirror. She ran her hands up and down her reflection, then turned her face flush to the glass and kissed her own image. She kissed it savagely, roughly, keeping her eyes open, wanting to know, needing to understand, why *he* wanted her and why Strega didn't.

Strega. He was classy. Upright. By the book. A golden rule boy.

Well, what would he do if his perfect Princeton profile was destroyed? What would he do *if and when* he was stripped of *it*—*it* being his protective Ivy League coat, the one that made him feel superior, bigger, and better than all the rest?

What would Jon Strega do if he was stripped down bare?

If he looked in the mirror and saw a face of shame there?

The shame, the shame, the shame.

Jon Strega didn't understand the word *shame*. It wasn't part of his Princeton vocabulary. But it would be now.

Maria spun away from the mirror and picked up the phone. She dialed 911.

The pounding started around five o'clock in the morning. It was hard. Insistent.

"Police," a man yelled. "Open up."

Strega woke. He pulled a robe on and looked out the living room window. A car from the Two-Four was parked out front, siren winding down, red and white roof lights gyrating. A patrol car at five a.m. meant bad news. Strega opened the door, wondering who had died. Two officers crowded the little landing. His elderly landlady stood behind them, wrapped in a chenille robe. Her eyes were wide with fear.

"Jon Strega?" one of the cops barked.

"Yes."

"We got a 911 call from a woman reporting a disturbance here," the cop said. The name tag under his shield read PEREZ. His partner's name tag read D. RIORDAN. Perez had three stripes on his sleeve, Riordan had none. "The woman said a man named Jon Strega was beating her up." Perez fondled his gun and craned his neck, trying to see around Strega's big body into the apartment. "Mind if we come in?"

"I'm a cop," Strega explained, blocking the doorway. "I'm in the One-Nine. My partner's Ed Gavin."

"Good for you," Perez said.

"There's no one here," Strega said.

"Then you won't mind if we have a look around," Perez said. "Ever since the Simpson case, we're under pressure to take reports of domestic dispute more seriously than we might have in the past." Perez put a hand out and pushed the door.

Strega stepped back. The two cops walked by. His landlady trailed in after them. She looked up at Strega sheepishly and whispered: "I wasn't the one who called them."

"I know," Strega assured her. "Must have been a crank call. The Department gets them all the time."

Perez and Riordan split up. Riordan took the kitchen. Perez toured the living room. He yanked curtains back, looked under the couch, and grimaced at the mutilated clay head. He went over to the alabaster statue and tweaked one of her stone nipples. "Now, this is what I call art." Perez grinned at Strega, then worked his way down the hall.

Strega followed. Riordan went through the bathroom while Perez checked the closets and under the bed. Riordan wandered out of the bathroom. "Nothing in there," he said.

Perez ran his hands over the intricately carved antique armoire. He opened it and rifled through Strega's good-quality civilian clothes. "Ralph Lauren," Perez observed. "Constructed jackets. Custom slacks." He slammed the armoire doors shut and went to the computer. "IBM. State-of-the-art. High-ticket stuff you got here, *Officer* Strega." He fingered the sheets and checked the label. "Ralph Lauren again."

Perez signaled Riordan. They went back into the living room. Perez looked around again. "Slick place," he said, "How long have you been with the Department?"

"Two weeks," Strega answered.

Perez studied the art collection and touched the good fabric on the custom couch. "You live this good, Riordan?"

"Nope," Riordan said.

"Me either and I've been with the Department five years." Perez sneered at Strega. "Looks like they're paying rookies more in the One-Nine than in the Two-Four. You moonlighting, *Officer* Strega?"

"Something like that."

"I see. Well, have a nice day, now. We can see ourselves out." They left.

Strega turned to his landlady. "Did you let anyone in last night while I was out?"

"Just the policewoman you sent over."

"Policewoman?"

"She came late," she admitted. "Around ten-thirty. She said you had some files in your computer that you needed printed out. You were on duty and couldn't get over here, so you sent her. I saw you go out this evening in your uniform. I let her in. She stayed upstairs about an hour or so, then left with the little kitten she said you were taking care of for her while she'd been away."

"Did she tell you her name?"

"Of course. She's the police commissioner's daughter. A pretty girl, and nice too. Polite." She looked up at Strega's expression. "She *is* the police commissioner's daughter. I saw her picture with her father in *New York* magazine. Did I do wrong?"

"Never let anyone into my apartment. Not unless I ask you to."

"But she was wearing a uniform. She had a badge."

"She had no right to enter my apartment. I didn't tell her to come here."

"My heavens, did she steal something?"

"Not exactly. But don't let her in here again. No matter what she says."

"I'm terribly sorry."

"It's late. Let's both try to get some sleep now." He gave what he hoped was a reassuring smile. His landlady backed out.

Strega closed and bolted the door. The mutilated face of Vincent Strega mocked him. The 911 call had been a prank call, all right. The question was, why was Alvarez continuing the siege?

The phone rang. Strega answered it. After a beat of silence, a kitten cried.

"Alvarez?" Strega shouted into the receiver.

"Morning, Jonnie," she rumbled. "Did you have a little visit from the Two-Four?"

"Alvarez, the joke's over."

"I'm not laughing, Jonnie." She wasn't.

"Will you be so cool when Internal Affairs hauls you in?"

"No, I'll be upset. After all, this new cop Jon Strega has been hassling me. I went out with him twice, then told him I didn't want to see him again. He's rough with women. He hit me. I'm not the first woman he ever hit. A woman called 911 once and reported him. I don't want to go out with him, but he doesn't take no for an answer. He bothers me. Makes nasty comments, even sent me a vicious letter. It's typed, but I know it's from him because the stationery's personalized. It says Jon Strega, right there on top of this fancy blue note paper.

"I'm scared now. Thinking of going to IAB myself. He's been threatening me, and now he's turning the whole story around and trying to get me fired. All because I won't sleep with him." The kitten cried again. The line went dead.

Maria Alvarez had set him up.

His gut told him to go to Internal Affairs anyway. It would be his word against hers. He was a Princeton grad. On the other hand, would IAB really believe the *police commissioner's daughter* was stalking him? Wouldn't they be predisposed to believe a man was stalking her? Would anyone in Internal Affairs take him seriously, or would they send him straight over to Psych Services?

Strega picked up the phone and called Gavin.

Fifteen

The early morning sky was hazy. Thunderclouds crowded the horizon. Gavin watched them while he waited for Strega in front of the precinct house. He sipped an iced coffee from a styrofoam cup and wondered when the next summer storm would hit. Gavin missed the crisp autumn air and bright, cold skies. He missed the brisk fall breezes and the smell of chimney smoke. He missed the winter snow.

Strega rapped on the window. Gavin opened the passenger door. Strega got in. It was six o'clock in the morning. The rookie was sweating and looked like he was going to explode. "Talk to me," Gavin ordered.

"I'm going to Internal Affairs with this Alvarez situation."

"You don't want to do that."

"She called me at *your* house last night! She's following me! How else could she know I was there?"

"Lucky guess. You can't go to IAB because of a phone call. Maria's the P.C.'s daughter."

"I don't care who she is. She was in my apartment."

"Still not enough to go to IAB with."

"Misrepresentation in uniform for personal reasons is."

"How does that mouthful of legal babble apply to Alvarez?"

Strega told him the story.

Gavin sipped his iced coffee. "You're right," he finally said. "Alvarez crossed the line. But if you go to Internal Affairs, the first thing they'll suspect is a romantic altercation. They're going to ask Alvarez *her* side of the story. Alvarez will lie. She's already told you what she'll say. It sounds convincing. The bitch of it is, IAB will believe her. Twenty-three officers at roll call witnessed her act, not to mention Wilson and the P.C. himself at the Met."

"Theatrics," Strega protested. "Anyway, it's IAB's job to deal with problems within the Department."

Gavin snorted. "You're a rookie. You're brainwashed to believe the Department systems are there to support and back you up. They're not. They'll screw you every time."

"Then what do I do?" Strega said in a dead voice. "I need help."

"Let me think a minute." Cops were bound tightly together. They worked things out amongst themselves, without outsiders. It was a clan, a brotherhood, one the IAB and other departmental divisions like IAB weren't a part of. It was a hard concept to explain to a rookie.

"It's definitely gotten out of hand," Gavin said. "I agree with you there. I just don't think Internal Affairs is the best place to go. I hate to see you branded at the start of your career as a troublemaker. The stigma will never leave you. And if IAB knows, then the P.C. will know, and you sure as hell don't want that."

"I have to do something."

"Wilson," Gavin said. "Let's talk to Wilson."

"I hear Wilson's a good friend of the P.C.'s."

"Strega, everybody likes to think they're a good friend of the P.C.'s. Wilson's calm. He's rational. He'll understand about keeping the P.C. out of it."

Wilson shot out of his chair. "This is a fucking bomb waiting to go off. It's the kind of thing the tabloids will gorge on. *Rookie Cop Charges P.C.'s Daughter With Sexual Harassment.* Don't think for one minute I'm not going to tell the P.C. about this *situation.* I happen to be a close friend. Any altercation, any *situation,* involving Ramon Alvarez's daughter involves him."

Wilson was immaculately dressed despite the early weekend hour. His shoes were spit-polished, his hair combed back tight and neat. A silver Omega watch flashed on his wrist. Wilson tapped the watch face while he studied Strega. "Frankly, Strega, I find it hard to believe Maria has done any one of the things you suggest. And I find it fucking impossible to believe she's responsible for the dead cat in your locker."

Strega stood up. "If that's the way you feel, I'll take my complaint over to IAB."

"Sit the fuck down and hear me out."

Strega sat.

"Maria's a smart and ambitious officer," Wilson explained. "Ramon thinks she can be the first female P.C. in New York one day. She's a dedicated cop, a good cop, and a hard worker. I know she has a reputation for sleeping around. If she were a man, frankly, I don't think anyone would be keeping track of who she sleeps with. Maria's young. She hasn't learned the importance of separating her personal life from her professional life." Wilson sat back. "Any problems you've got with her are the results of mixed signals. You must've encouraged her somehow, given her a reason to think you were interested in dating her. Who knows? What I do know is that Maria doesn't have a malicious bone in her sexy little body."

Wilson let his words sink in, then continued. "The fewer people who know about your *misunderstanding,* the better. I want to solve this situation quietly, and that means no Internal Affairs. If you go to IAB and make a public scandal out of this, Ramon Alvarez will wring your neck, Strega. You embarrass his daughter, you embarrass him. He's not going to stand for that. He's got cast-iron balls." Wilson turned to Gavin. "Gavin, tell him. You remember his performance in the Three-Four. You were there!"

Gavin nodded. "Ramon Alvarez busted up a drug den on his own. He went in with no backup because he had reason to believe an important informant was about to be executed. Alvarez went in shooting, one against five. He saved the informant's life, made five arrests, and was

subsequently decorated for his actions—all in his first
month on the job."

Wilson smiled. "There was no stopping him after that.
Alvarez went on to collect commendations and decorations the way the rest of us collect our paychecks." Wilson's smile faded. "Strega, if you go to IAB, I guarantee
you Ramon will make you wish you weren't a cop."

Gavin nodded. He remembered the look on Ramon
Alvarez's face at the Metropolitan.

Wilson swiveled around in his chair and looked out
the window. "I'll talk to Maria. Maybe she's just trying
to be a ball buster like her dad, and she's going about
it the wrong way. Dismissed."

Maria Alvarez was not present at Saturday morning's
roll call.

Strega wondered where she was and what she was
doing.

The tour sergeant ran through the daily business.
When he finished the roll call, the sergeant frowned.
"Kelly's scheduled for this tour. He's a no-show. The
way this schedule's been jerked around with vacations,
it's a wonder anybody remembers what tour they're on.
Alvarez is out sick. That makes us light by two officers.
There will be no foot post at Seventy-sixth today. Moon,
you pair up with Chang and handle Kelly's sector. That's
all. Dismissed."

Emma drifted back over Manhattan Saturday afternoon, much calmed by her trip out over the Atlantic.
She floated back in a blanket of thunderclouds and a
whisper of wind. But when the rain started at three
o'clock, it came down in solid sheets. Strega stopped the
patrol car at a corner near Bloomingdale's to wait it out.
He flipped the wipers on.

"You feel better after talking to Wilson?" Gavin
asked.

"Sure," Strega said. Gavin knew he was lying.

A young woman dashed across the street. Her skirt
was pasted to her thighs from the rain. The thin wet

fabric revealed her fleshy behind and a pair of round, full thighs that would score a nine on Donovan's *thigh meter*. The *thigh meter* worked like the *crunch meter,* on a sliding scale of one to ten—ten being the highest rating possible—but of course, the aesthetics were different as was the principal sense used to gauge the rating. The *crunch meter* was based on noise. The *thigh meter* was all visual pleasure, the aesthetic joy of fleshly linear grace. Donovan's meter would have rated this girl a nine.

Gavin watched her trot over to the opposite sidewalk. She stopped and tugged at her skirt. Gavin could see the outline of her underwear through the skirt. *Visible panty lines,* Donovan used to marvel, *are one of man's greatest pleasures. They're a reference point; they give you the north, east, south, and west all at a single glance.*

Donovan's observations were always benign. He was a shy man with women, fumbling and sweet, the kind of man that provoked strong maternal feelings in females of all shapes and ages. His shy way brought women to his side like flocks of birds, and once there they melted down into wholly maternal creatures plying the big Irishman with cookies, pies, cups of coffee—everything but polishing his shoes, and Gavin had had a sneaky suspicion that the captain's secretary in the Three-Four had been hankering to do even that.

Danny always had a shoelace untied or a button missing. He needed attention, and when the girls gave it, he would smile his Buddha smile, pat the girls sweetly on their freshly combed heads, and mumble thanks. Nothing sweeter, Gavin thought, than seeing the secretaries around the station house mother the big, shy cop. There never was an untoward thing in their behavior, not one thing at all out of line, just good old-fashioned fussing and clucking, and then the proud observation of Danny beaming under the shower of attention.

Donovan had been the same kind of shy when he was a boy. The shyness stayed with him through his teens right into his twenties, and it always drew women to him. Danny turned every girl down but one: Jillian. He felt safe with her. Danny, Gavin, and Jillian had grown up on the same Brooklyn block. Something about Jillian was *girl next door safe* to Danny. He fumbled less around her than other girls.

Gavin stood up for Danny at his wedding with Jillian, happy to see his best friend find the courage to take the aisle-long walk into manhood. Jilly took to her wifely role like ice cream to apple pie, but it changed her, and the change in her changed Danny. In the years after the wedding, Danny tried his best, but the dynamic shifted with the exchange of plain gold rings, and somehow the wifely demands, the wifely needs, the conjugal *duties,* made Danny shy with Jillian, and nervous in his own heavily mortgaged house. From the start, before her bridal bouquet had even dried, Jillian complained: *Why are you just a cop, Danny? When are you going to make detective grade? My father was a detective. Aren't you as good as he was?*

Danny was smart enough by far to have gone the detective route, but like Gavin he just didn't want to. "Detectives," he said, "crawl around in their fancy suits trying to figure out what happened *after* the crime's occurred. I want to *prevent* crime from happening in the first place. And the only way to do that is to be on the street." So he stayed put and worked it his way, which was working with the kids.

He loved kids. The ones in the Three-Four used to bring pictures around for Danny to look at. They were drawings in primary colors full of singing frogs, smiling flowers, dancing trees—full of hope those pictures were. Donovan invented all kinds of games for the kids in the Three-Four, deputizing them with fake gold shields and teaching them to sing *just say no to drugs.* He also trained them to dutifully present their report cards. When the grades were good, Danny beamed. When the grades were poor, Donovan's whole face sagged with disappointment. *Make your life count,* he would thunder.

Donovan was a counselor, a role model, a brother, and a father all rolled into one. He was a one-man jungle gym, taking the little ones for rides on his broad uniformed shoulders, twirling them around, then setting

them down and teaching them to plant saplings in the
sparse bare batches of earth in the Three-Four. Donovan
gave the kids a reason to be good and something more—
he gave them hope. So how many young lives had
Danny steered right over the years? Five? Fifty? A hundred? There was no way to know for sure, but Gavin
guessed the number was a big one—big enough to make
it all worthwhile.

Aside from kids, Danny had been comfortable only
with other cops. The complexities of women and marriage confused him. Little by little, over the years, Jillian
browbeat him down. He would tell Gavin how Jillian
had said he was fat, or how she'd declared that sleeping
with him was like being trapped on the underside of a
rubber boat. Danny always laughed when he repeated
her unkind words—he laughed, but Gavin knew Danny
hurt.

Digging, digging, chipping away, a pickax for a tongue,
chipping away at the fragile self-esteem Danny had as a
man, and when she had that obliterated, she started in
on his performance as a father. By this time the three
sons were teens, and it was clear they were screw-ups in
every possible way. Jilly tossed the blame on Danny.
*The boys are your fault. You were never here to guide
them. You were always more worried about the slum-
rat kids in the Three-Four than about your own flesh
and blood.*

Lies, all of it lies.

Sure, over the years Danny's tour calls had interfered
with some with the big moments of growing up—a
school play missed while Danny was up in the Three-
Four slamming a thieving punk against the side of a car
for selling drugs to eight-year-old kids, or a baseball
game unattended because Danny chose to stick around
overtime on a tour to help pick up body parts when a
car load of drive-by shooters decided to open fire on a
school playground.

No, Danny had been there plenty for his boys, but
Jillian had been there more, poisoning their young minds
over the years as her marital discontent festered and

grew, letting the boys witness her mushrooming contempt for the big, gentle man who was her husband and their father. Contempt is contagious, and Danny's boys got an overdose.

By the time Jillian slipped the neighbor's teenage son into the Donovan matrimonial bed, Danny's self-esteem had been destroyed. His whole sense of *manhood* had been squashed, and he swore he'd be a looker, not a toucher for the rest of his God-given days—her shrill accusations rang that loudly in his ears.

So, when he'd see a pretty girl running across the street with *visible panty lines* and an even yard of youthful leg, Danny would sigh and say: *The memory of her will keep me company tonight. Just the memory of her's enough.*

Gavin shook himself. For an instant, there in Emma's deluge, with the windshield wipers slap-slapping and the linen-skirted girl disappearing into the crowd, Gavin thought that maybe Danny had been sitting at home on June the twelfth, alone with just the memory of a short-skirted girl to keep him company. Maybe that night the emptiness and the loneliness hurt so much that after easing his needs in his own private way, he had indeed picked up his service revolver and blown himself out of this life into the next.

Looking out the rain-sluiced windshield, even as he thought it, Gavin knew it wasn't so. *It hadn't happened like that.* Someone had shot Danny, and suddenly Gavin knew that there was more to the semen on Danny's thigh than a private act of self-gratification or even a woman for hire. The puzzle pieces didn't fit that way. Something in the arrangement of the events that June night—the pants off, the tension eased, the door unlocked, the gun pressed to flesh and fired—had to reveal something worth knowing, something that would help Gavin change the verdict from suicide to murder.

Strega was tight-lipped and silent next to him, watching the rain come down. Gavin watched the clock, waiting the last long hour of duty out, wanting only to get to Ballantine with the new theory that was bubbling up inside him.

Gavin rapped on the glass window of Ballantine's fish-tank office. Inside, the detective was perched on a corner of his desk, talking into the telephone. His face was screwed up with frustration. An unlit cigarette wiggled between his lips. He waved Gavin in.

The paper mountain on Ballantine's desk had grown. A floor plan of the Metropolitan Museum blanketed stacks of folders. The walls were covered with sketches of the two shooters. A map of the Nineteenth Precinct filled the bulletin board. Color-coded push pins punched the map where crimes had been committed.

Ballantine slammed the phone down and turned to Gavin. "Know what they're calling the One-Nine? Club Dead. Club Med turns into Club Dead. Fuck." Q-Ball lit his cigarette. "What can I do for you?"

"Clarify a few issues."

"If I can."

"Did CSU dust Danny's place for prints?"

"No." He noted the accusing expression on Gavin's face. "Ed, it wasn't a crime scene. The Department's spread thin enough without us going and making up crimes where they don't seem to exist."

"Answer this. Why didn't any one of the neighbors in all of these shootings call the police when the fatal shot was fired?"

"In this city most people who hear gunfire run the other way. And remember, in each of our nine cases it was a single gunshot. Could've been mistaken for a car backfiring. If the TV volume was turned up high, the shot might've sounded like it was part of the entertainment. That would account for the TVs being on in each of the apartments. Two, three, four shots, someone would've called it in. One shot? No one calls." Ballantine shrugged. "What else?"

"A woman."

"You want one, you need one, you saw one. Finish the sentence."

"A woman killed Donovan."

Q-Ball sat very still on the edge of his desk, the cigarette frozen in midair between the ash tray and his lips. "You found a witness." Hope and disbelief.

"Not yet," Gavin admitted. "But the evidence in Danny's file tells us a woman killed him."

"What evidence is that?" Disappointment. Skepticism.

"The autopsy report. The dried semen on his leg. Why else would it be there if it hadn't been a woman?"

Ballantine moved from the desktop to his chair. He put his feet up and sighed. "We've been over that. Could've been a hooker who was hired by the killer."

"A woman killed Danny," Gavin insisted.

"Nope. Serial killers are men. If we're looking for anybody at all, it's a man. I'm sure of that. Donovan either indulged in a little self-gratification, or the killer brought along a hooker and threw a sex party before he killed Donovan."

"Take your second theory. Assume the killer showed up with a hooker. Do you really believe a man can achieve orgasm when he's got a gun pointed at him? Talk about performance anxiety."

"I hadn't thought of that," Ballantine admitted.

"Okay. Now let's look at your first theory, that Danny had indulged in a so-called act of private self-gratification before he got killed. Was there semen on Danny's uniform trousers?"

"No. He wasn't wearing them."

"Okay. Let's play it out your way. Danny sits on his couch with his pants off and indulges himself. The doorbell rings. He gets up *without* putting his pants on, answers the door, and lets his killer in. That make sense to you, Ballantine?"

Q-Ball chewed on his cigarette. "No, it doesn't. What's more likely is that the killer surprised him, caught him *in the act,* so to speak. The killer could've been waiting *inside* his apartment. Could've played out like this: Danny comes home, puts his service revolver on the dresser, undresses, sits down to watch television, plays with himself, then wham. The killer jumps out of a closet or out from under the bed, uses his own gun to keep Danny immobile, then snatches the service revolver off the table and plays whatever pre-death games he wants with Danny. Eventually, he puts the nine-millimeter in Danny's hand and fires the fatal shot. Then he walks out the door and the big city swallows him up."

Gavin was unconvinced. "Were the apartment front doors locked in the other eight cases?"

Ballantine shuffled through the paper mountain. He pulled out a stack of files and went through them one by one. When he finished, he looked up at Gavin. "All of the nine suicides were discovered a day or two after the estimated time of death. In five of the cases, like Danny's, the cops had missed a tour or two, and the partners went looking. In the other four cases relatives got worried when the cops weren't where they were supposed to be at a given time. They called the NYPD to investigate.

"In all of the cases the front doors were locked. In four cases the building super had a master key and opened the door for the NYPD. In the remaining five NYPD had to bust the door in. I assume you busted into Danny's place." He shoved the files back under the museum floor plan. "That's what bugs me. Every time I have myself convinced there was foul play, a nasty little fact like the locked doors pops up and scuttles my theory. With the exception of Donovan, who lived on the second floor, all these guys lived ten floors up or higher. If there was a killer, where did he go? Out the window? Did he sprout wings and fly away? No, a locked door *reinforces* the argument that these were legitimate suicides. It doesn't support any of my theories at all."

"I didn't bust Danny's door down."

"How'd you get in?"

"I turned the handle and walked in. His door was unlocked."

Ballantine pondered this new information. "So what? The other eight *were* locked. My theory's still screwed up."

"Come on, Ballantine," Gavin challenged. "You're

the detective. You can do better than that. Think harder. Think about the eight *locked* doors."

Ballantine's face clouded. Gavin's sarcasm bordered on insubordination. Suddenly, the anger vanished and Ballantine's eyes lit up. "It's so stupid, I never thought of it."

Gavin smiled smugly. "The killer took the key."

Ballantine went on. "Of course. He locked the door from the outside, walked away, and tossed the key down a sewer, laughing. Laughing because he knew the locked door would drive home the message that the death was a suicide. No sign of forced entry, no sign of a struggle. No money or electronics missing. And *a locked front door*. It was part of the plan."

Gavin pressed. "Then why was Danny's door unlocked?"

"Simple. The killer couldn't find the key."

"Which brings us full circle. How did the killer get into all eight apartments in the first place? There was no sign of forced entry in any one of them."

"There's where my theory goes screwy again," Q-Ball complained. "I don't know how the killer got in. You're giving me a headache. Where are you going with all this?"

"Let's focus on Danny. What if Danny knew the killer? What if he got up and let the killer in?"

"Ed, you said so yourself. No way he went to the door to let someone in *without his pants on.*"

"My point exactly. He had his pants *on.* He went to the door and let a *woman* in, Ballantine. A *woman*. It plays out. There's some sort of sex play. While Danny's still in dreamland, she grabs his service revolver, wraps his hand around it, and fires. Then she takes a shower, dries off with the hula girl towels, but something spooks her before she can find Danny's keys. She takes off fast, forgets about the door in her panic to leave. She forgets and *leaves the door unlocked*. She makes a stupid mistake."

Ballantine flipped the bulletin board over. He studied

his pin map of the suicides. "Or, Danny might have just forgotten to lock his door."

"You believe that if you believe he killed himself. I know he didn't. There's only one arrangement of events that works, and that arrangement depends on a woman. A woman killed him."

Ballantine swiveled around to the bulletin board and flipped it over to his suicide map. "If you're right, all nine cops let a woman in." Ballantine pointed at each of the red push pins in the map, emphasizing how far and wide through the boroughs they were spread. "Who the hell is she that cops in all these different precincts, all over the city, opened their front doors and let her walk right in?"

"She's someone they know. Someone they know well enough to let her in and, later, to jerk them off. She puts a porno flick on the VCR and jerks the cop off. After she does that, she picks up their service revolver and plays Simon Says, only Simon's a girl. Put yourself in one of those living rooms. She's holding a nine-millimeter. All you're holding is a beer can. She tells you to give her your arm. Simon Says. You do. She sticks you with a needle and feeds a little liquid candy into your veins. It's her game. She's Simon. You sit there, helpless. Then maybe she plays more sex games with you. You go along, because you've got no choice. Finally, she puts your gun in your hand, holds it to your head, and fires."

Ballantine studied the suicide map again. "If you're right, we're looking for a woman who has some reason to launch a private war against male cops."

"The question now is, why? What kind of woman would want to do that?"

"There are a hundred theories. I'll name two. Could be a woman who watched someone she loved, a father or boyfriend, sent to prison by a cop. Or, maybe a woman who watched her boyfriend take a bullet from a cop's gun. Any way you look at it, she's a cop hater. If she wanted to just kill them, she could've given them an overdose of cocaine and left them to die. You have any idea how intimate an act it is to hold the nose of a handgun to a man's head and pull the trigger? To be so close you feel the man's body take the impact of the fatal shot? Whoever she is, she hates cops."

"So you agree with me that we're looking for a woman."

"You've come up with a good, strong theory," Ballantine admitted. "I won't rule it out, but the fact is we're still just guessing, aren't we? We need more than our own invented stories. We need a fact. One fact. One witness. Something solid."

Gavin pulled into his driveway at nine o'clock. Shelly's car was gone. Inside, he found one of her curt notes stuck to the refrigerator. *Went to the movies. S.* And, below it, another note from earlier in the day: *A Walter Paxton called asking for you. Said he lives in 1-A and that you'd understand. He works nights. He left his home number—754-9890. Call days only.*

Gavin picked up the phone and punched the number in. After thirteen rings he hung up. Gavin cursed the fact that he was on the eight-to-four tour the next day. He wanted to be sitting on Walter's doorstep at sunup when Walter the night worker came home. *Walter the night worker.* Was Walter sleeping when Danny was killed? Did he have a black sleep mask stuck over his eyes and plastic plugs stuffed in his ears? Was he snoring, lost in dreamland, oblivious to the nightmare unfolding in the apartment upstairs from him?

What kind of sleeper are you, Walter?

Sixteen

Maria woke up late Saturday night. She felt paper-thin, transparent. Her head hurt. Her stomach hurt. It was all getting out of control, the drugs and the game. Everything seemed to be speeding up. The more blow she took, the more she needed. The more she played the game, the more she wanted. The game was like the blow. She needed it. And now she needed it more often. Now she had played the game twice in one week. That was careless. The game was dangerous, like the drug. Too much of it would get her in trouble.

She got up slowly and tottered around the bedroom. Maria was scared. He would come again, soon. *The fear. The fear. The terrible fear.* Even Jonnie's kitten was afraid. It crouched, hissing, in the back of her closet. Fear was a funny circle. The kitten was afraid of Maria. Strega was afraid of Maria. But Maria was afraid of *him.*

She dug in the dresser drawer for her stash. She had played the game, and now she needed a hit. The game and the soft white snow went hand in hand. She found the baggie. It was empty. She had used it up in the last game. "Fuck," she shouted, slamming the drawer shut.

Grains of white stuck to the plastic. She licked them out and her tongue tingled, but it wasn't enough. She needed more. Angel would have more. Angel dealt. Maria stumbled down the hall. Her uniform was wrinkled and stained. She hadn't been careful in the last game, and now she needed a new uniform. She would buy one later. Now she needed the blow to make her feel a hundred feet tall again.

She clambered down the stairwell to the fourth floor, to Angel's apartment.

"Angel, honey?" Maria shouted, rapping on the door.

Angel didn't answer.

Maria rapped again, harder. "Angel?" She jiggled the doorknob. It was unlocked. The door swung open. Maria walked in, calling Angel's name. She found a manila envelope, fat with cocaine, where Angel always kept it, under the couch. Maria tucked it in her waistband, under her shirt, then wandered down the hall, thinking Angel was asleep. Maria found her in the bedroom, sprawled nude across her soiled bed.

The soiled bed.

The bed soiled with Angel's blood and tufts of her ripped hair, puzzle pieces that matched the big bald circles on her beautiful head.

Maria fell across her.

Angel, Angel, lying so still.

Maria rolled off, then rolled Angel over and cradled Angel's head in her arms. Maria saw the silvery earrings torn from Angel's ears. Then she registered the torn ears themselves, one each on Angel's two pink pillows. She saw the grin too late, the terrible grin carved into Angel's sweet throat. Maria squeezed her eyes shut, but she still saw the grin. She was five years old again and the gaping grin was her mother's. Then the grin was her father's, but it wasn't a grin because he was mad. He was shaking Maria, shaking and yelling that it was her fault. Maria was the one who should have died, not her beautiful young mother.

Her father, her proud, handsome father, broken with despair, shaking his little girl as though she had been the one to carve the grin, shaking her hard, hating her, then teaching her. He taught her the knife first and after that the gun. Combat weapons. The weapons of war. *Life is war,* her handsome father had said. *You must learn to fight back.*

It was too late, too late to fight for Angel. Maria hadn't been there to save her from Zeke's messenger. Maria had failed Angel the way she had failed her mother. She had failed again to protect the one she loved. And now, with Angel dead, there was no one at all left to love.

Maria picked up the phone and dialed 911. She left Angel on the soiled bed and went outside to sit on the stoop, in the rain, waiting for the ambulance to come.

An old man shuffled down the sidewalk, carrying a tattered black umbrella. He was dressed for winter in a fat green parka and baggy flannel pants. His shoes were ragged Birkenstocks, two sizes too small. His big toe poked over the edge. The nail was talon-long. Yellow. His face was dotted with liver spots, and he had a hundred lizard-like folds around his eyes. He sat down next to Maria.

He worked his thick liver-colored lips one against the other and put his palms together, spinning his thumbs first in one direction, then another. "The world's ending," he said. "Hurricanes and floods, plagues and pestilence, it's all in the Bible. Yup, it's right there for you to read. The world's ending, so you better make your peace with Jesus now."

"You waiting for someone?" Maria hissed, wishing he would go away.

"Second coming, that's all." He wiggled the big taloned toe. His lizard eyes flickered slowly shut; then his head rolled back and he started to snore.

Maria heard the ambulance before she saw it. She heard the shrieking siren, and moments later she saw the spinning lights far off, coming her way, coming close, coming fast, coming to carry her Angel away.

Gavin woke up at six o'clock in the morning and tried Walter. He let the phone ring thirteen times. Gavin imagined those long, unanswered rings in the apartment facing the stairway, one flight down from where Danny had been murdered, and he wondered where Walter was. Gavin tried again at six-thirty and listened to the same thirteen unanswered rings. He hung up, dressed quickly, and drove into the city. He tried again from the station house and got a busy signal. Walter was there.

Walter was home. Gavin tried off and on through the
first hour of the tour and got a busy signal every time.
Strega waited in the car while Gavin tried again from a
pay phone at nine o'clock.

"Still busy," Gavin complained, getting back into the
car.

"Walter must take his phone off the hook so he can
sleep," Strega observed.

"Yeah. That must be it." Gavin spent the rest of the
morning staring out the window, trying to think Walter
awake.

Central's rapid-fire voice interrupted his late-morning
thinking. "Sector Ida John."

Gavin picked up. The assignment sounded routine.
Check out a disturbance at an apartment building up on
the north border of the precinct. The building super
claimed he had a problem that required the police. He
wouldn't say what. Gavin wrote down the street address
and confirmed the call while Strega coasted up the center of First Avenue, free as a bird on the empty Sunday
morning city streets.

"What's your fiver say on this one?" Strega asked.

"Probably a little family argument," Gavin speculated.
"John Doe comes home from an all-nighter, and his wife
lets him have it. He slaps her around some, she throws
pots and pans at him, breaks a few glasses, and makes
enough noise to prompt someone to call the police. Your
standard domestic-abuse call." He glanced at Strega.
The aftershave-ad jawline was set hard and angry. He
remembered Alvarez's 911 prank. "Sorry."

Strega flashed a wry smile, made a hard left turn, and
slowed, checking the building numbers as they flipped
by. Ninety-sixth Street was the precinct boundary, and
the neighborhood here was far less genteel than the rest
of the One-Nine. It was as though when the precincts
had originally been carved out, the knife missed and
went too far north, including a wedge of Manhattan that
was worlds apart from the golden grid of avenues between Fifty-ninth and Eighty-ninth streets.

Strega pulled up to the curb in front of a gritty brick apartment building.

Gavin reached for his hat. "No wonder John Doe didn't want to come home."

Strega cut the engine. They got out and went up a narrow cement path. The lobby doors were glass. The super was waiting, holding one of the doors open. "Glad to see you guys," he said as they stepped into the dingy lobby.

He turned his short, squat body around and stuck a hand out in greeting. "I'm the super. Franklin's the name, first and last. My folks thought it was funny. So you can call me Frank Franklin, or Franky, or just Franklin. It's all the same." Franklin was dressed in dirty gray coveralls. His hand was black with grime.

Gavin ignored the proffered hand. "What seems to be the problem?"

"There's always some kind of problem here." Franklin stuck his hand in his pocket and jangled his change. "Today it's trash."

"Trash," Strega repeated.

"Yup, trash." Franklin grinned. "Tenants stick their trash in dumpsters in the stairwell. I empty the dumpsters out, take the bags down to the big dumpster in the alley. I do it every morning. This morning I was late to the nineteenth floor on account of I overslept. Saturday night's my card game night, and sometimes things get rowdy."

"You were telling us about the trash," Strega said.

"Right. Anyway, I worked through all the floors like I always do. When I finished the eighteenth, I took the elevator to nineteen, then got out and walked down the hall to the stairwell, but I didn't make it past 19F. The stench is enough to knock you over. I think first it's the garbage. There's no a.c. in the building, so the hallways are a hundred and ten degrees, and unless you're lucky enough to have your own window unit, your apartment ain't gonna be much cooler, especially if you're high up. Heat rises, right?"

"You were telling us about the smell," Gavin prodded.

"Right. Like I said, I'm thinking someone left a whole lot of garbage inside and went off on vacation like a dumb fuck. The garbage is going to rot more and the smell's going to get worse, and—Christ—the last thing we need here is more bugs and a new population of rats. I just got rid of the old ones. So, I'm standing outside the door, trying to think of what to do. Then it hits me. I can't go in because I got no key.

"The management office has the master keys, and they're closed on Sunday. No way the neighbors are going to be happy with that smell. They got my home number. Something like this, they'll be calling me all day complaining. Ruin my Sunday. So what am I going to do, break in? I got no authorization to go in. The guy might get mad and sue me or get me fired. Maybe he's into garbage. Anyway, like I said, then it hits me. I can't go in, but *you* can."

"Why do you think that?" Gavin asked. "We've got no cause and no warrant."

"You can go in because one of your buddies lives in 19F. A cop. NYPD. I see him all the time, coming and going in his uniform. He moved in four months ago and told me how it was funny that he lived on the nineteenth floor because he worked in the nineteenth precinct and he was born on the nineteenth of November. All those nineteens, he said, must be karma." Franklin grinned and laughed dryly. "Nice guy. A Mike Kelly."

Gavin's vision blurred. He saw two Franklins standing in front of him, grinning ear to ear. "Mike Kelly?" he managed.

The grins got bigger. Four greasy hands clapped together. The sound was like a gunshot. "That's the one," the two Franklins said.

Gavin's tongue felt swollen when he spoke. "Take us up."

"Great," the Franklins said. "I knew you guys would help."

On nineteen, the stench was overwhelming. Franklin

led them down a narrow hall. The floor was dark brown linoleum tiles. The walls were dirty white. 19F was identified by a peel-and-stick letter F stuck a hundred years ago on the grunge-gray door. It had been chipped in enough places to make Gavin hope it was really an E that had been scraped into an F, and that Kelly didn't live there at all.

Gavin checked the door to the left. It had a peel-and-stick E, a nice new one. He turned back to the F and rapped loudly, then put his ear to the door. He heard a faint hum inside, like someone had left the radio on without tuning it in properly. He had heard the sound before. He looked down at the threshold. It was unfinished, bare of weather stripping or moldings, and where the saddle should have been, a sliver of space gaped between floor and the bottom of the door. The space was big enough for a single fly to wedge its engorged body under the door. Once out, it crawled onto Gavin's foot.

The flies. The godawful flies.

Gavin covered the doorknob with a handkerchief and jiggled. It was locked. He looked up at Strega through a curtain of tears. "Bring the battering ram up from the squad car. Call Ballantine. And call the M.E. Kelly's dead."

Seventeen

Gavin leaned against the hallway wall and waited.

Franklin sat down on the floor. He emptied out his pocket of change. A single marble rolled out with the coins. Cat's-eye glass and blue as the tropical sea. Franklin picked the marble up and stuck it in his mouth. He then concentrated on making stacks out of the coins, quarters on the bottom, dimes at the top. Pennies and nickels in between. He spat the cat's-eye marble out and rolled it into his new city of metal coin towers. The marble bounced around like a pinball and rolled back to him. He giggled gleefully and rolled it again.

Gavin watched him with disgust. The flaccid face, the child's absorption and delight in his shiny glass, in the little metal towers. The village idiot, Gavin thought. He stuck his foot out and knocked the towers over. Franklin began to shout in protest, but the elevator opened and Ballantine appeared.

"You been in there?" Ballantine bellowed from ten doors away.

"I waited for you," Gavin said.

"How the fuck do you know he's dead?" Q-Ball shouted, slamming the wall with his fist. Ballantine approached, rubbing his sore knuckles and looking down at the floor, at the fat flies oozing out from under the threshold space. He punched the wall again. "Fuck." He slipped a plastic glove on and jiggled the doorknob. "It's locked. Why didn't you bust it down?"

"I waited for you," Gavin repeated.

"Who's this guy?" Q-Ball asked, noticing Franklin for the first time.

Franklin rolled the cat's-eye between his thumb and forefinger, and held it up in front of his natural eye.

"The super," Strega answered. "He called it in."

"Hey, buddy," Q-Ball said, "take your marble downstairs and watch the front for the M.E.'s wagon. Tell them to come up to nineteen."

Franklin grinned. "This is just like *NYPD Blue.*"

"Yeah, and I'm Jimmy Smits," Q-Ball sneered. "In my next life I'm coming back as Don Johnson. Now, get the fuck out of here and take your toys with you."

Franklin scooped up his coins, dropped them back in his pocket along with the marble, and stood up. He drifted off to the elevator, jangling his change and whistling a tune.

The elevator doors opened again. Strega stepped out, past Franklin. He carried the battering iron. Cybil Hansen followed. She hurried down the hallway. "Ballantine," she said, "I just heard."

"Get out of here, Hansen," Ballantine ordered. "Go back to the station house."

Hansen stopped cold. "What?"

"I don't want you seeing this."

"I'm a *homicide detective,* Ballantine. I have a right to go in."

"This is my crime scene," he shouted. "Now get out." Then he said more softly: "Do me a favor and call CSU. Tell them I want the whole fucking team down here. Then go back to the station house."

The color rose fast and high in Hansen's cheeks. She looked from Ballantine to Gavin, and seeing that there was no support for her, she wheeled around and marched out, ignoring Strega's compassionate tap on the shoulder.

"Why are you keeping her out?" Gavin asked.

"I don't want her involved in this investigation," Q-Ball said. "I have my own reasons."

Gavin knew Ballantine had already gone way out over his authority investigating the cop suicides, and now that he had one right in his own backyard he was going to

break a lot of rules. Gavin guessed that Q-Ball wanted
Hansen far away if and when the roof fell in on him.

Ballantine jiggled the doorknob again. "Strega, get
over here with that thing."

Strega moved to the door.

Q-Ball gestured impatiently. "Well, go ahead. Open
it up."

Strega hoisted the lead-weighted ram. He used an
underhand grip with one hand placed at either end of
it, and began a gentle swinging motion, working from
his shoulders, building up a good momentum. When the
feel of it was right, he swung the ram as far back as he
could, then threw it forward into the door lock. The
wood split. He swung again. Wood cracked. He swung
again and again, back and forth, the force of the impact
sending the ram back with a power that fed the return
blow. The door cracked and splintered, Strega heaved the
ram forward one last time. The door split away from the
bolt and swung open. It flapped loosely for a moment,
then shuddered slowly back to the buckled doorframe.

"Good work," Ballantine commended. "Now go
guard the elevator. Keep the curious neighbors away
from the crime scene, but keep them around because I
want to question everyone who lives on this floor. Gavin,
you come with me."

Strega noted the set expression on Q-Ball's face. He
backed away wordlessly and moved down the hall.

Q-Ball pushed the door back with his foot. He stood
rooted in the doorway, staring. "Jesus, Mary, and
Joseph," he whispered.

He buried his nose and mouth in a handkerchief.
Gavin unbuttoned his uniform shirt and yanked it up to
cover his nose. The smell was worse than when he had
walked into Donovan's place.

Ballantine moved into the room. Gavin followed,
dimly aware that he was walking over a carpet of flies.
They buzzed up off the floor and around his ankles, their
bodies sluggish from so much feasting. One or two
drifted up to eye level. Gavin waved them away with his
free hand.

The apartment was an L-shaped studio. The doorway opened into the main bar of the L. The skinny part of the L stretched long and narrow off to the right, and was lined with a Pullman kitchen, a row of closets, and a door that looked like it opened into a bathroom. The arrangement of furniture in the main space of the studio had a sleeper sofa facing the door, a high, wide shelving unit with a television set facing the sleeper sofa, and a butcher-block table with four square-backed chairs shoved up in a corner.

The sleeper sofa was unfolded into a double bed. Gavin saw the tangle of sheets and pillows on the thin spring mattress. Then he registered the blood and human insides left out to dry, and his eyes followed the trail down to the floor.

What was left of Mike Kelly lay clothed in nothing more than his uniform shirt, and that—unbuttoned and thrown back away from the body—revealed more than it covered. The body had gone slack beyond rigor, blistered and bloated, and turned green-red in color. Kelly's once living fluids leaked from every orifice, snaking over the swollen skin and pooling—death's putrid waters—around his unrecognizable form.

Gavin had seen this kind of decomposed death before. He had walked in on it a dozen times a year during his long service in the Three-Four. Sometimes it was a body left half buried in a vacant lot, sometimes one tossed away in a garbage dump left to rot under a pile of refuse, sometimes inside a tenement building, often undressed like this, often mutilated beyond recognition, carved up with a knife or burned with gasoline, but never, *never* had he walked in on this kind of decomposition when the decomposed had been a colleague, a friend, a fellow officer with five stripes worth of duty time on his sleeve and forty-eight hours worth of death registered on his now unfamiliar flesh.

Danny had been bad to see, but then, Gavin had arrived only twenty-four hours after the time of death. From all first appearances and the visible progression of decomposition, Kelly had been dead forty-eight hours, which the extreme heat made look like seventy-two. Those extra hours made all the difference. Danny's general form had been clearly recognizable as *Danny*. But Kelly's form resembled nothing natural or known in live human beings.

Death was not a great, sweet blanket of sleep that turned a familiar body heavy with gentle, eternal rest. Death moved swiftly, marching over and erasing facial features, altering physical proportions, painting with its horrific colors, perfuming with its own foul scent, claiming its own with an army of insects. Thousands of fly eggs had hatched, and the new generation wriggled and waved out of Kelly's every facial cavity—the eyes, the nose, the mouth and ears, and of course, out of the fatal wound itself. It was there, on the temple, burned into the now green flesh. The star-shaped entrance wound, as unmistakable and damning as the gun next to Kelly's bloated hand.

Gavin gagged. He turned around and stumbled through the broken door, back into the hall. He threw himself against the wall and beat it with his head, hoping to beat the grisly images from his mind, hoping to beat away the cresting nausea that was wrangling him to the floor. He fell and clawed his way along the hall, threshold to threshold, trying for the stairwell and not making it. At the elevator bank, Strega watching helplessly, Gavin retched. He crawled another foot and retched again. When he finished and there was nothing but air left to heave out from his insides, he wiped his mouth with the back of his hand, looked up at Strega, and said simply, quietly, with deadly intent: "I'm going to find her."

Gavin waited in the hall, watching the procession of CSU techs arrive, heavy gear boxes bumping at their knees. Lang arrived next, then Wilson, and finally Ramon Alvarez himself.

Alvarez had been at a Westchester country club, enjoying a bloody Mary when he heard the news. He raced straight back to the city and arrived at the scene wearing

pristine tennis whites. The bright tennis whites were out
of place in the dim, steamy hallway of Kelly's building.
They implied a genteel joviality and a well-mannered
cheer that had nothing to do with Kelly's apparent self-
inflicted death and subsequent corporeal rotting.

Ramon Alvarez disappeared into 19F. He came out
later with Q-Ball in tow. As Gavin observed from a distance, Alvarez paced the hall, agitated and annoyed, anticipating the press frenzy a seventeenth suicide would
provoke. Alvarez questioned Ballantine quietly at first,
then his voice rose. Gavin watched the P.C. prod Ballantine in the chest with one finger, demanding to know
why Ballantine had ordered the full CSU contingent.

"Why did you order fingerprint dusting in a *suicide,*
Ballantine? You think CSU doesn't have enough to do
crawling over the Met? Why do you have forensic ex-
perts crawling around in there tweezing fibers out of
the carpet and pulling hair samples out of the bathroom
drains? I don't need a crime-scene investigation to tell
me that these cops are blowing their own fucking brains
out. What I do need is a shrink to tell me *why.*" Ramon
ran a hand through his thick hair and waited for Ballantine's response.

Gavin heard Q-Ball mutter something about *getting a
thorough documentation of evidence,* then Alvarez
shouted *Evidence against who?* and steered Ballantine
back into the apartment before Gavin could hear the
detective's answer.

The P.C. emerged much later, looking less genteel and
full of rage, although his tennis whites were still spotless.
He elbowed his way down the crowded hall, into the
elevator. As the doors were sliding closed, he focused
on Strega, and an expression of recognition and anger
spread across his handsome features. "You!" he said,
pointing a finger. The doors closed tight, and the elevator whisked Ramon Alvarez away.

Strega flashed Gavin a strained smile. He knew how
it had gone. Wilson had talked to Maria. Maria had
talked to Ramon. Strega would hear from Wilson, or
possibly the P.C. himself, before the week was out.

Gavin sat down on the hall floor and waited. He waited for hours. Finally, Ballantine stuck his head out of 19F. "Gavin."

Gavin edged over. "What do you have?"

"No towels," Ballantine reported. "TV set's on, programmed to VCR. The VCR's on, but there's no tape. Cause of death: single gunshot to the right temple, apparently fired from his service revolver and apparently self-inflicted. We'll have to wait for the autopsy to know if there was evidence of sexual activity or drugs. Estimated time of death, fifty-two hours, give or take a few on either side. With this kind of heat, it's hard to pin it down."

Ballantine mopped his sweaty brow. "We pulled the shower drain, looking for foreign hair on the chance the perp showered. It was clean, too clean. Someone beat us to it. We're still looking for the apartment key. No sign of it. One other thing. We found a cigarette butt in the sink. No cartons or packages of cigarettes in the apartment, no lighters either. Some cheap matches in the kitchen next to the gas stove. You have any idea if Mike smoked?"

"He quit eight years ago. Doctor's orders."

"Lot of good quitting did him," Q-Ball observed. "Go on, Ed, you look like hell. Get out of here. Go home. Have a drink."

"Think I'll do just that, Ballantine," Gavin said, working his way back down the hall away from the crime scene. Away from the flies.

Gavin didn't wait to get home to have his first drink. He had it at a tight, dim Midtown bar that catered to office workers, but lured in weekend traffic by offering a two-for-one Sunday night special and a generous spread of all-you-can-eat appetizers, toothpick freebies, Cheez Whiz on Ritz crackers, honey-roasted peanuts, buttered popcorn, and mini-pizzas.

Gavin straddled a stool at the bar and piled a plate high with the mini-pizzas. He ordered up a shot of whisky on the rocks, clear and cold and strong enough, he hoped, to flush out the smell and memory of Kelly's death. He tipped the first shot back in one smooth motion and signaled the bartender for a refill. He nursed the freebie slowly. Halfway through, he remembered Walter. The clock over the bar said it was five o'clock. He slid off the stool, pumped a handful of change into a pay phone on the wall, and listened to Walter's phone ring fifteen times. He hung up. Walter worked Sundays.

Gavin mounted his bar stool again and worked his way through the stack of mini-pizzas while he watched a newscast flicker silently on a corner television set. The scene was too familiar. Kelly's gritty apartment building. The swarm of emergency vehicles outside, the parade of brass marching in and out—Alvarez in his bright tennis whites, Ballantine, Wilson, the lieutenant of Manhattan Detectives, Chief Medical Examiner Lang, they were all there. The news cameras zoomed in on the CSU boxes bumping along at the knees of the techs. Gavin watched the reporters' lips and believed he could read them: *Why are there so many CSU techs at a suicide?*

Ballantine was hanging in the wind, all right, and now it was public.

Gavin stared into his whiskey glass, pondering the puzzle pieces, sliding them around into different sequences. He arranged and rearranged, but always came up short. He just didn't know enough. Finally, Gavin paid his bill and left. In the time it had taken him to finish his two golden shots, the afternoon outside had eased into early evening. The city streets were Sunday night quiet. Emma's torrential downpour had sputtered out into a hot, spitting rain, and the winds had died down to nothing.

Gavin drove home. In between the bar and his Ozone Park driveway, the two whiskeys wore off and he started to smell Kelly's death again. He walked straight into the kitchen and mixed another drink, a scotch this time, straight up, and tipped back fast to burn the smell of Kelly away.

Shelly stood at the stove, wokking up more of her low-sodium veggies. She tossed and flipped with contented

violence, scraping the metal Chinese cooking shovel hard
against the sizzling wok basin. Her back stayed turned
to him all through the drink-mixing ritual and the first
stir with his finger.

"Mike Kelly's dead," he said.

The ferocious wokking subsided. She tilted her head
but did not turn. "How?"

"Shot himself in the head." Gavin upended the scotch
and took it in one easy swallow. He sucked the sheen
of alcohol off an ice cube, spat it back into the glass,
and poured himself another. "I ate in the city. Don't
save any of that stuff for me." The stir-fry action started
again, more violent than before.

He carried his drink into the bedroom and snapped
on the television. Kelly's death led the local news. Gavin
sat down and watched the footage all over again. This
time the camera angle changed to a tight shot of the
building entrance. Gavin picked out Franklin standing
off to one side, watching the parade of cops trekking
back and forth in the pouring rain. Franklin was grinning. His right hand was stuffed in his pocket, and Gavin
could tell he was jangling his change. Grinning and jangling while Kelly's remains were hauled out on a gurney,
hidden from sight inside a heavy rubber body bag.

Franklin's expression bothered Gavin. It was smug,
secretive, and Gavin had the feeling Franklin was laughing at everybody. The camera cut back to the reporter,
and Franklin was out of the frame. But Franklin's grinning face stayed with Gavin. Maybe the village idiot
knew something. Gavin swallowed his drink and decided
to swing by Kelly's building the following day. He
wanted to turn Franklin upside down and see if something besides coins and a cat's-eye marble could be
shaken out of him.

Strega sat alone Sunday night at his sculpting pedestal.
He worked shirtless and barefoot, wearing only a pair
of old Princeton running shorts. The pedestal was fitted
with a flat square of varnished wood that turned to allow
for three-hundred-and-sixty-degree rotation. He placed

a fresh block of white clay in the center of the wood and began to work the clay with his hands. Usually he worked from a photo of his subject, but tonight his memory was enough. His hands worked quickly, building planes and angles in the clay, then shaping and molding a high forehead, a full pair of lips, wide, deep eyes, strong cheek contours sweeping high. He worked fast and sure, transforming the clay into the small, well-shaped head and finely featured face of Maria Alvarez.

She was right about one thing. He was thinking about her. All the time.

The fear. The fear. The terrible fear.

He came for her that night. Late. She knew he would. He took her in the living room, roughly, standing up, then left without a word. Maria felt so dirty. And shamed.

The shame. The shame. The shame.

Maria watched her bathtub fill. She was going to wash her shame away. The water gushed out, fast and hot. Her cramped bathroom was run down. Peel-and-stick squares of mirror covered the walls and ceiling. A hundred Marias, dressed in the dark regulation uniform, stared out at her from a peel-and-stick prison. She looked down at the tub. The water had risen to the lip and was dripping over the side of the yellowed porcelain. She turned the faucets off, stepped in fully dressed, and stretched out in the water. She unbuttoned her uniform top. The sides flapped up to the surface. Maria patted them down tight to her skin. The small hairs on her forearm lifted and wavered in the water.

The wet, dark uniform pants pasted to her limbs looked eel-like and eerie. She tugged her uniform pants down. Her pubis was a dark scar against the pale of her skin and the white of the tub. The hairs down there uncurled in the water. Maria unsheathed a fresh razor blade. She held it to the flat top of her pubic triangle, just away from the hair edge, where the skin was more baby white than anywhere else on her full body. She

rocked the blade from left to right, feeling the bite of
sharp metal against her flesh.

She stopped the rocking and applied a strong, steady
pressure. The fatty pubic skin folded up to either side
of the blade. She pressed down harder, then dragged the
steel blade across, watching intently. A single red line
snaked up. The blood billowed out, and the waving field
of black hairs disappeared in a watery cloud of red. Red,
red, smoking out around the tops of her marble thighs
and the white of her belly skin, feathering brightly across
the water's surface. Maria skated the blade across the
soft of her stomach, following the dusky blue vein that
ran straight down to the field of black hair, to the center
of her sex.

To her sin.

To the pulsing, aching part of her that had brought
nothing but disgust and pain and fear.

Maria released the blade. She groped for a bottle of
blue bubble bath and unscrewed the top. She turned the
bottle upside down. Blue streamed into her bath water,
running into the red. She dropped the bottle on the
floor. Glass shattered. She twisted the faucets open
again. The tub ran to overflowing, red and blue, the
colors of her own desired self-destruction. The abandoned blade floated near her nipples. She snatched it
and laid it against her left wrist. The vein there was
thick. It sprouted high and hard against her flesh. She
sliced the blade lightly across the arc of the vein and
plunged her bleeding wrist into the hot bath water. The
skin was split, but the vein was unharmed.

She sank down under the surface and looked up
through the bloody bath water at the mirrored ceiling
above. Maria Alvarez smiled. Bubbles escaped from her
wide, proud mouth. The mirror reflected her perfect
body submerged, molded and pale, awash in the red of
her own blood. She saw how she would look if they ever
found her like this. How *he* would see her. How the
crime-scene photos would picture her.

Maria Alvarez ran the blade down from sternum to
pubis in a fast straight line, wishing she was ready to cut
all the way through, to cut deep enough to die.

Eighteen

Maria Alvarez did not show up for the eight-to-four tour Monday. The tour sergeant was annoyed. Strega was relieved.

Ballantine stood in the front of the room, brandishing the *Daily News*. "THE SHOOTING GALLERY," he shouted. "That's the headline! Creative writers, aren't they? It gets better. 'The Nineteenth Precinct's latest victim is the Department's own officer Mike Kelly, who Sunday became the seventeenth suicide in this year's NYPD suicide epidemic. Add to that nine fatalities in the Massacre at the Met, two fatalities in the attack on Emilio's restaurant, two fatalities in the attack on Melissa Stewart's Bridal, and there goes the neighborhood.'"

Ballantine tossed the paper aside. "The pressure on the mayor is substantial, which means the pressure on me is worse. It's up to you to keep the precinct calm. Be visible. Get out of your patrol cars, walk around. Let people *see* you. That's all." Q-Ball rolled out.

Roll call broke up quietly. Mike Kelly's death was fresh in every cop's mind, as were the silent questions: What does it take? How bad does it have to be?

Strega ran into Hansen in the hallway. "Morning, Cybil. You still burning over yesterday?"

She tucked a curl of hair behind her ear and shrugged. "I'll get over it. Sometimes I think no matter what Q-Ball says, he still thinks I'm more fragile than the rest of his team just because I'm a girl."

"Woman, Cybil, you're a woman."

"Well, thank you for noticing, but I'm trying hard to be one of the boys."

And she was. She wore loose cotton trousers, a baggy blazer, and button-down shirt. Her shoes were flat and dull, and her blond hair was combed away from her face and tied back in an old-fashioned ponytail. Her green eyes sparkled, though, and Strega thought with his sculptor's way of seeing things that there was no way she could hide that face, those great, arching cheekbones, and graceful mouth. Not unless she stuck a paper bag over her head. Her face was animated as she explained her workload problem to Strega. The animation made her more beautiful. "Anyway," she was saying, "it's not like I don't have enough to do trying to track down our shooters."

"Any leads?"

"Not yet. We're still out there trying to come up with something on your tip about the suit. I'm dealing with every store in Manhattan that sells Armani. I got a style number match on that Armani suit your witness gave us. Now I'm knee-deep in receipts, backtracking to May, when the new summer collection hit the stores. Wherever a sale of that style number's recorded, I'm pulling names and addresses off the receipts.

"Problem is, the store only records names and addresses for credit card or check purchases. I can't track cash sales. They do a big cash business, bigger than you'd imagine. Funny money, probably. Right now I'm just working on the Manhattan stores. Next it's the outer boroughs, then as far out as D.C., Boston and Philly. You ask me, Strega, it's a complete waste of time. Those Joes paid cash. And with the money they raked in from the Museum, they're probably long gone by now. Mexico. Barbados."

"Not necessarily."

Hansen cocked her head to one side. "What's going on inside your Ivy League brain?"

"After the bridal shop hit, they pulled off one of their car hustles. Then after the restaurant hit, they pulled off two more car scams. I'll think they'll do it again in the next day or so."

"After the fortune they lifted at the museum, why would they risk it?"

"The operative word is risk. They get a high from taking chances. And what could be riskier than walking down Madison Avenue in broad daylight if you're one of the nation's ten most wanted? What bigger thrill than to fleece a couple more rich ladies *right under the NYPD's nose*?"

"Ballantine swears they won't be back."

"He's wrong, Hansen."

"So what if he is? We can't have cops every two feet. How the hell do we prevent them from hitting again?"

"The question should be, how the hell do we catch them?"

"You say that like you have an answer."

"I do."

"Well, don't just stand there, Strega. Talk!"

Gavin waited for Strega in the patrol car. It was after eight, and he wanted to get rolling. Gavin suddenly realized he actually *looked forward* to spending the day with Strega. He looked forward to the kid's affable ways and even his Princeton chatter. Yes, Strega with his easy, earnest talk and his head full of knowledge was refreshing. Gavin found, if he listened, he almost always learned something he hadn't known before. Like how to cook sauce for pasta. Or why modern art was *valid*. That was a word Strega liked. *Valid*. He watched his young partner lope across the street. *To be that good-looking and so smart*. If Strega wasn't so affable, he'd be intimidating.

The fact was, Gavin figured, he had lucked out having Strega around for his last days of duty—a pleasant presence while he was spinning the days out, killing time until retirement. A funny expression, killing time, as though time were something living that could be killed, as though wasting time was a grave act, as grave and morally reprehensible as murder and subject to the same moral judgments.

With so little time on earth, Gavin supposed a man

could do somewhat better than to *kill time,* especially him. Killing time was an apt expression, a cliché for the cliché that was rapidly becoming his life, with his predictably fragile marriage, his deteriorating body, and his attitude souring like milk on a summer day. A cliché, wasn't it? The young cop-old cop thing? The Mutt and Jeff thing? Whatever it was, there he sat, Edward S. Gavin, mumbling and grumbling his way into admitting he had a bright new friend. Yes, Strega was now a friend, as different as the two cops were—Strega was a Renaissance man while Gavin felt stranded in the Middle Ages.

Strega ducked into the driver's seat and buckled up.

"You're late," Gavin announced.

"Sorry," Strega offered, turning the ignition. "Where to?"

"Take a run up to Kelly's building."

"What's there?" Strega asked, pointing the car uptown.

"Franklin. I got a feeling Franklin's got something he wants to tell me."

"Hey," Strega said when they were rolling uptown, "you ever reach Walter, the night-shift worker?"

"Forgot all about him," Gavin admitted. "There's a phone there."

Strega pulled up next to it. Gavin hopped out, punched in Walter's number, and listened to the buzzing busy signal again. He smacked the phone with a fist, hung up, and got back in the car. "Off the hook," Gavin said.

Strega's Genie went off. He flipped it open. "West Entertainment. It's ticking up."

"You selling?"

"Not yet." Strega pulled away from the curb and headed uptown to Ninety-sixth Street. He parked in front of Kelly's building. A man was visible through the glass lobby doors, mopping the floor. He wore gray coveralls, like Franklin's.

"Bingo," Gavin said, jumping out and hurrying up the walk.

Strega followed him. The man had his back to the

doors. He was short like Franklin, but too skinny by far. Gavin rapped on the glass. The short man turned around. He was Asian. His name was stitched on his coverall chest, LING in red script, and Gavin wondered if that was the first name or the last name, or like Franklin, if it was both. Ling leaned his mop in the pail and opened the door.

"Where's Franklin?" Gavin asked.

"Day off," Ling replied. "Every Monday."

"Where can we find him?"

Ling lifted his shoulders helplessly. "Don't know. Come back tomorrow." He closed the door and went back to mopping.

"Fuck," Gavin said.

"So we'll swing by tomorrow," Strega said, putting a hand on Gavin's shoulder in consolation. "One day isn't going to make Kelly any less dead."

"Spoken like a poet," Gavin complained half-heartedly, staring up at Kelly's building.

The fact was, he knew Strega understood loss.

"Come on, Ed," Strega said gently. "Let's go. We'll come back tomorrow."

Gavin looked away from Kelly's building and moved heavily down the walk to the car.

Maria woke up, rolled over, and looked at her digital clock. Eleven o'clock. She was late. She stumbled out of bed, pulled her soiled uniform on, and left the apartment, not caring that her hair was matted and her face unwashed. Her hands shook as she pulled the door open to the station house.

"You're late," Officer Bell thundered when she swept past his tall desk.

"So what?" she snapped, feeling dizzy.

"Wilson wants you in his office, *forthwith.*"

Maria hesitated. It had to be serious for Wilson to issue a *forthwith* command. She swung up the stairs and down the hall into his office. He was pacing. Maria slouched in a chair. She felt nauseous. Wilson wore black

and gold cuff links like her father's. He was wearing
pink cashmere socks, even though it was summer.

"Maria."

Said like that, her name was an order to stand at attention. She slid out of the chair and faced him. The
room was spinning. She gripped the chair for support.

He looked her over, taking it all in. Her tangled, matted hair, pale face, bloodshot eyes, and her wrinkled,
soiled uniform. "You look like shit," Wilson said more
gently.

Wilson was the enemy, with his leonine face and smart
white smile. He was a politician first and cop second;
worse still, he was her father's friend. *Sycophant,* she
thought. *Spy.* Wilson kept an eye on her for her father.
That's why she was here in the One-Nine, so he would
know every move she made.

Wilson approached.

She stared at his feet and wondered if the cashmere
made his feet sweat. He stood up next to her, close
enough for her to see where his stiff shirt collar cut into
the skin on the side of his throat. Close enough to smell
his aftershave. The Listerine on his breath.

"You're screwing up, Maria. Coming in late or not
coming in at all. Having *altercations* with other officers.
I had to apprise your father. I had no choice. Now, I'm
only going to tell you this once. Whatever's going on, if
you have an alcohol situation or a drug situation, *pull
yourself together.* And stay the hell away from Jon
Strega. Understood?"

She nodded dumbly, fighting back the nausea, the
dizziness.

"Dismissed."

"Oh, God," Maria cried. She whirled around and ran
out of the office.

She couldn't have heard Wilson's voice calling out
after her, *Are you okay, Maria?* or his puzzled voice
whispering to his secretary, *I've never seen her look like
this, I think she's sick,* or the measured words with which
he spoke to the P.C. *apprising* him of the latest *situation.*

She couldn't have heard Wilson talking to her father

because at that exact moment she was stumbling into the bathroom, locking herself in a stall, slamming her fists into the metal door, and kicking the porcelain toilet bowl. She sank down to the cold tile floor and gripped the sides of the bowl, feeling sick, feeling afraid.

The fear, the fear, the terrible fear.

It never left her now.

Things were spinning out of control.

She was out of control.

Maria hung her head over the sanitary blue water—water that got bluer with every flush—emptying her sickened insides out, emptying and flushing in a steady rhythm. In between flushes she shouted *fuck you* as loud as she could, hoping the sound of rushing water would drown out her shouts. It didn't. Someone came running in. That someone was rapping on the metal of her locked stall. "Maria, are you okay?"

Maria inclined her head slightly and saw the gleaming, tasseled shoes pacing back and forth, the flash of pink cashmere socks, and the perfect break of the inspector's Italian wool slacks. "Are you okay?" Wilson asked again. She answered him with a flush.

"Maria?" Wilson tried again. "Do you need a doctor?"

"Fuck you. Get out," she cried. "Leave me alone."

"Take the day off," Wilson said, the concern wiped from his voice. "Pull yourself together. Report in tomorrow, on time." He walked out, leaving Maria alone with her bowl of blue.

Blue, blue, blue. It was supposed to be a good color, wasn't it? Surprising, as in *out of the blue,* rich as in *blue blood,* adventurous as in *the wild blue yonder.* For Maria blue was a curse. The Mediterranean blue of the patrol cars, the same cheerful blue ringing the precinct house windows, the blue neon of the blinking bail-bond sign, Kelly's terrified blue eyes, the steel blue of Wilson's accusing eyes—*Stay away from Jon Strega*—and now the blue of this water.

She flushed again and waited for the bowl to refill. Then she reached in and churned the water with her

hands, searching for the part that was clear, not blue.
She trawled through like a kayaker, her hands flat-faced
oars, slapping into the water, windmilling out, churning,
turning, looking for white, but finding only the antiseptic
blue of treated water and her own blue despair.

Blue and red, both were blood. There was blue blood
and red blood. What if she opened the slim blue veins at
the base of her wrists right then and there? What color
would gush out? Blue or red, or maybe both and white
too. Red, white, and blue, the colors of America, the colors
of the flag. Maybe stars would tumble out in her blood.

Yes, she thought, fifty-two stars shooting out of her
opened wrists, shooting stars, white-hot, sinking to the
bottom of the blue porcelain sea. She would flush them
away. She wanted to open her wrists right then and
there. Suicide. The forbidden act. Well, Maria wanted
to exercise her God-given right of free will, of conscious
choice, but she wasn't ready yet.

Not yet.

She had unfinished business.

She dug in her pocket for the plastic bag she had
found in Angel's apartment. There was one good hit
left in it. She shoved the bag up tight to her nostrils
and inhaled.

The sickness lifted. She felt clear-headed. Strong. A
hundred feet tall.

Maria flushed one last time and stood up. She went
out to the row of sinks, bent over, and put her mouth
over a faucet. Her lips formed a perfect seal around the
steel. She ran ice-cold water down her throat, then
pulled her lips off the faucet and looked up at her rav-
aged face in the mirror. She smiled.

She had two games left.

Maria left the precinct house and drove out of the
One-Nine, across town, back to Hell's Kitchen. She
parked in front of an electronics store. The display window was filled with twenty-five television sets, all tuned
to the same channel. The sets were aligned in symmetri-
cal rows of five up and five across. The symmetry was

broken by one ultra-wide screen TV in the middle. Maria's face looked out from the wide screen. A video camera in the display window was pointed out, at her. She waved at it. The Maria in the wide-screen TV waved at her.

The twenty-five smaller sets were all tuned to the local news. The subject of the show was Ramon Alvarez. The screens were filled with pictures of him standing on the great staircase at the Metropolitan Museum. A speaker in the window piped out the sound. "We will not let terrorists run rampant through our city," he raged. "We will not be hostages of fear." He was raging at the perpetrators of the Museum Massacre. And at her. Maria knew he was raging at her. For not protecting her mother. For not protecting Angel. For being alive when she should have been dead, when her mother and Angel should have been alive instead.

She stood riveted, eyes cutting back and forth between the twenty-five raging Ramons and her one terrified face. Maria walked abruptly away from the store to a magazine shop. *New York* magazine filled the window. Ramon Alvarez was the cover story for the second time in as many weeks, the cover headline trumpeting THE P.C.'S WEEK OF HORROR.

Maria went inside and bought all two hundred copies.

She hauled the magazines back to her apartment and arranged them in neat stacks on the bedroom floor. She dumped a pair of scissors and a couple of rolls of scotch tape on the floor next to them, then sat down and began to cut.

Hours later, Maria stood in the middle of the room and admired her work. Every inch of wall space was plastered with pictures of Ramon Alvarez. Grinning, waving, now intent, now triumphant, candid shots, posed shots, dressed up at society events, and laid back in his elegant apartment, slick Ramon, fashionable Ramon, proud Ramon, always making love to the camera, and looking out now with a thousand pair of unseeing eyes into Maria's bedroom.

Maria stretched out on the floor and looked up. The

stars were gone, covered by the collage of Ramon Alvarez. There was one picture of the two of them, father
and daughter, in uniform. Maria looked at that picture,
at the way his proprietary hand lay on her shoulder, his
slim fingers curling slightly at her neck. She looked at
her own stiff, stilted smile and wondered if anyone else
could see the hatred in her eyes. Was she the only one
who hated the hero Ramon Alvarez? Was she?

Maria rolled over and stood up next to a wall, eye to
eye with a smiling Ramon. Maria touched the picture of
the familiar face. She traced the features lightly with her
fingers, and her touch was tender. Suddenly she slapped
the smiling face. Then her hand was a fist and her fist
was pounding her father's proud face.

She turned to the picture of Jon Strega. He was starting to look a lot like Ramon.

"I've been thinking about how we're going to catch
them," Strega said late in the day, when they were driving slowly up Madison Avenue.

"Catch who?" Gavin asked.

"The shooters."

"Catching them's not our job. That's what we have
detectives for."

"Hansen says they're stuck." Strega explained his
theory.

"So what if you're right?" Gavin replied. "Madison
Avenue has forty blocks of prime shopping on both sides
of the street. There's no way Ballantine's boys can cover
it all."

"I didn't say they should."

"Then what are you saying?"

"We use Hansen to draw the shooters out."

"Cybil?"

"Q-Ball would look a little silly prancing down Madison Avenue dressed up in a skirt. Hansen's perfect. She's
ambitious, she likes challenge, and she's a woman. We
dress her in expensive clothes, load her down with paste
jewels and a wire, and send her out on Madison Avenue.

Then we'll tail her in an unmarked car, see if anyone follows her."

"Fish bait?"

"You got it."

"Sounds to me like you're handing Hansen to them on a silver platter. How do you know they won't kill her?"

"Because they've never changed the way they operate. The blonde is trigger-happy, not the Latin, and the Latin's the driver. So, the way I see it, if they bite, if Hansen's hustled into a car, she'll be in there one-on-one with the partner who hasn't hurt any one of the women he's taken for a ride."

"Yet. He hasn't hurt one yet. Go on."

"We'll set up chase cars at quadrants around Madison. As soon as Hansen's car takes off, we follow in one of Ballantine's unmarked Chevys. We'll have two other teams standing by to take the blonde."

"Meanwhile, Hansen's locked inside with Giorgio Armani."

"She'll be armed. If things go wrong, she nails him. If they go right, he takes her for a quiet drive, then lets her out somewhere, and we get him after the drop. One way or another, we get both boys in one neat haul and Hansen walks away untouched, like all the other ladies did."

"Good idea," Gavin admitted. "But it's high-risk. I don't think Cybil sees herself as a sitting duck."

"Wrong." Strega smiled. "She already said yes."

"I'm impressed. Must be your Italian charm."

"She's married."

"All the more reason for her to be charmed. One other problem."

"What's that?"

"No way Q-Ball's going to let us play I-Spy," Gavin said, shaking his head.

"According to Hansen, Ballantine thinks the shooters are long gone. He says if he's wrong and they try another hit, it will be something bigger than the Met, not smaller. He's got his team staked out in luxury hotels and high-ticket jewelry stores. He doesn't have enough detectives to go around as it is. He'll be happy to have us."

"If you can convince Q-Ball, I'm with you. Even the Lone Ranger had a partner."

"If I'm the Lone Ranger, guess what that makes you?"

"I'm no Indian. I'm Anglo-Saxon with an emphasis on the Saxon. I can't ride a horse, and I'm not interested in playing detective."

"You're already helping Ballantine with an investigation."

"That's different. I'm doing it for Donovan. I ran out of hero juice a long time ago. I want to wake up on retirement day with all my body parts intact."

"Something tells me you're going to miss the action when you leave the Department."

"I get lonely, Strega, I'll call you collect from my golf cart in Florida."

"You play golf?"

"Not yet, but I'll have plenty of time to learn."

Strega checked his watch. "This tour's over. Let's go back to the precinct house. We'll take Cybil in and see if we can't convince Q-Ball to let us go hunting."

"No fucking way." Ballantine pounded the desk for emphasis. "Is that clear enough for you?" He looked from Hansen to Gavin to Strega. "Two weeks out of the academy, and Strega here wants to be promoted to detective grade." Ballantine surged across the desk and prodded Strega in the chest. "Didn't they teach you anything at the academy? You have to *earn* detective grade, *Officer* Strega. You perform your sector duties well, you demonstrate the correct respect for your senior officers—and that includes your partner here—maybe you even act brave enough to get decorated a couple of times. Then and only then do you come and talk to me about moving up to detective. I don't need a rookie's help. I've got some of the most experienced detectives in the Department working on this case."

"What kind of ideas do they have for you?" Strega asked.

"Is that sarcasm I hear?" Ballantine bellowed.

Gavin winced. Strega's blowing it, he thought. He should just let it go, shake Ballantine's hand, say, *"You're right, sir,"* and let it go. But Strega didn't.

"It's not sarcasm," Strega said. "It's concern for the people who live in this precinct. I have a plan that will work. It shouldn't matter much what title or job assignment I have."

Ballantine's mouth twisted in displeasure. "If anybody's going out as fish bait, let it be one of the ladies from the major case squad. Better yet, let it be one of the Feds."

Detective Hansen stood up. She usually tried hard for Ballantine to see her as one of the guys, but Ballantine had a soft spot for her. Once in a while, when she shot him her mile-wide smile, he just came unglued. So when Cybil wanted something from him, she flashed him *the smile.*

She sat down next to him. "Ballantine," she said, "you don't mean that. What if it works? You're going to let the *Feds* get all the glory? It's a wonderful idea. I'd like to take a shot at it." And then she smiled.

Ballantine's big, tense face went soft. A smile of his own quivered at the edge of his lips. He played with his pencil and brushed a hand over his bald head.

Cybil had him. She moved in for the close. "I have the skill to pull this off, and I'm willing to try. I'm asking you to do me a favor. You owe me after throwing me out of Kelly's."

Ballantine picked at an edge of paper. He looked at his shoes.

"Ballantine?" Hansen coaxed.

Ballantine cleared his throat and looked at her. She was smiling *the smile* again. "Okay," he said. "You have one week to play with this half-assed scheme."

Cybil put out a hand to shake his. "Thank you very much. We won't let you down."

Ballantine swiveled his chair around and studied his

push-pin crime map. "You're all excused. Except you, Gavin."

Gavin hung back. When they were alone, Q-Ball shut the door and paced out the small perimeter of his office. "Dr. Fields came to see me today. Kelly talked to him just last week. Part of the P.C.'s shrink-in-every-precinct plan. Looks like the P.C.'s preventative medicine failed." Ballantine referred to a sheaf of papers. "Anyway, according to Field's notes on Kelly, there was no sign of melancholia, depression, or self-destruction. Not a one. Some unexpressed rage, but Fields claims it was normal and that it was all directed at the soon to be ex-Mrs. Kelly. Bottom line? Fields didn't come up with anything you and I don't already know." Ballantine put the papers back in the new file marked KELLY, M. The file was thinner than the rest, still awaiting autopsy reports, photos, crime-scene evidence.

"What else?" Gavin asked.

"Lang determined that suicide was the manner of death. Kelly had cocaine in his blood, dried semen on his hands and thighs, but not on his genitals. Lang said the semen could have come from masturbation or, of course, intercourse with a partner who washed his genitals off after the act, eliminating foreign body fluids. If there was intercourse, then the perp was really thinking. Not only was Kelly washed, there were no stray pubic hairs picked up either. Lang insists that if intercourse had taken place, there would have been foreign pubic hairs on his thighs or genitals. Lang said someone would have to use tweezers and a magnifying glass to pick them out, and if someone did that, they had more than an average knowledge of forensic science.

"Kelly's hands were full of powder stains, the bullet in his head was a match from his service revolver, and, of course, he had the star-shaped entrance wound. Most killers don't stand close enough to make a contact wound. They like to shoot from a nice safe distance. Like I said before, our killer must be one sick motherfucker." Ballantine reached around and flipped his bulletin board over. The city map was covered by a twelve-month calendar—all the months of the current year, starting in January, running to December. Certain days of certain months had bold red X's drawn in. Others had black X's.

"This is the time frame for all the suicides this year," Ballantine explained. "I went back through the files from last year, but nothing came up a match with the details of the deaths we're questioning. The run started this year. On January first. New Year's Day."

"Significant?"

"I don't know. You can ask the killer if and when we ever find her." Ballantine turned back to the map and pointed to the X's as he spoke. "Red X's stand for the suicides we think were homicides. Black X's stand for the legit suicides. You can see there's no pattern at all for the black X's. They're random as can be, scattered around on different days of the week, different weeks of the month. The red X's are another story. There's a distinct pattern for the first five killings.

"The first day of each month was consistent up to May. But then she hit on the fifteenth too." He pointed to a red X on the first and the fifteenth of the month. "The new pattern continues in June with a killing on the first, then Danny's on the fifteenth. He was the eighth victim." He pointed to Danny's red X. "The pattern changes again. There's nothing at all in July, nothing on the first of August or the fifteenth. Then out of the blue, we got two X's, one for Prince and one for Kelly, both within a week of each other."

"What's the point of the first-of-the-month thing if it was dropped halfway through the year?" Gavin asked.

"That's what was bothering me. This is how I think it goes. Serial killers always have all kinds of patterns and rituals. The date pattern's not unusual. I think our killer started with a pattern, then wised up and decided leaving a distinct trail wasn't so smart. Our killer seems to be fighting the need to be utterly consistent in every detail of each murder and the need to not have the killings identified as murder at all. But taking her trophies, the shields, is risky. It's as though part of the killer wants to be acknowledged and the other part wants the murders to remain secret." He flipped the bulletin board back to face the wall. "My guess is the killer is at war with herself, assuming it's a woman. There's some split in the personality. Who knows how or why it got there, but the killings seem to be gratifying and pushing the two sides apart at the same time."

"How's all this dime-store psychology going to help us find her?"

"It's not. For the moment, the part of her that doesn't want to be found is winning. She is meticulous in how she leaves the crime scene and in how she arranges the evidence. She has to make a mistake. But she's a smart one. So far it doesn't look like she made any mistakes in Kelly's murder, with the exception of the cigarette, and there are a hundred possible explanations for how that got there. We have to hope she'll screw up the next time and leave us something. Now that the date ritual's broken, there's no telling when she'll hit again. Two killings in one week may have satiated her compulsion, her need to kill. Who knows how long it will take for her need to build up again? We may have to wait a couple of months."

"I hope we wait forever," Gavin said.

Strega ran into Maria Alvarez on his way out of the precinct house. She was swinging her way up the welcoming-arms stairway as he was swinging his way down, and it was too late to back up. She had him cornered. The look on her face told him it pleased her. She blocked the staircase, tapped the baton at her hip, and eyed Strega. She was wearing oversized, long silver earrings. They touched her shoulders and tinkled when she moved her head. Maria looked pale and worn, like she really had been sick.

Another cop from the precinct loped up the stairs, around her. "Hey, Maria, long time no see. Where you been?"

"Philly," she said, looking hard at Strega.

"What's in Philly besides the Liberty Bell?"

"Family friends," she said, still looking at Strega. "I had to visit some family friends regarding a recent tragedy in my family."

"I'm sorry to hear that, Maria," the cop said. "Didn't know there'd been a tragedy. You don't look so good. You holding up okay?"

"You know me. A regular brick house."

"I wasn't referring to your body, Maria," he ribbed.

She laughed goodnaturedly. "See you around."

The cop went on up into the precinct house.

"Philly, Jonnie. You should go. You don't even know what happened in your own family, do you? I do. I really know you now. I feel close to you too. But you made a mistake going to Wilson. He asked me a lot of uncomfortable questions. I'm going to make you pay for that." She skipped up the last few steps and ducked inside.

Strega jogged home.

Philly, she had said. *I had to visit some family friends.*

He went straight to his desk drawer and dug out an old Christmas card. On the front, on heavily embossed stock, an angel floated against a sky full of stars. One star shone brighter than the rest. Inside, the message was simple—*Glory to the newborn king.* The signature was even simpler. In a childish scrawl, her first name only, no love always, or your loving sister, or even with best wishes, just Catherine. Plain and simple, like the girl herself.

Below that she listed her latest Philadelphia address and phone qualified with the sour instructions that the information was for emergency use only. Catherine had cut the cord a long time before. She refused to talk to anyone in the family, even her mother, *especially* her mother, yet it seemed to Strega that Catherine disliked him more than the rest.

Catherine's animosity had always puzzled him, more so now they were both grown. He had tried reaching out dozens of times over the last five years, but she slapped him away time and again with cutting words, accusing eyes. When he asked his mother why Catherine hated him so, she just shook her head and said *Cather-*

ine's found Jesus. As if that was the answer. Finally,
Strega gave up asking the questions the way he gave up
the periodic trips to Philadelphia to see Catherine. He
never gave up wondering what had driven such a hard
and cold wedge between brother and sister.

Now he picked up his portable phone, punched in her
area code and number, and waited out ten long rings
before hanging up.

Gavin drove from the city straight to Donovan's apartment building. He parked out front and settled in deep
in his seat, waiting for Walter, ready to wait all night if
he had to. Walter the night-shift worker had to come
home sometime.

Strega tried Catherine off and on through the night.
At three o'clock in the morning, he went to the sculpting
pedestal and pulled the plastic bag off his new clay piece.

The head of Maria Alvarez was turned toward him. It
was clay, but it looked alive. The fine shape of her head,
the arrangement of the features, and their relative scale
were all true to life, yet he had captured emotions he
had never seen on Maria Alvarez's face. Sorrow and
vulnerability. *Help me,* the face seem to say. He stroked
her clay cheek. Then he remembered Vincent's red-
balled eyes, the neck arching up in agony, and the mouth
gaping in terror. The teasing voice came back to him:
The answer's in Philly, Jonnie.

He punched Catherine's number in again and listened
to the same ten long rings.

Nineteen

"I talked to Walter last night," Gavin said to Strega as they were walking up to Ballantine's office Tuesday morning. "I waited on his doorstep all night. He came home at five o'clock this morning. It was a waste of time."

"Why?"

"Old Walter's a security guard. He works the tomb shift at a factory. The afternoon of the day in question, he had switched shifts for the week with some guy who needed days free. Walter worked days the whole fucking week. He wasn't in apartment 1-A when Danny died. He wasn't there to see or hear anything." Gavin stepped into Q-Ball's office and stopped cold. "I don't fucking believe it," he said. "Excuse my language, Detective Hansen."

Strega edged past him and stared at Cybil Hansen.

She did a slow three-hundred-and-sixty degree turn. "Surprised?" she asked.

"Let's put it this way," Gavin said. "Only seeing Superman step out of a phone booth would surprise me more."

"What surprises you exactly?"

"You look so female," Gavin exclaimed.

Cybil laughed. A pair of three-inch heels put her near the six-foot mark. A mid-thigh pale pink linen skirt and short fitted jacket left nothing to the imagination. Sheer stockings didn't cover so much as they enhanced a mile of well-shaped leg. Her ash blond hair was swept up and back, in a new soft, polished style.

"Your hair makes you look different," Strega observed.

"It's called a French twist," Cybil said.

"All these years I thought a French twist was a doughnut," Gavin remarked.

"Hansen, you're a knockout," Strega said. "The ambulance chaser scored a home run."

"You haven't seen the ambulance chaser," she said smugly. "I scored the home run. Anyway, don't get used to this getup. I'm a detective, and when this fishing expedition's over, I'll go back to looking like one."

Q-Ball sat stony-faced behind the mountain of folders on his desk. "The suit's on loan from Chanel," he grumbled. "It retails for three thousand four hundred eighty-five dollars. The Department has insurance, but try not to screw it up, okay?"

"I promise," Cybil said. "Now, what about the jewels?" She grinned with anticipation.

Ballantine pushed a small velvet jewel box across the paper mountain.

Cybil opened the box and let out a low whistle. Inside, on a bed of satin, lay a five-carat square-cut *diamond* ring. "Ballantine," she said, "if this is a proposal, the answer's definitely yes."

Q-Ball's face turned beet red. "It's not real, and it sure as hell isn't a proposal. These aren't real either." Q-Ball pushed two more jewel boxes across the table.

Cybil opened them.

"Zelda's Fantasy Jewelers kindly supplied us with paste copies of Harry Winston diamonds," Ballantine explained. "They look real enough to me, but I don't have a practiced eye."

Cybil looked up at him. "I do. This is top-of-the-line. Really convincing." She slipped on the ring. "I'll wear it on my left hand just to see how it feels to be married to a tycoon for a day." She flashed him *the smile*.

Ballantine flushed a deeper shade of red. "Let's get on with it."

Cybil took a pair of earrings out of the second velvet box. They were two carats each, cut square like the ring.

From the last box she pulled out a thick gold neck piece with a nice-sized square-cut diamond set in the middle. "With fake jewelry this good, who needs the real stuff?"

"Our shooters," Strega said. "That's who. Let's run through it."

"I'm wired for sound under this suit," Hansen said. "Double- and triple-checked the unit. It works."

"Good," Strega said. "You start the day by taking a nice long stroll up Madison from Sixty-ninth to Eighty-sixth Street. You have coffee and a croissant in one of the expensive cafés, then wander in and out of a few boutiques."

Q-Ball interrupted. "The shop owners are anxious to help. Sales on Madison Avenue have dropped fifty percent. Violence is bad for business. We've made arrangements with Versace and Armani to give you shopping bags when you stop in so it looks like you're out on a genuine spree."

Strega continued. "At one o'clock, go to a restaurant named Le Bistro on Madison at Eighty-second Street. The front of the restaurant is solid glass. Take a window table."

Ballantine interrupted again. "Try to keep the bill down. Stick to a salad, something simple. Don't go for the caviar and blinis."

"After lunch," Strega went on, "stroll back out, shop for another two hours, then hail a cab and return to the precinct house."

"How do I know one of the shooters isn't posing as a cab driver?"

"A cab wouldn't work for them. The shooters want you in the front seat where the driver has total control, not in the back. If you're behind the driver, he's vulnerable."

Cybil considered the information. "I'll buy that. Now, where will my backup be?"

"A block away in one of Ballantine's unmarked Chevys," Strega promised. "We'll have you in sight at all times. If anyone's following, we'll alert you."

"Gavin and Strega won't be the only ones covering

you on Madison," Ballantine said. "Three more shadow units will be standing by. If you're picked up, two of those units will go after the blonde. The third will fall in with Strega and Gavin to tail the pick-up car you're in."

"Since you're wired," Gavin added, "we'll hear everything. If it plays out like all the other hits, you'll be dropped off safe and sound. If something goes wrong, the cavalry will ride to the rescue."

"Not that I'm less than impressed with the cavalry, but Hansen goes out armed," Ballantine said, looking at her. "You've got your duty piece in your handbag?"

"Better than that," Cybil said. "I want my weapon where I can get to it fast and easy. I'm registered to carry an Intratec nine-millimeter ultra-compact. It fits right into a garter-belt holster designed especially for women."

Q-Ball's eyebrows shot up. "You're wearing a gun in your garter belt?"

"Would you like to see?" She stood up and reached for her hem.

Ballantine flushed again. "No. I'll take your word for it."

"One last question," Cybil said. "My W-2 says I can't afford lunch at Le Bistro."

Ballantine pushed a stack of fresh twenties her way. "From petty cash. Get a receipt for your lunch, and like I said, try to not spend it all."

Cybil tucked the bills into a small Chanel handbag. "I love blinis, Ballantine." She flashed him *the smile*, then turned to Strega and Gavin. "Let's go."

Maria rolled out of bed and stumbled into the bathroom. She looked at her thousand reflections in the peel-and-stick mirrors. She stood up close to one of the squares and saw that her face was changing. Her eyes were black pebbles, hard and shiny. They seemed narrower, brighter, colder. She ran a hand through her matted hair. She felt her neck, the pulse thumping under her skin, and she put her hand over her heart and felt the great muscle beating, pumping life into her limbs, pumping purpose too. She breathed in, then exhaled. Her breath clouded the mirror. She wiped a circle of the steam away. A single eye stared back at her. The eye was afire with hate.

She turned the cold-water faucet on and dampened her forehead and neck. Her apartment was so hot. Horns honked outside, the sun beat in the bedroom window. Maria turned her palms up and put them over her eyes. Something had changed. She was going to be ready soon. Finally. She choked back a sob of relief. Finally. After all this time. She was going to be ready.

When she finished her work.

She spun out of the bathroom, past the hissing kitten, into her bedroom of the thousand faces. She looked up. Ramon smiled down at her. Wasn't it right that he was up there on the ceiling? Didn't he belong up there with the stars? Wasn't he a star himself?

Maria stood on the bed, took her scissors, and carved one of Ramon's smiling Spanish eyes.

An eye for an eye, Ramon, that's what you taught me. You taught me to never be a hostage to fear. To protect myself. So I will.

She shook. She wasn't brave enough. She would never be brave enough to hurt him. Maria looked at Jon Strega's smiling face and stopped shaking. She stuck his picture up on the ceiling. He belonged up there. He was a star too. A hero. Strega, the hero rookie. Maria was brave enough to finish what she had started with him. She reached up and carved one of his eyes out. For Strega the game was different. The way she was playing it was different from the other games, but it would have the same conclusion. The conclusion was sacred.

I'm going to shoot you down, Jon Strega. When I watch you fall, like a shooting star, I'll hold my breath and make a wish.

Maria smiled. It was game time.

Twenty

"If I were a rich bachelor, I'd definitely hit on her," Gavin said, watching Hansen walk out of Armani.

"It's after four, and no one's hit on her, rich or poor," Strega observed. "And it's starting to rain. Let's call it a day."

Gavin picked up the two-way radio. "Quitting time, Hansen."

Hansen answered without looking his way. "I'll cab back to the precinct house, like we planned. Here comes one now." She waved it down. "We'll try again tomorrow."

Strega and Gavin heard the click as she shut off the transmitter. They watched her duck inside. Strega radioed the additional chase units and dismissed them.

"Let's take a run back up to Kelly's building," Gavin said, watching Hansen's cab drive off. "Franklin knows something." He said the words like a wish.

Strega pulled up in front of the brick building. They got out and went up to the buzzer. Gavin rang the bell marked SUPER. There was no answer. He pushed it again and held it for two minutes straight. Franklin's voice came scratching out of the little speaker box. "Okay, already. Who's there?"

"NYPD."

"I was in the john. Give me a minute."

They waited five minutes. Gavin was ready to lean on the buzzer again when Franklin came shuffling out of an elevator. He opened the front door. "Oh, it's you two guys again. You look different without your uniforms. Come on in."

Strega and Gavin stepped inside. Franklin waited for them to move past him, to the elevator. Gavin stood rooted, staring at Franklin's grinning idiot's face. "Well, go on," Franklin said. "You know the way up to 19F by now. I don't want to go back up there. I got work to do."

"We're not here to go to 19F," Gavin said flatly.

Franklin looked beady-eyed with interest from one officer to the other. He stuck his hand in his pocket and started jangling his change. "Well, what in the heck *do* you want?"

"To talk to you, Franklin," Gavin said, his voice full of implication.

"What do you want to talk to *me* for?" The change was jangling faster, the grin was fading.

"You know things, Franklin," Gavin stated.

"I don't know nothing." The grin was back, wide and wet. "I'm just a dumb-ass super. At least that's what all you hot-shit cops thought Sunday. Pushing me around, shoving me outta the way, telling me to stand here, stand there, like I was some kind of dog."

"Time to talk, Franklin."

Franklin shook his child-man's head back and forth furiously. "Nope, not talking. That fat-ass detective kicked me out Sunday, talked to me like I was trash. I got nothing to say."

Gavin grabbed his collar and slammed him against the brick lobby wall. Franklin's head cracked, his eyes went fuzzy, and spittle dribbled out of the corner of his mouth. The jangling and grinning stopped. He looked up at Gavin, and his face flushed with fear. "You going to kill me? You're a cop. You can't *kill* me."

"I can do whatever the fuck I want to do to you. You're holding out, Franklin. And holding out information is breaking the law. That makes you a criminal. I'll have you thrown in jail so fast you won't know what hit you. Then I'll make sure the boys in your cell take good care of you. I'll pay them to do it to you, Frankie. That man in Nineteen-F was my friend. You know something?

You tell me now. You got to the count of three." Gavin
twisted Franklin around into a choke hold. He pulled
his arm tight around Franklin's neck, cutting off the
air supply.

"Gavin," Strega whispered in his ear, "lay off. Choke
holds are against regulations."

"Fuck regulations."

Franklin slapped at Gavin's fists. He choked out one
word and tried to nod. "Okay."

Gavin dropped him. "Talk, Franklin, now."

"I know something," he wheezed, "because Friday I
was sweeping up the hallways."

"Where?" Gavin pressed.

"On nineteen. That Kelly cop came home around
eight in the morning, when I was sweeping. He was in
uniform. Looked real tired. Said he'd been out all night
at that museum raid. He was a nice guy. It was already
over a hundred degrees in the hall, and I must of looked
hot. He asked me if I wanted a cold beer. Sure, I said.
He went inside his place and came out a minute later
with a can of ice-cold Bud. Silver Bullet, the big one. I
thanked him and he went back into his apartment."
Franklin stopped talking. He noticed Strega taking
notes.

"Hey," Franklin complained, "you can't tell nobody
what I'm saying. I'll get in trouble."

"What for?" Gavin asked.

"Well, that's part of it," Franklin paused, reluctant to
go on.

Gavin reached for Franklin's collar. "Talk to me, unless you want to feel the side of the wall next to your
skull again."

Franklin paled. "All right." He shook loose. "I could
get in trouble if the management company finds out I
was drinking. And that's what I thought of that morning
too. So I ducked into the stairwell to wash my brewskie
down in private. I sat down on a step, took my time.
When I finished, I stood up with my empty beer can,
ready to go back into the hall where I left my broom
and bucket. But the stairwell door has a square of glass

in it. It's security glass run through with chicken wire, just so you can take a peek into the stairwell before you open the door, make sure no one's there. Anyway, through the square of glass I saw someone walking off the elevator and down toward the opposite end of the hall. She stopped in front of that Kelly man's door."

"She?" Gavin interrupted.

Franklin nodded his head vigorously, up and down. "Oh, wow, and what a she. Boobies out to here, big ass, not skinny like those models who look like they're starving to death. Nope, she was a beauty, made for loving. When she turned to knock on the door, I saw her face." Franklin grinned and jangled his change.

"Come on, Franklin, give us the rest. What'd she look like? Could you recognize her again if you saw her?"

"Sure. And so could you," Franklin giggled.

"Cut the shit. What do you mean?"

"She's one of you coppers," Franklin snickered. "She was wearing a uniform, just like you, but it was tight and it showed all her illegal curves."

Gavin's heart skipped around in his chest. He shot Strega a glance. He had stopped writing. Gavin turned back to Franklin. "You remember what her face looked like?"

"Who could forget? Pile of black hair pulled back. I could see real good. Spanish. Red lips. Looked like she could give a hell of a blow job with those lips."

"She go into Officer Kelly's apartment?" Gavin asked.

"Sure did."

"Did he let her in?"

"Yup. She knocked and said something. He opened the door, she went in, he closed the door." Franklin made an obscene gesture with his fingers. "You don't have to be a cop to know what was going on in there."

"What else do you know?" Gavin ordered.

"That's it. I hurried out, got my broom and bucket, and took the elevator to twenty. Didn't go back to nineteen until the next day."

"Did you see her leave?" Gavin asked.

"Nope."

"Did you hear anything? Fighting? A gunshot?"

"Nope. Like I said, I was up on twenty. Hey, your buddy looks funny. He okay? He better not get sick here in the lobby. It'll stink the place up."

Gavin steered Strega out of the building, down the walkway, and into the Chevy. He turned the air conditioning on. "You'll feel better when you cool off. It's just the heat, Strega."

"No, it's not. She *killed* him. And if she killed Kelly, she killed Donovan, and all the other ones you and Ballantine are looking at. I'm next. That's what this has been about."

Gavin looked up at the inhospitable brick building and curtain of gray clouds behind it.

What was the last thing you saw before you died, Danny? Was it a face, Danny? Was it Maria's face?

"We're going straight to Ballantine," Gavin said. "Now. Drive."

"No fucking way, Ed. Forget it." Ballantine put his head in his hands. "First you come in yesterday with your hopped-up scheme for playing hero detective. I cave and let Cybil have her way. Now you come in and tell me to haul in Ramon Alvarez's daughter and charge her with ten counts of murder one. I'm going to forget that we ever had this conversation. I'm going to do you the biggest favor of your career and let you walk out that door, and I'll never bring this subject up again. You know why?"

"Why?"

"Because I think you've lost it. I think you've tipped right over the edge and that maybe you should go visit Dr. Fields down the hall there. It was a mistake to involve you. You were too close to Donovan. You're jumping for any goddamned explanation you can just to get your friend off the meat hook called suicide. You're so desperate to vindicate him, you've just gone and leaped off the deep edge. Maria Alvarez, for Christ's sake."

"Strega's next," Gavin insisted.

"Come on, a lover's quarrel ain't murder! So she's

giving him a hard time. So what? You said yourself that
Strega insulted her." Ballantine's hand curled into a fist.
"Maria Alvarez murdering Mike Kelly. Fucking
outrageous."

"I have proof."

Ballantine shot out of his chair and leaned forward
across the desk. "What you have is some dumb-shit janitor who lives in la-la land most of the time, and who
drinks the rest of the time. You got him grinning at you,
saying he saw little Maria go into Kelly's place Friday.
So maybe he did. They were partners Thursday night
when the Met got hit, remember? Maybe Kelly forgot
something in the patrol car. Maybe they just needed to
talk the horror of what they saw out, the way partners
do sometimes. Or maybe they were getting it on. So
what?" Ballantine thundered. "Good for Kelly. She's a
hell of a package, little Maria. What your idiot janitor
doesn't have is a single piece of information on what
happened *after* Maria allegedly went in Kelly's apartment. He didn't see her leave. He didn't hear them fight.
And by your own admission, he didn't even hear a friggin' gunshot.

"First rule of playing detective, Gavin, is evidence.
Evidence that will stand up in court, evidence that will
convince the D.A. to indict. A fucking loony-bin alco-
holic marble-shooting janitor is not that kind of evidence. One more thing. You stay away from Maria
Alvarez. No sly innuendoes, no following her around, no
confronting her with your penny-ante theories. Now get
the fuck out of here before I lose my temper." Q-Ball
sank back into his chair.

Gavin stalked out. He cut through the station house
and passed Strega, who was sitting on the steps waiting,
looking at him expectantly.

"Ballantine told me to go to hell," was all Gavin said.
He made a beeline for the Tempo, fired the engine up,
and roared off down the street.

Ballantine's accusations hammered in Gavin's head.
He stopped off at the Midtown bar and knocked back

two whiskeys. The accusations still hammered away. He slouched against the bar counter and watched the television set. Some enterprising young reporter was doing a feature on the string of cop suicides. The footage from Kelly's death flickered by, and there in the corner of a wide shot, Gavin picked out the grinning face of Franklin.

He ordered a third shot and knocked it back.

Gavin wanted to confront Maria Alvarez right then and there. He wanted to twist her black hair out of her skull and make her confess to the murders. How does it feel, Maria, to press the gun to flesh and fire? Were Danny's eyes open, watching you? Or did he close them, squeeze them shut tight against the horror he knew was coming? Then did you hold his great slack body in your arms like a baby? How much of Danny got on you, Maria? A little? A lot? Or nothing at all, nothing to stain your murdering hands. How did it go? A promise of sexual fun and games, followed by a silver needle slipping into a vein, then a quickie hand job, then the shot? Were you kissing him when you fired? Did you send him away with a good-night kiss, Maria? Afterward, did you stay awhile? Have a beer? Play with the body the way some sick killers do? Smoke a cigarette and listen to some music? Did you look at Katy's drawings? Did you then have one single pang of remorse for leaving the little artist fatherless? Did you, Maria? Did you?

He dropped the empty shot glass on the floor and watched it shatter. Q-Ball had warned him. He couldn't go near Maria, but he could find the evidence that put her there in those nine apartments. He would find the proof, and then he would hunt her down and watch her face when she heard the sirens coming, the cop cars converging on her to arrest her, to haul her away and lock her up forever.

Gavin paid for his three drinks, left a tip for the broken glass, and left. He drove slowly and carefully, aware that his reactions were muzzy and his vision unclear. When he pulled up in his driveway, the dashboard clock winked eight o'clock. Lights were on. Shelly's car was there. He wanted to avoid her and keep the burning truth to himself. He wanted to guard the secret of Danny's death a little while longer, lest she also accuse him of jumping too fast for any explanation that vindicated Danny.

The truth was, he wished he could talk it out with her the way they used to. He wanted the wall down, but he didn't know how. He wanted his *wife,* not the rigid, unresponsive back that seemed to always be turned against him.

She was in the kitchen, peeling carrots for the wok. He pulled a beer out of the refrigerator, twisted the top off. "I ate in the city," he mumbled. "Eat without me."

Upstairs in his bedroom, Gavin pulled his service revolver out of its snug shoulder holster and placed it on the end table, next to his beer. He loosened his shirt, then leaned over to untie his sneakers. An edge of a white box poked out from under the bed.

Part of his gloom lifted, and Gavin smiled. The violent wokking, the rigid wifely back were a hoax. Proof was here in a white box, shoved secretly under the bed. Shelly was ready to pull the wall down too. The box was a surprise for him. Surprise gift giving had been Shelly's special ritual for showing love. She used to wait until they were tucked into bed at night. Then she would reach over and pull a box out from under the bed. It was always a big, festive box tied with gold ribbon. Nestled inside reams of crisp white tissue paper would be a new bathrobe or a comfortable sweater. The gift giving stopped abruptly when Alex disappeared.

Gavin nudged the box with his hand. It was deep and big, a nice-sized peace offering. He started to push the box back under the bed, then impulsively pulled it out and admired not only the size of it, but the smart black type running across the box top—SAKS FIFTH AVENUE. There was no ribbon this time. Peeking would be easy. Gavin lifted the top off, fished around in the tissue paper, and found the garment. It wasn't a sweater or a

bathrobe or even a smart shirt. It was a sequined strapless ball gown, glittery gold. Size six. Shelly's size.

Gavin fingered the gown dumbly. There hadn't been
any invitations to black-tie events—no charity balls or
weddings or Department parties. He and Shelly lived a
quiet suburban life. Prime-time television and Kmart
sales. So what the hell was a gold sequined strapless
evening dress doing under their bed? The price tag still
dangled from the dress. He looked at it. $1,780.00. Al-
most two thousand bucks for a dress.

Gavin leaned over and lifted the bed skirt. Shopping
bags and boxes full of clothes crammed the king-size
space. He got down on his hands and knees and pulled
them out.

There were more evening gowns, a dozen of them, all
with designer labels—Armani, Valentino, Versace, Chanel, Ralph Lauren. There was a big Victoria's Secret bag
stuffed with lacy bras and g-string panties. There were
ten shoe boxes from Gucci, Fendi, and Christian Dior,
and five more from Ferragamo. There was a black velvet
Dior cocktail dress, a short, flirty Givenchy skirt, and
three more short cocktail dresses from someone named
Donna Karan. There was a wig too, long red-gold hair
and styled the way Shelly used to wear her own. Gavin
crawled under the bed to get to the last of the stash, a
big white shopping bag marked Ferre. When he wiggled
back out, Shelly was standing at the door looking at him.

Their eyes locked, his rock hard with accusation, hers
brittle bright with fear and another look he'd seen a
thousand times in the eyes of junkies: *Help me.* But
Gavin didn't feel like helping. Outrage and indignation
rolled right over mercy. He scooped an armful of clothes
and threw them at her.

"What is this?" he roared. "What the fuck's going on
here? You wake up one day thinking you're Ivana
Trump? Or are you having little afternoon dress-up parties? Who with, Shelly? Who? You and Ellie Barrone
make a package deal on the UPS boy?"

"Ed, don't."

He stood up. "Don't what, Shelly? Don't worry about

what all my hard-earned money is getting pissed away on? Our *retirement* money, for Christ's sake?" He threw the wig at her. "Or don't worry that you've just maybe lost your mind and I'm living with the thirteen faces of Sheila or whoever the fuck the world-famous schizoid was. Well, guess what? I'm worried. And I'm mad. And I expect a goddamn good explanation for this."

The phone rang and went unanswered.

Shelly cowered against the door.

Gavin crossed the room. "I deserve an explanation, and it better be damn good, like you took a part-time job to pay for this shit." He slapped her once across the face. Then, when his open palm was curling into a fist, he stopped himself. He had never raised a hand to her. Never. She looked at him in shock and disbelief. Her reddened, swelling skin sickened him—that he had done that to her. He dropped his hand. "I deserve an explanation," he said quietly, hating himself.

She put her fingers on her fiery skin and whispered. "*I, I, I, I.* It's always about you, Ed. About *your* career, *your* problems, *your* day. Even this is about you now. *Your* outrage, *your* betrayal."

Gavin stared at her, speechless.

"You ignore me." Her voice was little-girl small. "You're lost in your own world, and you don't even know I'm here."

Gavin stared at the floor.

"Thirty years, Ed. Keeping house. Matching colors, carpets, and tile, your slacks and shirts, plates and glasses. My life is over, and I have nothing to show for it, not even a child. You? You have pride and honor. You perform a thousand little heroics every day. You come home and you're tired, but you feel good about yourself and about what you've spent your life doing."

Her words were coming fast now, in a torrent.

"You get up and have someplace to go, people to talk to. You have the Department, and when you leave, you'll have your memories. I have nothing. I have no-where to go. I can't come home because I'm already here, and since Alex disappeared it's a pretty shitty place to be. You changed. We both changed losing Alex."

She laughed bitterly. "Somewhere along the way I stopped feeling like a woman. So it started with a pair of lace underwear to make me feel more feminine. Then bras and slips and finally evening dresses, the most expensive ones I could find. It made me feel giddy and good, standing in those pretty shops, surrounded with salesclerks. It made me feel whole, to put those dresses on—like I was a woman again. I bought one and swore to end it there. I couldn't help myself. I went back and bought another, then another. It felt so good! I made up stories to tell the salesgirls about who I was, where we were going, the parties and balls and opera openings, when the only place we're going is to Florida."

"I thought you were looking forward to retirement," he said, amazed.

"You never asked what I thought. I'm not even fifty years old yet, and you want to park us in some Florida retirement town where we'll sit around with a bunch of people blinking in the sun, waiting to die. Now, when you get up every morning, you have someplace to go. When you don't have anywhere to go but the shuffleboard court, you'll want to die too." She lay back on the bed. "I don't want to go to Florida."

"Where do you want to go, then?"

"I don't want to go anywhere," she whispered. "What if Alex tries to come home? I don't want her to find us gone. I can't go anywhere, not while there's a chance she's still alive. Now I spent so much, we can't leave."

"How much?" he asked gently.

"I went through half of the savings. I guess I just got mad. Got mad or went mad. Sometimes they're both the same thing. You have been so far away from me for such a long time, and more so lately. I have felt so alone."

"It's been rough on me, having Donovan die like that."

Shelly laughed bitterly again. "Donovan, God rest his soul. Dead, alive, it's always been Donovan. You loved him more than your own wife, and you still do."

"That's not true," Gavin said.

"Isn't it? We were in trouble long before Danny died. You always put him before me."

"We worked together."

"It was more than that. When I lost Alex, I lost you too. You shut me out. You turned to Danny when you should have turned to me. I loved Danny, but part of me hated him. If you hadn't given so much to him, maybe there would've been something left over for me. I needed you when we lost our girl. I needed you to talk to me."

"I didn't know what to say."

"No, it's that you did all your talking to Danny. By the time you got home, you'd said it all."

He looked at her helplessly. "I'm a cop, Shell. He was my partner. He helped me look for Alex!"

"And you couldn't find her, could you? All the king's horses and all the king's men. You and all your cop friends couldn't find Alex."

There. She'd said it. The words hit Gavin like a body blow. After all these years she'd finally said it. The truth hurt. He left the room. The phone rang. He ignored it and went downstairs to the kitchen. He rested his elbows on the lemon yellow counter tiles and looked at his reflection in the big plate window. All his coply bravado was stripped. The emperor, he thought, has no clothes.

The suspicion that he was not a great cop, or even particularly good, had always lurked around in his mind. Thirty years and no commendations, no medals or decorations or honors. What kind of cop was he if he hadn't even guessed the truth behind Danny's death? And wasn't Shelly right? What kind of cop was he if he couldn't even find his own daughter? The knobs on his elbows wobbled and hurt against the hard tiles, but he leaned on them anyway as he went in close to his own reflection and whispered, "Loser."

Gavin backed away and took a handful of beers out of the refrigerator. He went out to the small wood deck and sat down listening to the summer night sounds, wishing they were loud enough to drown out the accusations

in his head. He had failed Danny and Alex, and now
he had failed Shelly. He finished his beer and opened
a second.

Clouds churned in the sky. Emma wasn't leaving.
From time to time the clouds slid apart, and Gavin got
a good look at the fat moon hanging low on the horizon.
He took a long swig of beer.

A gunshot cracked the night. Gavin hit the ground
instinctively, pressing his body flat to the deck. His
brain shifted sluggishly into cop mode and processed the
information.

A single shot.

Sounded like it had been from a 9mm, like his own
gun.

But where did it come from?

Inside the house, his brain told him. *Inside, you idiot.*

He scrambled to his feet. Shelly. Sweet Jesus. He had
left his piece lying on the nightstand. Inside, the staircase
stretched in front of him, impossibly steep. He stumbled
to the top, then, using the walls to stabilize himself, he
lurched down the hall into the bedroom.

Shelly lay curled on the bed. His revolver was clutched
in her hands. The closet door was ajar. The gold ball
gown hung from the top of the door on a padded hanger.
A single neat bullet hole punctured the dress.

Shelly looked up at him through her tears. "I wanted
to do it to myself," she whispered. "I wanted to be Donovan, to hate life so much that I could just turn it off.
But I can't. I can't do it. I hate my life, but I don't want
to die. I feel dead and I just want to feel alive." She
pulled her knees up to her chest and pushed the gun off
the bed.

Gavin made it to the bed before his knees gave out
again. He covered her shaking frame with his massive
body. She felt so small beneath him, small and delicate.
He had always thought Shell was strong. When had she
become so frail? He stroked her short hair, studied her
face with his hands, then pulled her tight to him and
held her hard.

"Don't leave me, baby," he murmured. "We're going

to work this out. We're going to start over. Somehow we're going to start fresh."

For the first time since Alex disappeared and Donovan died, Gavin cried in front of Shelly. He cried for his lost girl and friend, for the wife he nearly lost, and for himself, wondering what kind of man he really was.

Maria crouched on the floor of her cramped bathtub, limbs all akimbo, teeth chattering, full hips hurting from the long time spent sitting on the hard tile. Cold water from the shower head spat down on her. Her service revolver rested on the edge of the sink, in her line of sight. For just a moment she was afraid. Then she looked out into the bedroom, at the ceiling where the one-eyed Strega stared down at her. Anger replaced fear. She took the gun and fired. The bullet ripped a hole in the picture at Strega's right temple. Head shot scores ten. The target rarely survives it.

Twenty-one

Gavin's face had changed. It was marked now with the grief he had so narrowly escaped and, too, with desperation for how to make his life whole again, how to replace what had taken a decade to save—how to replace it in a matter of weeks. His cheeks appeared sunken, as though the skin beneath his eyes collapsed off the ridge of bone. His round cheeks had been slapped flat with fear. His eyes burned fever bright and a fine blond stubble covered his chin.

Gavin's hands shook as he buttoned his uniform shirt over the Kevlar vest. How many times over the span of his career had he gone through these familiar motions? How many times, steady-handed and sure, with the confidence that his life was clipping along in control? Chaos had stripped him of equilibrium. All his boxer's balance was gone. He tottered like a brittle old man when he stepped into his pants, and grabbed the bench to keep from falling over when he bent over to tie his shoes.

He straightened up. Alex's picture mocked him. His eyes flickered over to the small mirror on the inside of his locker door. His lower lip trembled like a child's. He bit down and the trembling stopped. He tasted blood. In the reflection he saw Strega walking down the locker row. Gavin leaned into the mirror and focused on the tiny black iris in the center of his fever blue eyes, and willed himself to ask for help.

"Morning," Strega greeted.

Gavin slammed his locker shut and rested his sunken cheek against the cool metal door. Strega tapped him on the shoulder.

"Hey," the rookie said, "you okay?"

"No," Gavin croaked. "I need a favor." There. The words were said, the white flag raised.

"Sure. Name it."

He turned around and knew by the lightning flinching of Strega's face that his partner saw the change in Gavin. He saw the fever, the hollows, the stubble, and the marks of desperation and despair. "You know your stock market hocus-pocus? I need you to invest a chunk of change for me, tell me where to put it, what to do to get the quick pop."

"Quick pops are usually high-risk. You might lose it all."

"I already have." That lower lip went AWOL again, shaking and flapping. Then tears inched out of his eyes and ran down his face. Gavin felt like a fool for having let his marriage run aground, and for not having the fortitude to hold himself together for this necessary and uncomfortable confession. He was a private man. The only one he had ever considered a friend enough to let in had been Danny. Reaching out took all Gavin's pride and courage.

Strega took a step back, as though to give his partner privacy, but Gavin put a hand out and touched his elbow. "No. Hear me out."

Gavin sank down on the locker room bench and haltingly strung the words together that made the story for what had happened with Shelly, for how she had tried to commit a different kind of suicide, turning self-destructive, wrecking silent havoc in their lives, ripping down the unspoken bond of trust—which was what spending the money had been about. Then Gavin recounted her savage, aborted attempt to end her own life, ironically, with his own service revolver.

Strega listened intently, interrupting once or twice to clarify a point. He listened well, Gavin had to admit, managing to convey sympathy without pity, concern without condescension and the fact that he cared and would help.

"I just don't have it in me anymore," Gavin concluded, "to stick it out another five or ten years in uniform. Maybe if everything had fallen differently, if Danny hadn't died, if I still had Alex, maybe then I could work it all back penny by penny."

Strega spared him the amateur's psychological analysis and simply asked him when he wanted to start.

"Today, now. This morning. Just tell me what to do."

"Hansen doesn't go on the street until ten. Banks open at nine. We'll go by your branch, wire the funds over to a trading account in your name at Merrill Lynch. Then we take a quick run down to Rosemary's office. You sign all the appropriate papers, including a power of attorney giving me the right to trade on your behalf."

"What makes you think Rosemary will take my account?"

"She never turns new business down. Never."

"I need your magic, Strega. I need you to pull a rabbit out of a hat."

"I can only try. I'll put you in West Entertainment. It's prime for a takeover."

Maria Alvarez was present at Wednesday morning's roll call. She stood up front, holding her hat gracefully in her hands, her hair pulled back tight and neat, showing off the long column of her neck and the silver earrings which tinkled like chimes when she moved.

Gavin didn't trust himself not to throw her up against the wall and openly accuse her, so he stayed put, at the rear door to the squad room, his eyes drilling into the back of her head, thinking of all the ways he wanted to rough her up. At the end of roll call, as Gavin watched Maria walk his way, Q-Ball barreled in and grabbed his arm.

"Gavin," he thundered, "in my office, now."

He followed Ballantine out, wondering if Q-Ball could read his mind. Did he know what Gavin wanted to do to the P.C.'s daughter? Could he hear the wheels turning inside Gavin's head, reeling and spinning, trying to figure out how to *get* Maria Alvarez?

Ballantine ushered him into the office and slammed

the door. "At four o'clock this morning," Q-Ball said, "officers in the Ninth Precinct answered a call from an apartment building on the lower East Side. A building resident reported a gunshot from one of the apartments, one in which Patrolman David Walker lived by himself. The officers busted the door in and found Walker on the floor wearing nothing but his uniform shirt. His piece was on the floor next to him. He was shot once in the head."

"Number eleven," Gavin whispered, feeling sick.

"Not yet."

"What do you mean, not yet?"

"Walker's still alive. They took him over to New York Hospital. He's in a coma, but he's alive. The doctors are saying it's a miracle. So am I. If Walker wakes up, we've got our first and only witness."

"What if he doesn't wake up?"

"You can answer that stupid question yourself. I've got a round-the-clock guard posted outside his door just in case our perp decides to sneak in and finish Walker off. And I left instructions with the guard that no other officers are allowed inside, not without me."

"This one's outside the One-Nine. How can you call the shots?"

"Like I once told you, a few of the right people owe me favors. I pulled one in."

Gavin stood and moved to the door.

"One more thing," Ballantine said. "I'm sorry about yesterday. I was out of line. I just think you're barking up the wrong tree."

"If Walker wakes up, we'll find out, won't we?" Gavin pulled the door open and left.

They made good time on the run down to Wall Street. Strega parked in a tow-away zone in front of Merrill Lynch, tossed the NYPD plate in the window, and shuffled Gavin up to Rosemary's office.

David made Strega wait in the foyer. When Gavin came out later, Strega caught a glimpse of Rosemary shaking his hand and thanking him for his business. She

was dressed in a smart red jacket and matching pleated
skirt, and Strega knew she was the only broker on the
street who could get away with showing that much leg.
She looked at him. Her expression was charged. Then
she tossed her copper hair and disappeared down the
hall.

Gavin came out shaking his head. "She's one amazing woman."

"I know," Strega said glumly. "Come on, Cybil's
waiting."

Strega raced back uptown trying to not think about
Rosemary, about how she looked or the raw emotion in
her eyes. He pulled up in front of a café on Madison
and cut the engine. A second unmarked car slipped away
from the curb and disappeared around the corner. Strega
knew it would reappear two blocks up. Strega checked
the rearview mirror and saw the third unit taking up the
rear. He confirmed the position of the fourth chase car
over on Park. Hansen was covered, Strega reassured
himself.

The sidewalks were active and the streets busy with
morning traffic. Apparently, most people felt, like Ballantine, that the Met was the final act for the shooters.
Looking around, at the normalcy of the morning, Strega
knew this was exactly what the shooters were waiting
for. He knew they would be back.

"She's moving," Gavin observed.

Cybil was clearly visible through the bay window,
smiling up at the waiter and peeling off one of Ballantine's crisp twenties to pay for the cappuccino. She collected her change, put her sunglasses on, and walked
out, turning left on Madison Avenue.

"Morning, boys," she said smartly into the two-way.
Her voice crackled out of a little portable speaker in the
car. "How do I look?"

"Very enticing," Gavin replied.

She laughed softly. "I feel like a sitting duck."

"You're a swan, Cybil," Gavin said. "A swan."

Twenty-two

"Hansen's getting used to the good life," Gavin commented at the end of the day, as Cybil drifted into one of the fine boutiques on the opposite side of the street. Five minutes later, she drifted out. Traffic was heavy, but she was right in view. Gavin and Strega were parked at a corner intersection, a half block behind her. They watched a passing teenage boy admire Cybil's legs.

"Hansen, you're wreaking havoc with the male population," Strega warned into the two-way. "We're going to have to arrest you for inciting civil unrest."

She chuckled. "It's not as much fun as it looks. I'm not used to real girl shoes. My feet are killing me."

She was now more than a full block away, and walking past Maria Alvarez's foot post. Gavin watched Maria appear out of the building shadows, tip her hat, and cross the street.

Strega checked his watch. It was almost four. "Let's call it a day, Hansen."

"Great," she said, crossing to the facing corner. "I'll cab back like I did yesterday."

A bus sailed by, momentarily blocking Gavin's view. Then Cybil was in sight again and a cab was veering her way.

"Got it," Cybil said into the two-way. "See you at the station house."

They listened to the click of her transmitter switching off. A second bus lurched to a stop, obstructing their view.

Strega silently cursed the red light and intersection full of traffic that kept him from getting closer to Hansen.

Then the bus pulled away. Hansen was gone. Strega relaxed. "She got that cab," he said. "Let's go in." He dismissed the other backup units, then turned west off Madison, to Fifth Avenue.

Hansen snapped the transmitter off and breathed a sigh of relief when the cab swung her way. She had a blister on her left heel and two on the right. As she made a move for the cab, a woman cut in front.

"I was here first," the woman snapped, leaping into the taxi and slamming the door.

"Shit," Hansen mumbled. A bus blew in, spewing exhaust in her face. Madison Avenue was clogged with traffic, an inordinate amount of buses, and too many hot, tired pedestrians looking for cabs. Thinking there would be less competition on Park Avenue, she ducked around the corner and walked slowly, grateful to be out of the sun. Tall, full trees lined the sidewalk. This street was quiet and free of traffic, blocked off at each end by Con Edison utility trucks. Manhole covers gaped open. Machines hummed from deep inside. Hansen felt safe.

Halfway down the block, Hansen heard rapid footsteps behind her. She dropped her hand down to her thigh. The weight of the small gun was reassuring. She glanced over her shoulder. A Con Edison worker hurried after her. He looked nothing like the Latin or blonde, almost white, and his lean handsome face was unshaven. Rugged. He wore regulation coveralls and a hardhat. Hansen relaxed.

"Hi," he said, falling into step beside her. "I couldn't help but notice you walking by." He was in his mid-twenties and had a winning smile. "Are you a model?"

She blushed. Dammit all, she thought, it was nice to be admired. One of the problems with trying to be one of the boys on Ballantine's team was that eventually you felt like one of the boys. "No," she said, "but thanks for the compliment."

Suddenly, he was spinning her around, off the sidewalk and into the side of a building, slamming her face into the wall. Her head cracked. She groped, clumsy and

slow, for her gun, but he was fast, locking her arms painfully behind her back. "Don't hurt me," she gasped.
"Take the jewelry."

His powerful torso pressed into hers. "Why? It's fake.
You can't buy the real thing on a cop's pay, can you?"
he challenged, roughly twisting her arm.

"I'm not a cop," Hansen wheezed.

He bucked her head into the wall. Hansen felt her
nose crack. The mocking voice whispered: "Lesson number one: Never ever lie to someone smarter than you.
Lesson number two: Never ever walk away from your
backup."

A shot exploded. Her eardrums ached. *Where had it
come from?* She touched her abdomen. Her fingers came
away wet.

Cybil sagged against the wall. An enormous exhaustion rolled over her like the Atlantic surf. The cloudy
sky above her grew blindingly bright. She squeezed her
eyes shut, but the brightness burned right through her
eyelids, white and strong. Then the white exploded
into black.

Maria heard the gunshot.

She bolted around the corner and across the street, in
the direction Hansen had walked. At the end of the
block Maria glimpsed a blond man hurtling around the
corner. Hansen was nowhere in sight. Maria ran, looking
all around as she went. When she found Hansen's body,
she dropped down next to it and radioed for help.

"Officer down," Maria shouted across the open band.
"Ten-thirteen, officer assist *forthwith.* Seven-eight, Madison and Park. EMS and backup, *forthwith.*"

Gavin and Strega heard Maria's call. They looked at
each other.

"Hansen," Strega said grimly, gunning the unmarked
Chevy down Fifth. He looped back around to Madison,
then turned hard at Seventy-eighth Street, swerving
around the open manhole, and clipping the Con Ed
truck with his fender. He slowed to a crawl, searching.

"There," Gavin said, pointing at a narrow alley where Maria watched over Hansen.

Strega pulled up. Gavin jumped out.

"She's alive," Maria announced, rising and running for the car. She ducked into the passenger seat, slammed the door.

Strega stared at her, shocked.

Maria looked at Strega's frozen face. "What the fuck are you looking at?" she shouted. "Drive! Now! Go!"

Strega stepped on the accelerator.

Gavin knelt by Hansen's side. A crimson stain flowered across the lower front of the pink suit. Her skirt was bunched up around her waist, and he could see her gun was still in the garter. Her stockings were ripped. One shoe was off, and she lay at an odd angle with her legs tucked up under her. Gavin checked for a pulse. "She's alive," he said out loud, to himself.

He took his hand from her neck and gently tucked her skirt around her thighs, knowing she would appreciate the gesture. Listening to the wail of an approaching ambulance, he cradled her head in his lap, and couldn't help but think how pretty she still looked in pink—perfume ad pretty—with the French twist hairdo that didn't look anything like a doughnut.

Strega stopped for a red light at Fifth and searched the crowded sidewalks, his heart racing, both from the fear of having Maria in the seat next to him and from the panic he felt looking into the sea of people and cars.

"Long white-blond hair, hardhat and a Con Ed uniform," Maria said, scanning the crowd. "Where the fuck did he go?" she shouted, banging her fist against the dash. "Left, right, straight ahead into the park? Where?"

Strega saw the man, a half block away on the side of Fifth edging the park, moving rapidly downtown.

"He's there," Strega said, pointing.

But Maria had seen him too. She was already springing out of the car and down the street. Strega abandoned the Chevy and followed.

Maria dodged through the crowd, locking her eyes on

the yellow hardhat. The man was moving swiftly. She dropped her own hat and quickly turned her uniform shirt inside out, oblivious to the fact her breasts were bare there on Fifth Avenue and that people were staring. She let the shirt hang loose over her gun belt and hoped she looked like a normal Manhattan girl.

Her man looked back. Maria dropped back to a normal pace, wanting him to think he had gotten away, wanting him to relax and slow down so she could close the gap between them.

Strega came up next to her. "Cross the street and cover the subway entrances," she ordered, thankful he was in plainclothes. Maria knew if her man saw his pursuers, he could too easily duck down into the underground and lose himself in the crowd on the long multiple platforms.

She wanted to shoot, she wanted to take him down *now,* but there were too many pedestrians between them to risk a shot. *Closer.* She had to be closer. All of her senses were sharpened now, by adrenaline and her last generous hit of blow. She felt invincible, powerful, unstoppable.

Maria checked Strega's position across the street. He was moving parallel to her, and he was moving fast. In his street clothes he appeared to be just another harried New Yorker.

She moved briskly ahead, weaving in and out of the crowd, closing the gap little by little. Her man looked back at her. His expression changed.

He made me, she cursed. Suddenly, her man cut across the street, mid-block, darting in and out of the sluggish afternoon traffic and disappeared behind a city bus.

Maria followed, dancing smoothly through the cars and up onto the opposite sidewalk. She stopped. Her man was gone. Strega rushed up to her. "Where the fuck is he?" she shouted at him.

"A bus blew by. I lost him."

Maria looked left, then right, panicked. Her heart kicked in her chest.

Strega, taller by far than she was, had a clear line of

sight over the crowd. "There!" he cried, pointing at her target a long way down the block, crossing a side street and turning the corner.

Strega ran. Maria followed, elbowing people aside, one hand on her holster, drawing her weapon. A woman saw her coming with the 9mm in hand and screamed. People stopped and gawked, stepping back, clearing the way for the wild-eyed madwoman running with a gun.

Up ahead, she saw Strega dash across the side street and cut around the corner.

Maria kicked forward and followed. This was her collar, not his. She wanted badly to beat Strega at his own game.

She whirled around the corner, hard on Strega's heels. The blonde had a good lead. He was moving fast. Maria felt fire running through her veins. It was the thrill of the chase—and the blow. She exploded forward, lagging only slightly behind Strega. The blow gave her incredible speed and stamina.

She shoved people aside. Another woman screamed. The blonde looked back, and saw Maria and Strega charging at him, guns held high. He sprinted ahead. Strega was running like a fullback, fast and hard, his long legs pumping and his broad shoulders dipped low.

The blonde sprinted again, but the gap was closing, and Maria guessed he was tiring. She would never be tired, not with the fire running through her, powering her forward. She heard Strega's deep, rhythmic breaths next to her and the man ahead grunting with effort. Her own heavy panting mixed in, and the sound was something almost sexual.

"Freeze!" Strega shouted. "Police!"

The blonde sped up and spun around a corner.

Strega cursed.

Maria willed her body to run faster. She wanted this. She wanted to outrun Jon Strega and nail this man. He was hers. They were both hers. And she was going to get them.

Rounding the corner, she broke away from Strega's side, cutting into the street, welcoming the long stretch of empty asphalt. Her man was slowing imperceptibly, and little by little Maria closed in on him.

It was impossible to fire an accurate shot moving at this speed. *Wait.* She had to wait. Inching up, close enough to hear her target's coveralls snapping in the wind, close enough to smell his sweat and hear the frantic beat of his shoes on pavement, Maria suddenly exploded off the sidewalk in a long jump born of frustration and desire. She sailed through the air, one hand gripping her gun tightly, the other reaching for the flapping coveralls.

Her fingers touched fabric. Her body slammed into his. They hit the ground. His hardhat flew off. Maria's face was jammed up close next to his head. She smelled mouthwash and sweat and heavy cologne, and saw fat balls of wax clinging to the inside of his ears. She knew instantly the Nordic hair was fake. She tugged the wig off, revealing the close-cropped yellow blond hair beneath.

He slammed an elbow into Maria's ribs. Pain sliced through her. She wanted to grab the rib and hold it, but didn't. She straddled him, then drove the nose of her gun hard into her prisoner's open, gasping mouth, choking him. She heard his teeth clack against the hard gun metal. "You're under arrest," she panted, her lungs burning, her head pounding, and the exhilaration fanning the fire inside her as she stared into his wide, panicked eyes.

Then Strega was suddenly next to her, sucking air into his starved lungs, snapping handcuffs around the man's wrists, and grinding them down tightly.

They were face to face, Maria and Strega, inches apart, Strega staring at her with a wild mix of admiration and terror. Maria brushed her lips across his. She smelled his sweat, and she tasted his fear. Her own breath was hot, her tongue silky.

"Accidents happen," she whispered. "What would happen if my weapon accidentally discharged right now, into you? Accidents happen. They do happen." She bit his lip gently. "I could have done it, Jonnie. I could have killed you today."

Strega shoved her away and wiped his mouth.

Maria reached in her pocket and stroked Kelly's shield.

Ballantine's enormous frame filled the waiting-room doorway. "Just for the record, Gavin, it wasn't worth it. Even if Cybil comes out of this one hundred percent okay, it wasn't worth it. I'm holding you and Strega personally responsible for what happens to her." He lumbered in. "You should've been covering her right up to when her high-heeled shoes stepped back inside the precinct house. What the fuck do you think backup means?"

"She hailed a cab," Gavin attempted. "We had every reason to believe she got in it. A bus blocked our view."

"There are always a hundred excuses when an officer goes down. In my book, not one of them's worth a damn. We're trying to find her husband. He's in Boston somewhere on business. For the moment, you and I are all the family she's got."

Q-Ball folded his impressive size into one of the green plastic bucket chairs. After a beat of silence he spoke again. "Your rookie partner hauled the son of a bitch in, with a little help from *Maria Alvarez.*" He ignored Gavin's incredulous expression and delivered the information in his own deadpan way. "Scab by the name of Baxter. He's one half of our two most wanted shooters. He was wearing a wig. The Con Ed uniform was bogus. He's down at the precinct house now, sweating, and it isn't because there's no a.c. He lawyered up, but by the time my team of homicide detectives is done with him, he'll be confessing to the Met hit, the bridal shop hit, the restaurant hit, and to the murder of JFK as well."

"Shouldn't you be there?"

Q-Ball threw him a deadly look. "Stupid fucking question, Gavin." He folded his hands over his stomach. "I'm sitting right here until they're done working on Hansen."

"Mind if I wait with you?"

"I don't give a fuck what you do," Ballantine stated. His tone made it clear he was finished talking.

Ballantine got antsy after a time, tapping his feet, tugging on his tie, buttoning and unbuttoning his shirt cuff ten times over. Finally, he shot up out of his chair and huddled at the pay phone, where he dropped in enough silver to buy him an hour's worth of telephone time to the station house. He spent the hour asking questions and barking orders to his team of boys, and orchestrating the interrogation of his valuable prisoner in absentia. Q-Ball was like that. Good as his team was, he always thought he was better, and he was never really happy unless he was stirring the pot. Got some of the team piqued from time to time, but most shrugged it off as the price of working for a genius. Gavin had seen the magic. Q-Ball could make anyone talk. Witnesses when they were in shock, victims when they were dying, and the perps themselves, even when a confession to murder one was going to buy a one-way ticket to Attica.

Gavin listened to him cajoling and swearing at his boys, and wondered how the big detective would score without the substantial intimidation factor of his impressive bulk in the rom, staring the prisoner down, eye to eye.

Gavin waited precisely sixty minutes to find out. Ballantine slammed the receiver down and thundered across the waiting room with his fist thrust high in the air. "We nailed the scab," he shouted, "and he even helped us hammer down the last couple of nails in his own G-D coffin."

"He confessed?"

"Nope," Ballantine stated smugly. "He cracked open like a piñata. His lawyer all but stuffed a wash rag in his mouth, but Baxter told his lawyer to go to hell and then he gave it all up. Boasted how he made Hansen as a cop yesterday, then how he figured out where the stakeout vehicles were. Said he knew she'd be back today. Boasted again about how it was his business to know everything about how cops work. He was espe-

cially proud of how he slipped out of the Met right under
our noses. A fucking master of disguise."

"What about his partner?"

"Gave us the scabbie's name, address, phone—everything but his Social Security number and his mother's
maiden name. He used to work for Con Ed. That's
where the uniform came from. They were planning to
drive into Mexico, then maybe South America. Shit, they
had enough to live forever on. But Baxter said they were
going to hit a couple of more lunching ladies just for
fun. Their last hurrah. Big egos just like Strega said."

"How'd you get him to talk?"

Ballantine smiled serenely. "A little old-fashioned politically correct coercion, all legal, of course. It's amazing
how you can get a grown man to pee in his pants when
you describe what'll happen to him if he gets sent away
to a specific prison facility as opposed to other more
user-friendly facilities. Then, when he's wet as a day-old
baby, you intimate that if he cooperates, perhaps the
D.A. will whisper in the judge's ear and see to it he
spends the next few decades in a user-friendly facility
where his chances of staying a virgin are zero, but where
his chances of staying alive are better than fifty-fifty."

"Who are they?" Gavin asked.

"Who the fuck are any of them?" Ballantine bellowed.
"Scumbags! These particular scumbags were smarter and
ballsier than the rest." Ballantine sat down and folded
his hands again. "Your young partner's going to make
a hell of a detective someday. Good head on his shoulders, and fearless too. He scored a big one. I'm sure
the P.C. will present the commendation himself. Hell, he
might even kiss Strega on the cheek."

Gavin thought of Ramon Alvarez's deadly expression
on the elevator at Kelly's death scene, the long, fine-
boned Spanish finger pointed at Strega, and the venom
when he said, *YOU!* "A kiss, Ballantine? I don't think
so."

"Maria scored big today too, Gavin. Don't mean to
bring up a sore subject, but you're going to need Jesus
and all his apostles as witnesses now if you want to con-

vince *anyone* in this city she's anything less than a goddamn saint."

Fuck you, Gavin wanted to say, but he couldn't. Ballantine had been there for him with Alex. He had to let
the jab slide.

Ballantine sat back down and resumed his vigil. He
hopped up from time to time to check on this or that,
chatting with the D.A., barking out orders on how to
find the second perp, but Gavin lost track of time. The
droning of the TV and Ballantine's baritone voice put
him to sleep.

Gavin awoke, hours later, to Ballantine tapping him
on the shoulder.

"She came through," Ballantine announced. "The doc
says we can look in on her."

Gavin followed Q-Ball down the hall and into Hansen's recovery room.

"She's so pale," Q-Ball said, his big face crumpling
with concern. He stepped in and took Cybil's small hand
in both of his. He kissed her on the forehead and whispered, "Hansen, you're a hero. You make the rest of us
look like wimps." He turned back to Gavin. "Let's go."

Ballantine steered Gavin down the hall. "I want to
stop by, see how Walker's doing." A uniformed officer
sat outside the room. He rose when Ballantine approached. "Anyone try to come by to see him today?"
Ballantine asked.

The officer shook his head. "No. Just a couple of doctors and the duty nurses."

Ballantine pushed the door open. Gavin followed him
in. Walker lay surrounded by life-support equipment.
Tubes snaked into his nose and mouth. His lips were
stretched back by the tubes, giving the impression that
he was grinning. Bandages wrapped his head. He looked
like an Egyptian in a turban, a happy Egyptian, lulled to
sleep by the gurgling and whooshing of the big machines
surrounding him.

The grin mesmerized Gavin. *Do you find it funny,*

Walker, that she did this to you? Or are you just happy to still be alive?

"Come on, buddy," Ballantine was saying in a soft voice to the comatose figure. "Wake up long enough to tell me who it was. Give me a name, buddy, one name." He stared at Walker, searching for the flinch, the blink, the twitch, that promised consciousness. Finding only the stillness of a man more dead than alive, Ballantine turned and left. Gavin followed him out. In the elevator on the way down, Ballantine gave Gavin the once-over. "You look like shit, Ed."

"I'm hearing that a lot from you lately, Ballantine."

"Go the fuck home and get some sleep."

Gavin slept.

The rain beating down against the windows helped him sleep. That and the fact that Shelly was wrapped around him with her head buried in the middle of his chest, holding on, hanging on fast for dear life. Or was it him hanging onto her? His chin rested on her head, his arms wound around her. Two people lost, trying to find their way back to each other. He woke once and shifted his face so he could kiss her sleeping lips; then he tightened his hold on her. Somewhere far off in the house the phone rang. He let it go unanswered and drifted back into sleep.

He and Shell had stayed up until five trying to get to know each other again, and Gavin had finally talked. He told her about Danny's death and the other eight murders, of his part in Ballantine's investigation and all that he had learned. He spoke of the guilt he had for believing Danny had killed himself, and the outrage he felt when he learned it was murder.

He reeled back in time and spoke of the fear and the grief when they lost Alex, of the long, aimless, night-long drives looking for her and the things he'd been thinking on his solitary searches. He told her about his friend at the morgue, about all the dead girls he'd looked at and the relief he'd felt when he saw they weren't his daughter. He spoke of the fear he had that one day he would throw the sheet back and see Alex's face, white and waxen and still. He talked about his nightmares, the pale-faced girls moving endlessly through his dreams. He described their icy breaths and the wordless whispers. Then he told her about his war with God and the desert in his soul.

From time to time he ran out of words, and in the silence stretching between them, there had been only the sound of the rain, always the rain, drumming down, beating hard on the side of the house. When he finished talking, Shelly cried quietly for a while, then asked, *Where do we go from here?*

Not to Florida, he quipped. For the first time in a long while Shelly laughed, and then he looked into her lovely green eyes and said: "Forward, Shell, somehow we just go forward."

Around the time the black sky was brightening from pitch to gray, they shut the light out, lay down to sleep, and still there was the sound of the rain, drumming down, beating hard, like his own heart.

The alarm woke him two hours later. Shelly stirred and mumbled something in her sleep. He wiggled out of her embrace and traced his fingers lightly over her lips. They trembled and mumbled something again—something that sounded a lot like love.

The phone went off on a ringing jag. Thunder cracked outside. He eased out of the bed and tiptoed across to the bathroom. He closed the door, turned the shower on, and when the temperature was right, he stepped in. In the middle of soaping his boxer's chest, a pair of arms wound around him and a cheek pressed against his back. He let the arms sink low and touch him. His desire grew. He turned around. Standing there naked and soaking wet, proud and wounded but working her way back, was his wife, Mrs. Edward S. Gavin. There were no walls between them, nothing at all but his own evident desire. All the cold, lonely years fell away there in the warm shower. Shelly reached out, and husband and wife became man and woman again.

*   *   *

Strega stood over Cybil's bed. Her face was pasty and her eyes fuzzy from the painkillers, but she managed a small smile. "Hey, Princeton boy. Your plan worked."

"I never thought you'd be in danger."

"Neither did I."

"I'd give anything to have me lying there instead of you."

"He wouldn't have hit on you, Strega."

"In this city, you never know." She laughed and reached for his hand. He held it tight. Her face clouded. "Cybil?"

"He made me, Strega. He knew I was a cop. Was I that bad? That unconvincing?"

"No, you were good. Maybe he saw you on the news, at one of the other hits, and recognized you. Maybe he saw us or one of the other shadow cars tailing you. The important thing is that it's over and you're okay. I owe you, Hansen."

"No, you don't. Thanks to you, we're heroes. The P.C.'s going to decorate both of us."

"How's the ambulance chaser holding up?"

"Wants me to quit. Go teach school. He says it's safe. I told him I'm safer on the street than in a classroom given all the guns kids are walking around with these days. I'll never quit. I love being a detective." She took a breath. "Anyway, the ambulance chaser's downstairs getting coffee right now. He hates you, by the way. Said something about killing the son of a bitch who came up with the bright idea of using me for bait." She smiled again, then began to mumble.

Strega leaned close to hear her.

"Most murders are crimes of passion," she mumbled, "and in most instances the victim knows their killer. If I were you, I'd get out of here before my husband comes back." She let go of his hand. "I hurt like hell, but you know what? I'm a hero now. This is good for my career, Strega. Really good."

Maria lay across her bed, nude, on her back, turning Kelly's shield around and around in her hands. She pressed the shield to her belly, then to her thigh, remembering how first he had been restrained, his movements slow, almost reluctant, looking away from her, while she unbuttoned his clothes. Then she tipped his head around and saw his eyes were hazy with desire.

Maria pressed the shield to her thigh, remembering the ecstasy on his face, the small, shy smile, as though he was still surprised at his good fortune—at his very good fortune—of having her fit, able body hungry for him. She thought of how he placed his two hands on her hips, shut his eyes, and rocked into her. Maria said, *I want you to watch,* and he did. She held his face tight, watching him watch. He was mesmerized, his bright blue eyes dark with lust, watching them rock together. He moved her hands to his solid hips, and she held him as he bucked and moaned and whispered her name.

Maria.

They had all whispered *Maria.*

Even *him.*

Maria, Maria, Maria.

She held the shield in one hand, touched herself with the other, and whispered: *Maria.* The telephone rang. She picked up on the fifth ring.

"Maria?" a voice said. "Maria Alvarez?"

The voice was a stranger's. "Who is this?" she asked, still dreamy from looking at Kelly's shield and touching herself, remembering.

"A friend."

"What friend?"

"Kelly's friend."

She dropped the shield. "What do you want?"

"I saw you."

Maria sat straight up.

The voice went on. "I told the coppers I saw you go into that Kelly cop's place the day he died. I picked *New York* magazine out of the trash this morning and saw your picture inside, with your daddy. I recognized you."

"So what if I went into his place?"

"I'll tell them more. I'll tell them I heard a gunshot and saw you go running out after. I can say a lot of

things to make trouble. With a daddy like you got, you
can't afford trouble."

"Who did you talk to?"

"Couple of regular coppers. Don't remember their
names. Old guy, young good-looking guy. Old guy said
he was Kelly's friend."

"How much do you want?"

"Five thousand bucks. Then I'll forget what I saw and
I'll change my story. They think I'm nothing but a stupid
super anyway."

"You're right," Maria said, with promise in her voice.
"I don't want any trouble. Come see me now, tonight.
I'm sure we can work things out."

Franklin giggled. "I have your address. You're listed
in the white pages."

Maria hung up. She lay on her back, looking at the
ceiling. The crack in the ceiling had grown. Now it
touched the other side. Maria dressed quickly in a new
uniform. She slipped her Spanish blade in her pocket,
put her hat on, and waited for Franklin to come.

Strega worked at the sculpture pedestal into the early
morning hours. His hands moved automatically, knowing
just where and how to build the clay up, where to skim
it down. His fingers knew the angles of the facial planes
and the line of the lips. He worked to the rhythm of
the rain slashing against the window panes, adjusting the
features, changing the expression on the face of Maria
Alvarez, erasing the sorrow, the vulnerability, the
beauty, until what was left was hard and ugly and
violent.

At three, the phone rang. He picked up, hoping to
hear Rosemary's voice.

"Jonnie," she purred.

"Alvarez."

"It's late for you to be up working. You making a
sculpture of Rosemary de Cesare?"

"Leave Rosemary alone. This isn't about her."

"You're right. It's about you and me and Vincent. But
Rosemary could be part of it. We could make room for

her." She laughed softly. "I went to see her late today, after our big collar. I wanted to tell her how great you did, Jonnie. She's a beautiful woman. Accomplished, educated. All the things I'd like to be, actually. What would you give to protect her, Jonnie? Would you give your life?" Alvarez hung up.

Maria stood at a phone booth on the corner, a block away. She saw the big plate window lit up, and Strega standing there, motionless, searching the night for her.

She smiled. Her uniform was wet. She had just come from the river.

Maria rolled the blue cat's-eye marble from hand to hand, and even though she was far away, she could taste Strega's fear.

Twenty-three

Strega spent the few remaining hours of night in his Jeep, waiting outside Rosemary's East Side apartment. He didn't need coffee to stay awake. The adrenaline rush was enough. He watched the streetlights go out and the night sky brighten to a steel-colored haze. At seven-thirty sharp, Rosemary came swinging out the door and hailed a nearby cab. Strega jumped out and crossed the street, calling her name.

She ignored him and ducked inside the waiting cab.

Strega tried for the door. His hand brushed metal, but then the cab accelerated away. He had a fleeting glimpse of Rosemary's angry, tear-stained face turned to the rear window looking back at him.

Strega knew by the time he got home, she would be behind her desk. He steered the Jeep across town, parked in his garage, and jogged up to his apartment.

Her assistant answered on the first ring. "Rosemary De Cesare's office."

"Jon Strega. I've got to talk to her."

"You're dead, Jonnie. It's over." Even David sounded shell-shocked. "She trashed all the pictures of you yesterday afternoon."

"Why?"

"Maybe it had something to do with you sending your new girlfriend in."

"I don't have a new girlfriend."

"Right. So how come she had a picture of you and Rosemary?"

"Tell me what happened."

"A woman called up saying it was a referral to open

an account. Rosie agreed to meet her, thinking it was another of your cop friends. Once the Spanish bombshell got in here, she raked Rosie over the coals and told her what you were like in bed. Then your *mamacita* went *coco-loco* telling Rosie how she's got bad taste in sheets. She threw a picture of you and Rosie on the desk, and Rosie threw *her* out of the office." David sighed. "Rosie cried, Jonnie. She really liked you, maybe even loved you. You're history here, personally and professionally. She's transferring your account over to another trader, Owen Varick. Your cop friend's too. Owen's on vacation until Monday, after which time you call there, not here. Happily never after. Cheerio." David hung up.

Strega threw his phone on the couch and went to the clay head of Maria Alvarez. He pressed his hands on both graceful temples and squeezed. The damp clay gave way. He moved hands all over the face, squeezing and contorting. When he was finished, Maria's face stared at him.

Her mouth was agape in horror.

Her neck was arched up in agony.

And her fine Spanish cheekbones were crushed.

Strega knew he had to see Rosemary, face to face. He raced downtown, in uniform, used his shield to get past the main reception desk, then swept into Rosemary's office, ignoring David's protestations. He slammed the door behind him and locked it.

Rosemary pushed her chair back from her desk, stood up, hands on hips. Her cheeks were flushed. "Get out." Her voice was ripe with hurt.

Strega hoped the hurt proved she still loved him. "I'll leave when I'm finished talking."

"I'm not interested in lies."

"You were sure interested yesterday. Aren't you curious to hear what I have to say?"

She blinked. He had her. She sank back into her chair, looked him over from head to toe. "You look like shit," she finally said.

Strega's pulse raced. Despite her smart navy blue silk

suit, she looked like she hadn't been sleeping well. He realized Rosemary was as miserable as he was. All the old electricity was there between them, stronger than ever.

"I've missed you," Strega said softly, watching her, loving her, fearing for her.

Rosemary's green eyes flashed away from him. "Like I said, you look like shit."

Strega pulled a chair around to her side of the desk. He sat right up close to her, close enough to smell her cologne. He tucked a curl behind her ear. She didn't resist.

"I've been up all night," Strega started, taking her hands in his, looking her strong and straight and sure in the eye. "Let me tell you why."

Gavin walked into the station house at three in the afternoon.

Desk sergeant Bell glowered down at him. "The M.E. left a message for you. Said to stop by when you have a minute. And Ballantine wants to see you *forthwith.* Said he's been calling you all night and all morning."

"Good afternoon to you too," Gavin quipped.

He went up the stairs and through the detective pool to Ballantine's office. The shades were shut, but a light was burning inside. He rapped on the door. "Gavin here."

"It's open," Ballantine barked.

Gavin stepped in and stopped short. Ballantine had pinned all the CSU photos from the suicide files to the wall. It was a gruesome gallery, but most stunning was the row of ten pictures documenting the gunshot wounds. Ten perfect stars, bright red, on the pale temple skin of each dead cop. Ballantine paced in front of his display.

"I've been calling you since early this morning," Ballantine said.

"So Bell told me."

"Ten men, Ed. Ten good men, with their brains blown out and the eleventh in ICU with his head wrapped up

like an ice cream cone. I been here all night looking at
these pictures, trying to understand. What do these
eleven men have in common besides the hole in their
head? Who did this to them?"

"Is that why you called me? You already know my
opinion." He turned to the door.

"Wait!" Ballantine barked.

Gavin stood with his hand on the doorknob and
listened.

"I went looking for your loony-bin janitor this
morning."

Gavin dropped his hand and turned around. "Why'd
you do that?"

"I wanted to talk to him myself. Anyway, I struck
out. He didn't show up for work." Ballantine shifted
uncomfortably. "Look, I don't want to be telling you
what I'm about to tell you, but I need your help. CSU
called me late last night. The first print run's in from
Kelly's place. We got a full index fingerprint that came
up on his gun." Ballantine cleared his throat. Loosened
his tie.

"And?" Gavin prompted.

Ballantine looked at him for a long moment, then said:
"The print belongs to Maria Alvarez."

Gavin felt electrified. His fingers tingled and his head
buzzed. "Arrest her. Now."

"Slow down. So she was inside his apartment. That's
all we know. As far as the D.A.'s concerned, all I've got
is a fingerprint and a loony-bin janitor. It isn't enough
to even put a tail on her, and it sure as hell isn't going
to be enough to convince the D.A. to bring Ramon Alvarez's daughter up on murder one charges. Like I told
you, I'm not even sure I buy it. If she was having an
affair with Mike, maybe she picked up his gun. Or
maybe she took it out of his holster while she was undressing him. Maybe she was fucking him, maybe she
was fucking every cop in the NYPD. So what? That's
not murder. There are a hundred legitimate reasons why
her fingerprint is on Kelly's gun."

"You're going to just ignore her?"

"No. But I need more than a fingerprint. I need an eyewitness, preferably two." He leaned across his desk and looked intently at Gavin. "If you really believe she's guilty, help me. Go back and rap on every door in Donovan's building one more time. Take her picture with you. And if you don't find a witness there, start in on the apartment buildings of these other dead cops. You get me those witnesses, I'll think about going back to the D.A. and asking for an indictment. Not until then, not on the shit speculation you're giving me. Got that?"

"Loud and clear." Gavin grabbed the door handle.

"And, Ed? Did I tell you to stay away from Maria?"

"You mentioned it," Gavin said. Then he was out the door, going through the squad room and down the stairs, his blood hammering in his head, hot with the need to shove her up against a wall and ask her point-blank: *How did it feel to kill Danny?*

Bell shouted out at him as he passed the big desk. "Lang called again. Said it was important you stop by."

The desk clerk at the morgue waved Gavin in. "He's expecting you. Go on back." Moving down the long, cold mortuary hall, past the steel bins, Gavin couldn't help looking up at the blinking temperature gauges. Thirty-five degrees. It was still winter.

He walked into the autopsy room. A white sheet covered a steel examining table. Lang crossed over and clapped Gavin on the shoulder.

"A farmer out in the country found her when he was tilling some new earth at the end of his field. The age and height are right, so is the timetable. Decomposition puts the murder back five years. I want you to look at the personal effects found in the grave. Tell me if they were Alex's."

Lang moved to a side table and picked up a plastic bag. Sealed inside was a pair of gold hoop earrings. Same size and shape Alex had been wearing. Gavin nodded. Lang presented a second sealed evidence bag. Inside was a Bart Simpson key chain. Gavin blanked out.

Was it hers? He thought so. "I'm not sure," he finally said, feeling queasy. "Could be hers."

Lang presented a third sealed evidence bag. Inside was a tattered nylon blue book bag, the same kind Alex had carried to school. Gavin shook his head. "No," he managed. "Alex's was bright pink. That is definitely not hers."

Lang replaced the bag and sighed. "Okay. Looks like we're finished."

"What happened to this girl?" Gavin had a sudden sick fascination to know.

"Don't do this to yourself, Ed."

"Tell me. Talk to me like I'm a cop and not a father."

Lang blinked. "Okay. She was buried in three feet of dirt, on her right side, with her legs bent. The bag was found on top of her, as though it had been tossed in as an afterthought. From the trace fibers I've looked at on the bones, I think it's safe to assume she was buried with her jeans on. She was wearing sneakers. We know her top was on because that item of clothing was intact. Polyester lasts forever.

"Five years in the ground. Five summers and five winters. There's not much left. We have a perfectly intact skeleton of a young female, five feet one inches tall. The bones are in good condition and total eight pounds ten ounces in weight. We have fragments of her clothing, but I don't think it will tell us anything about who killed her." He showed Gavin an evidence bag containing a pair of rotted sneakers. "The canvas decayed, but the rubber soles endured.

"Her earrings were intact, of course, as well as several items in the backpack. Her schoolbooks and notebooks had disintegrated, but we have a plastic comb, five dollars in coins, and the key chain which you saw. Metal buttons from a pair of Levi jeans and a jean jacket were also recovered at the burial site. We've gone over every item looking for possible evidence, fibers or hairs her abductor might have left. We came up with nothing."

Gavin nodded. Alex had been wearing jeans, sneakers,

a jean jacket, and gold earrings too on the day she disappeared. Lang knew that. No wonder he called. "Go on."

"She died of a single bullet wound to the head. The entrance wound is a single round hole with inward beveling in the center of her forehead. There was no exit wound. We recovered the bullet from inside the cranium and know the weapon was a .38. Her wrists were both broken, probably in a struggle. There were no other broken or fractured bones. I have no way of telling if she was abused in any other manner."

Murder seemed abuse enough. Gavin spotted an evidence bag Lang hadn't showed him. It was half covered, as though someone had hidden it quickly. "What's that?"

Lang flushed. "Nothing."

Gavin pulled the bag out and flinched. The bag was full of long auburn hair, almost but not quite the same shade as Alex's.

"The hair remained intact," Lang explained. "That's not unusual."

Gavin replaced the plastic bag. "I want to see her."

Lang hesitated.

"I have to see her."

Lang pulled the white sheet off. Gavin approached.

The bones were stained from the earth and spotted with patches of fungus. Here and there little bits of clothing stuck to the skeleton. Her arms lay at her sides. He reached out and stroked her pitifully broken wrists, then her small hand bones. He looked at her head. The skull was small. In front of the face, in the center of the forehead, a single round hole pierced the bone. He moved slowly down the table, running his hands over the arc of her ribs, the length of her arms, her legs, and finally, her feet.

It could have been Alex, but it wasn't. Was he happy? Relieved? Disappointed? Did he want to know for once and for all that Alex was dead? *Did he really want to know?* Or did he want to leave it unfinished, so he could live out his life with the tireless flame of hope flickering in his soul?

"Alex," he whispered. Was she out there in a field, the lycra lasting forever, her long hair perfectly preserved, hoop earrings hard and indestructible in the dirt?

He remembered her so alive, dancing around his boxing bag, light as a feather, fleet and agile. *Come on, Dad! Bet I'm faster than you!* And then how her little fists shot out into the heavy bag. *Bam, bam, bam. Upper jab, lower jab. Right cross, left cross. Look at me, Dad! Look! Bam, bam, bam and her bright, bubbling laugh.* Gavin remembered her laugh and her smile. Gavin remembered her well. His own sweet Alex.

Gavin stepped back from the table and nodded.

Lang pulled the sheet up. It billowed out, white and spectral, then floated down to cover the small stained bones.

"I can see myself out," Gavin said.

Down the hall, he stopped and touched the steel bins, thinking of all the dead girls with their strange perfume. He thought Alex's baby breath, warm and moist against his cheek. Then he thought of the white-faced girls of his dreams, their wordless whispers, and the touch of their chilly, lifeless lips dry against his skin.

Gavin looked up at the blinking temperature gauges over the steel bins. Thirty-four degrees now. Cold enough to snow.

Twenty-four

At one o'clock in the morning, Maria Alvarez stepped off the elevator on the ICU floor of New York Hospital. The nurses' station was empty. She walked quickly by and turned down the hall. She wore her new uniform and hat. Her lips were carefully glossed red, and her hair was tied smoothly back. Her gun belt felt heavy and official around her hips. The night guard outside Walker's room was Moon. Maria smiled. He would be easy to roll. Moon looked up as she approached. "Hey," she said, "these all-nighters are no fun."

He grinned and stretched. "I must be dreaming. What are you doing here, Maria?"

"Just finished the four-to-twelve. Thought I'd look in on Walker." She paused, took her hat off, and looked intently at his eager, ugly face. "I was seeing him for a while."

"Lucky him," he replied, sincerely.

"Not really. I broke it off. He was a nice guy, but too old. You know, I finally realized I should be going out with guys my own age." She flashed him a smile.

Moon flushed. "Yeah? What if I asked you out again?"

"I guess you'd just have to ask and find out." She moved past him to the door, careful to brush his arm with her hip. She put her hand out to open the door. Moon grabbed her wrist.

"You can't go in there, Maria," he said apologetically.

"Who says?" she asked evenly.

"Ballantine. No one goes in there without the Q-Ball."

Maria turned her big eyes on him and asked, "Why's that?" in a way that expressed casual, offhand interest.

Moon shrugged. "Don't know. Those are the orders."

She crouched next to his chair and put her hand on his arm. "Walker and I were sleeping together. That makes me family, in a way. I just want to pay my respects."

Moon looked doubtful.

"Come on," Maria implored, squeezing his arm. "I won't tell the Q-Ball you let me in. It'll be our secret."

"Guess you could go in," he said reluctantly. "Just for a minute, though."

"Thanks," she said softly. She stood up and stepped inside. The door swept shut behind her. Walker lay in the dark, surrounded by machines. Monitors glowed and beeped. She moved to the bedside and tenderly touched the white wrappings around his head. She leaned over and kissed the left temple, where she knew the star-shaped wound was.

If anyone were to walk in, she thought, they would see a young grieving woman kissing her former lover. It would be a tender and touching sight. No one would see her right hand working the syringe out of her pocket, puncturing the IV drip high up and feeding in the dose of digitalis that would drip into Walker's veins and shut down his stubborn pumping heart instantly and forever.

If anyone looked in, they would simply see a handsome woman in uniform, paying her last respects.

On her way out, she leaned down and kissed Moon lightly on his pocked cheek, then put her finger up to his lips. "Remember, this is our secret." Her breast pressed up against his head. "Let's have dinner sometime soon. I'll show you then how much I appreciate this."

She moved away, lightly down the hallway, knowing he was watching the roll of her hips. She felt flushed and excited. The violence always did that to her, and when she felt this way she changed out of her uniform and went to the West Side piers.

*   *   *

The rain made Strega restless. It drummed against his living room window panes. He looked out into the night, wondering if she was out there, watching him. Strega studied the sidewalks and corners, the phone booths and parked cars, half expecting to see Alvarez standing there, uniform pasted to her full body, oblivious to the rain, watching him, waiting for her chance.

At least Rosemary was safe, Strega thought, turning away from the window. He had hired a bodyguard to follow her around on the odd chance Alvarez might make a move for her. Rosemary let him do it. Fear was palpable. She must have seen and felt how afraid he was of Maria Alvarez—how afraid he was that Alvarez would get to Rosemary again and hurt her.

He picked up a framed photo of Rosemary off his bookshelf. She was wearing a long batik skirt and flat Grecian gold sandals. He remembered that day earlier in the summer, when they were lovers, flushed and new, wandering the city, tied to each other by a hundred tiny unconscious moves—his hand resting on her flank, her fingertips sliding across his cheek, her hips bumping his thigh, his palm open and flat and sure on the small of her back. Her skirt was cut long and full. It swung with every step she took, brushing Strega's leg. Her gold sandals were made of fat gold leather that laced up past her ankles, crisscrossing her calves. The sandals slapped the sidewalk in rhythm to the swinging and brushing of her skirt. *Slap-slap, swing, brush.* Strega could have walked forever.

He picked the photo up and studied it—not that he needed a picture to bring her up. Her voice, her smell— Rosemary was always right there with him. If he closed his eyes, he could feel the exact weight of her thigh thrown across his in sleep. He recalled the ache he always felt watching her unhook her bra. How she dropped it to the ground. How she would then lose patience with undressing. How she would then lay back and twist a band of panty lace between her thumb and forefinger, edging it out of the way, clearing the way for him.

*   *   *

Maria Alvarez cruised slowly up Twelfth Avenue. She kept the Celica tight to the curb and studied the sidewalks. The pickings were slim. The rain had chased most of the street crowd in. A tall black girl blew her a kiss. A tired blonde straddled a trash can and lifted her breasts as the Celica passed. Hands reached out for the windows, trying to scratch their way in. The Celica's glass was tinted dark, and no one outside could see in. No one outside knew if the driver was a man or a woman, and on this block no one cared.

She watched him standing apart from the girls, leaning uneasily against a warehouse wall. He was young and muscular. He shifted his weight several times in the thirty seconds Maria studied him, crossing his arms, then uncrossing them, chewing his fingernails, looking unsure and desperate enough that Maria knew she could get him to do anything she wanted.

Suddenly he was aware of being observed, and his body language changed. He stood straighter, hooked his thumbs through his belt loops. He thrust his pelvis out in an aggressive manner and ran his free hand through his thick blond hair. His chin tipped up, his foot tapped, and he posed, showing off the impressive bulge in his tight shorts.

Maria stopped the car in front of him. He swaggered over with a practiced self-conscious gait, and the hand was reaching up again, sweeping all that hair out of his vapid eyes. He leaned down next to the window and tapped his finger against the smoked glass. He smiled. His teeth were stained and bad. His skin had a drug addict's pallor. His arms were a child's connect-the-dots puzzle—old needle scars mixed with fresh punctures, angry and pink. His eyes were unfocused, but she could see the need in them. He would do whatever she wanted for any amount of money as long as it was U.S. currency. She got out and hustled him into a corner.

"Hey, what do you know?" he slurred. "A real live cunt. Mostly I get men. Haven't had a bitch in so long, I hope I remember where to stick it."

Maria grabbed him by the collar and twisted hard. He choked. She slammed him against the warehouse wall and heard the satisfying crack of his skull against cement. She drew her service revolver with her free hand and shoved the nose of it into his throat.

His eyes rolled around, his chin pulled in, and he went cross-eyed trying to identify the metal. He focused on the butt of the gun and put that form together with the feel of metal sticking in his skin. "What the fuck?" he sputtered.

She leaned close to him and nearly choked on the cloud of cheap musk mixed with the unmistakable smells of unwashed flesh and human fluids. "Twenty bucks," she said.

He giggled. "Fifty."

"Twenty."

"What do you think I am, cheap?" He giggled again.

She slammed his head into the cement. His breath rattled in his throat.

"Bitch," he wheezed. "Threatening to shoot me if I don't fuck you for twenty."

"I don't want you to fuck me." She pulled the gun back and slipped it into her holster.

He scratched his crotch. "Well, what do you want me to do?"

"Hit me. Hard enough to mark me, not so hard as to knock my teeth out. You fuck up and knock them out, I shoot you. Got it?"

He swallowed hard and whispered: "Can't. Can't hit a girl."

"Yes, you can."

"Shit." He turned his head and looked off at the empty street. He swallowed again, and just as he was getting ready to explain how he was too much of a gentleman to do it, Alvarez pistol-whipped him with the butt of her gun.

He reacted instinctively, slamming a fist forward into her face. His arm became a piston. Her head exploded with white-hot pain, and her skin ripped open. Maria's hands clawed the air, trying to grab his wrists. "That's enough. Lay the fuck off," she screamed. Her face was full of blood. The reflex piston did not stop. The fist came at her, tireless and strong. He was hitting in a blind frenzy. She managed to twist her gun around in her hand and fire a warning shot off at the wall.

The fist dropped. He stared dumbly at her. When she saw the shock spread over his pocked face, Maria knew the boy had done a good job. She reached in her pocket, pulled out a twenty, and stuffed it in the waistband of his shorts. "Don't spend it all in one place." She got back in the Celica and drove away.

Her head was woozy. She drove slowly, inching along. Now that the rain had stopped, the sidewalks were filling up.

A big woman ran crazily up to the Celica. She had long wheat-colored hair that didn't fuzz up in the humidity. Maria knew it was a wig. The woman threw herself on the hood. A short pink vinyl skirt Saran Wrap tight against her small ass revealed long café-au-lait legs. Ten pink fingernails scraped the Celica's windshield. The woman pressed her mouth against the glass. Her red lips squashed up, and Maria could see the big white teeth receding into pink-brown gums. A long, skinny tongue snaked out and licked the glass.

Maria flicked the wipers on.

The woman pulled back and giggled, batting the rubber blades like flies. She sat on her heels, remarkably steady on the rain-slicked hood even when Maria hit potholes and the whole chassis rocked from side to side. Slowly then, with the suppleness of a contortionist, she eased back on the hood until she lay flat. She spread her knees, the pink vinyl skirt gaped open. A rigid male organ, potato thick and angry, stuck up into the sky. It swayed slightly with the rocking motion of the car.

Maria accelerated. The Celica shot forward. The he-she scrambled up to the windshield, blanketed it with the he-she body, and clawed the roof for a hold. Maria heard the fingernails scratching metal. She drove blinded by the press of the bare mocha stomach against the glass—the belly button rubbing up in front of her, the

line of black hairs leading down to the still engorged
organ, and the organ itself thrusting against the
windshield.

Maria hit the brakes. The he-she body fell back and
tumbled off the hood. The car was skidding out of control. Maria gripped the steering wheel hard and felt the
sickening thump of her tires rolling over flesh and bone.
Instinctively, she accelerated again and cut her eyes up
to the rearview mirror. A heap of pink vinyl lay motionless in the road behind her. Maria was far away,
but she knew by the slack of the body that the he-she
was dead.

She took the first right and raced away. She was within
the boundaries of the One-Three. The precinct was
short-staffed. They wouldn't expend much effort, if any,
trying to find witnesses to a hit-and-run—not when the
victim was a transvestite hooker. There were too many
crimes to solve in the One-Three and not enough detectives to go around. The he-she would be quickly
forgotten.

When she was a good ten blocks away, she stopped
the car and counted out loud to slow her heartbeat. The
he-she haunted her. Maria was a he-she too, only for
her the *he* was separate, outside of her but still part of
her—a part she couldn't destroy. This he-she thing had
broken Maria. A broken person was different from the
rest of the normal world, with a different sense of right
and wrong, or sometimes none at all.

She remembered the old-fashioned white wood window frame in Jon Strega's bedroom. She remembered
how she had filed down the wing lock so it didn't catch
in the locked position. Maria thought of the old fat vine,
thick as a tree trunk, running up from the ground to
that window, and she smiled.

She checked her face in the mirror. The skin was puf-
fing up around her eye, and the color was ripening to a
rich purple. Her lip was split wide. Her cheek was ripped
and bleeding. She drove the last twenty blocks in a haze,
flush with excitement, panting and wet and ready.

The violence always made her feel that way.

*   *   *

Strega was sleeping, dreaming of the Sicilian, of her lush body pressed to his. The weight of her heavy breasts pressing against him. He dreamed her female sex was over him, massaging his forehead and his mouth, showing him how wet she is, how ready for him she is. Then she was covering him with her full body, and her tongue was learning the curves of his ear, poking gently in, feeling the inside. Her mouth was moving lower over his chest now, covering him with wet, circular kisses trailing down, and then her hands were spreading his thighs and her mouth was gently probing while her hands weighed him tenderly. Her long fingernails were tickling him lightly. He reached down and buried his hands in her hair. There was so much of it and it was straight, not curly.

Jon Strega stirred in his sleep. The dream felt real, as though his hands were really buried in hair. He opened his eyes. This was not Rosemary's curly copper hair. This hair was black and long and straight. His mind raced dumbly, searching for information. Had he gone out, gotten drunk, and brought someone home?

He smelled cinnamon and musk. Strega pulled on the hair and forced the face away from its midnight feeding. He tugged again, snapping the head back, and looked down fleetingly at the shining, triumphant profile of Maria Alvarez.

He heaved his body out of the bed. "Get out."

"Why do you sound so mad when you're obviously so happy to see me?" She pointed maliciously at his sex, pulsing and erect, shiny from her mouth.

She sat up in the bed, on her knees, and ran her hands over her body. Her face was hidden in shadow and by the tangle of her long hair. He couldn't focus on it anyway. His attention was riveted on the things she was doing to herself, there in his bed. She was arching back, spreading herself with her fingers, giving him a clear view, talking softly all the while. "I wanted you, Jonnie, as much as you wanted me. I had to show you. You refused to listen to your own body. This was the only way." Her hands were squeezing her nipples and pulling them up to meet her mouth.

Her clothes lay in a pile on the floor. Strega picked them up and threw them at her. "Get dressed," he said in a dead voice.

She shook her head no and patted the mattress. "Come back, Jonnie. Let's finish it." Her hand was moving in a circle now, wider and wider, over her soft belly, back down into that thick black forest, her face still obscured by the tangle of hair.

Strega reached for the phone. "Get out or I'll call the police."

"Go right ahead, Jonnie." She flipped her hair back and watched Strega's reaction. The shock must have registered on his face because she was laughing again.

"What happened?" he asked hoarsely.

"You beat me up, Jon Strega. You beat the shit out of me. Go ahead and call the police. You'll save me the trouble. I'm going to have you hauled in. It was a hell of a fight." She was dressing as she talked, slipping a bloodstained fuchsia blouse over her bare breasts, shimmying into bloodstained skintight white jeans. "I don't know what set you off, Jonnie. You have a bad temper, so it could've been anything. Jealousy maybe, from the way a guy looked at me on the street. You lost it and went at me like a crazy man."

She rolled off the bed. She reached up and tore her blouse, roughly ripping the silk, revealing a healthy portion of those lush, heavy breasts. "I tried to stop you. You said you were going to rape me. You said you were going to show me what a real man felt like." She shook her tangled hair until it was wilder still. "I tried to say no, I don't want you to, but you pulled at me anyway. I said no again and you went ballistic," she screamed, yanking the sheets off the bed, "hitting me over and over and over."

She threw herself against his desk, swept a pile of magazines off, and pushed the computer to the floor. "I tried to climb out the window, I was so scared, but you were on me, one hand between my legs, the other hand pulling my hair, pulling me back to you, back to your swinging fists. I hung onto the shade." She pulled and it came crashing down. She turned then and slipped through the door, down the hall, into the living room. He ran after her.

"See?" she said, holding up two of his champagne glasses, half-filled. "We were having champagne. You invited me up here for champagne." A bucket full of ice, a half empty bottle of champagne, sat on the coffee table. "You were a perfect gentleman, but then you went crazy. You were all over me. I tried to get away from you." She threw the champagne glasses to the floor. They shattered. "You pushed me across the room." She hurled her body over to the bookcases and swept a row of books to the floor. "You threw books at me first, calling me an illiterate bitch."

She pulled a cigarette and a cheap plastic lighter out of her pocket. She lit the cigarette. Instead of putting it to her lips, she lifted her ripped fuchsia blouse and pressed the orange glowing butt on the exposed flesh of her stomach. Her lips tightened, her eyes blinked rapidly. Then she stoically slid the burning cigarette in a pattern across her dusky, satin belly. She lifted the cigarette away and smiled triumphantly. Strega's own initials, *J.S.*, were seared into her skin.

Strega was stricken and shocked, locked in the horror of her self-mutilation. He should have seen her next move coming, but he didn't. He was still focused on the red, raw letters, bloody and charred, burned into her flesh.

Suddenly, she was across the room, standing next to the alabaster lady, hefting the stone piece up off its pedestal, groaning with effort, straining, lifting, hoisting the rock up over her slim shoulders and then grunting, then heaving the hundred-pound block of carved stone through the living room window. The plate glass shattered. Maria dropped to the floor, panting.

In the second of silence afterward, she whispered: "You said a stone woman was a better fuck than I was. You said you were going to teach me how to screw like

a whore." She stared up at him, wild-eyed and accusing.
Then the dead quiet broke. She rolled over, grabbed his
portable phone, punched in 911, and began to scream
hysterically. "Help me, he's going to kill me. His name
is Jon Strega and—"

The sound of his name shocked Strega back to life.
He dove across the room and tackled her, groping for
the phone. She bucked and heaved, trying to knock him
off her back, all the while holding the phone tight to her
mouth and screaming into it. "He's going to kill me!
He's trying to kill me!" She shouted out his address,
then reached back with one hand and clawed his face.
Her aim was good, she ripped her nails down his cheek,
and Strega felt fire. She pulled his hair, found his lips,
and tugged on them hard. He bit down on her fingers.
She thrashed under him and brought a foot up into his
head. He rolled over, gripping her body tight to his
chest.

Then they rolled, one over the other, across the floor,
into the coffee table. She scrambled up onto the glass,
gripping the phone to her mouth, screaming and crying,
knowing the whole act was being recorded on a master
911 tape.

Strega knew too. He ripped at her hands, pried the
phone free, and sent it sailing out the broken window.
He was dimly aware of the sound of sirens.

She was laughing at him now. "You pulled the phone
out of my hands when I tried to call for help, but it was
too late. They already had the address, and they were
on their way."

It was true. The sirens were getting closer.

She pulled his service revolver out from under a sofa
cushion. "And then you pointed this at me," she said,
turning the gun on herself.

He lunged across the glass table and knocked her to
the floor. He grabbed her hand and tried to twist the
gun out of her grip. She rolled. He stayed on her. She
rolled again and again, taking him with her. She rolled
one more time and came out on top, straddling him,
pointing his 9mm at his face. "You tried to kill me with

it, Jonnie." She eased the gun nose over, pressed it to
his right temple, and wrapped his right hand around it.
"Or did you try to kill yourself? Were you trying to
become number nineteen, Jonnie? Were you? Were you
going to end up *just like your father*?"

He felt the cold gun barrel against his skin and waited
for the explosion.

Suddenly, she was off him. She tossed his gun across
the room. It scuttled under the couch. She went to the
window and looked out. "They're here now, Jonnie,"
she said softly. "They're here. I'm safe now."

Red and white light flashed through the dark apartment.

She erupted again, screaming, heartbreaking piercing
screams, begging for mercy, pleading with him to stop
hurting her. She tore at her jeans, tugged them down to
her knees.

Doors slammed outside. A floodlight went on in the
garden. Strega crawled to the window and looked out.
A patrol car was jackknifed up on the sidewalk, doors
flung wide open, roof lights spinning, spinning, spinning,
and the crazy shrieking wail of the siren going on and
on, not winding down at all. Two cops were running up
the walkway with their guns thrust out in front of their
bodies. Strega's knees gave way. He slid down the wall
and crouched on the floor.

Alvarez was screaming hysterically. She grabbed a
vase and threw it against the wall. She tossed the crystal
ice bucket into the television set. She overturned chairs,
tore his paintings down, smeared her blood against the
white walls. She threw herself on the floor. Wedged her
body under the table and turned the table over on
herself.

Then they were pounding at his door. "Police, open
up." His knees wouldn't hold him upright. Strega
crawled across to the door. He pulled himself up, opened
the door, and looked down the barrels of two 9mm service revolvers.

"You can make this easy on yourself or hard," one of
the cops said.

Strega focused on the cop's name tag. Perez.

Alvarez was crying hysterically. "Help me, please, I'm in here. Help me. Don't go away."

Perez slapped a pair of handcuffs around Strega's wrists. His partner pushed past Strega to where Maria lay on the floor. Her ripped blouse was artfully arranged so startling breasts were bared. Her pants were tugged down over her hips. The full expanse of her scarred belly showed and, below it, a tuft of the black forest. The cops reacted first as men. It lasted only a second, but Strega recognized it. He saw the lust and appreciation there for the lush female form in front of them. Then the men recovered and the faces went blank with the practiced mask of a coply indifference.

Strega leaned against the wall, forgetting he was nude. They were helping her up.

"Can you tell me your name?" Perez was gently asking.

Maria clung to him, and pressed her full brown breasts into his chest. She looked up into his eyes and said in a loud, clear voice: "I am Officer Maria Alvarez of the Nineteenth Precinct. Police Commissioner Ramon Alvarez is my father."

Twenty-five

Gavin walked into the precinct house at seven-thirty Friday morning. Bell glowered down at him and for the second time in as many days bellowed: "Ballantine's looking for you. Says he's been calling you all night again."

"Good morning to you too," Gavin tossed back. "Ballantine got me as I was stepping into the shower." Gavin felt like Humpty Dumpty putting himself back together again with Shelly, and they needed quiet and privacy to do it. He had taken his phone off the hook for the night. When he put it back on the hook at seven o'clock that morning, Q-Ball had blasted through with ten rings, Gavin finally picked up, and all the Q-Ball said was: *Get here now.*

Gavin went swiftly up the stairs, swearing under his breath. *This better be good, Ballantine.* He rapped twice on Ballantine's door.

"It's open," Q-Ball shouted.

Gavin went in. "Ballantine, you look like hell." And he did.

"That a fact?" Ballantine stated. "Maybe it's because Walker died last night."

The raw sentence stunned Gavin. "How?" he managed.

"Right now the doc claims natural causes. Heart attack. But I'm getting a second opinion. Walker's body is down at the M.E.'s. The rookie cop who was standing guard last night looks to me like he's scared out of his mind about something. I think he's got something to say, and I'm going to lean on him until he pees in his pants and tells me the truth. Something went down last night. I think Walker had a midnight visitor, and I think this rookie knows who it was."

"You talk to Alvarez yet?"

"Funny you should bring that up."

"I don't see anything funny about Maria Alvarez."

"Neither does your young partner."

Gavin sank down into the bucket chair. "Not Strega."

"Oh, he's alive, Ed. But right now I bet he wishes he were dead."

A half hour later, when Ballantine had finished the whole incredible story as he knew it, Gavin said: "Don't you believe me now? What's it going to take?"

"For me to believe you, I've got to believe that Maria set Strega up. You haven't seen her face. She didn't get to looking the way she does with her own two fists. Someone did it to her, and frankly, it's hard for me to accept that Strega was an innocent bystander. The 911 call came in from *his* apartment. You listen to little Maria screaming on that tape and tell me shivers don't go up your back."

"You think Strega's lying," Gavin whispered.

"I don't know what the fuck to think."

"You think Maria's innocent," Gavin said, incredulous.

"I find it hard to believe she beat herself up."

Gavin exploded out of his chair. "If she can kill, why can't she beat herself up? You think about that, Ballantine?"

"It doesn't matter what the fuck I think," Q-Ball thundered back. "I've got no evidence. I'm stuck. Even if I take Strega's situation out of the mix, I'm stuck. Even if the rookie outside Walker's door talks and tells me Maria went in there last night, I'm stuck. I've got nothing but a handful of circumstantial evidence."

"And a print and a witness that puts her inside of Kelly's apartment the day he was killed."

"I can't find your goddamn witness! He's off on some beer binge, and I can't fucking find him! And what happens when I do find him? Say I've got your janitor and a print that puts Maria inside Kelly's place. Say Moon comes clean and admits Maria went into Walker's room last night. Say that's enough to get her indicted. A jury will kick her loose in five minutes. That's the way the system works. She's too sympathetic. Raised by her widowed father who happens to be a hero—who happens to be the goddamned police commissioner—a cop herself who happened to help make one of the most important arrests in the history of the One-Nine. Nope. No way Maria Alvarez spends one night in jail. We need a witness to one of the killings, and I'm not even sure that would be enough." Ballantine flipped the bulletin board over and stuck a red push pin in for the Walker killing. He rubbed his eyes. "Fuck."

Strega showed up at the precinct house late morning. Not knowing what else to do or where else to go, he went looking for Ballantine. As Strega walked through the detective pool, conversations stopped. Jaws dropped. He imagined he was some sort of folk hero, the idiot rookie who had the guts to punch Maria Alvarez in the face. He imagined all the men there had wanted to do that to her at one time or another. She had probably teased them all, but tortured only him and the men she had killed.

Q-Ball's door was open. Strega stopped short. Maria Alvarez was sitting opposite Ballantine, smoking a cigarette and tapping her shoe. "Kelly and I were having a fling," she was saying.

Ballantine looked up at the doorway. "Strega!"

Maria turned around and looked at him. Her battered face was blacker and bluer than he remembered. The flesh around one eye had puffed up the size of an egg, sealing her eye shut. She looked at him out of her one good eye and flashed him a secret conspiratorial grin. "Jonnie can stay," she said, still looking at him. "We had a misunderstanding, but it's cleared up now."

She turned back to Q-Ball and continued her speech. "Like I was saying, Kelly and I were having a fling. Nothing serious. We partnered together for a couple of days, and he told me about how he was feeling all broken up over his divorce. He still loved his wife. But he was lonely, so I made him a little less lonely, that's all." She paused, then leaned forward as though it had just dawned on her: "Are you saying I'm some kind of *suspect*?"

"We're just having a friendly conversation here, Maria. Routine. Your prints came up in his place."

"The way you say that makes me think I should call my lawyer."

"This is routine. I can't cut you any slack because you're Ramon's daughter."

"Okay. I'm guilty. I'm guilty of fucking him. But he didn't get fucked to death. Mike Kelly *killed himself*. With his own gun. The case is closed."

"Are you so sure of that, Maria?"

"You're trying to shake down the wrong person, Ballantine," she said evenly. She stood up and marched out of the office.

Ballantine moved to the doorway, next to Strega. "If she turns around and looks at me," he whispered, "she's guilty."

Strega and Ballantine watched her wind her way through the busy squad room. Her back was straight, her black hair was spilling down her back, and her hips were swinging. At the door she stopped, turned around, and looked back. Although she was a good distance away, Strega saw her one good eye narrow and her nostrils flare. He heard Q-Ball's sharp intake of breath. Maria pushed the door open, then she was gone.

"Heard you had a hell of a night last night," Ballantine said, still looking at the spot where Maria had been standing seconds before.

"Hell of a night," Strega agreed.

The door swung open and Wilson stormed in. He cut straight through the room to Ballantine's office. He waved the rookie and the detective in and kicked the door shut. "Talk, Strega."

"I didn't do it. And Maria had a change of heart at the station house last night. She refused to file charges against me."

"I know that. I also know she's saying it was all really a misunderstanding and partly her fault. Suddenly she's intimating that you weren't the one who beat her up. That she went to your place *after* she'd been beat. Tell me this. Someone beat the hell out of her, and if it wasn't you, who the fuck was it? And what was she doing in your apartment last night? And how the fuck do you explain the 911 tape?" Wilson rubbed his chin and worked hard to calm down. "You were first in your class at the academy. This is your third week on duty, and you helped make one of the most important collars in the history of the One-Nine. The press has already canonized you. Ramon Alvarez is stuck between a rock and hard place. He can't very well fire you, at least not right now, especially since Maria's saying you didn't do it."

"What do you think?" Strega asked.

"I don't believe you were the one who beat her up. If I find out I'm wrong, I'm going to give you a face to match hers and throw you the fuck off the job. Now get out of here."

Strega swallowed his indignation and yanked the door open. Standing on the other side was Ramon Alvarez, hand on the doorknob, ready to march in.

He grabbed Strega's collar. "You motherfucking son of a bitch," he spat. "I'm going to have your shield for this. I'm going to chase you the fuck out of this Department and out of this city."

Wilson intervened. "Ease up, Commissioner. Maria dropped the charges. She said he didn't do it. They had an altercation, but she said someone else beat her up. Strega's clean. Let him go. It was a misunderstanding, that's all. Maria was upset. She accused the wrong guy."

Ramon let Wilson peel him off Strega.

Strega didn't wait around. He had seen and heard enough. It was time to go to Philly.

Twenty-six

Strega pulled his Jeep into a service station on the out-
skirts of Philadelphia. He filled the tank, bought a coffee,
and went to the pay phone. She answered on the first
ring. It was nine-thirty in the morning, and she sounded
like she'd been sleeping.

"Catherine?"

"Who is this?"

"Your brother, Jon."

"What do you want." Matter-of-fact. No elation. No
emotion at all.

"I'm in town. I want to see you."

"Why?"

"I have this crazy feeling our father didn't die the way
everybody says he did."

The line was so quiet, he thought she had hung up.

"Catherine?"

He heard her sigh. "Don't stir things up, Jonnie."

"You know the truth, don't you?"

"Let him go. He died a long time ago. It's all over."
Her voice broke. "Just let him go. Please. He's dead.
There's nothing more to say." She hung up.

He tried the number again but got a busy signal. He
stepped outside and leaned against the booth. The sun
beat down on his face, and the voice echoed across the
years: *Your father was a hero, son, and don't ever forget
it.* Riley. Vincent Strega's partner. Who would know the
truth better than Dave Riley?

Strega crammed his big frame back inside the glassed-
in booth and spent the next hour feeding the pay phone
quarters, working his way down the substantial list of

Rileys in the Philadelphia white pages. The problem was, the Dave Riley he wanted had either left Philadelphia or had an unlisted number. Strega's next call was to the Philadelphia Police Department. He asked for accounting. A young woman answered the phone.

"Accounting, Jeanie Harlin speaking."

"Good morning, Jeanie," Strega coaxed. "My name is John Smith, and I'm calling from the Equitable Life Insurance Company. Jeanie, I hope you can help me out. I've got a check here I'm trying to get to someone. The company lost a lawsuit over some past rate hikes, and we owe some of the long-term policy holders substantial refunds."

"Some people have all the luck," Jeanie sighed. "I never get a refund."

"Yeah, me neither. Anyway, this lucky guy won't get his because the computer's fouled up and there's no street address listed for him. All I got is his name and the fact he was a detective eighteen years ago with the Philly P.D. I'm hoping you still send him benefits or a pension or a newsletter. Heck, maybe he's still with the Department. Can you help?"

"My pleasure. What's his name."

"Dave Riley."

"Spelled like it sounds?"

"R-I-L-E-Y." He listened to the sound of her tapping on the computer keyboard.

"I started with active-duty officers. We've got one David Riley, but he's a rookie, so I don't think he's your man. I'll change the search string and run through every officer who worked for the Department in the last twenty years." He listened to her tapping the keyboard again. "Bingo," she said. "I think I've got your man. John, are you still there?"

"I'm listening."

"David Riley. And the dates look right. He's not retired. He was relieved of duty in 1971 after eleven years on the job. That's a nice way of saying he was fired. Riley was a detective in the special narcotics unit. Last known address, 175 East Ridge Drive. No telephone

listed. That's all I've got for you. The last piece of corre-
spondence the Department sent him was in '72. No telling if the address is still any good."

"It's a place to start. Thanks a lot, Jeanie."

"Sure. If you don't find him, send me the check. I'll
use it to take you to dinner."

He laughed obligingly. When he hung up, his hands
were shaking. The address was in the same suburb where
the Strega family had lived up until Vincent's death. Jon
had never been back. He went inside the mini-mart and
bought a local map.

A few wrong turns and a half hour later, he was crawling down a sleepy-looking street named East Ridge,
checking curb-side addresses, looking for a match. The
houses were all rundown clapboard single-story numbers, peeling paint, tired chain-link, and beat-up American cars sitting on most front lawns. Once it might have
been a clean, tidy middle-class neighborhood. Now it
looked as though the creeping crud of the inner cities
was crawling over suburbia. A couple of long-haired
teenagers in baggy jeans and bandannas lounged on the
hood of a canary yellow Chrysler. The back end was
souped up with drag wheels, and the windows were
tinted black. The car body rocked with the bass vibration
of rap coming from a tape deck inside. The bandanna
brothers whistled and honked when the Jeep went by.
Strega reached for the automatic door-lock button.

The next block of East Ridge was no better. A rusty
swing set, a kid's plastic wading pool gone green with
slime, iron bars over all the house windows, more
souped-up Chryslers, and a lot of overgrown grass gone
to weed. America the Beautiful.

On the third block of East Ridge, the numbers ticked
up to near matches. Riley's was an odd-numbered address which, by the logic of the suburban planner, put
his house on the right. Strega found it sitting mid-block,
a gray-green version of the same clapboard structures
around it, only this one made the others seem positively
palatial. The low chain-link fence was rusted out and
fallen in. The grass had long ago dried up and blown

away on a winter wind, leaving hard-packed dirt for a front yard. The dirt was scarred with holes where something canine was trying to dig his way to China. Not that Strega blamed the hound. China had to be better than this Philly front yard. A collection of bent-up metal garbage cans covered with spray-paint graffiti littered the drive. The porch was low-roofed and sagging, and the travel-hungry canine in question was sprawling on the first step. He was a German shepherd, scarred and skinny, but big enough to make a casual visitor think twice. Strega felt anything but casual, especially when he deciphered the peeling initials *D.R.* taped on the rusting mailbox.

Something told him East Ridge had a couple of chop shops within walking distance. He didn't want his brand-new baby stripped down and sold to a coffee farmer in Costa Rica, so he parked the Jeep in the drive and set the alarm. Strega got out and stepped over a tumbled-down portion of the chain-link. He stepped slowly, but it was movement enough to set the shepherd off. The pooch was up and over in a split second, dripping saliva, baring stained teeth, ears flat with bad intentions.

"Hey, boy. Easy, now," Strega wheedled. The dog sniffed Strega's Top Siders, and must have smelled the kitten on the khakis, because the next thing Strega knew, the ears went even flatter and the barking turned to a back of the throat I'm-going-to-chew-you-the-fuck-to-death growling. One thing was clear. Dave Riley wasn't much interested in having visitors.

The front screen door slapped open, and a tall figure hung back in the shadows of the house, poking a fat rifle nose into daylight, shouting with the kind of authority you hear only from cops. "Hands up where I can see them. Now. Spread your legs and tell me who the fuck you are and what the fuck you want. You got ten seconds. Talk."

"Jon Strega." His hands were up, his legs were spread. He hoped his name would do the rest. The rifle nose didn't budge. Strega tried another tactic. "Vincent Strega's son."

The rifle nose dipped. "I figured that much out," the surly voice said out of the screen-door shadow. "Civilian life hasn't made a complete dumb shit out of me. Not yet, anyway." The lanky figure stepped out onto the porch. His hair had gone to shock white and his face had turned leathery from hard living, but he was still wiry and strong. Tucking the shotgun under one arm, Dave Riley loped down the crooked steps, kicked the shepherd aside, and put a hand up to shield his eyes from the morning sun while he looked Strega over carefully. "Christ. You look so much like him, I thought he was paying me a visit from the other side." He stuck his hand out and touched Jon's cheek. "Last time I saw you was the day your daddy was buried. You were what, five?"

Strega took that to be a peace offering, so he lowered his hands. "Six," he corrected.

"Good-looking kid too. Some guys have all the luck. Born beautiful and they stay that way. Some of them, like you, even get more goddamned beautiful. Me? I was cute once, but now I just look like one of my dog's chewed-up rawhide bones." He laughed roughly. "Well, Jon Strega, come on in out of this damn hot sun." He ushered Strega up the steps, into the house, and steered him into the living room. "What'll you have—domestic or imported?"

"Just a Coke."

"No beer? On a day like this? You sure you're Vince's kid?" Riley leaned the shotgun in a corner and shuffled off into the kitchen, laughing at his own joke.

Strega took a look around. The inside of the house didn't look much different from the outside. The floors were cracked linoleum, yellowed with neglect, and the furniture was standard-issue bachelor cop crap gone to seed. Big vinyl easy chair with the stuffing poking out of one arm. Nice-sized TV facing the chair. Old coffee cups and beer cans littering an early American coffee table. Gun magazines and enough far-right militia propaganda scattered around to make Strega wonder if Riley had gone into a different kind of law enforcement. The walls were cheap press board, and they were dotted with Bruce Willis posters tacked up with push pins. A side table was filled with dozens of framed photos, all shapes and sizes, all of Riley and Vincent Strega. Unlike the rest of the unkempt mess, the framed pictures were dusted and polished to gleaming.

Strega went over and picked up a black-and-white eight-by-ten. A much younger version of Dave Riley, fit and good-looking in uniform, smiled out. His arm was slung around Vincent Strega's shoulders. Vincent was laughing at the camera—laughing at the world, it seemed—younger than any pictures Strega had ever seen. He was wearing the same uniform as Riley. Strega read the inscription. "Graduation from the academy. Vince and Dave. The partnership begins." The loyalty, the love, showed on their faces.

Strega put it down and picked up another. Riley and Vince Strega again, but in smart suits, big trench coats, and wide-brim hats, smoking cigars, celebrating the promotion to rank of detective. In the shot Riley looked more the way Strega remembered, and his father's face showed the passage of time. He was still young, but there was experience stamped on the fine features—experience and a certain wild, wolfish confidence that fit the images stashed away in Jon Strega's own grainy memory bank.

Riley interrupted Strega's browsing. "Oh, you found those." He handed Strega a can of Coke and kept the beer for himself. "We went through the academy together, split up for a while on the job when we were rookies. Then later we partnered up and made detective grade together. The detective thing was a big moment. We thought we were a couple of regular Perry Masons." Riley laughed. "Come on, sit down. Take a load off." Riley fell back into the easy chair and let the foot rest drift up.

Strega remained standing.

"So," Riley continued, "who's the lucky girl who married you, Jonnie?"

"Haven't married anyone yet."

"Oh, hell. Be careful, now. Time passes fast. You don't want to end up an old creaky bachelor like me, do you?" He chuckled, then went on. "What kind of business you in?"

"I'm a cop."

"No shit. A cop." Riley washed this information down with a long pull on his beer. "Not here in Philly. I would've heard."

"New York. NYPD. It's my third week on the job."

"Well, they sure as shit must be paying rookies a whole lot more in New York than they are in Philly, judging by your slick set of wheels and those sharp-looking clothes."

"I'm doing okay."

"It's good that you're a cop. Following in your daddy's footsteps and all that." Riley's voice trailed off. Then he leaned forward and pushed the footrest down to the floor. He looked hard at Strega. "What'd you come here for, son?"

"The truth."

Riley's eyes cut away. "What truth's that, Jonnie?"

"The one you know."

"Don't have a clue what you're talking about."

"I think you do. Tell me how my father went down."

Riley tugged on the beer. Picked at his trousers. "Well, it's still hard. Seeing your partner go down in the line of duty—shit, that's something that haunts you for the rest of your natural life."

"Wrong story, Riley."

"Okay," he said with a wide, guileless grin. "You got me. It didn't happen like I first told you."

"Then how did it happen?"

"Oh, hell. Okay. I'll tell you, ancient history anyhow." He paused. "It was a big-time drug bust. We shouldn't have gone in by ourselves, but your daddy didn't want any backup. Wanted all the glory for himself."

Riley went on, spinning his story, tapping the beer bottle with one finger. "He was a grandstander, Jonnie, and I was a follower, not a leader. So I said okay. Shit, the idea of glory, decorations, and all the rest sounded good to me too. We nailed the sons of bitches, all right, but we were plain outnumbered and your daddy took a bullet in the heart. He made a mistake and paid with his life, but he died a hero, Jonnie. That much is true."

Strega knocked the beer bottle out of Riley's hand. The beer ran over the yellowed floor, pooled in some of the cracks, and spread out at the baseboards. "I'm sick of lies."

"Now, I know it's hard to take," Riley said, putting his hands palms up in a gesture of surrender, of having given it all up. "But that's the God's honest truth, son."

Strega snatched Riley out of the chair. "No, it's not."

"Get out of my house," Riley ordered, trying to pry Strega's strong hands off his collar. "You asked me. I told you. Now get out."

Strega glanced at the pictures again. The two men had been close, closer than brothers. It was a wild assumption but not implausible: Vincent might have wanted his partner there to witness his last mortal act. Strega remembered Maria's taunting words. *What was it like, Jonnie?* He tightened his grip on Riley and went for it. "What was it like? How did it feel to watch him put the gun up to his own head and fire the shot?"

"Now, that's a damn lie," Riley stubbornly swore.

"What did the hole look like? Did he put the gun right up to his head so it was touching his skin? Was he looking at you when he fired the shot? He was, wasn't he? He was looking right at you. His eyes were wide open. And you just stood there. Stood there and watched him die."

"You've got it all wrong," Riley protested, his eyes filling with tears.

"Where did he do it? Right here in your living room? In your backyard? How far away were you standing? Did some of his blood get on you, Riley? Were you wet with your best friend's blood?"

Riley shut his eyes.

"What kind of hero kills himself?" Strega said softly, in Riley's ear.

"I couldn't stop him," the older man sputtered, finally

looking up at Strega. "I swear to God I couldn't stop
him. You weren't ever supposed to know. Your mother
took you away so you wouldn't ever know."

"Looks like she didn't take me far enough." Strega
let him go.

"Leave it alone," he pleaded. "Go home. Take a
pretty girl out to dinner. Forget about me. Forget about
all of this. It was a long time ago."

"You're the second person to tell me that today.
Start talking."

Riley staggered back into the easy chair, took a deep
breath, then spoke. "Your father found the big-time
drug dealers, all right. He found them and made deals.
Went something like this: a weekly cash contribution to
the Vincent Strega Fund and a nice weekly supply of
heroin to go with it. Said he was going to use the fund
to send you to one of those Ivy League colleges and
said he was going to use the heroin to send himself to
the sun."

"You were part of this?" Strega accused.

"Don't look at me like that," Riley whined. "You
didn't know him the way I did. He was a charmer. He
could convince you that the world was flat and that Columbus never made it around, that he just slid right off
the end with his fucking army of boats. Vincent Strega
was all wild kinetic energy. I was—well, we *all* were—
just blown away by him. Like I said, he was a leader.
He had a way of telling you to do things so that you
just did them. Had a way of making even the worst kind
of wrong thing feel right. He made you *want* to be with
him. On his side. Everything seemed so rational, so goddamn right.

"Eighteen years ago, our precinct was drug central for
the whole city. What's the point, Vince said, of shutting
the dealers down when we know someone else will move
in and take over where they leave off? He wanted to
control them instead. Take a big chunk of their profits
for our trouble. The way Vince had it worked out, most
of the money was going for a good cause: your education. And the rest, well, cops were underpaid as it was.

We were shutting a lot of other dealers down, just not these main guys. So it's not like we weren't sending guys to prison. We were just being selective about it."

"You went along with him."

"At first," Riley conceded. "The extra cash was nice. And he was right. There were more drug dealers out there than the DEA or the Philly buy and bust could ever bust, so why not get a little extra compensation for risking our lives putting scumbags away? The trouble started when Vince got into sampling the merchandise. He wanted to *understand the enemy.* I didn't know he was shooting up regular until it was too late and he was hooked as bad as any downtown alleyway junkie. By then he was needing to stay high around the clock, never wanting his feet to touch the ground, and when they did, he turned ugly. Violent and shaky. A wild man. A madman. Once, Vince gunned a kid down in a bust because he was hallucinating that the kid was a giant spider coming to spin a thick white web around his body. Vince shot the kid in the face." Riley paused.

"I loved your daddy," he finally said. "I lied for him. I testified that the kid shouted, *I'm going to shoot you pigs,* and that he went for a gun. The kid had really said, *I surrender, take me in!* He had dropped to the pavement with his empty hands out at his sides, legs spread-eagle wide, screaming, *Don't shoot me!* Vince walked up, stood over him, and put a bullet in his face. The kid had a couple of kilos of heroin and a Saturday night special. We were given a pair of meritorious awards for the bust. I went home and cried. But I backed your daddy up. I thought it was a freak accident, a one-time thing.

"For a long time Vince managed to hold himself together. But when he started deteriorating, he went downhill like a runaway freight train. Started making dozens of clumsy mistakes. Couldn't hold a pen steady enough to do his paperwork. I did it for him. Internal Affairs got tipped off that things were out of whack with us. They started following us around, keeping tabs, looking into arrest complaints, listening hard to guys we had put behind bars, guys who were only too happy to help put the noose around our two cocksure necks. Internal Affairs stacked up enough evidence to make us look really bad, but it was mostly aimed at your father. IAD leaned on us. I got wind the investigation had gone outside of the Department and that DEA was going to nail us. Meanwhile, your good old dad was shooting up, trying to find the sun. He swore he had almost made it there, swore he was so close he had touched the burning golden globe. You know what, Jonnie?"

"What."

"He was so charismatic, I believed him. *Vincent Strega has touched the sun.* Not bad for a mortal, I thought. Anyway, it wasn't too long before DEA was knocking at my door here. Said I could deal, but it was a deal with the devil. DEA promised that if I gave Vince Strega up, I could save myself. I was supposed to go in to the group we were protecting—go in wired—get the hard evidence on tape of Vince taking the kickbacks, then give the signal and stand back while DEA stormed the warehouse. If I didn't, they promised to nail Vince anyway through one of the drug-ring insiders who was ready to save his own neck. Difference was, they figured my testimony on the stand would be worth more than a scumbag drug dealer. They promised I could save myself or go down with Vince. What kind of choice did I have?

"I agreed. But I loved your father like a brother. I couldn't just walk him in to his own slaughter like an animal. So I drove to him out to a parking lot near the river and told him it was over. I told him it was a blessing in disguise for him. He needed help. Professional help. The drugs were going to kill him. Vince looked me cold in the eye and said no, I had killed him. Whatever happened to him, he said, it was on my shoulders. I could accept that. Part of me really believed he would be better off alive behind bars than dead with a needle in his arm. Hell, I even convinced myself I was doing it for Vince, and not to save my own sorry ass.

"Your dad asked me to drive him home that afternoon. I did. He went into the house, and from what I can piece together, he put his patrol uniform on and shot up one more time. You came home and burst in on him. You saw him *taking his trip to the sun*. He got in his car and drove to the front of this house here. Stood on the porch and rang my bell. I opened the door. He looked at me like he was stone-cold straight and said: 'Riley, tell Catherine I'm sorry. Jonnie saw me going to the sun. Tell him he was dreaming. Just tell Jonnie I was a hero. Leave me with that at least. My boy needs something in this world to look up to. Let it be me.' Then he pulled his service revolver out, put it up to his own damn head, and fired. It happened so fast. I couldn't stop him."

Strega stumbled to the springless screen door. He pushed it open and stood in the blinding sunlight, trying to pick out the stains on the porch boards that would mark where his father had fallen. Then the light triggered something. The light and Riley's information pushed the puzzle pieces of his fragmented memory together. The full images came at him, flashing through his mind like a strobe.

The afternoon Riley spoke of, Jon had come home from school. The house was quiet. His mother had gone out grocery shopping with the baby. Catherine was home. He saw her book bag on the living room sofa. He heard music. Jazz music, old and scratchy, coming from down the hall, from his parents' room, where his father kept an old turntable and his collection of jazz records. His father was at work. So who was playing his records? Jonnie walked down the hall. The carpet was blue with corn-colored flowers. It was bad luck to step on the corn-flowers, so Jonnie walked carefully, picking his way around them. A door at the end of the hall was ajar. He thought Catherine was in there, secretly listening to the records. He was afraid she would break one and get in trouble. He wanted to go make her get out. There were voices coming from the room. One voice was Catherine's, and she was crying, *No*. Jonnie edged forward to the door. He heard his father's voice. *I love you so much, baby. You're my perfect lady, my perfect little lady, and I want to take you to the sun. You won't tell anyone, will you, about our secret trips to the sun?* And then Catherine crying again.

Jonnie looked in through the wedge of open door. He saw the profiles of his father's face and his sister's. Catherine's, contorted in fear and shame. Their father's in ecstasy. Vincent Strega was kneeling, wearing his uniform shirt and nothing else. He had the sleeve to his uniform shirt pushed up, and he had a funny rubber hose wrapped around his upper arm. Catherine stood in front of him. Her pretty summer sundress was crumpled up on the floor. Her father had his face pressed to her tummy, and his hands were out of sight, in places Jonnie knew a boy should never look and certainly never ever touch. His father was smiling. *The sun, baby, we're going to fly to the sun.*

"Daddy?" Jonnie asked.

His father looked up sharply. The ecstasy was gone, replaced by rage. *Get out of here,* he bellowed. The anger smoking on his father's handsome face scared him. The bellowing scared him. But his father's nudity and his sister's tears scared him more. Jonnie turned and ran down the hall, not caring if he stepped on the cornflowers, not caring at all that he slammed out of the house, leaving the door wide open, that he ignored his father's commanding voice and kept running in spite of the order to stop.

He ran down to the end of the block and hid in a hedge of overgrown bushes bordering the yard of an abandoned house. He squatted under the scratchy branches and felt bugs crawling up his legs, but he stayed. He watched his father, fully dressed now, run out of the house, uniform shirttails flying, the one sleeve pushed up high to the bicep. He stood in the driveway, turning his body in a full circle, adjusting his uniform slacks and yelling Jonnie's name into the bright Indian summer afternoon. The last call was a cry. *"Jonnie?"* A question answered with silence.

Vincent Strega ducked into the old family Buick and slammed the door. Jonnie heard the engine fire up. He watched the car back down the drive and roar down the street, past the abandoned house, past the overgrown hedge where young Jon Strega cowered and saw his father's face for the last time, screwed up with tears, hand banging the steering wheel, shouting something inside the Buick.

Jonnie Strega stayed in the bushes, crouching in the dark, crying. He had been bad, going into his father's room, seeing parts of his sister he wasn't supposed to see. He believed if he could *forget* what he saw, it would make everything okay again. So, he sat pushing the images out of his six-year-old mind, forcing the images out until when he thought of the incident he saw nothing but bright cornflowers lit up by a ray of sun.

He fell asleep in the bushes. Hours later, when the late-afternoon shadows fell long and deep, he was awakened by the sound of his mother calling his name. *Jonnie! Dinnertime!* He dragged himself home. Catherine sat pale and quiet on the living room sofa. She looked up when Jonnie went in and put a finger up to her lips. *Shhhh,* she whispered. They were conspirators bound by a secret, but Jonnie couldn't remember what the secret was. He remembered only something about blue cornflowers and a shaft of light. The big old grandfather clock struck six. The family sat around the dinner table, waiting for Vincent to come home. At the stroke of seven, the doorbell rang and Dave Riley gently pushed his way in to tell Jonnie that his father had died a hero.

"Jonnie? Jonnie?" Riley was leaning down now, shaking Strega by the shoulder.

Strega ran his fingers over the porch boards.

"He never wanted you to know," Riley said. "Catherine and your mother were the only two who knew the truth outside of the Department. Funny how after all these years both of you should come asking in the same week."

Strega stood up. "Both of us? You said Catherine knew."

"Your baby sister didn't. She came around last week."

Despite the heat of the sun beating down on his back, Strega felt chilled.

Riley went on. "She showed up asking questions. I had no idea who she was. Last time I saw her she was still in diapers. She sure grew up into one hell of a good-looking woman. Different-looking than you and Catherine, nothing of Vincent in her face or your mother either, and short where the rest of you are tall. Almost more Spanish than Italian. Funny how the family-tree thing works, isn't it? How things jump a generation, then there they are again. You must've had someone Spanish in the family a long time ago."

Strega grabbed Riley again. "Why did you talk to her?"

"Hey, calm down, Jonnie. It was your sister, for crying out loud. Somehow she'd gotten hold of the IAD file, classified stuff from the Department. She already knew most of it. I filled in the blanks, told her not to tell you. But she must've said something anyhow. I tried to keep my promise to Vincent, dammit. Can't say I didn't. And don't you go blaming me for what happened to your dad. He had a death wish from the start."

Strega ran across the dirt yard, over the broken down fence, and into the Jeep. When he pulled out of the drive, he took one look back. The mangy shepherd was growling and pawing at the dirt, digging to China, and Riley was just standing there, arms hanging awkwardly at his sides, blinking in the bright sun, calling out Jonnie's name.

Strega knew where he had to go next. Catherine lived in a marginal area downtown. Strega guided the Jeep out of the suburbs and picked up the main highway running into the city. Traffic was light on the downtown streets and the sidewalks were empty. Emma had missed Philadelphia, but the heat wave hadn't. A local bank time and temperature billboard blinked cheerfully a hundred feet in the sky. The temperature was a hundred and four degrees. It was eleven-thirty in the morning. Strega referred to his map from time to time, winding his way along, making the correct turns, which eventually put him on a street that matched the street name on the Christmas card. He slowed to a crawl and checked building numbers.

Catherine's was a rundown, low-budget modern structure with a presumptuous name—*Liberty Gardens*. The building was one of those standard prefab quickies that had been popular in the seventies. It wasn't wearing well. Rust stains ran down the yellow facade, and Strega knew the jagged vertical cracks running from roof line to base were going to get the building condemned one day.

Strega parked the Jeep in a no-parking zone and threw his NYPD ID on the dash. Cops never hassled other cops, even when the departments were an entire state away. He walked up the entrance path, which was flanked by plastic yuccas in concrete planters. The yuccas were twelve feet high, and Strega guessed they had been put there by someone who was sick of living in Philly and dreamed of wide-open desert spaces out West. Some kid had left his G.I. Joe hanging by a string noose from the stem of one of the branches. The implied anti-American sentiment upset Strega. He untied the action figure and shoved him in his pocket. The buzzer list was four panels wide and crowded with a hundred apartments' worth of names. He found *Strega, C,* on the last panel, apartment 5D. He rang.

Catherine's sleepy voice drifted through the cheap speaker. "Who is it?"

"Jon." Then after a beat of silence, "Your brother."

He waited out the second beat of silence. When he heard the buzzer hum, he pushed the glass entrance door open and walked in. The walls of the lobby were decorated with a giant frieze depicting all the founding fathers and their heavily inked scrolls proclaiming LIFE, LIBERTY, AND THE PURSUIT OF HAPPINESS. A life-sized replica of the Liberty Bell crowded the center of the lobby. Strega paused and tapped it with a finger. It was plaster and didn't ring. No sounding the bell of freedom, not here in *Liberty Gardens*. He patted the silent bell and thought of his sad sister living all alone upstairs with her ghosts and her guilt. Liberty and the pursuit of happiness did not include the freedom to wreck a young girl's sense of self. Strega hoped the founding fathers had been better to their daughters than his own had been to Catherine.

He called the elevator. The doors opened into more kitchy Americana—a back panel covered with an enormous needlepoint piece depicting Betsy Ross sewing the flag, all cross-stitched in the proper red, white, and blue colors. Stars and stripes. Only now, for Strega, stars stood for the star-burst temple wound, the suicide's tattoo.

The elevator opened on five. Strega walked down a narrow hall. Catherine's door had a plastic Jesus hanging from a plastic cross centered over the plastic symbols 5D. Strega hesitated. He hadn't seen her in seven years. Now he understood her headstrong desire to avoid him had been born of shame, not the usual sibling envy or hatred. He crossed himself out of habit and knocked.

Catherine pulled the door open. Her face was disconcerting for Jon to look at. Her features were identical to his, only they were arranged differently, on a more angular face where, jutting and colliding, they became hard-edged, finishing out in something asymmetrical that missed all of the harmony of Jon's own face.

She wore a JESUS LOVES YOU sweatshirt that bagged shapelessly over her scarecrow frame. It went down to her knees, which, Jon observed, were as knobby as they'd been when she was just a girl. It seemed as though her body had refused to go forward with time, keeping her locked in a permanent adolescence—one complete, he imagined, with all the nightmares and the guilt and the busted self-esteem that went along with these kinds of homegrown horrors.

She wore her black hair shoulder-length and straight. Her face was scrubbed. She wore no makeup. She had one fist balled up to her teeth, and it seemed as though she was chewing on her knuckles. Jon's own wide brown eyes looked out at him, but her glance was shifty, uneasy, not direct and clear like his own, and it kept slipping and sliding away from his. She took the knuckles away from her lips long enough to wave him into the apartment. She shut the door behind him and leaned against it while Strega paced around, taking in the whole miserable one-room place that his sister called home.

"It's not much, I know," she snapped. "I didn't go to Princeton."

Strega looked at her sharply, surprised by the bitterness in her voice.

Those elusive eyes slid away. She looked down at her bare feet. "Sorry," she mumbled, and Strega imagined she was. "I'm a tour guide," she added. "Underpaid, overinformed, and I'll be obsolete soon because the city of Philadelphia is putting in computerized automatic gadgets that give visitors the same spiel I do, only with the choice of Japanese, Korean, Spanish, and Russian. I figure I've got a year left before the pink slip shows up in my unimpressive pay envelope." She shot a quick look up at him, then went back to looking at the floor.

"*Then what,* you'll want to know." She shrugged her slim shoulders and stuck her big toe up in a child's game of piggy. "I have no idea. Guess I'll end up living with Mother, taking her to church twice a day, being a good Catholic, which isn't so different from being a good tour guide. You learn to say the same thing day after day until you say the words without even hearing them. You repeat those well-learned words and poof, you're magically taken care of, either with a low-grade government-employee remuneration package or eternal life." She choked out a laugh. "Truth is, I'm a pretty lousy tour guide. I keep getting stage fright and forget the words halfway through the spiel. Do you think I'll make a better full-time Catholic?"

Strega reached out and took her hand. He led her to her dingy sofa bed and made her sit down. She yanked the baggy sweatshirt over her bony knees and stared at him for a full two minutes.

"You look great, Jonnie," she finally said with a lot of awe and wonder in her voice. "Really. Like you walked out of a magazine. Guess Princeton does that for a guy—polishes him up to a high shine, to something precious and brilliant. Well, old buddy, you got a rock for a sister. A nice piece of shale. It crumbles when you try to hold it. Crumbles into a thousand dirty bits that get blown away in the first faint breeze."

Strega reached over and put his hand lightly over her mouth to shut her up. She was looking at her feet again, sticking that big toe up. He forced her head around so she was looking at him. "I talked to Dave Riley," he said. "And then I remembered."

Her eyes went cat wild with terror, the same look his kitten had the day he fished it out of the dumpster. She tried to wrestle away from him. His hands dropped, and he took her by the shoulders. "Talk to me, Catherine." She clapped her hands over her ears. He peeled them away and held her by the wrists. "Why did you and Mother keep everything a secret? Why did you *lie* to me about his death?"

"It wasn't about him, Jonnie. It was about *you*," she spat. "It was always about *you*, the one and only son. The precious male child. The gifted one. Sweet little Jonnie, so bright and beautiful." The rage bubbled up, and she lashed out, pummeling him on the chest with her weak hands, slapping at his face. Missing the target, she began to slap her own face instead. "You, you, you," she chanted in a child's temper. "Jonnie, beautiful Jonnie mustn't know, Jonnie mustn't ever know, Jonnie mustn't ever, ever, ever know."

Strega caught her wrists. Red palm marks welted up on her pale face. "Why?"

She rocked and cried. "Because you needed a *hero*— someone to look up to. They said it was unfair to let you grow up knowing you had a monster for a father, a thief, a criminal—a suicidal drug addict whose pleasures were all illegal and illicit. Little girls and glass syringes. I had to live with the truth. They said it was more noble for you to live a lie."

"Who said that?"

"Riley. Mother," she said softly. "Mother believed Daddy was damned for eternity and that she might be damned too because she knew."

"She knew?" Strega asked incredulously.

"Everything," Catherine whispered. "From the start.

She took the drug money and stuck it in a shoe box. First there was one shoe box full, then two, then three, then ten. *For Jonnie's college one day,* she said. So you could grow up big and bright and strong and smart. She took it greedily, happily, thinking all her Hail Mary's would clear the slate. She believes God is like a used-car dealer, that you can bargain and trade.

"After Daddy killed himself, she was desperate for a bargaining chip with God. She was afraid she would be damned for not stopping Daddy from stealing or taking drugs. She believed she was as guilty as he was for his suicide, so she gave God you. She made you a cop. She wanted you to relive Daddy's life, only you would do it right and that would make up for Daddy's crimes. Sick logic, isn't it? But it was *her* logic and Daddy's last request. And it almost worked. You're a cop. And knowing you, you were going to treat it the way you treated Princeton. You were going to be the best. A record breaker. A star. A fucking hero."

She looked up at him with wide, clear eyes. Strega knew the look in them. It was the kitten in the dumpster again, a look put there by a big, heavy hand coming down hard too many times against that soft cheek. It was put there by a hand twisting the fabric of a young girl's dress, tearing, and then helping itself to whatever was uncovered.

Strega stroked her head and asked the question gently. "Did she know about you?"

"Yes. She knew from the start. It went on for years. She talked to me once, in the beginning, and said I had to understand Daddy. She said it wasn't really Daddy doing the bad things. It was a bad spirit that got into him sometimes, and it would take love and understanding to chase the bad spirit away. She said Daddy was a special man with special needs. He worked hard. He made the world a better place. He provided for us. It was our job to help him, to keep him happy."

"She allowed this to go on in her own house?"

"You still don't understand, do you, Jonnie?" Catherine looked up at him, marveling. "She loved him more than anything or anyone. More than me, certainly. She was terrified of losing him. It wasn't a sane kind of love, what she had for him. When he died, she transferred it all to you, and you took his place in her heart. She was going to make you over into the perfect image of what Daddy should have been."

Strega's lips tightened. He held her close and rocked her. "Catherine, Catherine. How could she?" He rocked her and remembered the look of shame on her face that day, the shame that was still there now, that he had all these years mistaken for something else. Now he understood the dark circles under his sister's eyes. They had always been there, and he had always assumed they were there because she was a sullen girl. Now he knew they were from shame and sleepless nights. He pulled back and shook her lightly. "Catherine, listen to me. You can't hide anymore."

She looked at him strangely. "You don't understand the shame, Jonnie. I don't want to hide. I want to die."

"He took enough of you. Don't let him take your entire life."

"It's too late. It's always been too late for me."

Strega had studied the abuse issue in college. He knew that it drove some victims to violence. Other victims repressed the incidents and went through life in a relatively normal way. Still others retreated into private quiet fantasy worlds where they were safe. These victims were usually unable to compete in the day-to-day world. There simply wasn't enough self-esteem left to motor them along. Catherine fell into the third category.

Sometimes, with a talented and dedicated therapist, the damage could be healed, especially if it was caught early on. Catherine had spent her entire childhood, all of her formative years, and her adolescence under the cloud of Vincent Strega's abuse. It was late now for Catherine to start the healing process. Strega wondered if she wasn't right—that it wasn't already too late for her.

He tilted her face up and studied her features. He put his hand on her cheek. It was as if her facial planes were drifting continents that were frozen before their correct and final arrangement had been completed. He wanted to unfreeze them and finish the work. He wanted to soften the line of her chin, sweep her cheekbones back, and smooth her forehead down. He wanted to reach out with his sculptor's hands and erase the hurt and pain, but he knew that job ultimately belonged to Catherine herself.

He stayed with her until late afternoon, letting her talk it out. She ranted and raved, cried and screamed and whispered the horrors. At the end she took Strega's big hand in her own, curled up, and slept, hanging on to him for dear life. It was a start, a weak one, but a start. Maybe with Strega's help, the right doctor, and time, Catherine could make herself whole again. She had already died once, he thought, and that was before she had ever lived. Maybe she could do it in time to do a whole lot of living before the second and final dying, in time to make this life count instead of waiting for some promised ever after.

This one, Catherine, this one. Make this life count.

How bright did love have to shine to chase the shadows from the dark corners of her life, to chase the shadows out from under her wide, sad eyes? Was this one brother's love bright enough?

Strega left Philadelphia late and drove to Queens to confront his mother. He spent the travel time making up versions of the speech he planned on giving, meticulously placing the accusations in a certain order, cataloguing her sins, and announcing the punishment. Yes, the price of her lying, the price of her paying for his Princeton education with dirty money, the price of her conspiracy of silence while Vincent Strega ransacked Catherine's body, the price would be big. It would cost her her son.

As he pulled into the driveway of her modest bungalow, Strega swore he would never see her again.

He dug the extra key out of a flower pot next to the front door, unlocked it, and walked in.

The house was dusty and dim. He almost missed seeing her sitting in the corner, in an old wing chair. She wore a print dress, yellow flowers on a field of black. Her thick black hair was pulled back. The years and guilt had taken a toll on her Madonna's face. The skin was lined and slack. Beauty had been erased by sorrow. There was defeat in the line of her slumping shoulders, surrender too. Strega's resolve flagged; then he remembered Catherine's face, her chewed-up knuckles, and his outrage rode high again.

She shook her head slowly before he could speak. "I know why you're here," she said in a voice that was a hundred years old. "Catherine called."

The despair with which she uttered those two simple words—*Catherine called*—knocked Strega's anger out of him. He knelt down in front of the bent, slight figure and put his hand on her face. She sat stone still with the rosary falling through her fingers like rain.

"How could you?" Strega accused. It came out a whisper.

"There's a higher justice than you, Jon Strega." She squeezed her eyes shut and pulled the rosary to her lips. "I'm keeping my answer for judgment day."

Suddenly he understood that she was an old, tired woman with enough fear and guilt to last the rest of her life. Nothing he could say would make a difference; no words could change the past. Strega turned and walked out the door, wishing he had the strength to forgive her. He wondered if a man that strong walked anywhere on the face of earth.

He left Queens, stopping once to call Gavin, hoping he was in a listening mood. Gavin was. He suggested a bar in Midtown where they promised two-for-one drinks and all the freebies a hungry man could eat.

Twenty-seven

Gavin hunched over the bar, staring into the first martini of his two-for-one special.

Strega pulled a stool up next to him. "Alvarez was right about my father. He didn't go down in the line of duty. He killed himself."

Gavin looked up, stunned. "How?"

"Single gunshot to his left temple." Strega ordered a beer and told Gavin what he had learned in Philadelphia.

Gavin listened, asking questions from time to time for clarification. As much as he hated crooked cops, he understood the temptation of hard, cold cash and the reasoning that stealing from a drug dealer isn't really stealing at all. Cops were underpaid and unpopular, and they risked their lives every day they wore the uniform.

Yes, Gavin thought, he certainly understood the machinations that bent a cop and turned him crooked, and sometimes that was forgivable. But the second crime, the sick abuse of a female child, was inexcusable and unforgivable for all time. It was dark and heinous and, in Gavin's book, the same thing as murder—only the victim lived.

Gavin hoped Vincent Strega was burning in Hell. He felt Strega looking at him, waiting for a response. "Hell of a story," he croaked.

Strega nodded, then started thinking out loud again, trying to make sense of it all. "The irony is that Alvarez was right. That's what gets me, Ed. She was *right!*"

"Maybe she did you a favor. You would've never found out."

"The question is, *why* did she go digging into my past in the first place?"

Gavin shrugged. "Easy. You pissed her off. I think first she took a look through your personnel file because she *liked* you. She saw the thing about your dad being a hero. Then, when she got *mad* at you, she took a wild guess there was something worth digging up. She made a phone call to the Philly P.D. She probably posed as Ramon Alvarez's secretary and gave some song and dance about a special investigation going on into a new NYPD rookie cop named Jon Strega. *What can you tell us about his father, Vincent Strega?* Using Ramon Alvarez's name and rank, she got it all with one phone call."

"And the irony is, she freed me."

"How's that?"

"I know now I don't have to be a cop. I can walk away."

"Why? You're in the fast lane. Christ, you could probably be the P.C. one day."

"No, thanks. I'm a free man now, free to resign."

"Suit yourself." Gavin picked at a bowl of mini-pretzels and glanced up at the TV set over the bar, at the sharp-looking female anchor giving the business report. A picture of William West popped up over her shoulder.

Gavin pointed at the set. "Maybe there's more good news before the day's out."

The anchorwoman frowned. "The big surprise loser on Wall Street today was West Entertainment," she announced. "The stock plummeted to two dollars a share before trading was suspended on reports that the SEC has charged Chairman William West with tax fraud and embezzlement of company funds. Details after this message."

"My Genie," Strega remembered. "I didn't take it with me today."

Gavin gripped the bar edge for support. "I'm finished."

*   *   *

Strega huddled up to the bar pay phone and punched in Rosemary's number.

"Miss De Cesare's office. David speaking."

"David. Jon Strega."

"Jonnie? Jesus Christ, where've you been? Rosie's been trying to call you all day."

The line went silent for an instant, and then Strega heard her rich throaty voice. "Hello, Jonnie-come-lately, nice of you to phone home. I've been trying to reach you."

"So David said. I was in Philly learning some pretty ugly truths."

"Nothing as ugly as what could have happened here with your trading accounts."

"What do you mean *could have*? I just saw the news. West is ruined. I don't need a calculator to tell me I am too."

"Well, Jonnie, I saved your ass. The West stock has flown too high, too fast. High fliers make me nervous. Last night I dreamed it crashed. I tried to reach you this morning but couldn't, so I did what you pay me a nice fat commission to do: listen to my intuition. I sold your stock off before the story hit. You'd never get this kind of service with a discount broker."

"You sold it because of a *dream*?"

Rosemary got defensive. "Sicilians are superstitious. Anyway, I told David I had a power of attorney to trade for you at my discretion. A little white lie. I'm hoping no one at the SEC gets suspicious about my extraordinary timing. They could make things uncomfortable for me if they do. I put my job and my ass on the line for you today, and I happen to be very fond of both."

"Why'd you do it, Rosemary?"

"Like I said, I trust my instincts." She hesitated. "I should tell you something else. My instincts tell me to believe you about that Alvarez woman."

Strega felt his eyes sting. He cleared his throat. "Does that mean you'll have dinner with me?"

"I happen to be free tomorrow night."

Suddenly, Strega felt reckless. He felt like doing what he had really wanted to do when he first laid eyes on her. "De Cesare," he said quietly, "I was thinking of a more long-term situation."

The line went silent. He thought she had hung up. When she spoke again, her voice was heavy with emotion. "Don't make any promises you can't keep."

"I never do."

"Let's go slow. Start fresh. See what happens."

"I love you, Rosemary."

"That's a good place to start." The line went quiet again for a long moment, then she said: "I almost forgot. One more item of business. The shares in the new trading account your partner opened this week?"

"What about them?"

"When we were setting the account up, your partner told me it was an all-or-nothing bet. He wanted to be as aggressive as possible. Everything in the account was invested in West, so I got aggressive this morning. I sold a big block of the stock short and cashed out when the stock hit two bucks, just before the trading suspension. Your partner made a healthy chunk of change."

"How healthy?"

"Three hundred thousand."

"You're an amazing woman."

"Tell me that tomorrow night. Eight-thirty. My place. I'll cook you some *penne arrabbiata*." She hung up.

Strega strolled back to the bar. Gavin was slumped over. His skin tone was bad, and his martini glass was empty. Strega flagged the bartender. "Do you have any good champagne by the bottle?"

"Hundred bucks a bottle good enough for you?" the bartender asked.

"Bring it over with two glasses," Strega ordered.

"That what Italians drink at wakes?" Gavin mumbled.

The bartender put a big silver ice bucket in front of them. He uncorked the champagne bottle and poured two flutes. Strega put a glass in front of Gavin and wrapped the older cop's reluctant hand around it. He held up his own glass and said: "A toast. To beautiful,

smart Sicilians. They are magicians in bed and out. Rosemary made you a hell of a lot of money today, my
friend."

"This is not a joking matter."

"I'm not joking. Drink up. You're golden." Strega's
face was glowing and earnest.

Gavin didn't understand. "What'd she do, pull it out
of a hat?"

"No, she sold you short before the stock was
suspended."

"What the hell does that mean?"

"It means you're a rich man. Rich enough to retire,
anyway. Enough there for a new set of golf clubs and a
daily martini at the club."

"No shit?"

"I told you she was smart," Strega affirmed. He
grabbed a pen off the bar, scratched the digits out on a
cocktail napkin, and pushed the napkin over to Gavin.

Gavin traced the zeros with a finger, then looked up
at his young partner and grinned. "Strega, I think I
love you."

Strega raised his glass. "Cheers."

Gavin raced home and up to Alex's room, looking for
Shelly, wanting to share the news. The room was empty.
He lingered in the doorway, wishing his newfound
money could buy Alex back. Then he thought of the sad
small bones on Lang's table, how they must have looked
in the shallow three-foot grave out there in the fields.
He knew in his heart Alex was dead.

In his dreams he would see the shadow of her killer
lingering by her unmarked grave. It was always a
shadow, never more. Gavin would wake then, with his
heart slamming against his breastbone and his body
bathed in sweat, his rage rising fast and hard, thinking
of her killer still out there, walking free, walking tall,
while Alex was lost forever. He would turn on his side
after such a dream, the grief heavy on his body, like
those three feet of dirt might be pressing down on his
girl, and weep. Gavin knew he would never forget how

those bones looked on Lang's table. Never. They would haunt him more than any other thing he had seen in his long life.

Standing there in Alex's room reminded him of when she was five and suddenly scared of some imaginary monster under her bed. She used to scream—terrified, shrill screeches—until Gavin came charging in, in full uniform to search the room.

"Daddy, Daddy, the monster is here!"

He played along with her, searching the closet, under the bed, behind the curtains.

"Look in there, Daddy," she begged, pointing at the toy chest, her eyes bright with tears, and her tiny hands balled up into fists as she chewed on her knuckles.

"No monsters here, young lady," he always said in his best cop voice. He would shout orders into an imaginary radio, pretend to listen. Then, bowing neatly and smiling at her broadly he would say: *They got him, three doors down.*

She would giggle and throw her arms around his neck. *"You saved me, Daddy! You saved me from the monster!"*

I guess I didn't, Alex baby, Gavin thought now. *I guess I didn't save you at all.*

He thought of the lifetime he had spent looking for the real monsters, hunting them, arresting them, locking them away. A whole lifetime dedicated to that, and yet somehow one of them must have reached out, snatched his girl, and taken her away. Shelly appeared at his side, startling him. "I miss her, Ed."

"I do too." He reached for her hand, folded her into his arms, and held her tight.

The phone rang just then. Gavin left Shelly and went down the hall to pick it up.

"Ed? It's Jillian."

"I don't have a word to say to you."

"Wait. It's about Katy."

The magic word. Gavin listened.

*   *   *

Gavin watched the headlights swing up the drive. He opened the front door and waited on the porch. Jillian sat in the car with the engine idling and her face full of Kleenex.

She got out and took five tentative steps forward, then stopped. "Thank you, Ed. I'm not a good mother. I never was. Danny didn't want me to have her. He was right. He'd approve of you two, you know he would." She waited for him to say something.

Jillian. Brittle hair, bleached overly blond. Thick-waisted and falsely tan. Everything about her was over-done. There was too much fake gold at her neck, around her wrists, stacked up on the columns of her puffy fingers, and glittering in do-bobs that scrunched her hair together and held it straight up on top.

Her skirt was too short for those graceless legs, heels too high for any decent woman. She was shabby too, with little nicks and tears in the leather on the back of her shoes and runs in her stockings. Her nails were too long and too orange. The sum total of her parts was a desperate, exaggerated reach to hang on to something she once had. All the trappings with none of the fresh-ness of youth. Jillian, as if gripping a teenage boy be-tween your angry heavy thighs might make you young again.

Jilly, Jilly with the heart of stone. Wasn't it enough, having a man who loved you and who didn't mind all the inevitable tracks time would leave on you? Wasn't it enough, having a man who found your stretch marks *beautiful,* the laugh lines on your face funny—a man who believed that all those marks proved the two of you had lived a life together?

Jilly, Jilly, you never stopped the chewing discontent. You never slowed it down long enough to know your own husband, to know the treasure you had in Danny.

Jillian retreated to the car. She opened the passenger door. Katy clambered out.

Katy.

Everything Danny packed into three feet of new

blood, childish innocence, and a special mischievous way all her own.

Katy walked up the drive with a suitcase bumping against her skinny legs. It was half again as big as she was. She stood on the porch, ill at ease in her starched white Sunday dress with its ruffles and sashes and dainty roses embroidered in pink. There was too much tomboy in her, too much free spirit for ruffles and roses. She tugged at her collar and looked up at Gavin, her five-year-old forehead bunched up in consternation. "Mommy says I'm going to live with you now."

"Yes, that's true, Katy. Does that make you happy?"

"Will you teach me to box?"

"Sure will."

"Good. Then I'm happy. I'm going to be a policeman one day like my daddy was." She grinned. It was an ear-to-ear grin that lit her blue eyes up. "He was a hero."

"He was indeed, Katy bird, he was indeed."

She set the suitcase down and hugged Gavin around the knees. Shelly appeared beside him. Katy opened her little arms and brought Shelly into her embrace. Shelly stroked Katy's blond curls. Tears of joy filled Shelly's eyes.

Why was it, Gavin wondered, the number three felt more even than two?

Jillian backed her car out of the drive and vanished around the corner.

Gavin looked up at the sky just as a mass of clouds parted, revealing a star.

Is that you, Danny, with your bright stellar eye looking down on us? Can you see the whole galaxy at a glance, the sun burning mightily while the Earth tumbles around it? Can you see the sunrise from an eagle's view? Can you see all the oceans and seas at a single glance? Are you really out there watching over us? Can you see us here, missing you?

He looked back down at Katy. She was unrolling a new crayon picture and holding it up. It was a picture of a house. Smoke curled out of the chimney; three stick figures lived inside. One was a round, jolly man wearing a policeman's uniform. The next was a brown-haired woman with a big red heart. The third was a little blond girl stick figure standing in between the man and woman, holding hands, linking them all together. Floating up in the bright blue sky where the sun ought to have been was a flying policeman looking happily down on the crayon house. He was made from big circles drawn and stacked one on top of the other, snowman style.

The top circle was filled in with a pair of squinty blue eyes and a crooked smile.

His crayon arms were open wide in an all-encompassing embrace.

And the word Daddy was scrawled on the yellow star-shaped badge he wore over his red hero's heart. As if that wasn't totally clear from the start.

Strega cabbed home, his head buzzing pleasurably, body warm with a champagne glow. Manhattan looked magical. The world spins on a dime, he thought. One day, twenty-four hours, and everything changes. A killer behind bars, the Alvarez thing over, his past reconciled, a bankable profit for all, and Rosemary. *Rosemary.* He couldn't help grinning like a fool.

The taxi stopped in front of his brownstone. "Six-fifty," the driver announced.

"Here's ten. Keep the change," Strega said, feeling effusive, magnanimous.

"Thanks, man," the driver said.

Strega got out and wandered upstairs to his apartment. He was shocked. His brawl with Alvarez seemed like a lifetime ago, but the place was still a shambles. He moved through the destruction to his bedroom. The answering machine light was blinking. He played the message back.

"Strega, Ballantine here. The mayor wants a picture with you and Gavin in Hansen's hospital room tomorrow. You're back on the eight-to-four tour, so we'll do it just after roll call in the morning. A little birdie tells me the three of you are up for a fistful of decorations. Congratulations."

Strega played the message again just for fun, then
went into the living room, flicked the CD player on, and
cranked the volume. Three tenors sang lustily. Strega
sang with them as he started to clean up the mess. He
picked up a handful of books. Plato, Socrates, Sophocles.
The Greek classics. A world of wise men to help him
understand his own life. The phone rang. He picked up,
hoping for more good news.

"Jonnie." The voice was low. He had trouble identifying it at first.

He dropped his books. "Who's this?" A terrible suspicion seeped through his champagne haze.

The voice laughed. "Who do you think it is?"

Alvarez. "I have nothing to say to you."

"I have something to say to *you*."

"I'm not in a listening mood."

"You should be. I have something that belongs to you.
So why don't you take a walk outside to the corner of
Eighty-sixth and Columbus?" A kitten mewed pitifully.
Alvarez hung up.

Strega went back out into the summer night. His euphoria was fading fast, and by the time he got to the
corner it had vanished. A queasy feeling took its place.
He stood next to the curb and looked up and down
Columbus Avenue, not knowing what he was looking
for. A dirty low-rise white Celica slid up alongside him.

The windows were tinted dark. He tried to look in at
the driver, but all he saw was his own reflection. The
window slid down. He pulled back. Alvarez. Dressed in
her smart, starched uniform. She slouched, smoking a
cigarette. She blew a series of smoke rings up at him.
Her eyes were hooded and lazy, and she looked like she
was on something. The bruises on her skin had turned
purple and yellow. The kitten was in her lap, wrapped
up in a towel. Alvarez held it tightly.

"I've been to Philly," Strega said. "I know about my
father. It's over, Alvarez."

"It's not over, Jonnie. Not yet." She smiled lazily at
him and stroked the cat. "You live pretty nice for a
rookie. Maybe some folks around the Department are

wondering how you can afford such a snazzy place. Cool furniture, lots of electronic gadgets. You know what I'm saying?"

"I have no idea."

"Maybe you're dealing a little on the side." She took a long drag on her cigarette.

Strega wanted to turn and walk away, but he waited with a sick fascination to hear what she had to say.

"You've had some time to think about how vulnerable you are, Jonnie. What was the worst thing you thought could happen to you? A woman might rape you? Not likely. But she might rob you, kill your cat, or fool with the brakes on your Jeep so you have a little accident. You thought of all those things, didn't you?" She looked up at him. Her eyes were full of malice. Her split red lips curled back in a sneer. "The way I see it, the worst thing that could happen to you is prison."

She had his attention now.

"What if the Two-Five got a tip you were dealing cocaine, Jonnie?" She paused, letting the full weight of her words sink in. "What if they came after you because of that tip and found it? Maybe it's in your Jeep. Maybe it's behind your refrigerator. Wherever it is, let's say they find it. Then what?" She tapped her long fingernail on the door frame. "Like father like son, history repeats itself, only this time Strega doesn't kill himself. The good Princeton boy gets hauled off. Try hanging your fancy diploma on the wall of a prison cell. See what good it'll do you there."

"I know what you did to Kelly and the others."

"I like to fuck. That's not a crime, and that's all you and your nosy partner know for sure about me."

"We have a witness who puts you in Kelly's apartment the night he was murdered."

"No, you don't." She held up a pair of gray coveralls, the kind Franklin wore. "Franklin went swimming. He won't be back."

He shook his head in denial. "You're finished, Maria."

"No, but *you* are," she replied. "Possession with intent to sell cocaine is a crime. Someone could come knocking on your door tonight or tomorrow night or the next night, and when they do, they'll have a warrant. They'll turn your place upside down, and they'll be glad they came. Good night, Jonnie. Sweet dreams."

She unwrapped the towel and threw the kitten out the window. The kitten came at him, fighting and scratching. He held Sigmund tight and shoved him under his sweatshirt. Needle-sharp claws dug into his skin. The Celica window slid up, and Strega was looking at his reflection again. The engine revved and the car sped away.

Strega watched the Celica disappear in the thick evening traffic. He forced himself to think rationally, consider her threats. Alvarez had had plenty of opportunities to plant drugs. There was the day his landlady let her in and the night she climbed in while he was sleeping.

A siren wailed in the distance.

What if she had already called? What if there was a patrol car outside his apartment, waiting for him?

Strega ran. The garage came up on the right. Strega veered into it. José was on night duty.

He looked at Strega's shirt. The bulge wiggled and mewed. "You got a *cat* in there?" he said incredulously.

"Where's my Jeep?"

"All the way in the back. You looking for another tape?"

"What do you mean another?"

José's smile faded. "Couple of hours ago, a lady cop came on down. Said she worked with you and that you wanted one of your tapes. She was a cop for sure— uniform, gun, badge. I've seen her face in *New York* magazine. She was the P.C.'s daughter. Beat up pretty bad in some bust, but what a dish. Spanish dessert. Anyway, I let her down there to get the tape for you."

Strega bolted past him.

"Did I do wrong, Mr. Strega?" José called out.

Strega went down the garage ramp, to the first level, where the Jeep was stashed away against a far wall, blocked in tight by other cars. He shimmied between them to the Jeep, opened the door, and got in.

Alvarez had trashed the Jeep. A dozen cassette tapes were thrown around, the tape pulled out in long, curly sheaths. She had unfolded maps and ripped them apart. She had opened a six-pack and poured the beer over the seats, then tossed the empty cans on the floor. The Jeep was trashed but not destroyed. If the police looked it over, they might assume Strega was a sloppy house-keeper. Nothing more. There was no evidence of rob-bery. The tape deck was still there.

He felt around in the door side pockets, ran his hands under the seats, then along the backs and under the carpet. He patted down the entire interior, then popped the hood and inspected the engine. There were a thou-sand possible hiding places for an envelope of white powder—a thousand places and this was just a car. He tried to not think about his apartment, about what Inter-nal Affairs or DEA might find there.

He climbed up out of the garage, sprinted past the frightened attendant and down the street.

There were no patrol cars in front of his building, and his apartment was as he had left it. He let the kitten loose, turned the CD player off, and started to search.

He turned the couch upside down. A long manila en-velope was taped to the underside. Alvarez was too smart to leave her prints on it. Strega was too. He went to the kitchen for a pair of plastic gloves, slipped them on, and opened the envelope. A fat plastic baggie slid out. Strega carefully opened the zip lock and tasted the white powder inside. It was uncut cocaine, and there was enough of enough to put him away for a long time.

Strega's pulse raced. He smacked the baggie down on the table.

This was too easy. Too obvious.

Think like Alvarez.

Alvarez had a twisted mind.

Think! Think!

Finding the bag was supposed to give him a sense of

378   *Jeannine Kadow*

false security. She would have planted more somewhere else.

But where?

And even if he did find it, there was no guarantee
she hadn't planted more in his locker, and there was no
guarantee she wouldn't be back.

Strega felt helpless. *She can do it,* he thought. *She can
destroy me.*

Alvarez was sly and smart. If she was smart enough
to kill and get away with it, she was smart enough to
get him too. Maybe not tonight, maybe not tomorrow,
but she would get him. He knew it. Until then he would
live his life in fear, and that was another kind of prison,
wasn't it?

Maria Alvarez had won.

Strega picked the phone up and dialed Gavin's number. Shelly answered on the second ring.

"Jon Strega, Shelly. I need Ed. It's an emergency."

"Hang on," she said.

A moment later, Gavin was on the line, laughing.
"What's the emergency, you run out of champagne?"

"Alvarez." Strega spoke quickly. When he finished,
Gavin was dead sober and in charge.

"Sit tight. I'll pick you up in an hour," Gavin said.
"Bring the envelope. Handle it with gloves. Wipe it
down if you touched it." Gavin hung up.

Strega flipped the lights out and sat in the dark, with
his head in his hands, waiting for his partner to come.

Gavin placated Shelly, then rummaged in the back
of his closet for the unregistered snub-nosed Colt .38
Detective Special he had stashed away. Most cops kept
an unregistered piece tucked in a hidey-hole somewhere.
Gavin had a feeling he might need his on this night. He
put a shoulder holster on, fit the Special in, and picked
a cassette-sized tape recorder out of a dresser drawer.

Alex had given it to him one Christmas. It was from
the Eye-Spy shop, and Alex thought Gavin might need
it one day if he decided to become a detective. He was
glad now for the gift. He checked the batteries, then

dropped it in his shirt pocket and put a light jacket on over the shirt.

Gavin stepped outside. The night was hot and still, the neighborhood dark and quiet. He started up the Tempo, pulled out of his driveway, and drove to the expressway. Traffic was light. He pressed the accelerator to the floor and made good time to the city.

On the approach to the Fifty-ninth Street Bridge, he slowed, rumbled across the bridge and onto the city streets. There was no traffic in front of him and a string of green lights. It was too good to resist. Gavin gunned the Tempo and raced from the East to West Side, listening to the car chassis protest when he rocked roughly through the potholes. He eased up on the long stretch of Central Park West and slowed to a crawl when he turned left on Strega's street, hugging the curb and straining to catch the building numbers.

Strega's brownstone was halfway down on the right. Gavin stopped in front and tooted the horn three times. Moments later, the front door opened and closed, and Strega loped gracefully to the car. He swung into the passenger seat. He held the large manila envelope tight in his gloved hands. It was now midnight.

"The cavalry's here," Gavin announced.

"Glad to see you," Strega said. "We going to see Ballantine?"

"Better than that," Gavin answered, rolling slowly away from the curb and down the street. At Broadway he turned left. Although he had the wide street to himself, Gavin observed the speed limit, driving like a model citizen past empty Lincoln Center, down through the theater district, where the sidewalks were never empty, and past the big flashing billboards at Times Square.

"You taking me back to the academy?" Strega quipped. The academy was downtown.

"Nope," Gavin replied. His expression was enigmatic as he searched the street signs. At Forty-third Street, he turned right, then crossed Eighth Avenue and Ninth Avenue, driving into the heart of Hell's Kitchen. He drifted slowly here, checking building numbers. He crossed Tenth Avenue and pulled up to the curb in front of a squat, grim ten-story modern apartment building. The back ends of window a.c. units stuck out like bad acne.

Gavin put the gearshift in park and turned to Strega. "Wait here," he said.

"Mind telling me what I'm waiting for?"

"If you haven't noticed, this is a shitty neighborhood."

"I noticed."

"You guard the car. If we both go in, it won't be here when we come out."

Strega looked unconvinced. "Any other reason I'm out here while you're in there?"

"Yes. I may not follow procedure, and that might upset you." He slipped on a pair of latex gloves, then pulled the .38 out of the shoulder holster.

"That's not your duty piece," Strega remarked.

"Right. It's not registered, and it's not traceable. Could be useful tonight." He reached over and took the envelope from Strega.

"Anything else I should know?" Strega asked.

"If you haven't guessed, I'm paying a visit on Alvarez."

"She lives *here*?" Strega took another look at the ugly building.

"I'm surprised too. P.C. for a dad. You'd think she'd be in a doorman building. Unless, of course, she's spending all her dough on blow." He shook the envelope.

"Why are you doing it this way?" Strega asked. His tone said he accepted Gavin's decision.

"Because I've got no faith in the system."

"Revenge or your own idea of justice?"

"A little of both, plus the fact I don't want to see her take you down too." Gavin got out of the car. "Keep the doors locked and the engine running." He slammed the door neatly and walked up to the building entrance.

The door operated on a buzzer system. He scanned the list of names. Alvarez was at the top. He skipped it and randomly pushed a button marked Silvers—10B.

A sleepy voice answered. "Yeah?"

"5-D. Took my dog out to pee and forgot my keys. Sorry to bother you."

"If you forgot your key, how are you gonna get in your own front door?"

"I left it unlocked."

"Stupid fucking thing to do," the voice muttered.

The door buzzed. Gavin pulled it open and stepped in.

The foyer was a continuation on the shabby modern theme. Brown, stained couches and a beige armchair crowded around a low kidney-shaped glass table. A pair of naked fluorescent light tubes flickered overhead.

Gavin took one look at the filthy casket-sized elevator and decided to walk. He yanked the stairwell door open and climbed up. The air was hot and heavy. When he reached the eighth floor, he made a mental note to go back to the gym.

Gavin stepped into the hall. The carpet was a sickly shade of green. The walls were papered with a shiny foil-striped number. Another sickly shade of green alternated with broad stripes of reflective silver. Gavin could see his reflection in the silver. The walls must have been crooked because the reflective stripes had a circus effect. Gavin's face was stretched out two feet wide, and his body compacted down into a midget-sized version of the real thing.

He turned away and walked down to the last green door. This one had a fake gold metal letter G stuck on. There was no peephole. Gavin reached down and tried the knob. It turned, but the door was bolted from the inside. He rapped several times hard, then waited. He wasn't disappointed.

A sleepy female voice called out. "Who the fuck is it?" Alvarez. She had a way with words.

Gavin raised his voice a pitch. "Silvers up on ten. You dropped your wallet in the lobby. Lucky no one else found it first." It was a thin story, but he counted on her foggy state of mind. He counted right. A chain rattled, a bolt slid back. The door opened.

Gavin pushed hard and knocked her back. He threw himself into the room and slammed the door behind him, bolting it. Maria Alvarez lay on the floor, rubbing her elbow, looking up at him in confusion. She wore a melon-colored nightgown that brushed the tops of her thighs. Once it might have been pretty, but now it was torn, and the front was spotted with old coffee stains. The lace plunged to a low V in front, putting her substantial cleavage on display.

"Wake-up call, Alvarez," Gavin said.

"What the fuck are you doing here?" she mumbled. Her eyes were unfocused and her limbs uncoordinated as she tried to scramble to her feet.

Gavin stuck a leg out and pushed her back down to the floor. "I'm here to find out the truth."

"The truth?" She laughed roughly. "There's no truth in this world. You telling me you haven't figured that out at your age?" She lay back on the floor and closed her eyes.

Gavin looked around the apartment. It was shabby, surprisingly so for a girl. Funny, he thought, his expectation that a girl always had girlish things—flowers, wispy curtains, bright knickknacks. The fact was, girls were no different from men. Some of them were sticklers for cleanliness, detail, and ambiance; others, like the girl sprawled in front of him, were hell-bent on disaster. When a girl was a slob, it seemed almost obscene. One look around told him Maria Alvarez was a slob.

The furniture was secondhand shit. An old sagging couch the color of sand, spotted in places with suspicious stains. One of those butterfly chairs from Pier One Imports, cheap lemon yellow canvas stretched across a butterfly-shaped iron frame. Gray shades pulled down over the windows. Lamps made out of Chianti bottles, ashtrays stolen from some lesser-known restaurants around town, and a bad imitation of an Indian dhurrie in muddy colors. Couple of wood wine cases turned upside down as a makeshift cabinet on top of which sat a big thirty-inch television set with VCR. Next to it was a state-of-the-art music system. Big Bose speakers stood up like six-foot doormen in two corners of the room.

One thing about Generation X—their lives were seedy,
but their electronic gear was not.

Maria Alvarez ran a hand through her tousled hair.
"Get out of here." She was looking more alert.

Gavin crossed over and placed a foot in her belly. He
pressed hard.

"You're hurting me," she said in a small voice. Her
eyes teared up.

"Good. Answer my questions."

"I want a lawyer."

"I don't remember arresting you," Gavin replied.
"However, if you insist, I'll be happy to say I came in to
question you about the campaign of harassment you've
instigated against another officer in the One-Nine. I'll
be happy to testify that in the middle of our discussion
you offered me this." He waved the manila envelope.
"Your attempt to bribe an officer." He threw it down
on the butterfly chair.

She ran the back of her hand under her nose and
brought herself up to a sitting position, making sure
Gavin saw that she had no underwear beneath the dirty
melon nightie.

"You're walking a thin line, Gavin. All these years
with the Department, why are you trying to break the
law now? Why play hardball with me? I've got better
connections than you do."

He put the toe of his shoe against her sternum and
pushed. She gasped for air and fell back.

He leaned down next to her and twisted her arm
around until she clenched her teeth in pain. "Like I said,
I'm here to find out the truth." He watched little beads
of sweat pop out on her forehead. She bit her lip. In the
bad light he could see she hadn't bothered to take off
her mascara before going to bed. It was smeared under
her eyes. She twisted in his grip, trying to break free.

"Let me go," she whispered.

Gavin twisted harder and brought his foot down on
the soft part of her lower abdomen. "Talk."

"About what?" she hissed.

"Danny would be a good place to start."

To his surprise, she giggled. The giggle turned into a laugh, and the laugh turned into big, choking guffaws. "Donovan?" she sputtered.

"Yes."

When her laughing fit subsided, she looked up at Gavin and smirked. "Men are so easy to scare. Your buddy Donovan was no exception."

"Be more specific." He increased the pressure of his foot.

She flinched and paled. "He didn't tell you? I thought you two were like brothers." She was bragging now—as swaggering and proud as a woman could be who was lying down with her arm twisted up around her head and a man's foot driving into her private parts.

"We were like brothers," Gavin said. "Tell me something I don't already know."

"Did you know Danny liked to drink?"

"A beer now and then. So what?"

"More than a beer. Stoly was his drink. He liked it frozen, straight up in a tiny, tiny glass. He even named it after me. *Cocktail Maria.*"

"So?"

"So when he had a few pops, he liked to take me to bed. Maybe he needed a few pops to get up the courage. Anyway, once he was there, he was courageous enough. Danny liked to get wild. I taught him to want all sorts of things Catholic boys aren't supposed to want. He said sex with his wife had always been a lights-out kind of thing. You know, pure missionary, straight-ahead procreation, nothing sporty about it at all. He said he'd never fucked another woman. Can you believe that? In this day and age, a man who's fucked only one woman?"

She put her free hand between her legs. "I told him. Danny, I said, there are new worlds. Let me take you to them. He was scared at first, fucking the P.C.'s daughter. Then he was like a duck in water. He liked his sex wild and rough, and he liked it all sorts of ways—some of which are still illegal here in New York. He felt guilty about liking it. That's why he needed the vodka, the Cocktail Maria."

She looked up at him. Her eyes were flat and cold. "Poor Danny didn't know. I had the whole thing on tape. Every position, every word of his begging me to do it a different way. What a sight. Donovan's fat ass working away on top of me."

She laughed again. "I had a video camera rigged up in the closet. Home movies. I went to his place one night. He was happy to see me. We fooled around. I jerked him off, then I showed him the tape. I thought it would turn him on. It didn't. Danny got pale as a fish. Started crossing himself and dropped down to his knees and prayed. I guess he didn't like seeing what he'd been doing in full color. When I saw how scared he was, just for fun I told him I was sending a copy to his wife's lawyer. And a copy to Internal Affairs. I told him I was going to have him thrown out of the Department for sodomizing a fellow cop.

"You should've seen his face. Christ. The rest was easy. I shot him up with some coke, then I did the honorable thing. I helped him into the next world." She giggled. "Bang, bang! He banged me and then we banged him, and no one ever figured it out."

Gavin saw white. It all clicked. Donovan's embarrassment. Why he didn't want to talk about Alvarez. A man exploring his sexuality after three decades of a bad marriage and, most probably, bad sex. It was too intimate to tell even his best friend. The driving needs loneliness brings. It was just too intimate. Danny didn't know he was a pawn in Maria's sick game. He had no idea how the sick game would end.

Gavin pulled Maria's hair, forcing her head back. He shoved the barrel of the gun up against the pulse point in her neck. "I should kill you right now."

"You wouldn't dare," she whispered, oddly calm.

"Where's the tape?"

"What tape?"

"The tape of Danny."

"Dunno."

He yanked her hair and pulled her up to a standing position. "Let's go get the tape." He marched her down the narrow little hall and into her bedroom. He stopped short. The walls were covered with pictures of the P.C. He looked up. The ceiling was covered too, and up there with the P.C. was a picture of Strega, smiling down. Gavin stood on the bed, reached up, and ripped Strega's picture off. He crumpled it and shoved it in his pocket.

Maria watched him, curiously docile, limp almost, shoulders slumped, leaning against her bedroom door. Gavin kept her in his line of vision and pulled the top drawer of her dresser open. It was filled with NYPD shields. He searched the remaining drawers. There was nothing in them but nightgowns and T-shirts. Funny, he thought. She had no bras and no underwear.

He opened the closet. New uniforms were hung neatly in a row. Five new hats lined one shelf, and on a high shelf above that, set up on a small tripod, was a small video camera pointing out at her bed. Gavin guessed she used to leave the closet door ajar. No one would ever notice the little camera eye recording.

"Where's the tape?"

"Top shelf. In a little black box marked Danny. I'll play it for you. You'll see a side of your partner you never knew he had."

There were a lot of black video boxes, maybe two dozen, all carefully labeled with names. Gavin rifled through them and recognized a lot of names. They were all officers of varying ranks in the NYPD. Some of the ranks went as high as two-star chiefs. He found a box carefully labeled with Mike Kelly's name. The next box was marked simply, RAMON.

His discovery chilled him. He flashed back to the scene that rainy night in front of the Met. Ramon Alvarez brushing a strand of hair out of her face. Tipping her face up and kissing her on the forehead. Kissing her with a tenderness that wasn't at all fatherly. He remembered the way they had stared at Strega. Her handsome face stamped with hatred, Ramon's stamped with jealousy.

Gavin's stomach cramped. He put the Ramon tape to one side and continued sorting. He found it, shoved in the back. A black video box marked *Donovan*. He reached deep into the closet, standing up on his toes, off balance for a fraction of a second. It was all the time she needed.

Maria sprang forward and knocked the .38 out of his hand. He whirled around to face her. The docile girl was gone. The drugged-out girl was gone. She was savage now, enraged, and armed with a slim, vicious blade. Her foot kicked out, catching him in the groin. He doubled over. She came down hard with the knife, aiming for his heart. She was fast, but his old boxer's reflexes were faster. He ducked away and watched her move. He knew from her style she was trained and deadly.

Her foot snapped out again, this time at his nose. He pulled back and she missed. She came back at him, aiming for his throat, aiming to kill. Gavin pulled one hand away from his injured groin and whipped his fist into her wrist. Her hand popped open. The blade scuttled across the floor.

Maria grunted in frustration, then spun away from him. She grabbed a ceramic lamp and swung. Gavin heaved his heavy body against her. They crashed to the floor, Gavin on top. The lamp base exploded. Her hand closed around a ceramic shard, and she held it like a knife, going for his face. He gripped her wrist, but she fought him, wildcat strong. The ceramic shard swiped his cheek. He felt the skin break, the burn of blood, and then she was driving the sharp hard into his chest and dragging it down, carving a deep trench in his flesh.

Gavin rolled off her onto his back. She scrambled onto him, riding him, gripping the shard, bringing it down time and time again into the soft flesh of his belly. Gavin wanted to curl up in a protective shell and shield himself from her, but he didn't. He thrust his right arm up over his head, feeling for the blade. Maria drew the shard up high, ready to bring it down on his eye. Gavin's hand curled around the knife handle, but she was coming at him fast with the shard. He curled his left hand into a boxer's fist and jabbed up and out, slamming hard into her jaw.

She fell forward, over him, moaning. Her hand uncurled. The bloodied shard slipped out. Gavin straddled
her, one hand on her hair, pulling her head back, one
hand gripping the knife. He laid the blade against her
neck.

"Should I do it, Alvarez? Tell me to do it!"

She turned her head suddenly, and the blade split the
skin, leaving the long red line of a surface wound. Gavin
rolled her off, retrieved the .38, and shoved the bloodied
ceramic shard in his pocket. He removed his jacket, then
used it to wipe his blood from the floor and from Maria's
skin. Her melon nightie was splattered with his blood
too. He ripped the nightie off her body and wrapped it
in his jacket along with her blade.

Then he leaned down next to Maria, twisted her hair,
and pressed the gun nose to her temple. She was crying
softly. "Where'd you plant the rest of the drugs,
Alvarez?"

"Fuck you," she spat. She reached one hand up and
raked a long red nail down his face.

He grabbed her hand and, using his fingernail, he dug
his own skin out from under her nail, then drove the
nose of the .38 back into her temple. "Where'd you put
it? In his locker? In his car? In his apartment?"

Her lips puckered together. She made little kissing
sounds. Gavin imagined those lips laughing while Donovan hung his big head low in shame when she played
him the tape. "I'm going to fucking kill you, Maria," he
said softly in her ear.

"I don't care about dying."

"Tell me." He pressed a thumb against her windpipe.
She gagged and choked. He released. "Tell me." She
shook her head no. He pressed again, longer. Suddenly,
all the fight went out of her body. He released. She lay
slack on the floor. "Tell me."

"I cut the inside of one of his books out," she said in
a defeated voice. "It's in there."

"Why?"

"I wanted to watch Jon Strega fall. He deserved it.
Then I was going to kill him." Her face contorted. "All

of you deserve to die. I'm doing it, one by one, and there's no proof, Gavin, nothing to prove it's me."

"Where's Franklin?"

"He went for a swim." She giggled. "Franklin went swimming. You'll never find him."

Gavin dropped the .38. He wrapped his big boxer's hands around her neck and squeezed. Maria bucked and fought, but Gavin had her now and he wanted to see her red giggling lips go loose with death. Maria's face changed color. All at once Gavin saw the scene as a spectator would. He saw an enraged man killing a killer. He was many things, he thought, not all of them good, but he was not like Alvarez. He was not a killer.

Gavin let her go and picked his gun up.

"You're fucking crazy," she wheezed.

"Guess I am. I should've killed you. Would've done the world a favor."

She crawled up the side of the bed and sprawled out over it, displaying the bare expanse of her full hips. Gavin's gaze dropped down to look. Those round hips would have been compelling to a lonely, broken man. Donovan had looked for comfort there, for a fresh start. Gavin shook himself. "This is the deal, Alvarez. You confess to Ballantine."

"Or else?" she mocked. "Or else what? You come back and kill me? Why don't you just fuck me instead?" She rolled onto her back and spread her legs wide. Gavin reached out and threw a blanket over her exposed sex. It felt obscene, looking at the place Donovan had been, the place where he had lost his self-respect.

"I'm smart," she bragged. "You have no evidence. No witnesses. Not one. The D.A. will never indict. There's no proof, no evidence. I'm too fucking smart."

"Are you?" He pulled the recorder out of his shirt pocket. The red recording light was lit, the tape was rolling.

She sat up and eyed the little machine. "You're a regular detective, Gavin. I'm impressed. But it'll never hold up in court. You broke into my apartment. You're here illegally. Your tape is illegal. Worthless."

"This isn't." Gavin held up the videotape box marked *Ramon.* "This would get a hell of an audience on the evening news."

Alvarez paled. She started shaking. "You can't."

"I will. You confess to Ballantine, or I bring you down and take your father with you."

Maria's expression changed.

Gavin sensed he had her. "Or maybe that's what you want. To humiliate your father. Is that what this is all about? Maybe he humiliated you when you were a little girl. Maybe he kept on humiliating you, and this is all about getting back at the big, bad policeman. Is that it?" He shook the Ramon tape. "Is this about your personal retribution against him? Is it?"

"Maybe," she answered, with that new strange look on her face. She smiled sweetly. Then the smile slipped away and she turned savage again. Gavin stiffened, but she attacked herself this time, viciously, ripping and clawing her own face, clutching fistfuls of her own thick black hair and tearing it out at the roots, pulling at her earrings until her earlobes split.

Gavin watched, stunned by her shocking self-mutilation. Then he caught her wrists and held them tight. She twisted and pulled, but his grip was iron. He held her down, watched her battered face, and waited for her to calm. Underneath the bruises and the scratches and the clotted makeup, he saw a terrible pain that had nothing to do with her physical injuries.

After a time, Maria quieted and she lay still. Limp. Gavin cautiously released her wrists. Her hands fell to her sides, as though she were asleep.

"Maria?" Gavin shook her.

Her eyes opened. They were opaque. Unreadable.

"I'm going to call Ballantine now," Gavin said. "He'll come down and you'll give him your confession." He reached for the mobile phone.

Then, somehow, Maria was there, at the phone, smashing it against his head. Gavin reeled back, blinded. He went after her anyway, following the sound of her feet flying down the hall into the living room.

His vision cleared. She was smacking the phone into the wall, then opening it and gutting the electronics inside.

"Try calling Ballantine now," she said, panting and crying, hitting her own head with the phone shell. She stopped abruptly and dropped to the floor, wrapping her arms around her knees.

Gavin went to her, approaching carefully. "It's over, Maria." He touched her face. "It's all over."

She bowed her proud, finely shaped head.

He took her hand and led her back to her bedroom.

She turned her body easily around and sagged against Gavin. He felt her full, heavy breasts against his chest. She was small next to him, and close. Her eyes were closed. Tears slipped out and rolled down her cheek. Big, fat drops of water. Symbols of sorrow. Gavin found it hard to believe there was any sorrow in her malicious heart.

She stumbled away from him and fell across the bed.

Gavin tensed and watched her sprawling nude body, waiting for her to fly up at him again. She pulled her knees up to her chin instead and looped her arms back around them. She was humming a church tune and whispering the word *Angel*.

Looking at her sad, spent body, Gavin knew he had nothing more to fear. He picked up his balled-up jacket and the videos marked *Donovan* and *Ramon*. He walked out of the bedroom, down the hall, and out the green door.

Gavin moved past the silver-foil stripes on the wallpaper. The midget's face staring back at him was the face of a stranger. His bright blue eyes were dark as night. There was hatred in them, and murder too. He had been close. Too close. Gavin turned away from the stripes and hurried to the stairwell. He ran down the stairs, through the lobby, and out to the car.

Maria reached in her closet for a new uniform shirt and shrugged it on. She switched the video camera to record, then sat on the end of the bed, looking squarely into the camera eye, and began to speak. "I am a *he-she*," she stated. "I was broken a long time ago." As she spoke, she held and caressed her 9mm service revolver. "The *he* part of me has a name. He is Police Commissioner Ramon Alvarez, my father."

Gavin was sliding into the front seat of the Tempo when he heard the shot.

His cop brain processed the information.

A single shot.

From somewhere inside.

Sounded a lot like a 9mm.

A single 9-mm shot, you idiot, his brain screamed.

Alvarez.

He had forgotten to take her service revolver away.

Gavin put the car in gear.

"Where are we going?" Strega asked.

"To make a phone call." Gavin accelerated away from Maria's building. He made a series of sharp turns, looking for a pay phone. He pulled up next to one, left the car idling, and ran for the phone. He dialed 911, altered his voice, and reported shots fired from Maria's apartment. He gave the address and hung up.

He called Ballantine next.

"Maria Alvarez just shot herself in the head." He gave Q-Ball the address and hung up before the big detective started asking questions.

Gavin got back in the car and drove to an access road he knew of that put him out on the bank of the East River. At the river, he killed the engine and tossed his Eye-Spy tape recorder to Strega. "Rewind the tape," he said, "then listen to it. I'm taking a walk." He gripped the video box marked *Donovan* and his jacket with her nightie and knife.

He got out and picked his way over the rock shards and tin cans littering the river bank, to the edge of the East River. He kicked a stone. It skipped away down the sloping embankment and scuttled into the water. It was past midnight, and the lights of Manhattan were a thousand stars trapped on the river's surface. A siren wailed far away. Police, Gavin thought. He knew the sound. Ironic, his being a cop and unable to use the law to bring justice to Maria Alvarez.

There was a small, hot breeze coming in off the water. Out in the distance a big barge crawled along. The water surface was oily and black in the night. Gavin leaned on a broken-down cement post. He tossed his jacket out into the water, then waited for a time, turning the box marked *Donovan* over and over in his hands.

"Danny," he whispered. "You could have talked to me." He took the videocassette out of the box. His fingers fumbled on the plastic casing, feeling for the smooth face of the tape itself. When he found it, he began to pull. The tape spooled out easily. He pulled and pulled, until black tape curled all around his feet. Then he gathered the tape in his hands and threw it out into the water. It floated on the river for a long while, moving slowly, swept along by the slow tide. Little by little the long snakes of videotape disappeared beneath the surface. Gavin wondered if it would all sink to the bottom. He wondered if it would drift out to sea. He wondered how long it would take for salt water to eat through the tape and disintegrate it completely.

He wondered if Maria's last desperate act had been drug-induced, or if, in a moment of lucidity, she had realized she couldn't face up to her horrifying acts. He thought of the tape box marked Ramon. There was clearly another story to Maria Alvarez, a darker story, one in which she too was a victim.

Gavin didn't need a Princeton degree to understand this tragedy. A girl's fragile innocence destroyed by her father. Maria must have stored up a lifetime of hatred, then retaliated by destroying men, but never finding the courage to destroy *the* man. Sex was the weapon. She must have believed that which destroyed her could redeem her too. Her sick mind found its own logic. No matter the men were innocent. She had been innocent once too. He thought of Donovan's ill-fated exploration of his sexuality. Sex was not as simple as boy meets girl. Not so simple at all.

Sure, Maria Alvarez had been a victim. Donovan, Alvarez, Shelly, Alex, Strega, Gavin himself. In the end, weren't they all victims of something? He held the tape box marked *Donovan* in his hands, then tossed it high into the sky and watched it fall into the river. The box bobbed along on top for a time, filling slowly with the dark river water. He watched it sink.

He didn't know how much time passed while he stood at the river's edge, staring out at the black water. The sky seemed to have lightened in the distance. He looked at his watch. It was four-thirty in the morning. The barge had drifted out of sight. He ran a hand over his grizzled face, then turned and walked slowly back to his car, wondering if, by confronting Alvarez and pushing her over the edge, he wasn't as guilty as if he had pulled the trigger himself. He wondered too if that made him like Maria—if that made him a killer.

Strega had the FM radio tuned to a classical station. He appeared to be asleep. When Gavin slammed the door, Strega spoke without opening his eyes.

"Where to now?" Strega asked.

"Clean out your bookshelves. Have a cup of coffee. Shave. Go to work."

Twenty-eight

When Gavin and Strega walked into the precinct house, desk sergeant Bell leaned over and glowered. "Ballantine wants you both in his office. Now."

"Good morning to you too," Gavin mumbled as they went past and clambered up the stairs.

The blinds were shut in Q-Ball's office, and the door was open. Strega and Gavin walked in. A television monitor and a VCR player were on a portable cart in the corner of the room.

Ballantine had his feet up on the desk. His eyes were closed. "Sit down," he ordered. "And shut the door."

Strega and Gavin complied.

Q-Ball opened his eyes. He pointed the remote at the VCR and rolled the tape. Maria Alvarez's battered face filled the screen. She was wearing nothing but her uniform shirt, and that was open, revealing her naked skin. She held her service revolver with both hands, like a bouquet of flowers.

"I am a *he-she*," she began. "I was broken a long time ago. The *he* part has a name. He is Police Commissioner Ramon Alvarez, my father. He taught me to protect myself. He taught me that justice never takes a life without cause."

Gavin and Strega watched and listened intently. Maria Alvarez's confession was rambling and emotional and, at times, surprisingly composed. When she recited the specifics of each of her crimes, she did so in a cold, coherent, organized manner, as if she were filing a routine report. Gavin was reminded of her top-notch police work, her professional cool on the job. She was as cool now, including dates, times, and places. In all, she confessed to murdering eleven NYPD officers in the suicide string, to killing Franklin, and to setting Strega up with domestic abuse and drug possession as a preamble to killing him.

When she finished, she smiled a crooked, helpless smile. "I liked shooting stars," she said enigmatically. "I was building a constellation all my own, a constellation of twelve stars, one for each letter of my name. Jon Strega was going to be the twelfth and final star. My constellation was going to take me to heaven, away from hell. But now I know the perfect constellation has just one star—one perfect star, burning bright." She lifted the gun.

Ballantine snapped the machine off. "I'll spare you."

"Has Wilson seen this yet?" Gavin asked.

"He's on his way up."

"Ramon Alvarez?"

"Yes. Last night."

"Can we use this to change the manner of death on Danny's death certificate?" Katy had a fat insurance check due her.

"We can," Ballantine confirmed. He rubbed his eyes and sighed.

Strega stared at the frozen frame on the television monitor, at Maria Alvarez looking proudly out at them in the final second before her final self-destruction with a strange peace on her face.

"She was killing Ramon, over and over and over," he mused. "It was a kind of mind skip, a transference. She chose cops who shared certain traits with her father, like the Catholic religion, and at the moment of killing I honestly believe she thought she was killing Ramon. Something inside her, some kind of ancient moral code, stopped her from committing patricide which, in a way, is the greatest irony here. She had to keep killing, repeating the act over and over as long as the real Ramon lived and continued to terrorize her. Hers was a tremendously complex dynamic of need and loyalty and guilt and love."

"Love, Strega?" Ballantine exclaimed. "You lost me there. How the hell could she have loved Ramon?"

"He was her father. That bond was stronger than any other emotion she had, stronger even than hate."

Q-Ball looked over at the frozen video frame of Maria Alvarez. He nodded, then looked at his watch. "The mayor's waiting for you over in Hansen's room for the photo op. Get out of here."

They walked out the door as Wilson was walking in.

"I just had a very unpleasant meeting with Ramon Alvarez," Wilson stated. "He says his daughter would never turn her gun on herself, not unprovoked, not without a little help. He asked me if I knew anything that might help in his *personal* investigation of her death. I had to look him in the eye and say I didn't."

Wilson turned red. He stuck a hand out and jabbed Gavin in the chest with his index finger. "I'm wondering why you look like you've been up all night. I'm wondering why your partner looks haggard. I'm wondering where you got this lump on your forehead. I'm hoping this mark on the other side of your face is from a lousy shaving job and not some girl's fingernail.

"Ramon Alvarez tells me that her telephones were destroyed and the contents of her dresser drawers were thrown all over her bedroom. He tells me there were new contusions on her face, terrible ones. Her earlobes were ripped and her hair was torn out. There were signs of a violent struggle. One fingerprint," Wilson said, prodding Gavin in the chest again, "one fingerprint that puts you inside Maria Alvarez's apartment, and I'm coming after you. Do you read me?"

"Loud and clear."

Wilson dropped his hand and stalked into Ballantine's office.

Did Ramon Alvarez tell you about her sizable video library, neatly marked with names of NYPD officers? Gavin wondered. *Did he tell you about her drawer full of shields—her trophies—and the fat bag of cocaine on the chair, the blow in her nose?*

Wilson was about to see and hear it all.

The door to Ballantine's office slammed shut.

Strega tapped Gavin on the shoulder. "The P.C. didn't waste any time," he said, pointing at a television set across the room. The news was running a clip from an early morning press conference. Gavin moved close enough to hear.

Alvarez, appearing grief-stricken but composed, expressed his suspicions about the circumstances surrounding Maria's suicide. He described the state of her apartment, the evidence of a struggle, the contusions on her face, and then he dropped the bombshell.

"My daughter videotaped her suicide."

Ramon paused and let his statement sink in.

"I know she killed herself, but I don't know what went on in the apartment in the hours preceding her death. I have just learned that my daughter had a severe drug problem. A large quantity of cocaine was found on the premises, and in her body. I believe last night's violent struggle was drug-related and that my daughter was coerced into committing the act of suicide."

He spoke of the knife marks on her neck, and how suicidal women do not cut their own necks. They choose pills or slit their wrists, never their necks. He spoke of the destroyed telephones, as though someone there didn't want her to call for help. Her door was unlocked, he said, and her apartment ransacked.

"In the videotape," he said in a sad voice, "my daughter makes shocking allegations against me and against herself. The allegations against herself will warrant a full department investigation. The allegations against me are the worst accusations a father could face. I am here this morning to tell you I loved my daughter and was never anything less than a committed, caring parent to her.

"It was heartbreaking for me to watch the tape, heartbreaking for me to witness her mental confusion, her delusions, and hysteria. My daughter was a victim of drugs. They destroyed her mind and her life, and they are responsible for her hysterical allegations. Her finger may have pulled the trigger, but cocaine killed her."

Alvarez's eyes were bright now with an evangelist

shine, and his voice thundered with conviction. "I am devastated and I am angry—angry that my daughter was one more victim in a war our nation is losing, and I say to you now, I will dedicate the rest of my career to fighting drugs and crime. I will do it in the name of Maria and her mother, may they both rest in peace."

Gavin watched, incredulous. It was the perfect offensive move: tell the press about the tape before they learn about it from someone else. Alvarez was brilliantly twisting the truth, turning himself into the victim, positioning Maria's death as the second great tragedy to strike him. Guns and drugs—the P.C. had lost his wife to one and his daughter to the other. It was politically compelling, politically irresistible, and for the moment Ramon Alvarez was selling it. He was goddamn selling it. He was going to walk away with clean hands.

One thing Ramon Alvarez does not know, Gavin thought, watching the handsome, stricken politician's face and the fake tears rolling down it, *is that I have the trump card.*

"Let's go," Strega interrupted. "The mayor and Hansen are waiting."

"I have to make a quick phone call first," Gavin said.

He stopped at a pay phone on the street and dialed Alvarez's office. The secretary said the commissioner was not taking phone calls.

"Tell him I know something about his daughter's death."

The secretary went off the line. Strega gave him a questioning look.

A moment later, Ramon Alvarez picked up. "Who is this?"

"An acquaintance of Maria's," Gavin said. "I have a videotape you might be interested in."

"I already know about Maria's confession. It's in the hands of the NYPD, and I have made a public statement."

"I'm not talking about that tape. In the tape I have, you play a starring role."

The line was so quiet, Gavin thought Alvarez had

hung up. "How much do you want?" Alvarez whispered hoarsely.

"The tape's not for sale."

"Then what do you want?"

"Nothing."

"Nothing?"

"One day, *Commissioner* Alvarez, you'll look up at the news and wish you hadn't. Maybe today, maybe tomorrow, or the day after. I know who you really are. And one day soon, the taxpayers in this city will know too. Game, set, match. You lose." Gavin slammed the phone down.

Strega raised an eyebrow.

"Quit looking at me like that," Gavin complained, heading for his car. He got in and slammed the door.

Strega followed. "You surprise me, Ed. I thought, despite taking a few liberties with *procedure,* you were basically a law-and-order guy. Toe the line, respect the law, because it's the only system we've got. All that stuff."

"I don't trust the system to give Ramon what he deserves."

"You know," Strega said, "I studied the classics at Princeton. And never once did revenge ever get anyone even."

"The classics are wrong," Gavin replied, firing up the ignition. "Dead wrong."

It was 9:00 A.M. The mayor and Hansen were waiting.